Alex Gray

THE DARKEST GOODBYE

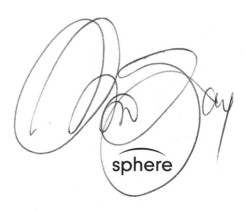

sphere

SPHERE

First published in Great Britain in 2016 by Sphere

1 3 5 7 9 10 8 6 4 2

Words from 'In the Snack-bar' by Edwin Morgan
from *New Selected Poems* published by Carcanet Press Ltd 2000.

Lyrics to 'Rainy Days and Mondays' by Roger S. Nichols,
Paul H. Williams. © Almo Music Corp.

A CIP catalogue record for this book
is available from the British Library.

Hardback ISBN 978-0-7515-5491-5
Trade Paperback ISBN 978-0-7515-5489-2

Typeset in Caslon by M Rules
Printed and bound in Great Britain by
Clays Ltd, St Ives plc

Papers used by Sphere are from well-managed forests
and other responsible sources.

MIX
Paper from
responsible sources
FSC
www.fsc.org FSC® C104740

Sphere
An imprint of
Little, Brown Book Group
Carmelite House
50 Victoria Embankment
London
EC4Y 0DZ

An Hachette UK Company
www.hachette.co.uk

www.littlebrown.co.uk

This book is dedicated to Alanna Knight MBE,
my beloved friend

Alex Gray was born and educated in Glasgow. After studying English and Philosophy at the University of Strathclyde, she worked as a visiting officer for the DHSS, a time she looks upon as postgraduate education since it proved a rich source of character studies. She then trained as a secondary school teacher of English. Alex began writing professionally in 1992 and had immediate success with short stories, articles and commissions for BBC radio programmes. She has been awarded the Scottish Association of Writers' Constable and Pitlochry trophies for her crime writing. A regular on the Scottish bestseller lists, her previous novels include *Five Ways to Kill a Man*, *Glasgow Kiss*, *Pitch Black*, *The Riverman*, *Never Somewhere Else*, *The Swedish Girl* and *Keep the Midnight Out*. She is the co-founder of the international Scottish crime writing festival, Bloody Scotland, which had its inaugural year in 2012.

And slowly we go down. And slowly we go down.

'In the Snack-bar' by Edwin Morgan

PROLOGUE

One hot day in August

He had to die. That had never been a matter for debate. The body at their feet was bleeding copiously from the stab wounds that had been inflicted. A young man's life snuffed out, but hey, they were used to things like that by now. Weren't they?

It had happened quickly at the end, the drug dealer shambling towards them down that hallway, eyes glazed as he'd tried to focus on who was banging on the door of the tenement flat, a look of surprise turning to shock as the first blow had made him sprawl on the carpet. After that it had been easy. Knowing just where to make that fatal cut, letting out the warm blood. Not so easy dragging his thin wasted body into the bathroom. And it could be weeks till anyone came looking for him.

It was also a warning to the others. Loose talk could bring everything crashing around their ears.

The two figures emerged from the dark close mouth into the daylight of one of Glasgow's busiest thoroughfares, soon merging into the crowds.

Nobody glancing at either of their faces would ever guess that they had just killed a man.

1

CHAPTER ONE

'*You're early.*'

The old woman's dark eyes narrowed as I entered the room, staring up at my navy blue uniform. Was there suspicion in those clouded eyes? Or was she simply trying to decide if this stranger standing in her bedroom was bringing the pain-killing relief she had craved through another long night?

'Ready for your meds, darling?' I asked, my laconic shrug and wide smile putting her at ease. 'Give you a bit of peace, eh?' I chuckled, inviting her to share in my little joke. She'd soon be at peace all right, enough to last for all eternity.

But the patient in the bed did not return my smile and for a split second I wondered if she could possibly have guessed my real intentions.

I put down the bag I'd been carrying and lifted out the plastic box containing the medication. Her eyes followed every movement as I unwrapped the sterile syringe and filled it with the contents of the phial. Surely she must be desperate for the release from her constant pain? If she'd had any choice in the fate that I was about to administer, wouldn't she see me as some sort of angel of mercy? My smile never wavered as I pulled up the sleeve of her nightdress, preparing a patch of wrinkled flesh with an antiseptic wipe.

Her head turned away as the needle pierced her arm, a reluctance to see what was happening. Then, as though she knew that sleep was about to follow, her eyelids drooped, her chest rising and falling in one huge sigh.

I sat back and waited, watching the faint movement, a gentle rhythm that would soon give way to one final struggle as she gasped for breath. I would continue to sit in this room where the curtains were rarely drawn back until after ten in the morning. Other hands than hers were required for such small acts nowadays; hands like mine, clasped loosely together on my lap as I watched the woman sleeping.

It had been easy enough to gain access. A simple matter to turn the key in the lock, the click hardly discernible. It would be returned later, shiny and clean, no traces on its yellow brass to identify me. Anyone happening to look at the figure who had walked into the house would have seen the navy blue jacket, standard uniform for most community nurses these days. It was expected that the old lady at number thirty-three would have someone coming to look after her, though perhaps not at this early hour of a September morning.

It would not be long now. I amused myself by imagining the contents of the used syringe travelling through these knotted veins on a journey that would end in the chambers of her heart. A sigh, a rattle, then it would be over. There was no need to stay until the end but something always kept me there, as though this final vigil was a thing that ought to be shared. I'd never had a word from any patient, no whispered 'thank you', no look of gratitude from eyes worn out with too much suffering. I'd have hated it if an eyelid had ever flickered; there was an inner need to have these moments of peace when the patient drifted away, mouth slackening, blood cooling as death came with its chill hands to carry them off.

All over this city there were silent, seated watchers just like me, waiting for their loved ones to pass over. But the difference between us was that these patients were not my close relatives, never people known intimately, even though I might have smiled at them and called them darling.

For a few minutes I turned away and yawned, stretching my arms behind my head, eyes closed for a moment, drifting into a half sleep, musing about Quiet Release ... When I jolted awake, blinking to stare at the patient, it was only to notice that there was no visible movement from the bed.

I clenched my fists in a sudden spasm of annoyance. She'd cheated me, the old bitch! It must have happened in those few seconds when sleep had dimmed my senses – the old woman had stolen away. Aye, death might be a process, the organs shutting down, the body cooling until rigor stiffened it, but there was something exciting about being there for that final intake of breath. And I'd missed it.

For one angry moment I was tempted to grab hold of her frail old body and shake it. But the urge passed, leaving me standing beside the bed, fists unclenching as I stooped to pick up the bag from the floor. It was only as I turned to leave that I gave her one last look.

'Goodnight, then, darling,' I crooned, putting two fingers to my lips and blowing a kiss in the direction of the bed.

CHAPTER TWO

For everybody else it was just a day like any other day.

Kirsty had almost passed the mirror when she took a step back, momentarily puzzled by the stranger whose frown so resembled her own.

It was, she thought, like seeing herself naked.

That quick glance each morning had seen a figure clad in the uniform of Police Scotland, PC Kirsty Wilson often pausing to adjust her hat, a piece of kit that she disliked intensely.

This morning was different. Today was a new beginning, a step away from the routine she had enjoyed as a uniformed officer in Glasgow into the heady atmosphere of CID. In truth, since joining the police, Kirsty had always hoped to emulate her father, Detective Inspector Alistair Wilson, who was now on the point of retiring after thirty years of service. There would be a brief few weeks while father and daughter worked together as colleagues in the divisional headquarters at Stewart Street, something that was rarely allowed to happen within the force and was only being permitted because the DI would be leaving in early October.

Kirsty started to frown back at the girl whose reflection was caught in the long mirror in the hallway of her flat, then gave a laugh instead, her mouth curving in the grin that came more naturally to her. It was a face that had lost its former chubbiness after her spell of basic training and regular attendance at the gym. Anyone looking at the police officer would have noticed high cheekbones and a pale complexion, with dark, almost black hair – the young woman's features being typical of the ancient Celtic blood that ran in her veins.

Kirsty smoothed down the jacket of her new trouser suit, feeling the slenderness of her waist with satisfaction. Gone were the days of scoffing her own home baking and curling up with a mug of full-fat hot chocolate in front of the television, though in truth she still enjoyed pottering in the kitchen and turning out some delicious cakes, especially for her boyfriend, James, whose stick-thin frame never seemed to change, however many calories he consumed. James had sat up poring over his textbooks well into the night, his dissertation for this final honours year proving to be more of a task than he had anticipated. Kirsty would not wake him but simply slip out and greet this new phase of her professional life alone.

'Good morning, Detective Constable Wilson,' she whispered, savouring the name for a brief moment, acknowledging the thrill of excitement that she felt inside.

What would they make of her? It would be extra hard, given that her father's reputation preceded her own. She'd have to prove to them all that she had deserved this step into CID. Giving the girl in the mirror a desultory wave of her hand, Kirsty picked up the shoulder bag lying by the front door, turned the key in the lock and stepped out of the flat, careful to close the heavy door behind her as quietly as possible.

It was the sort of morning that suited new beginnings, she

thought, pausing by the kerb at Barrington Drive to breathe in the cool early morning air. Few people were about at this time in the morning yet there was always the sound of traffic coming from Woodlands Road on one side and Great Western Road on the other. An arrow-shaped leaf from the row of cherry trees fluttered down at her feet, a harbinger of the swirling flight of autumn foliage that would spread all over the roads and pavements come the next storm. Kirsty resisted the urge to pick it up and put it into her pocket, something she had always done as a child. *The first leaf of autumn, Kirsty*, she could recall her grandmother telling her. *It's the sign of a new season beginning.*

Grandmother Wilson had been right about that long after her voice had ceased to be heard this side of eternity. September was a month when Kirsty had made new starts in both university and police college. She loved this time of year when early morning mists appeared, bringing a chill to the air and robins whistling in the shrubbery. Although these were harbingers of the cold Scottish winters ahead, there was something about the transition from long bright days to the darker months that gave Kirsty a sense of renewed vigour after the lazy days of summer. Whenever the trees in the park turned from dusty greens into the autumn tints of yellow and gold, fond memories came back to her of crunching through drifts of leaves on her way to primary school and hunting for conkers.

It seemed a long time since she had come to the city, Kirsty thought, heading towards the path that would take her to Kelvingrove underground station. The flat in the quiet street that she shared with James was far handier for work and university than the one she had lived in when they had first met. That had been one of comparative luxury, the owner a Swedish girl whose wealthy father had indulged his daughter by purchasing a duplex apartment near Anniesland Cross. The time spent there had changed the course of Kirsty's life in more ways than one.

She thrust the thoughts of Anniesland aside, concentrating instead on what she had been told to expect this morning. An induction into CID, becoming assigned to a mentor whom she may or may not have met in the past and, best of all, a short meeting with the man who had inspired her to join up in the first place, Detective Superintendent William Lorimer.

As Kirsty Wilson made her way out of the fresh early morning light and into the depths of the subway with its familiar smoky smell, she had no inkling just what else might lie ahead.

For everyone else, it was just an ordinary day.

For the woman heading to Stewart Street police station it was destined to bring unspeakable horror and a dilemma greater than any she had yet faced in her young life.

CHAPTER THREE

Sarah sniffed the air, wondering why it felt so different. She had worked in the gardens of HMP Cornton Vale in fresh air for most of the summer, but here, outside the prison gates, there was a scent of something smoky that reminded Sarah of her childhood. Bonfires and piles of leaves, dressing up for Halloween, misty mornings ...

It had been a misty morning the day she had left for work, the day that everything had gone wrong in her life, she remembered, shivering as she waited for the taxi that was supposed to come and meet her in the car park. She pulled up the collar of her thin coat, the same coat she had worn to come in here all those months ago. Feeling in the pocket, Sarah found a crumpled tissue. It was the cold air, she told herself, blowing her nose and sniffling again. That was all. So why were her eyes filling up with tears, making the view of the houses nearby all blurry? She should be happy, ecstatic even. She was out, after all. Wasn't that what she had dreamed of every blessed night as she'd lain down in that narrow bed, trying to sleep, desperate to blot out all the images that had haunted her?

The sound of a diesel engine made her look up as a silver car slowly wound its way into the visitors' car park. Sarah stepped forward, knowing that this was a moment she had secretly dreaded. The car was coming to take her away from the place where she had been safe from the world outside.

'Taxi for Wilding?'

The driver had rolled down his window and was regarding her with an appraising look in his eye. Did he think she was on the game like so many of her fellow inmates? Sarah clenched her teeth, realising that this was the first of many tests she was going to have to face. She reached out a hand to open the rear passenger door, trying not to return the driver's stare. He might be used to picking up ex-cons here on this very spot for all she knew.

'Railway station?'

Sarah nodded. It would be all right. She was only going to be alone with this man for a short while then she would feel the freedom of being an anonymous person amongst hundreds of other commuters travelling from Stirling into the city of Glasgow.

She did not look back as the car swung away from the prison, nor did she glance across the bridge where the Wallace Monument rose from the mist like an admonishing finger.

CHAPTER FOUR

Stewart Street police station was hidden amongst a huddle of high-rise flats, office blocks and the nearby fire station, its chequered sign only visible as Kirsty Wilson turned the corner of the street. Memories of her first visit here when she had been giving a witness statement in a murder inquiry came flooding back. She shivered suddenly, remembering. Yet there were good memories too: her stint here in uniform in the run-up to the Glasgow Commonwealth Games had given her plenty of experience. But today the building seemed more daunting, somehow. This was where she would spend the next few months in CID and so she must begin to see the place through different eyes, ones that had become used to seeing the citizens of Glasgow in all shapes and forms.

Her eyes sought out the old Volvo estate car lined up in the car park at the rear entrance to the police station. With a smile and a nod, Kirsty acknowledged the presence of her dad. He would be inside the building, waiting to see if she were arriving, perhaps even looking out for her at this very moment. The thought made her look up, but there was no face at an upper window watching for her arrival. She pushed open the door and entered the waiting area, glancing to her right just in case anyone was seated, watching for the moment when they were summoned inside to speak to one of the officers. But the curved row of brown faux-leather seats was empty, the floor slick and damp from the cleaner's early morning work, a faint whiff of something that vaguely resembled pine lingering in the air.

She was about to open the swing doors when a thick-set man in a short-sleeved uniform shirt came to the window of the front desk.

'Can I help you?' His voice was a growl, his bushy eyebrows drawn down as though ready to admonish Kirsty.

'Ah ... It's me. Detective Constable Wilson,' Kirsty said. 'My first day here in CID,' she added, trying not to look as uncertain as she felt.

The eyebrows rose and the grim mouth turned up in a smile, transforming the man's face in an instant.

'Och, Alistair's girl! Come away in, lass. Haven't seen you in a while. Didn't recognise you out of uniform.' He grinned.

Kirsty heard the faint sound of a buzzer and the automatic doors in front of her swung open.

Taking a deep breath, she stepped inside, walking around to the door where the uniformed officer stood, regarding her with interest.

'First day with CID, aye, you'll be wanting to go upstairs to see Detective Sergeant Murdoch.'

'Who?'

'Len Murdoch,' the officer replied. 'He's your mentor. Did Alistair not say?'

It was Kirsty's turn to raise her eyebrows. 'No,' she replied, inwardly asking herself why her father had omitted to give her this snippet of information. After all, he'd been ready enough with other sorts of advice: *listen to everything that you're told; keep a written record of every single action that you undertake; never contradict your superior officers* ... the list seemed to have gone on and on, stuff that had echoes of the weeks spent at Tulliallan, that turreted mansion across the other side of the Kincardine Bridge that was home to the Scottish Police Training College.

Kirsty frowned for a moment: who was DS Murdoch? The name meant nothing to her. Perhaps that was why her dad had not mentioned her mentor. Was this Murdoch new to Stewart Street himself?

'You know your way about here, don't you? Along the corridor, up the stairs and you'll find the muster room past the interview rooms.' He nodded upwards. 'It's been a busy kind of night, by all accounts.'

'Oh?' Kirsty stopped and gave him an enquiring look but the officer simply grinned at her.

'You'll find out soon enough,' he replied, raising one bushy eyebrow. 'Aye, Alistair, come down to see this young lady?'

Kirsty turned to see her father hurrying towards them, his black jacket zipped up. In an instant she was enveloped in a hug. At his side was a young woman whom Kirsty remembered seeing on her last visit to Stewart Street, a detective constable, she thought, struggling to recall the officer's name.

'Sorry I can't stick around, m'dear, going out on a job.' Alistair shook his head and gave Kirsty's arm a reassuring pat. 'They're all upstairs. Busy morning,' he added, echoing the police sergeant. 'Oh, and Lorimer's off today. Family funeral.' He bent to give her a peck on her cheek. 'Best of luck.' He grinned, then they were gone, out to where the old Volvo was parked, two detectives in a hurry to be somewhere else.

*

As Kirsty opened the door to the muster room she could see several men and a few women gathered together and facing the far end of the room where an older man in a dark chalk-striped suit stood, talking to them. As Kirsty moved to join the crowd of officers, she observed his bullet-shaped head, its cropped grey hair giving him a distinctly military appearance. Was this DS Murdoch? A quick glance around brought a few smiles of recognition from the men and women who knew her as Alistair Wilson's daughter, amongst them DC Jean Fairlie who gave her a grin and a thumbs up. But the man at the front was a complete stranger to Kirsty. At the sight of the new arrival, the man stopped what he was saying, waving her in with a flick of his hand, making several of the other officers turn and stare.

The man cleared his throat noisily. 'As I was saying,' he began, the gruff tone not trying to hide its note of sarcasm, causing Kirsty to blush to the roots of her hair. 'It's imperative that we catch the buggers before they have a chance to get any further from the city. Traffic have given us up-to-the minute CCTV information that suggests they're still within the Glasgow area.' The man paused and stared out over the assembled officers as though assessing them. For a moment his gaze rested on Kirsty and a faint smile played about his mouth, a smile, the girl noticed, that did not reach that pair of hard grey eyes.

Kirsty continued to listen, catching up on the news about a break-in at Paton's, a city-centre jeweller's shop, something that commanded the attention of the CID officers gathered in this room. As she listened, Kirsty pieced the story together. Armed robbers had burst into the premises during the hours of darkness, cutting through the steel shutters and smashing the windows even as the burglar alarm had been set off. Kirsty looked at the pictures on the screen behind the man in charge, images of running figures captured on CCTV cameras. Dark, masked men carrying the proceeds of their crime in what looked like sports bags, they fled out of sight, probably to a waiting car down a side lane.

'DS Murdoch, sir, do we have any intelligence on other similar raids?' a voice asked.

Kirsty looked at the detective sergeant who was standing, arms crossed, chin tilted upwards as though assessing the officer posing the question. So this was DS Murdoch, her mentor for the foreseeable future.

'Nothing like it in Glasgow recently. A few raids down in the Nottingham area but can't say they were quite like this one. Buggers actually thought things out before they busted the shop.'

There was a ripple of laughter in the room but Murdoch's face displayed not a scrap of humour, his mouth a thin sour line as if the robbery was a personal affront and not just a part of his job. She felt a momentary qualm as she watched the detective sergeant's eyes wander over the room then lock on her own. There was nothing malicious about the weary sigh and the raised eyebrows but it made Kirsty feel certain that having a new DC to mentor was the last thing this man desired on a busy Monday morning.

Several actions were handed out and the officers dispersed to their desks, leaving Kirsty stranded in the middle of the room with the bullet-headed DS staring at her.

'Okay, Wilson, come with me,' he said at last. 'Might as well learn on the job. You can drive, I take it?'

'Yes, sir,' Kirsty replied, lengthening her stride to keep up with Murdoch. She bit back the temptation to add that she had recently passed her advanced driving test with flying colours. Murdoch obviously hadn't taken the time to read her appraisal from her previous division and the knowledge of this irked

Kirsty. Why hadn't her dad told her this was the man who would be her mentor? Was there something about Murdoch that he wanted her to find out for herself? The thoughts chased each other around her head as she followed him out into the car park at the back of the building.

'Here.' Murdoch turned abruptly and chucked a bunch of keys towards her. They flew through the air and Kirsty caught them with one hand, making Murdoch raise his eyebrows in the first gesture of approval that he had shown since her arrival. As she slid into the Honda Civic and adjusted the seat, Kirsty suppressed the desire to smile. This was where she felt most at home, driving around the streets of Glasgow.

'Where to, sir?' she asked, glancing at Murdoch who had opened a file and was reading from a paper he held in his hand.

'Scene of crime, of course,' he replied in a withering tone. 'Where else d'you think we'd be heading?'

There was the usual blue and white tape surrounding the front of the jeweller's shop when Kirsty pulled up beside the scene of the robbery.

'Keys,' Murdoch said, the first words that he had uttered since leaving Stewart Street, and Kirsty handed them over.

She watched as he opened the boot and rummaged in a large black bag, something that she recognised as a scene of crime manager's kitbag.

'Here.' He tossed a bag containing a forensic kit at Kirsty. 'One size fits all,' he said, a fleeting smile on his face. He looked at Kirsty's low-heeled court shoes with a frown. 'Don't tear the overshoes, for God's sake, will you.'

Kirsty struggled into the thin garb, feeling suddenly self-conscious. Every scene of crime demanded the same care and attention to detail nowadays. The least bit of contamination that an officer might bring to a locus could endanger the entire investigation. *Every contact leaves a trace*, the mantra that was Locard's principle had been dinned into the raw recruits at police college. A sneeze in the wrong place might result in an officer's own DNA messing up a particular area and so the wearing of full oversuits and masks was mandatory.

She followed him carefully as Murdoch stopped to examine the torn edges of the shuttering. 'Need to find out what did this,' he muttered, a gloved hand lifting the broken metal strut.

'Sorry?' Kirsty asked.

'We need to find out what sort of power tools they used to cut these shutters,' Murdoch said in a laboured manner, as if he were talking to a simpleton. 'Christ! Where do they get you lot from these days?' he sneered, rising to his feet and heading past the uniformed officer who was standing in the entrance to the shop.

Kirsty felt her face flame as he curled his lip at her. This was not a good beginning. *Watch and learn*, a little voice told her. *You'll not be with him for ever.* And somehow the voice reminded her of her old friend, Detective Superintendent Lorimer, the man she had known for most of her life, something that immediately made her feel better.

She followed Murdoch into the premises, past the uniformed police officer who was shuffling her feet to avoid the pile of broken glass that littered the dark blue carpet.

Kirsty looked around to see if there were any scene of crime officers already in the jeweller's shop but the place seemed deserted.

'Is it just us, sir?' she asked.

Murdoch turned with a crooked grin. 'Worried I might try it on with you, Wilson?' he asked, his voice thick with derision.

'No, I—'

'The SOCOs are on their way,' he sighed. 'As crime scene manager I have to be here first to determine exactly how this investigation should proceed.'

'The owners ...?'

'Are on their way to Stewart Street to have a nice cup of tea and talk to the officers there,' he replied. 'Need to get them back later to check the stock, see exactly what's missing.' Then he folded his arms and looked Kirsty up and down. 'How about getting me a coffee and a bacon roll from across the road,' he said, jerking his head in the direction of a greasy spoon that bore the dubious name Snax Attax on a white board above the double frontage.

But I've just kitted up, Kirsty wanted to protest, then her better self uttered, 'Yes, sir,' in her meekest voice.

As she stepped aside to remove the oversuit and shoes, Kirsty watched Murdoch out of the corner of her eye. The crime scene manager had strolled into a corner of the shop and was examining trays of watches that had been thrown on to the floor. As she folded the white clothing, she saw Murdoch drag the huge black bag that contained his crime scene gear and set it at his feet, partly blocking her view.

The man was crouched down on his hunkers, gloved hands running slowly across the tray. Was he making some sort of a mental inventory? Kirsty wondered as she turned to leave.

It was over so quickly that she hardly saw it happening. One moment Murdoch's hand was hovering above the watches, the next he was slipping something into the bag at his feet.

I didn't see that, was Kirsty's first thought as she hurried from the jeweller's shop, pausing to thrust her forensic suit into the Honda. *He couldn't have done that, could he?* Yet, as she crossed the road to the café, one hand fumbling for her purse, a cold feeling in the pit of her stomach told her that her eyes had not deceived her. She had seen her mentor, Detective Sergeant Murdoch, putting one of the watches into his crime scene bag.

The smell of rancid bacon and hot pies wafted out of the café as Kirsty opened the door, suddenly making her feel sick. Heart thumping, she waited in a small queue of early morning workers, glancing back across the road at the shop.

There was no way of seeing Murdoch from here, just the officer standing outside and the Honda parked by the kerb. Had she really seen her senior officer stealing a watch? Was it something he had done to test her, perhaps? Would he expect his new DC to bring up the subject?

Oh, sir, by the way, did you steal one of those expensive-looking watches? Was that what he thought she would ask?

Kirsty blinked and tried to recall the moment when Murdoch had picked up the watch. Had she really seen that? Or, she began to wonder, had it been a trick of the light? And her overactive imagination?

'Aye, hen, whit're ye wantin?' A woman in a white mob cap leaned forwards across the counter, shaking Kirsty out of her reverie.

'Oh, er, a bacon roll and a coffee, please,' she said.

'Whit kinda coffee?' The woman heaved a sigh, arms folded across her ample bosom.

Kirsty's mouth fell open. She hadn't even asked Murdoch how he liked his coffee.

'Um, white, please,' she decided. 'And can I have a sachet of sugar?' Then, biting her lip she added, 'Make that two coffees, would you? One black and one white,' she said. She'd take which-ever one Murdoch refused, she thought, desperate not to get into his bad books and even more terrified that he had known she was watching him.

The scene of crime officers were sitting in the van, pulling on their oversuits, when Kirsty crossed the road for a second time. A sense of relief washed over her as she unlocked the Honda and set down the cardboard tray on the passenger seat. She would not be on her own with Murdoch for the rest of the morning, Kirsty thought, clambering back into her white protective clothing. And, she told herself, what she had seen would be pushed to the back of her mind until such time as she could decide what she ought to do.

CHAPTER FIVE

As he glanced in the rear-view mirror, Detective Super-intendent William Lorimer smiled. There was not another car in sight. He slowed down as the Lexus took the bend, eyes on the unfolding panorama of mountains etched against this clear September sky. Queen's View, it was called, but any discerning traveller could heave a sigh of pleasure at the regal vista that spread itself before him. A momentary glimpse of Loch Lomond shining between the hills, then it was gone, the ribbon of road taking the detective superintendent downhill once more.

The landscape was changing with the seasons, he noticed; it was as if the very earth was preparing itself for winter with its coat of bracken curling into brown fronds and grasses dried yellow after the summer's heat. Swathes of willowherb lined the banks, their feathery seed heads soft and white after the ver-million that had stained the late summer hedgerows. Skeletons of Queen Anne's lace towered above, grey and dry now, their umbels picked clean by foraging birds. Soon the light would wane as the equinox balanced night and day and he would find himself travelling to and from work in the darkness for many months to come.

'I never tire of this place,' Maggie sighed as they left Stockie-muir behind.

'Need to come back for a climb one of these days,' Lorimer agreed. 'Some weekend,' he suggested.

His wife smiled and nodded, still gazing at the passing land-scape. It was a rare occasion for them both to be away from their respective jobs in the city. Maggie's school had allowed her a day's leave of absence to attend the funeral of her old Uncle Robert, Lorimer wangling time off from his own caseload of work. It was just a pity that it had coincided with young Kirsty's first day at Stewart Street, he thought. Still, she'd be there for long enough and he would see her tomorrow.

As they travelled on through the Stirlingshire countryside, Lorimer glanced at his wife. More than twenty years of marriage had dealt kindly with the woman by his side, her fine features and dark hair belying her age. Yet those years had not been without heartache, the loss of children robbing them of a longed-for family. Perhaps that was one of the things that had kept them close together, Lorimer mused; they'd had each other to cling to when life had dealt each harsh blow. And Maggie had endured the lot of a policeman's wife, putting up with his long hours and frequent absences with a patience that never ceased to amaze him.

'Last of that generation,' Maggie sighed, breaking into her husband's thoughts. 'End of an era, I suppose.'

'Aye,' Lorimer agreed, but said no more. It was hard to be sad on a day like this when the sun shone down from a clear blue sky on to the burnished trees, an autumn fire of scarlet and gold arch-ing overhead. Maggie's Uncle Robert had been Alice Findlay's only brother and now that last link with his late mother-in-law would be gone. He thought about Alice for a moment, remem-bering her smile. They had rarely seen Alice's elder brother, a farmer who lived more than an hour north of Glasgow, except at weddings and funerals. And now it was time to bid the old man farewell.

'You've got cousins, though, they'll all be there, won't they?'

'Mm.' Maggie nodded in reply. 'I expect so. Haven't really kept in touch.'

'Two boys, right?'

'Well, hardly boys now. David must be my age at least and Patrick a couple of years younger,' she mused, settling back and watching as the landscape unfolded before them.

The wind had freshened by the time Lorimer and Maggie left the crematorium and made their way back to the line of waiting cars. Leaves skittered along a narrow pavement, a fine cloud of dust following their progress. It had been a short service with many empty spaces in the small chapel, so many of Uncle Robert's friends and family already awaiting him on the other side, as the minister had told the small congregation. It had been a life well lived, according to the eulogy; Robert Imrie had been a man of the soil, a man close to the pattern of life dictated by the seasons, and the policeman found himself regretting that he had not really known his wife's uncle.

Lorimer had shaken hands with a dark-suited man whose face he scarcely remembered from Alice Findlay's own funeral: Uncle Robert's son Patrick, one of Maggie's cousins.

'Sorry for your loss,' he had murmured, words that had come to his lips so often in the progress of murder cases when he'd had to talk to members of the victim's family. And Patrick Imrie had nodded in reply. 'Thanks for coming,' he'd said, darting a glance at his cousin Maggie's husband as if reminding himself that Lorimer was someone important in Police Scotland.

'Where did he say the hotel was?' Maggie asked, fastening her seat belt.

'Middle of the town,' Lorimer replied. 'Up towards the castle. Used to be Stirling Royal Academy before it was changed to a hotel. You'll feel right at home.'

Maggie gave a short laugh. 'Typical. Away from that lot for a day and where do I end up?'

Lorimer smiled back, knowing that she wasn't serious. If ever anyone loved their job it was Mrs Lorimer. And the kids loved her back, that much was evident from the way she spoke about them. Teaching English was a genuine vocation for his wife and she never tired of finding different ways to open up the glories of literature to her pupils.

'Funny David wasn't there,' she remarked. 'I would have thought he would have been by Patrick's side after the service.'

'Maybe someone has to stay and see to the farm,' Lorimer suggested.

The hotel was located up a steep narrow street and, as he drove through a stone archway, Lorimer had the impression from the old building that he was travelling back in time. The stories these cobbles could tell . . .

The interior of the hotel was modern and warm, though part of the building's past still remained in the gilded names on the doors: Latin Room, Geography Room.

'The Imrie family is up in the Headmaster's Study,' the girl behind the reception desk told them. 'That's up at the top of the stairs,' she added with a sympathetic smile, glancing at their black clothes.

Maggie and Lorimer began climbing a curving staircase then she stopped suddenly. 'Look at that view!' she gasped, and Lorimer looked out of a small window set into the thick white wall to see a vista over the Stirlingshire countryside, the roof-tops of nearby buildings hazy as the sun cast its rays through the clouds.

There were a few black-suited people gathered in the room next to the bar when he and Maggie arrived to be greeted by a waiter proffering a tray of complimentary drinks. Lorimer chose orange juice, mindful of the need to drive back to Glasgow, and Maggie did the same.

'I better speak to Patrick,' she murmured.

Lorimer followed his wife to where her cousin stood, whisky glass in hand. Patrick Imrie had the look of a country farmer. Lorimer guessed that his ruddy cheeks and stocky frame were more at home in tweeds and a flat cap than the formal black suit.

Maggie took her cousin's hand in hers.

'And David? Could he not be here today?' she asked kindly.

Patrick Imrie shook his head, his eyes narrowing. 'You didn't know about David, then?' he asked.

'No, what's wrong?' Maggie frowned.

'Took a stroke a couple of years back,' Patrick sighed. 'He's in a nursing home in Glasgow now. Can't speak much, can't get about.' He shrugged.

'How awful,' Maggie exclaimed. 'The poor fellow!'

'Aye, well.' Patrick paused to take a slug of whisky. 'It's us that'll be poor soon enough,' he remarked. 'Cost of the nursing home's just about crippling us. Was a time when we could just sell a beast to pay for an emergency. Now ...?' He shrugged again. 'Farm'll have to be sold off before next spring,' he added sourly.

'Oh, no, that's terrible!' Maggie said, a sympathetic hand touching her cousin's arm. 'What will you do? Where will you go?'

'Ach, that's what I asked my father time and time again when he insisted that David be put into that place. Costs more than a thousand pounds a week,' he said, glancing up at Lorimer as if to gauge his reaction. 'We can't sustain that sort of expense for much longer. We'll have to move somewhere else. Hope the council can rehouse us. Unless . . . '

'Unless?' Lorimer asked.

'Well, he doesn't keep well, you know,' Patrick said, lowering his voice. 'David, I mean. A sudden turn for the worse and he could be away.' The farmer's eyes widened as he nodded. 'Could happen any time.'

Maggie said nothing, then, as an older couple made their way to greet Patrick Imrie, she and Lorimer walked slowly through to the main room where a buffet had been prepared.

'Goodness,' she said softly, once they were out of earshot. 'I didn't know about cousin David. Oh dear. I've been sending Christmas cards and wondering why we'd not heard back from him. Poor Uncle Robert!'

'Aye, and poor Patrick. What a state of affairs to be in,' Lorimer murmured, picking up a couple of triangular sandwiches and a sausage roll.

'Well,' a woman's voice broke into their conversation, 'it would be a God's blessing if *poor* David would just slip away in his sleep. Save us all a lot of grief!'

Maggie opened her mouth to reply but a nudge from her husband made her close her mouth again and glance up at him as the woman strode away, her black felt hat bobbing on top of a thatch of red curls.

'Isn't that Patrick's wife?' he whispered. 'She was by his side at the front of the crematorium.'

'I couldn't see,' Maggie admitted. 'Guess your height lets you notice something like that. Anyway,' she lowered her voice even more, 'she's Patrick's second wife. First one left him not long after they were married. We weren't invited to the second wedding. Probably a quiet affair in Stirling Registrar's Office, or we would have been.'

'I suppose your Uncle Robert left the farm to Patrick?'

Maggie shook her head. 'That's where you'd be wrong,' she said. 'I remember Mum telling me that the farm was to be left equally between the two boys. I guess that's why Patrick has to sell David's share to fund his nursing home.'

'No wonder she's in a state, then,' Lorimer murmured, licking flakes of pastry from his fingers. 'Can't be a nice prospect to lose your livelihood and your home all in one go.'

'I wonder whereabouts in Glasgow he is,' Maggie pondered as they sat down at a circular table next to some farmers who were deep in discussion about the prices at Stirling Market. 'David, I mean. Shall we find out and pay him a visit? If he's as bad as Patrick makes out we may never have another chance.'

Lorimer bit his lip. He wanted to return as soon as possible to the city and pick up the threads of his working week, but he could see his wife's point of view.

'Okay, so long as it isn't miles out of our way,' he agreed. 'Let's get the details from Patrick and give the place a call to see if it's okay to visit, shall we?'

CHAPTER SIX

Abbey Nursing Home was not very far from the city, close to
Bearsden and near enough to the Strathblane Road to make
the journey a reasonable one for members of the Imrie family. As
the sign came into sight, Lorimer slowed down to see the rooftop
of a long, low building set off the road, screened from view by a
high beech hedge that was beginning to turn to its autumn gold.

'This looks nice,' Maggie murmured as they drew up into the
bays marked out for cars to one side of the nursing home. And it
did, Lorimer mentally agreed, his eyes roaming over the façade,
noting the clever extensions either side of what may have orig-
inally been a country cottage, the whitewashed walls helping to
blend the old with the new. A quick glance showed that there was
a further addition at the back, then a glimpse of green grass and
more trees casting their shadows over that part of the grounds.

There was a security keypad and a bell push set into the thick
stone wall of the entrance, a heavy glass-panelled door beyond.

It did not take more than a few seconds before a figure
appeared and opened it, a kindly face beaming at them.

'Mr and Mrs Lorimer? I'm Mrs Abbott,' she said, offering her
hand to them. 'Do come in.'

'Mrs Abbott?' Maggie gave a puzzled frown.

The woman smiled at them as she led them through to a bright lounge where three of the patients were sitting in wheelchairs and watching television. 'Yes, the nursing home is named after my husband and I. There are no abbeys anywhere near here,' she laughed. 'And as our name is Abbott we thought it a good idea to name our nursing home after ourselves.'

Maggie returned the woman's smile. 'You're a nurse, then?'

'That's right. A retired nurse, although I do in fact have a lot to do with the patients here. Used to work in the old Stirling Royal before much of it closed down.' She made a face. 'My husband is in the building trade, or should I say *was*. He helps run this place now. Let me show you where your cousin's room is,' she added, leading them through another door and along a corridor, its walls painted canary yellow. White gauzy curtains graced every window they passed as they walked along behind her, light streaming in.

'The original building was a domestic dwelling house?' Lorimer asked as they turned a corner and came at last to the back of the building and another passage that gave on to several rooms.

'That's right. We were given permission to change its use into a business.' Mrs Abbott nodded. 'There are twenty beds here, all full, and we have a waiting list as long's your arm,' she said, raising her eyebrows. 'Victims of our own success, I fear. You'd be amazed how many people need round-the-clock care,' she added. 'And not everyone can cope with a severely disabled relative.' She lowered her voice. 'Stroke victims like your cousin need a special sort of care. And that's part of my own nursing background.'

She stopped outside a door that was slightly ajar. 'This is your cousin's room,' she told Maggie. The woman hesitated for a moment. 'He may not know who you are,' she began. 'He finds it difficult to process any new information and will probably

30

not remember that you were even here.' Her face looked from Maggie to Lorimer with a rueful expression. 'I'm sorry, but that's just the way he is. Mr Imrie gets the best medical attention every day and we do everything that we can to make him comfortable and as happy as a man with his condition can be,' she explained.

There was a pause. *But,* thought Lorimer. He could almost hear the word and the unspoken explanation: *but he will never be better, never walk again, never smell the new-mown hay or hear the noise of the combine harvester trundling over his fields.*

'We understand,' he said gently.

David was asleep, his head turned towards the glass doors that overlooked the side of the property with a view across the fields and hills. Lorimer nodded to himself. A thoughtful touch, to let this former man of the soil be as close to nature as he still could. The nursing home and its staff rose in his estimation as he looked around the well-furnished room.

'It's nice,' he whispered. 'Good quality stuff,' he added, nodding towards the curtains that were swept back from the French windows.

'Sanderson,' Maggie told him. 'No expense spared here,' she added with a sigh.

Then, as though becoming conscious of the people in his room, David Imrie gave a moan and opened his eyes.

'Oh, I wish I'd not persuaded you to take me there,' Maggie exclaimed as they set off once more for home. Lorimer glanced at her as she searched through her handbag for a clean handkerchief to blow her nose. There was absolutely nothing wrong with the nursing home, nor of the care her cousin appeared to be receiving. And yet it had been upsetting to see a person like that, someone of his own age, with white hair and the grey complexion of a much older man. One gnarled hand had lain on top of the counterpane, shrivelled and gaunt, a hand that was unable to reach for a cup or even to clasp another's hand in greeting. Vacant eyes had looked their way, slivers of drool spilling from his open mouth. Maggie had taken tissues from her bag and wiped them away, her natural instinct to help a fellow human being.

What was behind those eyes? How much intelligence was left after the episode that had damaged David Imrie's brain? As he drove towards the motorway, Lorimer said a silent prayer of thanks for his own good health, something he took for granted day after day.

CHAPTER SEVEN

Glasgow.

Sarah heaved a huge sigh as the train passed through the darkness of a tunnel. What was she going to find there after all this time away? It was where everything had gone wrong and yet there were still good memories associated with the city, memories that lingered like the aftertaste of a sweet wine.

Pete was gone. Her parents didn't want to know her any more, so why had she decided to come back? It had been home for all of her twenty-six years, she supposed, unless she counted the time spent at Her Majesty's pleasure. Anyway, Sarah told herself, zipping up her jacket, it was a question that could wait until she decided whether she was going to stick around here or move on.

The suddenness of light flooding into the railway carriage almost made Sarah gasp. As the train slowed down at platform three in Queen Street station, the girl glanced at the people beside her, gathering up their laptop bags and raincoats, ready to face whatever was taking them into Scotland's largest city. Sarah sat still, waiting until the train had come to a complete halt, not wishing to bump into any of her fellow passengers, deciding to hold off until the very last moment when she would pick up her

33

raincoat and the bag at her feet and set off on the next stage of her journey.

There was a damp smoky smell in the air as Sarah alighted from the train, as if an autumn fog had swirled its way through the dark tunnel and settled down on the concrete platforms and the metal rails below. She shivered, clutching her ticket, remembering that disembodied voice on the train telling the passengers that a barrier was in operation. So many details forgotten, so many things to think about. Only a few stragglers from the Stirling train were moving through the barriers now as Sarah placed her ticket in the slot. She watched as it was swallowed up and the little black gates opened noiselessly, letting her through. It was, Sarah felt, as if she were being properly released back into the maelstrom that was Glasgow's human population.

Her feet seemed to have a life of their own, taking her past the uniformed station staff, the Costa Coffee shop (was that white-haired barista who made such nice chai lattes still there?) then out past the Millennium Hotel and into the heart of the city.

For a moment Sarah stood on the pavement watching the traffic ebb and flow around George Square. Light bounced off the car windows, the rays of a September sun penetrating the clouds, a warmth that was pleasing after the chill of the station. If she could just stand here for a while, she thought, face turned up to the brightness . . .

Sarah only realised that she had shut her eyes when the beep from the traffic signal alerted her.

'You crossing here or what, hen?' a gravelly voice spoke at her side.

Sarah jumped then mumbled an apology to a cross-faced older woman with straggly grey hair as she let herself join the group of pedestrians heading along in the direction of Queen Street. She needed to keep her wits about her, not fall into the trap of standing out in a crowd, she thought, a sudden dread washing over her. She didn't want anyone staring, divining who she was and where she had come from. Perhaps she ought to have taken their advice back in Cornton, let them persuade her to talk to that woman from SHINE. *A mentor*, they'd told her. *Someone to help you when you come out.* But Sarah had rejected any offer of help, preferring to keep her own counsel, burying her darkest thoughts as deeply as she could.

The pavement underfoot was damp from an earlier shower of rain, the grey surface cracked and worn from many passing feet. She looked with interest at two red open-topped buses by the kerb, a few folk waiting patiently for one of the doors to open. Tourists, no doubt, wanting to sample the Glasgow atmosphere.

I could show you a few places that would make your eyes open, Sarah thought, glancing at them. But their eyes were probably turned towards the magnificent City Chambers, its neo-classical features dominating one entire side of the square. Sarah had been inside only once, a vague notion of brown marble and a sweeping staircase lingered in her memory.

She shifted her bag on to a different shoulder, the ache of its weight making her long for her journey's end. Not all of the landmarks around here were familiar, she thought. Some of the restaurants had changed, hadn't they? And there was a new building on that corner replacing one that had been demolished. What had it been? She simply couldn't remember. Then, as she walked along past the Gallery of Modern Art, Sarah's face creased in a grin: the Duke of Wellington's statue still had a traffic cone on its head. Some things never changed.

The light that had warmed her disappeared as Sarah walked down between the high buildings on either side of Queen Street, reminding her that summer was past and the chills of winter were only weeks away. In a doorway ahead she could see a bundle of grey rags that became a man's face, the eyes turned up in that self-conscious expression of pleading that street beggars always seemed to wear. He would tell her to *have a nice day* even if she passed him by without throwing a coin or two into the grubby upturned cap that lay beside the worn blanket. Sarah hesitated, unsure how she would react, thinking about how little she now had herself in the world yet hoping that fate might keep her from this state if she showed some kindness. She fumbled in her pocket, feeling the handful of loose change that she'd thrust there after the taxi had driven off, leaving her outside Stirling station.

It was the work of a moment to toss the coins into his cap then hurry on, not waiting to look in his face, not wanting to hear any words of gratitude. For who was she to receive thanks? The poor beggar sitting there was probably more deserving of kindness than she was.

Her head was down as she rushed along to the corner where the pedestrian precinct on Argyll Street opened up, so she did not see him until it was almost too late. A dark figure stepped sideways to avoid her and she gasped, horrified to see the uniform of Police Scotland, fearful that the look on her face would betray where she had been, what she had done. But the young officer hardly gave Sarah more than an amused glance as he strode on, leaving her with a sick, trembling feeling in the pit of her stomach.

Nobody appeared to notice the young woman walking hurriedly towards the street where she was to find the correct bus stop that would take her out of the city centre. Two women, each with toddlers in buggies, chatted to one another as they passed, snatches of their conversation drifting by.

'D'you think I really should?'

'Aw, go on! Tell him that . . . '

But whatever one of them was being urged to tell, and to whom, would remain a mystery for ever, the women's words lost in a blur of traffic noise as a bus braked nearby, its screech drowning out speech and thought.

Sarah wondered for a few seconds what they had been discussing. The break-up of a relationship? (She'd had plenty of those!) Or was it something more mundane, like blowing too much money on a fancy new dress?

Her thoughts made Sarah shift the bag again, its contents heavy enough but in truth the burden that she shouldered represented the sum total of all her worldly goods. She would not think of all her clothes and other belongings discarded by that mean-faced landlord, a fact that the prison officer had passed on. Her rent had been due and she had no means to pay it once the prison gates had slammed behind her, so the nasty old man had binned the lot, or so he had told the officers who had contacted him to ask. Sarah thought of her fake-fur coat with a sudden pang. Bad old bugger had probably sold it on eBay! Or given it away to one of his slim-hipped daughters.

The sigh that escaped her became a yawn as she turned the corner and searched for the number of the bus that she needed. At least where she was going there would be a room and a bed, somewhere that she could relax and call her own for a week or so. And she would need to sign on, find a job, get enough money together to . . . to do what? A wave of anxiety came over her as Sarah began to think how she might spend her future. And, despite the steady stream of people walking up and down Jamaica Street and the queue ahead of her at the bus stop, the former prisoner felt more alone than she had ever felt before.

However, Sarah was not alone. All along the route from Queen

Street station to the pavement here outside a cut-price store, the former inmate had no inkling that she was being followed, no hairs standing up on the back of her neck to alert her to the figure shadowing her every step. In her eagerness to take in all the sights, Sarah Wilding was quite oblivious to the person that kept to the shadows, pausing when she paused, head dropped to scan his mobile phone should she happen to look his way.

And when at last she stepped on board the bus that would take her to her final destination, there was nothing to make her turn and stare at the man who now sat two rows behind, his eyes fixed intently on the long blonde hair sweeping past her shoulders. Nor was there anything to alert her to the danger that lay ahead.

CHAPTER EIGHT

Sarah sat on the edge of the bed and looked out of the window at the street below. The bed and breakfast place was only temporary, she told herself, looking up at the rough patch on the corner of the ceiling where water must have dripped through. The woman shivered and drew her coat closer to her body. There was no heating that she could see and the windows rattled with every passing lorry, so no double-glazed units either. The yellowing candlewick bedspread was worn, several tufts of its swirling design missing. There was a desk and a metal chair, a lamp with a dingy white shade and a small rail set into an alcove with three wire hangers shoved to one side. She had been too tired, too depressed by the place to bother unpacking what few bits and pieces she had taken from the prison, and so the hangers lay empty still, waiting for garments to be placed on their thin metal shoulders.

Sarah had expected a surge of elation once she had closed the door to this room and taken possession of it, but all she could feel was the weight of her own guilt pressing down upon her. A headache was beginning to throb on either side of her head, the forerunner to a full-blown migraine, if she wasn't much mistaken.

She needed to eat, Sarah's wiser, more practical voice told her; the voice she used to employ when trying to coax her patients to take some nourishment. There was nothing in this room to use for preparing meals: no microwave oven or electric grill, only a white plastic kettle, its flex coiled like a fakir's snake to be charmed into something magical. The communal bathroom was down the corridor so she would need to leave her room whenever she wanted to fill it from the sink.

'Don't leave anything in there,' Mrs Duncan, the bed-and-breakfast owner had told her as she had shown her the bathroom. And, when Sarah's eyebrows had risen in a silent question, the woman had added, 'It'll just be nicked.'

Her words came back to Sarah now. Was this three-storey building on Glasgow's south side a halfway house frequented by female offenders, then? A place recommended by the social worker who had liaised with the prison about her release? Were there thieves, prostitutes and others here, separated from Sarah Wilding by a few plasterboard walls? The cornicing around the ceiling stopped abruptly, a tell-tale sign that a bigger room had been split into two or more. Once upon a time this might have been a lovely place, home to a prosperous Victorian businessman and his family. Years of neglect had rendered its red sandstone walls shabby and dark, the paint was peeling from every faded window frame and the creaking stairs up to this third-floor room bore testimony to the many feet that had climbed this way.

Mrs Duncan had not asked any questions of her newest guest, simply told her the times for breakfast each morning (seven till nine) and shown her the facilities, such as they were, before relinquishing the key and heading off back downstairs to her own part of this rambling old house. Was that because she knew of Sarah's history? Or was she simply uninterested in the young woman as a person, seeing her instead as a line of figures in a ledger, adding up as the weekly rent became due?

She gave another sigh and turned from the window, seeing nothing outside. A sudden yearning for sleep made her kick off her shoes and lie down on top of the yellow bedspread.

Outside, betrayed only by a thin line of cigarette smoke ascending in the cold morning air, the dark-clad figure stood, eyes fixed on the window up above where, until a moment before, the object of his scrutiny had stood.

CHAPTER NINE

What on earth was she going to do about Murdoch? The proper course should be to report him to someone in Professional Standards, of course. Failing to do that could cost Kirsty dearly, even see her sacked from the police. But, she reasoned, reporting him might see her hung out to dry as well; who knew what friends the DS might have in high places.

As she climbed the stairs to the CID rooms, Kirsty admitted to herself that the best course of action was simply to keep her mouth shut. After all, Murdoch could deny any accusation she might make and it would do her fledgling career as a detective no good whatsoever to point an accusing finger at the man who was mentoring her.

As if the thought of Murdoch had suddenly conjured him up, there he was, striding along the corridor towards Kirsty, a grim expression on his face.

'C'mon, Wilson, we're going back out,' he said sharply. 'Sudden death. And it looks like one for the Fiscal,' he added darkly.

A police car was outside the house when they arrived, an officer standing by the foot of a short flight of stone steps leading up to a dark green painted door. The house was one of the old-fashioned cottage-style four-in-a-block flats that were common in and around the city; the ground-floor homes were accessed by doors at the front of the building whilst the upstairs neighbours had to go around each side to enter their homes. Jane Maitland's home was one of those on the ground floor, and Kirsty noticed the small metal handrails that had been fitted either side of the front door steps. An old person, then, she guessed.

'District nurse found her this morning when she called in to give her the usual medication,' Murdoch told her as they donned their white suits for the second time that day. 'When the ambulance came to take her away, the neighbour from upstairs came down to see what was going on.' Murdoch gave a grin. 'Nosy neighbours. Don't you just love them!'

Kirsty struggled to fit the bootees over her shoes as Murdoch continued. 'Seems there had been an early morning caller. Another nurse who'd arrived at the crack of dawn. Not anybody on their rota.' He raised his eyebrows meaningfully. 'The body'll have to be taken down to the mortuary for a PM.'

Kirsty followed the crime scene manager into the house where a pale-faced woman with short dark hair stood in the hallway, a green cardigan draped over her navy blue uniform.

'Nurse Morgan,' she said as they approached. She looked at their white garb and nodded. 'I've only touched her wrist to feel for a pulse,' she said, tilting her chin up in a defensive manner.

'And the paramedics?'

'I asked them to come back later,' Nurse Morgan told them. 'When Mrs Doyle from upstairs told me someone else had been in early this morning ... well ... what was I supposed to do? A sudden death, that wasn't unexpected – she was a very sick woman – but with a complication like this ...' She tailed off as though the detectives would understand what she was trying to say.

'Is Mrs Doyle still there?'

'Oh, aye.' The nurse gave a faint smile. 'No show without Punch. She's just dying to see one of you to tell her story.' The hint of sarcasm in her tone was not lost on either of the officers.

'We'll need to see the deceased,' Murdoch told her and she walked a few paces along the hallway, motioning with her hand towards a door that was shut fast.

'Thought it should stay closed till you came,' the nurse murmured.

'Good thinking,' Murdoch told her, nodding as he opened the door with his free hand, the other holding the huge black bag containing his extensive scene of crime kit.

The room was still in darkness, a pair of curtains closed against the bright autumn day. There was a smell that Kirsty couldn't identify, a mixture of sweet pot-pourri and damp wool. Her eyes flicked over the shape underneath the bedcovers and came to rest on a radiator by the window where a Fair Isle jersey had been left to dry.

Murdoch nodded towards the window. 'Open them, can't see a damned thing in here,' he ordered.

Kirsty's gloved fingers felt along the side of the curtain until she found the pull cord. Suddenly the room changed as the brightness flooded in, dust motes dancing in a cone of sunlight.

Kirsty watched as DS Murdoch stepped around the body, checking for anything that seemed out of the ordinary, though how he would know what he was looking for was a mystery.

'Could be a simple enough explanation,' he grunted. 'Old lady might have taken a bad turn then called someone else.'

'But surely Nurse Morgan would know who that was,' Kirsty whispered.

'Aye, you'd think so. That's why we're here. Sudden deaths happen all the time. *Suspicious* sudden deaths not nearly so often.' He knelt down, lifting the edge of a pleated pink valance to check underneath the bed.

Kirsty's eyes were drawn to Jane Maitland's face. *The face of the deceased*, she thought to herself. Odd how being in the room with Murdoch, dressed in these white suits, depersonalised the corpse in the bed.

'She was bright enough yesterday.' Nurse Morgan's voice came from the hallway. 'Must have taken bad in the night. Like I said, she was a very ill woman.' She stepped into the room.

'And it would have saved you a lot of trouble just sending for her GP to sign a death certificate,' Murdoch said with a sigh.

Kirsty could see the woman bristle with annoyance at his words.

'Well, I would have had to be satisfied that Miss Maitland had died of natural causes,' she replied brusquely.

'And you weren't,' Kirsty finished for her, trying to sound sympathetic towards the district nurse and annoyed at Murdoch's insinuation that she'd caused more trouble for the police than this old lady was worth.

'No, I wasn't,' the woman insisted. 'My rounds are done at certain times of the day and there was definitely no other nurse meant to be here before me this morning. I checked,' she added, folding her arm across her chest and staring defiantly at the detectives.

'The home help's due at eleven-thirty. But I called their office to tell them not to come in today.' She sighed. 'God knows what I'll do if the Tesco delivery comes. It's due around lunchtime.'

'And have you called her GP?' Murdoch asked.

'Yes. He's been held up at the surgery but should be here any time now.'

At that moment Kirsty heard the front doorbell ring.

45

'That'll be him now,' Nurse Morgan declared, disappearing back along the corridor.

The doctor blinked at the sight of two white-suited figures in his patient's bedroom but Murdoch ignored the man's discomfiture, nodding towards the figure on the bed.

'She died earlier this morning,' Murdoch told the man who was hesitating in the doorway behind the district nurse. 'Seems there was an unauthorised visitor dressed like a bona-fide nurse.' He shrugged. 'How they got in and out is a complete mystery. Probably a simple explanation,' he growled.

'You want me to examine the deceased and write out a death certificate?' the man asked, a frown appearing on his brow.

'Aye, doc, you do that, will you? And our pathologist will no doubt confirm exactly what you decide was the cause of death,' Murdoch said wearily.

'Wilson, you go upstairs and see this Mrs Doyle, will you? I'll be with you directly.'

Kirsty was glad to leave the room and strip off her white suit in the hallway, though she kept on the gloves so as not to contaminate any fingerprints on the door handle as she left the lower cottage flat.

She slipped off the thin rubber gloves and stuffed them into her jacket pocket as she climbed the flight of stone stairs to Mrs Doyle's house. A nosy neighbour, Kirsty told herself, probably some old dear who couldn't sleep too well. So it came as a surprise when a young woman with short, cropped hair in tones of pink and a row of earrings studded along one ear appeared at the door. She was dressed all in black, a baggy T-shirt covering wide-legged trousers, a white muslin cloth slung over one shoulder.

'You polis?' she asked in the deep gravelly voice of an habitual smoker.

46

'Detective Constable Wilson,' Kirsty replied. 'My colleague, Detective Sergeant Murdoch, will be joining us shortly.'

'Ailsa Doyle,' the woman said, motioning Kirsty inside with a jerk of her head. 'The wean's asleep so dinna wake him, awright? In here.' She ushered Kirsty into the front room, which overlooked the street.

There were signs of a small baby's presence everywhere. A carrycot on a stand took up one corner of the room, the bedclothes spilling out on one side. A plastic nappy-changing mat had been left on the floor beside the fireplace, a blue quilted bag lying open beside it, all the creams and disposable nappies ready for use. A faint whiff of sick permeated the air and Kirsty tried not to wrinkle her nose as she saw the telltale yellow stains on the muslin cloth draped over the young mother's shoulder.

'Bad night?' Kirsty asked, a tone of sympathy in her voice.

'You got weans?' Mrs Doyle asked, looking sharply at Kirsty, eyeing the smart trouser suit with undisguised longing.

'No,' Kirsty replied.

'Had me up all bloody night,' Ailsa Doyle grunted, leaning forward and picking up a cigarette packet that was lying on top of a scratched wooden coffee table. 'That's how I saw the old lady's visitor,' she said, nodding towards the window. 'Used to seeing them come at different times of the day. Regular as clockwork, so they are. Till this morning, early on, like.' She paused to light up then closed her eyes, inhaling the smoke as though it were the best moment of her day. Perhaps it was, Kirsty thought, watching the woman while wondering just how his mother's smoking might affect a small baby.

'Can you tell us what the visitor looked like?' Kirsty asked, taking a notebook from her shoulder bag.

Ailsa Doyle tilted her pink head to one side, thoughtfully. 'It wis dark, like,' she began. 'Kinda misty mornin'. Saw him walking along the street. Navy jaicket, an' that.'

'He didn't get out of a car?'

'Naw. Like ah said, walked up tae the door and jist went in. Must've had a key, know whit ah mean?' She shrugged. 'Anyroads, the wean wis greetin fit tae burst so ah didnae see ony mair till he cam oot.' She frowned suddenly, flicking ash into a green glass dish on the windowsill. 'He didnae see me. Didnae look up. The light in here wisnae oan.' Ailsa Doyle shrugged again. 'Got tae watch the electric bills,' she said, lips pursing in a gesture of defiance. 'Besides, ah like tae see the sun come up ower thae trees.' Her voice softened as she nodded towards the line of golden-leaved chestnut trees across the road that screened the derelict industrial estate beyond. 'Went doon when ah saw th'ambulance. Telt that Nurse Morgan wummin what ah'd seen. Asked if that ither nurse hadnae been able to help old Miss Maitland earlier oan.'

Ailsa Doyle turned to face Kirsty, her sharp eyes crinkling thoughtfully. 'He wisnae supposed tae be therr, wis he?' she asked, a look of perfect understanding passing across her face. 'An' it's always women that come aroon; they're arenae any male community nurses at oor surgery.'

Kirsty stopped taking notes and tried to look as authoritative as she knew she should.

'You'll need to tell DS Murdoch all of this as well, Ailsa,' she said slowly. 'It's important that we find the man who came to see Miss Maitland this morning,' she added, trying to maintain a neutral tone of voice. How was it that Lorimer managed to talk to folk without giving them ideas? The man could discuss the grisliest facts and still sound as if he were talking about the weather! It was a trick that DC Wilson must strive to emulate, she reminded

48

herself, something that instantly put a witness at their ease so that they told their stories clearly, not missing out any details. Would Murdoch employ a similar technique?

The heavy rap on the door told her she wouldn't have long to wait as Ailsa Doyle gave a curse and headed back along the corridor to the front door.

She heard their voices as Ailsa Doyle and Murdoch came towards the front room then there came a piercing cry as the baby awoke, and light footsteps as the young mother went into the bedroom next door.

'Right, Wilson, get all of her statement?' Murdoch glanced at Kirsty's notebook.

'Yes, sir, but aren't you going to question her yourself?' *With me there to corroborate*, she wanted to add.

Kirsty bit her lip and wishing she hadn't spoken as Murdoch's face clouded over with disapproval.

'Let's see what you've got,' he replied, gesturing for Kirsty to hand over her notebook.

'Hm, looks like that'll be enough to go on meantime. Good. Let's get out of here.' He wrinkled his nose in distaste as the baby's cries grew louder. 'Probably a complete waste of police time,' he grunted. 'And there's plenty for us to do back at Stewart Street.'

Kirsty watched him stride along the corridor, only hesitating for a moment to look into the bedroom, aware that the baby's howls had suddenly ceased.

'That's us off, thanks for your help,' she said, smiling at the sight of the young mother nursing her child, a look of utter contentment on Ailsa Doyle's young face.

CHAPTER TEN

Kirsty watched as Murdoch closed the car door behind him and sauntered away, one hand already pulling a cigarette out of the packet. They were back at Stewart Street where the owners of Paton's jewellery shop, a father with his son and daughter, were to meet them.

Kirsty's heart thumped in her chest as she approached the rear door of the police station, keeping one eye on Murdoch who was leaning against a railing, tapping a number out on his mobile, the cigarette bobbing up and down between his fingers. His back was partly turned from her as she passed, but Kirsty decided that he'd probably have ignored her anyway.

There was just time for a quick freshen up before the meeting with the Paton family and Kirsty took the stairs two at a time, remembering exactly where the ladies' room was in this building.

A huge sigh escaped her as she closed the door behind her.

'Bad morning?'

DI Jo Grant looked up from the wash basin, an open make-up pouch on the worktop beside her.

Kirsty nodded. 'Feels like I've never stopped,' she admitted with an attempt at a grin. She was glad that it was DI Grant, an officer she had known since her university days. They hadn't always seen eye to eye, but Jo was a decent sort and Kirsty knew that both Lorimer and her dad shared the same respect for her.

'In at the deep end,' she told the woman, deciding on a phrase deliberately vague. 'Jewellery theft,' she added.

'Oh, I heard about that,' the detective inspector said as she turned to use the hand dryer. 'One of a series happening across the UK, by all accounts. Murdoch will have told you all of that, though,' she added. Then, stopping for a moment she gazed straight at Kirsty and asked, 'How d'you find him?'

'Murdoch?'

'Aye, Len Murdoch.' Grant nodded. 'Our latest crime scene manager.'

Kirsty tried not to show any of the doubts that were making her stomach clench with anxiety as she shrugged.

'Haven't really had time to get to know him yet,' she replied, avoiding Jo Grant's eyes and trying to affect a nonchalance that she did not feel.

'Has a decent track record,' Jo admitted, stepping closer to the mirrors. 'Not sure just how he'll fit in here, though. So many of our lot have been in Stewart Street for most of their careers.'

She was speering, Kirsty suddenly realised. Did Jo Grant have any reason to share her worries about the DS? Was she really asking for intelligence on the man? Or was this simply another sort of test? Officers were loyal to one another; that was the unspoken rule, wasn't it? Kirsty Wilson had learned that much since she'd first joined the force.

'I hadn't even heard of him till this morning,' Kirsty told the other woman. 'Dad never mentioned him.'

'No?' Jo Grant's eyebrows rose in a moment of surprise. Then she ran slim fingers through her short dark hair, gazing at her reflection in the mirror. She caught sight of Kirsty watching her and grinned. 'Well, I'm sure he'll be a competent enough mentor for you.'

The DI fished a lipstick from her make-up bag then paused, holding the lipstick in the air as though she were about to add something, her expression serious for a moment. Then she blinked as if changing her mind and started to fill in her lips in a shade of dark raspberry.

'See you in the canteen for a coffee sometime? My treat.' Jo grinned, patting Kirsty's shoulder as she gathered up her belongings and left the ladies' room.

Coffee would be nice, Kirsty thought, hearing her stomach growling. But she really needed something to eat. No time, she scolded herself. Shouldn't even have stopped to blether with DI Grant. But the DI's words had thrown up all sorts of questions.

Kirsty locked herself into one of the cubicles, her mind turning somersaults. What on earth had that been about? What was it that Jo Grant had been about to tell her concerning her mentor? Suddenly she wished that it was Lorimer who was to be conducting this interview with the Paton family and not DS Len Murdoch.

The smell of greasy bacon hit Kirsty as she opened the door to interview room two, reminding her again that she hadn't eaten since breakfast. Perhaps, she thought gloomily, eyeing the empty paper plate and the crumpled serviette, she ought to have bought herself a roll when she'd gone for Murdoch's. Someone else had been here before her, not stopping to clear up after themselves, she saw, sweeping the table clean with one hand and crunching up the greasy paper with the other before tipping the lot into the waste bin by the door.

A quick glance at the clock told her that there were only five minutes before the meeting was due to take place. Her first instinct was to have a quick look at the chairs, making sure they were clean and crumb free before the Paton family arrived.

Kirsty was just setting one of the metal chairs back down when the door opened wider and DS Murdoch ushered three people into the room.

'This is Detective Constable Wilson,' Murdoch breezed and Kirsty suddenly found herself shaking hands with a grey-haired man.

'Jacob Paton,' the jeweller told her then waved a hand towards a slim man of around her own age, his dark hair slicked back with gel. 'This is my son, Joseph, and my daughter, Samantha.' The daughter came into the room last, a busty blonde around mid to late twenties, Kirsty reckoned, with heavily made-up eyes and false lashes that were already fluttering at Murdoch. Her hand-shake was perfunctory, as though Samantha Paton was anxious not to soil her perfectly manicured fingers by contact with a mere police officer.

Never know where we've been, Kirsty wanted to tell her, taking an instant dislike to the woman. And those are definitely extensions, not your own hair, she thought, appraising the woman even as she pulled out a chair for her then took her place next to Murdoch.

'Right, Mr Paton, you were going to bring me the inventory of all the missing stock plus an idea of the damage caused in the break-in,' Murdoch said, pulling up his cuffs in a brisk let's-get-down-to-business gesture.

Kirsty wanted to gape but stopped herself in time. Wasn't that the same watch she's seen him sling into the crime scene manager's bag? She blinked, staring at the black and metallic wristwatch so blatantly on display. Murdoch's hands were lying clasped on the table, the watch face turned in her direction. A Tag Heuer Formula 1, she noted, then looked away swiftly. It wouldn't do to stare, yet even as she listened to the jeweller begin to read from his list of stolen items, Kirsty was memorising the make so that she could check it out on Google.

'... and one Tag Heuer, Dad, don't forget that.' Samantha Paton interrupted her father's voice, making Kirsty jump.

The blonde tossed her hair and glanced coquettishly at Murdoch as if ... Kirsty's heart missed a beat. *As if she knew!* But surely ... Kirsty glanced from one person to the next to see if they, too, were regarding Detective Sergeant Murdoch with the same sly smile. But father and son were both poring over the sheets of paper in Mr Paton's hand, serious expressions on each of their faces.

DS Murdoch simply nodded and listened coolly, seemingly unaware of Samantha Paton's obvious flirtation.

Maybe she was just like that, Kirsty thought. A man-eater. There had been a girl like that in her class at university, she remembered; Madeleine Something-or-other; a strange girl who was in the habit of making up the most fantastic tales, always sidling up to the lads, a sexual innuendo at the tip of her mendacious tongue.

'DC Wilson will see to that,' Murdoch was saying and Kirsty's mouth opened, alarmed at the realisation that she had missed his last few words.

'Thank you,' Mr Paton said, stretching across the table to grasp Kirsty's hand. 'It's such a relief to know that the police take care of details like that. Contacting the insurance company was going to be our next nightmare,' he added. 'Joseph, give Detective Constable Wilson the insurer's number, will you?' he said, turning to his son. Joseph Paton dipped into the top pocket of his beautifully cut charcoal suit (Armani, Kirsty thought, or something damn near like it) and produced a business card.

'Thanks for doing this,' he echoed his father. 'Goodness knows when we'll be able to open for business again. Whole place needs cleaning up and the shutters will need to be completely replaced.' He took one of the pieces of A4 paper from the table and passed it to her. 'That's a copy of what needs doing. Can we let our builder and the shutter company in to give estimates?' he asked, looking at Murdoch.

'Tomorrow,' Murdoch answered. 'The scene of crime officers will have finished by then. And hopefully there'll be some trace evidence, like fingerprints, to help catch them, though I'm afraid you'll find they came prepared with gloves on. It was a professional job,' he said, beginning to rise to his feet as a signal that the meeting was at an end. 'Thanks for coming in once again. DC Wilson will see you out,' he added, nodding at Kirsty before shaking hands in turn with each member of the jeweller's family.

Kirsty pulled her chair back and went to open the door, turning just in time to see Samantha Paton's simpering smile as she held the detective sergeant's hand. Murdoch's face gave nothing away though, Kirsty noticed, his nod to the young woman merely polite. Had she been imagining things, then? And, was it simply a coincidence that Murdoch was sporting a flashy-looking watch? Had she really seen . . . ?

Kirsty's thoughts were interrupted as Mr Paton strode beside her, his two children following.

'We're grateful for your help, you know,' he began, his voice low, as though it was forbidden to speak in anything other than hushed tones in a police station. 'It's been a terrible shock. Never happened in all my years in the trade. You always wonder, of course, take the proper precautions . . . ' He tailed off. 'Goodness only knows what this'll do to our insurance premium now.' He shook his head worriedly. 'Costs us a fortune as it is.'

Kirsty made a sympathetic sound. The jewellery business was a pretty lucrative one to be in, she knew, her father having told her once about the enormous mark-up on items of jewellery.

They were at the front door now and the younger Patons were heading towards the row of cars parked in the forecourt.

Mr Paton clasped Kirsty's hand. Then, giving her a shy smile, he lifted her other hand and for a moment she was startled, thinking he might raise it to his lips but he merely tapped her ring finger.

'If you ever need to find a decent jeweller, do come to us first, Miss Wilson,' he said softly. 'You'd be sure of a good discount, you know.'

Then he was gone, crossing the car park to where his children waited in a sleek grey Jaguar.

Kirsty walked back inside, puzzled. Didn't they know that officers couldn't accept stuff like that? Any sort of gift might be misconstrued as a bribe. And didn't the offer of discounted goods come into that category? She'd need to ask somebody. The thought conjured up an image of Detective Superintendent William Lorimer. If only she could speak to him, she thought wistfully. But he wasn't here today. A family funeral, her father had told her. Shoulders heaving in a sigh, Kirsty turned and walked back into the building, wondering what task her mentor might have lined up for her.

She didn't have long to wait. DS Murdoch waved to her from the muster room door, an impatient gesture that made Kirsty walk faster towards him.

'We're out again,' he said shortly. 'Another scene of crime. Over in Byres Road. Your neck of the woods, isn't it?' he added, striding back along the corridor.

'Yes ...'

'Body's been found in a flat. We need to be there now.'

The light was fading fast as they parked outside the row of tenement flats that lined the street, one of the busiest arteries in Glasgow's West End, a popular area for students with the city's oldest university close by.

Once again, a police car and scene of crime tape marked the doorway that had been closed off to the public. Kirsty parked the Honda close to the kerb.

'Looks like one of the pathologists has got here before us,' Murdoch murmured, nodding towards a light blue Saab.

Kirsty smiled, recognising Dr Rosie Fergusson's car. The Department of Forensic Medicine was close by, yet the pathologist would have had to bring all her own forensic gear with her.

In minutes, Kirsty and Murdoch were garbed up and heading up a flight of stone stairs.

The smell hit her as soon as she entered the flat, making Kirsty gag. *A decaying corpse gives off a pungent odour, unlike any other*, she remembered one lecturer at Police Training College telling the rookie officers, a grin on the woman's face. Back then the words had been something to write in a notebook but this foul smell was the reality behind them.

Kirsty followed her mentor into the flat, noting as she did the sprays of blood arcing against the beige wallpaper. There were streaks of dark brown along the cobalt-blue hall carpet, as though a dead or injured body had been dragged along.

Murdoch placed the metal treads carefully to one side, avoiding the trace evidence. It was vital that a pathway was made from these treads by the scene of crime officer for the investigators to walk upon lest the scene become contaminated by their footsteps.

'In here,' a voice called, its timbre cold and echoing.

'Bathroom,' Murdoch told Kirsty. 'Just look. Don't do anything until I tell you, okay?'

'Yes, sir,' Kirsty agreed, her reluctant feet padding from one tread to the next as she watched Murdoch's back disappear into the room at the far end of the hallway.

It was worse than she could have imagined.

The body of a man was lying beside the bath tub, his throat a gaping dark wound, the stain of old blood pooling the floor around his head.

Kirsty saw the movement on his neck at once and gagged. Maggot infestation had begun. She covered her mouth with one hand and turned away, wanting out of the flat, wishing that some other officer could have been there instead.

Murdoch was hunkering down beside DI Grant and the pathologist, as if this was something he saw and smelled every day of his working life. He gave a quick glance up at Kirsty and grinned at the expression on his DC's face.

'Better get used to this, Wilson,' he laughed, making both Jo Grant and Dr Fergusson turn from the corpse and follow his gaze.

'Kirsty!' Rosie exclaimed. 'What are you ... of course, you're CID now. What a baptism for you,' she sympathised, her eyes kind above the white mask.

'Bit crowded in here,' Rosie Fergusson murmured, giving Murdoch the chance to send Kirsty out of the room.

'Aye, but she needs to see how we do these things. I'm mentoring her,' Murdoch said with a firmness that brooked no opposition.

The next hour was the stuff of nightmares, white-suited figures moving in and out of the bathroom, photographs taken from every angle as the SOCOs carried out their work. And the smell, an all-pervasive stench of death that would linger on Kirsty's clothes afterwards. It was her job, what she had chosen to do, Kirsty kept reminding herself as she listened to Murdoch, finding out as she did that the deceased, Francis Bissett, was a tenant of this flat. Bissett was a known drug dealer, according to Jo Grant, who had come across the dead man in a previous case.

Eventually they were finished and Murdoch gave Kirsty a nod as he packed the crime scene bag. 'That's us for the day, then,' he said, giving her a hard look. 'Hope you learned something, Wilson. Even if only that you earned some overtime on your first day.' He gave a mirthless laugh.

Then he was gone, leaving Kirsty on the pavement of Byres Road. Home was a short walk up University Avenue and Gibson Street and she would be glad to be back with James, though she was dreading his questions about her working day.

'Here, get in,' a voice behind her said. 'I'll drop you off.'

Kirsty turned to see the blonde pathologist at the wheel of her Saab convertible. How could she do a job like that and still look so smart, she wondered, opening the passenger door.

'First thing you want to do is have a good hot shower,' Rosie advised as the big car swung away from the kerb. 'Plenty of nice scented stuff. Then pour yourself a decent glass of something.' She smiled at Kirsty sitting beside her. 'Works every time.'

'Thank God that's over!' Maggie exclaimed as she unlocked the front door.

'Cuppa?' her husband asked, taking her coat and draping it over the end of the banister.

'Please,' Maggie replied. 'Though, to be truthful, I feel like something stronger.' She smiled ruefully.

'A whisky, then?'

'D'you know what I really fancy? A hot toddy. How about you?'

'Well, since I'm not on duty for the rest of today I think I'll join you,' Lorimer agreed, heading through the long open-plan room that incorporated a desk by the window, a dining area and a large airy kitchen.

A click at the cat flap signalled Chancer's arrival, his furry marmalade-coloured body soon winding itself around Maggie's legs.

'Hello, you,' she said, scooping up their pet and rubbing her cheek against his silky coat. She sank into her favourite rocking chair, the cat turning on her lap, his thrumming purr a sign of welcome.

Outside, daylight had faded into dusky blue, the September evening promising a fine day to follow. What would tomorrow bring? Lorimer wondered, spooning honey from the jar into a pair of heatproof glasses. Maggie's job was so unlike his, the timetable of classes a set pattern to her working week. Tomorrow might bring any sort of crime his way, he mused, as well as the pile of paperwork that had to be endured and the meetings scheduled throughout the day. Yet he must find time to see young Kirsty Wilson. Detective Constable Wilson, he reminded himself with a proprietorial grin.

Busy fingers tapped a message on to the computer screen.

'Free yourself from the pain. Free your loved ones from all their unnecessary suffering,' the fingers wrote. 'Give them that quiet release they deserve.'

The right hand hovered over the keyboard as its owner reread the words. Then, as if satisfied, the middle finger jabbed a key, sending the message out into the ether. The repetition of that command was what made them respond to these words; it had worked before and would work again. Yet freedom, as anybody knew, always came at a price.

CHAPTER ELEVEN

Nancy Livingstone put down the telephone and looked out of the window of Abbey Nursing Home with a sigh. As the office manager it was her remit to look after everything to do with the staff, to ensure that there was always adequate provision of care for their residents. The nursing staff was a mixed lot; some local women, others from Eastern Europe, all suitably qualified with excellent references backing up their years of service in various medical facilities. Yet, despite her efforts to maintain the required numbers, there was always someone calling in to let them down. Anastasia, the Russian girl who had married a Scots lad the previous spring, was now suffering bouts of morning sickness. Nancy's sister, Grace Abbott, had tut-tutted and remarked that *she* had never taken time off for something as common as that until Nancy had reminded her gently that the Duchess of Cambridge had been hospitalised and that Anastasia's own GP had rung to confirm that the girl had the same sort of debilitating sickness. Now she would have to find temporary cover to replace the Russian girl, not such an easy task when the patients here needed such specialised nursing care.

Nancy closed her eyes and bowed her head in a moment of

prayer, asking for divine guidance to help solve her problem. When she opened them again, she gave a faint smile, a feeling of calmness returning. God would sort it out, the woman assured herself. He always did.

The Social Work Department was housed in a 1960s block, its flat roof a perpetual reminder of the utilitarian design that had failed this city for decades. There were stains running down the side of the building where water had dripped, the ever-increasing tendency for winter weather to bring high winds and flooding to every corner of the country. Square windows were set behind yellow-painted frames, brash outlines that only served to show up the dreariness of the entire worn façade, its grey pebble-dashed surface crumbling at the edges.

Sarah stood on the pavement, looking up at the four floors of offices, her spirits plummeting. The whole place seemed to exude an air of defeat as if the very effort of withstanding the elements had made it give up on life long since.

She sighed and made to push open the glass doors but, to her surprise, they opened silently as she stepped towards them, ushering her into a reception area where a young woman with dyed purple hair that matched her council uniform was busily mopping up the linoleum floor. Sarah skirted the wet patch and made for the reception desk where a man in jeans and a grey hooded top was standing, listening to a middle-aged receptionist as she directed him to his destination.

'Up to the fourth floor. Lift's over there. Ask at the window and they'll give you a time,' she was telling him. Her voice held a note of exasperation, as if years of dealing with the less fortunate elements of society had worn away any veneer of kindness.

The man grunted something unintelligible and turned away,

avoiding the cleaner, not even giving Sarah a second glance. The receptionist gave a weary smile over her half-moon spectacles as she took Sarah's letter, raising her eyebrows and shaking her head as if to include the young woman in a general despair at the hopeless fellows who came seeking help. Then, as she opened the letter and read its contents, her smile faded, the expression on her face losing any trace of friendliness. She gave a quick glance at the clock then a questioning look at Sarah.

'You're early. Mrs Reid is with another client right now. You'll have to wait.'

'Wasn't sure how long it would take to get here,' Sarah mumbled, the familiar cowed feeling that tended to come in the presence of any authority sweeping over her.

'Take the lift to the third floor and wait in the corridor outside Mrs Reid's office.' The receptionist handed Sarah's letter back to her then turned away to check something on a computer and Sarah waited, wondering if more explanation would be coming.

'What?' the woman asked rudely.

'I . . .' Sarah began. 'Nothing,' she added, turning away, flame-cheeked, towards a pair of dark grey doors set into the wall. She was conscious of eyes boring into her back as she waited, watching the red numbers descending – 2,1 – then with a ping the doors slid open and a teenager with a baby buggy pushed past Sarah, her thin face set and white, hair pulled back into a ponytail.

The lift closed behind Sarah with a sigh then rumbled its way upwards, shuddering to a halt at the third floor.

Perhaps it was because she had left the bed and breakfast early that there was no sign of any other person waiting on the row of blue seats fixed against the wall in the corridor, yet Sarah could hear the murmur of voices from behind the doors as she walked along, eyes searching for her social worker's office.

CATHERINE REID, the small white notice proclaimed and Sarah sat opposite the door, nervously running her fingernail along the edge of the letter. What would she be like? Was everybody here like that woman downstairs? Fed up with having to cope with the dregs of humanity? For, Sarah told herself bitterly, that's what she was now. No home, no job and very little in the way of prospects. She blinked back a tear of self-pity, a sign of weakness that she had never once allowed herself to have during her incarceration.

Sarah must have read the notices on the walls enough times to have memorised them before Mrs Reid's door opened at last and a thin young man with a shaved head and multiple tattoos on his bare arms emerged, his jaws moving rhythmically as he chewed a wad of gum.

'See you next week, Drew,' a voice called out from within, then the door closed once more.

It was only moments later that the door opened again to reveal a pleasant-faced older woman with greying curls, a pair of spectacles hanging from a slender gold chain around her neck.

'Sarah Wilding?' She smiled warmly and beckoned her new client inside. 'Sarah, I'm Catherine, how are you?'

The woman's handclasp was warm and her eyes bright as she regarded her newest client. 'Take a seat and we'll go through everything.'

Sarah sank into the black leather chair that the woman indicated, glancing at a matching one with a cushion embroidered with the words *God is Love*, entwined with flowers and butterflies. She stared at the words, stiffening, wondering why they suddenly seemed inappropriate in a place like this. What had God to do with Sarah Wilding? Hadn't He abandoned her long ago?

'Cuppa? Tea or coffee?' Catherine Reid asked, motioning

towards a small side table where a kettle jug sat on a circular tray surrounded by several mugs.

'Tea, please,' Sarah whispered, watching as the woman busied herself with the mugs and teabags. 'Milk, no sugar, thanks.'

She looked around the room, noting the calendar with masses of scribbled notes, a framed picture of a mountain scene and a tall grey filing cabinet with a pink orchid blossoming profusely next to a coat rack, a bright red raincoat hanging on one curled hook.

It wasn't what Sarah had envisioned: some stranger dealing with her from behind a desk, unravelling her life story, making value judgements about her crime. She watched, still wary, as her social worker brought the tea and came to sit beside her, masking the cushion and its unnecessary message. She hadn't expected this degree of informality with no physical barrier between them; hadn't been prepared for anyone to treat her differently from the way the prison officers at Cornton had with their bunches of keys and watchful eyes. She felt suddenly exhausted, as though all of her emotions had built up and were threatening to spill over.

'Here,' Catherine said, handing Sarah a box of Kleenex tissues. 'You'll be all over the place this morning. It happens,' she added kindly, moving closer to Sarah and patting her on the back as though she were a small child in need of comfort.

It was too good to be true, Sarah thought more than an hour later as she emerged into the sunlight once more. Mrs Reid (*call me Catherine*) had gone through the whole procedure necessary for newly released prisoners, making sure that Sarah was absolutely certain of every last detail. But it wasn't only the social worker's obvious concern for Sarah that had put a smile on the young woman's face, though that had lifted her spirits, especially after she'd had a good cry.

'Let's see what we can do,' Catherine Reid had suggested eventually, lifting the telephone and dialling a number.

Sarah had waited, listening carefully, not daring to raise any hope that this kindly woman could succeed in finding her a place to work.

'Nancy? I have a nurse here with me. Newly released from Cornton yesterday. Miss Sarah Wilding.' Catherine Reid had nodded at Sarah as she spoke. 'Yes, she's worked with all sorts, stroke patients too. Can I give you her details?'

Sarah had listened as the background to her nursing career was given. Then her crime was explained and the guilt that was never far away resurfaced to swamp her once more.

'She'll take you,' Catherine had said at last, putting down the phone. 'Subject to an interview, of course. It's a nursing home on the outskirts of Bearsden. Can you go there today?'

On the other end of the phone, Nancy Livingstone opened her eyes and smiled. She knew that the Lord worked in mysterious ways, yet something told her that He had a plan for this young woman who had made such a dreadful choice in her past.

'She's getting on to a train right now.' The man spoke into his mobile phone, watching the blonde woman as she stepped from the lower level platform at Queen Street station.

'Aye, I can. What d'you want me to do?' His eyes followed the woman as she entered the carriage then he slid his own ticket into the slot at the barrier and pocketed his mobile, the latest instructions concerning Sarah Wilding still resonating in his head.

He sat further back in the same carriage, watching the girl as the train slid out of the station. She would do as they wanted. She had to, he told himself with a grim smile. It was either that or ... his mouth twitched, making the scar that ran down one side of his face turn into a deep crease. Even just the threat of what he could do to her would make Sarah Wilding eager to play along with them.

CHAPTER TWELVE

Dr Rosie Fergusson looked at the list in front of her. Toxicology was in a separate department from her own within the Department of Forensic Medicine but thankfully they enjoyed a good working relationship. She glanced at the post-mortem arrangements for the rest of the day. One elderly lady whose demise was probably expected, nothing really for the Fiscal to worry about. Still, she mused, the report from DS Len Murdoch had been interesting. There was the matter of that odd visit from an unknown nurse in the early hours. Could it have been a case of voluntary euthanasia? These things happened. Doctors had to use their own judgement all the time, some of them only too willing to ease their suffering patients into an everlasting state of oblivion, everybody knew that. Could Miss Jane Maitland have made a private arrangement of some sort?

The sun was streaming through the mortuary windows by the time Rosie began the elderly woman's post-mortem examination. It was a routine that she had performed countless times, careful scrutiny of the external body before making that first incision that would reveal the inner parts of what had once been a living, breathing human being. Painstaking forensic work had already been carried out to search for fibres and hairs, anything that might give a clue to the identity of the mysterious nurse who had administered that final injection.

Some time later, Rosie wrinkled her nose. There was nothing conclusive to see, nothing at all, unless you counted the bruising from repeated needles finding these tired old veins to inject pain-killing drugs. And these had been expected, after all. Nope, she thought as the body disappeared back into the refrigerated cabinet, it was down to the Tox boys and girls to come up with their report. If, and it was a big *if*, they found anything out of the ordinary, then DS Len Murdoch would have a proper investigation on his hands. And so would Kirsty, she remembered, wondering just how the young woman was faring under the mentorship of the scene of crime manager.

'How did it go on your first day, then?' Lorimer smiled at his young friend as she sank into a chair next to his desk.

Before Kirsty could reply, the telephone beside Lorimer's computer rang and he made a face mouthing *sorry* as he picked it up.

It was only to be expected, Kirsty thought, feeling a little uncomfortable sitting here in the detective superintendent's office. He was a very busy man. She really shouldn't be taking up any of his time. And she certainly wouldn't be mentioning her suspicions about DS Murdoch.

Sleeping on it had helped to clarify Kirsty's thoughts and the young officer had decided that she had been completely mistaken about seeing Murdoch stealing a watch. Perhaps he had simply been taking off his own watch and putting it in the scene of crime bag? And it was pure coincidence that the missing watch was of

69

the same type that he wore. Nobody could be that blatant, surely? And yet . . . the look on Samantha Paton's face was the thing that had caused her most disquiet, the girl's expression changing into a nightmarish leer as Kirsty tossed and turned in a sleep punctured by fitful dreams.

'Okay, I'll get back to you.' Lorimer finished his call and beamed at Kirsty.

'Heard you were out for hours with DS Murdoch,' he said. 'Overtime on your first day. Well done.'

'Yes, we were busy,' Kirsty replied, trying to return his smile. 'Last one was a scene of crime with a decomposing body.' She wrinkled her nose before adding, 'Dr Fergusson was there.'

'The lad Bissett, I hear,' Lorimer said, frowning. 'Known dealer. Didn't expect him to be in with the hard men. Still,' he shrugged, 'you never know what goes on behind scenes like these. Could be they were high on dope and turned nasty on one another. An old story, I'm afraid.'

'Dr Fergusson was wonderful,' Kirsty said wistfully. 'Don't know how she can be so calm and straightforward with things like that.'

'Aye, our Rosie is something else, isn't she?' Lorimer chuckled. 'Your dad and I have seen many a sight that would have turned anybody green, but not her.' He paused and for a moment Kirsty imagined that she was about to be dismissed, allowing the detective super to get on with his job.

'How do you find Murdoch?' he asked quietly, fixing Kirsty with his blue gaze.

Her eyes slid away from his scrutiny even as she knew that avoiding his stare was a dead giveaway.

'Okay.' She shrugged. 'Early days yet. And we were really busy.'

Why do you ask? she wanted to demand, but the words remained unspoken.

It was a different Len Murdoch that Kirsty saw when she entered the muster room. Gone was the chalk-striped suit that had been covered over with scene of crime whites the day before. Now the DS was far more casually attired in a pair of dark jeans and a T-shirt, a black leather jacket slung on the back of his chair. As she approached, Kirsty noticed signs of exhaustion on Murdoch's face; dark circles under those cold grey eyes and the shadow of stubble made him seem a little less intimidating somehow. As she came closer, Kirsty wondered if this man had been up all night. What was his home life like? Did he have kids of his own? Somehow she doubted that. He'd been quick enough to leave the sound of a screaming baby in that upper cottage flat.

'Wilson.' He turned and nodded at her then indicated the sheaf of papers in his hand. 'The Bissett murder. Need to prioritise that,' he told her tiredly. 'Fiscal wants the PM done today.' He looked at his watch and pursed his lips. 'Need to be down at the mortuary in an hour.' He looked at her closely. 'You okay with that?'

Kirsty was taken aback. Murdoch had not asked once yesterday whether she was all right with anything. Had Lorimer had a quiet word, she wondered? Was that what his question had indicated? Or had her father been putting pressure on the detective sergeant? She hoped not. This was a job that she needed to do, standing on her own two feet, proving herself.

'Fine, sir,' she answered.

'Right. Here's the preliminary report from the crime scene. SOCOs made a decent job of it.' He handed her a pink folder. 'Have a look,' he added, motioning her to the desk beside his own.

Kirsty opened the folder to reveal a pile of photographs taken at the Byres Road flat. Seeing the detailed images of blood-spray patterns and the still body was far less awful than actually being there. No foul stench. No wriggling maggots. She shuddered, remembering.

'Upset you, does it?' Murdoch's tone was difficult to gauge. Was he being genuinely solicitous or was there still a sneer in that voice?

'Not really.' She gave a rueful smile. 'I was just thinking about the smell ... '

'Ach, you'll get used to that, Wilson,' he said. 'Everybody does.'

My dad says the same. Kirsty bit back the words. It was this man who was her mentor and she had to learn from him.

'Sir?'

'Aye?'

'I've seen a dead body before ... '

'The Swedish girl? Aye, I heard.' His eyes slid over her for a moment, making Kirsty shiver. 'A case Jo Grant would rather forget.' He grinned suddenly.

'Well, it worked out all right in the end,' Kirsty said, returning to her scrutiny of the photographs.

'If you want to make it in CID you need to become inured to the sight of death.' Murdoch shrugged. 'Doesn't make you a lesser person. Just more able to cope with the job.'

The sound of his mobile ringing made the DS stand up and walk away, his voice deliberately low as if anxious to keep his conversation private. Kirsty watched his back, curious to know more about this man, wondering once again how he had spent the hours since they had parted at Byres Road.

*

Catherine Reid had advised her that it was a fifteen-minute walk from the railway station to Abbey Nursing Home and Sarah found herself enjoying the exercise as well as looking at the large houses on either side of the road, many of them grand properties partly screened by high hedges. It was a far cry from the home that she and Pete had grown up in, Sarah thought, admiring the different styles of architecture as she walked away from the centre of Bearsden. Theirs had been a childhood spent in a Glasgow housing scheme, rows and rows of tenement flats with back greens where mums could hang out their washing on the lines and children were free to roam. She and her best pal, Flora Clarke, had sat side by side on the pavement at the front of their block, playing with their toys, Sarah turning the games even then into hospitals, their teddies and dolls silently submitting to all of the little girls' ministrations. And then there would be the rush and clamour of children at the sound of the ice cream van, its tinkling melody alerting them to rush and get *pennies for the van* then spill back out on to the street.

There would be no such events here in this leafy suburb, Sarah thought, eyeing a large red sandstone house with mock turrets and a crow-stepped gable. And where was Flora Clarke now? she wondered, wistfully. The Wildings had moved away when she and Pete were in their teens, out of the city and into a new town on the south of the river. Would it have made any difference if they had stayed where they had once lived? Would Pete have still gone down that fateful road? Sarah's eyes blurred with tears as she recalled her mother's words.

You're to blame. Just you! We never want to see you again!

There was a cough and the sound of footsteps behind her, making the young woman jump.

Sarah turned, one hand at her throat but the man in the red

73

jacket pushing a trolley was a harmless enough sight, a postman doing his rounds. She frowned for a moment, wondering at the state of her nerves. Was there anything other than the forthcoming interview at this nursing home to make her particularly jumpy?

Sarah looked along the quiet street. She was imagining things. There was nobody following her. She was just strung up, like Catherine Reid had told her.

The man shrank back into the space between the two high hedges, out of sight. He would have to be careful, he thought. The woman had almost glimpsed him as she'd turned around. Thank God that postie had blocked her view! The road ahead was rapidly becoming more countrified too; larger spaces between these great houses giving way to hedgerows and open fields. He'd easily be seen if he followed her too closely. Then, just as he was wondering what to do, he saw Sarah Wilding turn a corner into a side street, her steps quickening as if she were almost at her destination.

Where was she heading? The man trod quietly after her, ready to duck into any convenient opening should she turn around and see his face. Then he looked past the woman and grinned. So that was where she was going. The sign for Abbey Nursing Home was a dead giveaway and already she was turning into its driveway and out of his scrutiny. He took out his mobile and nodded to himself, walking slowly towards the open driveway.

'Think she must be going for a job. Place outside Bearsden. Abbey Nursing Home.' He waited for a response then gave a twist to his lips, muttering coldly, 'Aye. If you say so.'

Then, taking a final look at the white-painted sign outside the whitewashed building, he turned on his heel and retraced his steps. *Be patient*, the voice on the telephone line had ordered, but it was hard sometimes. There were other watchers who could dog the woman's footsteps, find out where she was and what she was doing. Then, when they were ready, Sarah Wilding would find them waiting for her.

He glanced back at the green hedgerow and the winding road disappearing into distant countryside, promising himself that he would be the one to make her do their bidding.

'I'm so glad to see you.' The woman beamed at Sarah, ushering her into a bright and airy sitting room with a kitchen area in one corner. 'Take a seat, won't you? Tea or coffee?'

'Oh, a cup of coffee would be lovely. Thanks,' Sarah replied, staring at the tall woman who had fetched a pair of mugs and was holding them up, a questioning smile in her eyes. Sarah noted the neatly cut hair shining in the sun, an indeterminate colour between grey and blonde, the glittery scarf around her neck catching the light as the woman bent to pick up a dropped teaspoon.

There was something familiar about her; she reminded Sarah of another woman from her past, someone . . . Sarah blinked as the memory faded, leaving only the trace of a smile and the feeling of being warm and cherished.

'We're short of a member of staff right now. Poor girl who's suffering severe morning sickness. Looks like she'll be off for a few weeks,' Nancy Livingstone explained, setting down a small tray. 'Catherine tells me that you have a lot of experience working with stroke patients and geriatrics.'

'That's right,' Sarah began.

'Milk?' The nursing home manager raised a little jug.

'Please,' Sarah replied, suddenly uncomfortable at being

served by this nice woman, wishing she could remember who it was that Nancy Livingstone resembled.

'How are you feeling?' The woman was looking at Sarah with genuine sympathy in these kind hazel eyes.

'What d'you mean?' Sarah mumbled, but she knew fine what this woman was asking; Nancy's eyes told her that.

'Must be hard, coming to terms with being back outside,' Nancy said. 'I can't imagine what that must be like.'

Sarah shook her head. 'Are you really sure it's someone like me that you want here?' she asked quietly, fingers clasped about the mug.

The woman gave a tinkling laugh. 'Someone like you? My dear, we are *all* like you.' Then her face softened. 'Nobody's perfect and some of us succumb to temptations that are more grievous than others, but we all fall under the same problem of being human.'

'But, I . . . '

'You were guilty of making a wrong choice and you have served a punishment for it. Now you have to go forward and live your life in a different way,' Nancy said, her words so gently spoken that Sarah felt the prickle of tears behind her eyelids. Was such a thing possible? Nothing would ever bring her brother back. And with the crime she had committed still hanging around her like a heavy weight, surely life could never be good again?

As if she had known the effect of her little speech, the nursing home manager sat back a little, regarding Sarah steadily. 'Right,' she said briskly. 'Now, tell me everything you've done since you qualified.'

Stepping on to the train once again, Sarah tried to tell herself that the last hour had been a dream. Surely she couldn't have been given a temporary nursing job as easily as that! Catherine Reid had obviously pulled some strings or else it had simply been a happy coincidence that her friend at Abbey Nursing Home had needed someone to begin work straight away. Yet it had happened, she thought, sliding into a seat by the window and staring into space. The Livingstone woman had made a few notes about Sarah's nursing career to date and then asked if she could begin working there tomorrow! Sarah had been taken from the sitting room (which was actually the staffroom, she was told) shown around the home, introduced to the owner, Mrs Abbott, and given a copy of the shift rota she would be expected to follow. A uniform would be supplied, the women assured her. And a week's pay would be given in advance so that Sarah need not worry about train fares or such things. It was, Sarah thought, too good to be true. And yet it had happened.

As the train pulled away from the station platform, Sarah saw her own face reflected in the glass and suddenly she remembered.

She was sitting with several other children in a sunny room and someone was playing a piano in the background. They were singing a song, something about a rainbow. And the face of the woman beaming down at them all was making Sarah feel such happiness. She must have been about five then. A time when she and Flora Clarke had toddled along to the Sunday school at the end of their street, a wooden mission hall where the lure of free fizzy drinks and a jammy biscuit had resulted in a weekly gathering of little children glad to join in the hour of singing and storytelling. Her Sunday school teacher's name had faded into oblivion but the shining eyes and loving expression lingered in her memory, a special something that this woman from Abbey Nursing Home seemed to share.

As the trees and fields gave way to rows of grey tenement

buildings, the reality of where she was going came back to her. If she could keep working then surely she could give up that horrid little room and find somewhere nicer? Somewhere ... her imagination took her inside one of the tall flats opposite the station where the train lingered, allowing passengers to spill out on to the platform. The large windows shone against the western skies, a few ledges adorned with boxes of late scarlet geraniums glowing like rubies. Then the train moved off, Sarah thinking hard as the flats disappeared from view. Surely she could find a room to rent near here? Anniesland was near enough to Bearsden for a commute and wouldn't be too expensive, not like her old flat in the West End.

Memories came flooding back. Pete on his knees, sobbing. Sarah holding him in her arms, making that promise ... She shuddered. No matter where she lived, Sarah Wilding knew that she would always be haunted by what she had done.

CHAPTER THIRTEEN

William Lorimer knew that it was only a matter of time before he needed to call Len Murdoch in for his initial staff appraisal, a part of his job that the detective superintendent heartily disliked. Putting down the scene of crime manager's file with a sigh, he rubbed his tired eyes and looked out of the window. It was just one of those things, he supposed; the sort of bad hand that fate dealt you. Why he should be happily married to Maggie with her dark curls and vivacious laughter when this man had the misfortune to have a severely crippled wife at home was simply a matter of luck, that was all. The staff file told the bare minimum; multiple sclerosis, carers in attendance several times a day, a husband who was immersed in the business of Police Scotland ... what kind of life was that for poor Mrs Murdoch? And how on earth did the detective sergeant cope outside his working hours? Well, at least his move to Stewart Street had helped a little, Lorimer thought. Irene Murdoch's hospital visits were becoming more and more frequent as her life drew to its sorry end.

Lorimer was not a sentimental person but he had a strong ability to empathise with his fellow man, a trait that sometimes saw him tossing restlessly in bed at night, his imagination transferring his own life on to that of someone else's. He had seen this sort of illness once before, he reminded himself. A woman called Phyllis, her life narrowed into that undulating bed in a room that had once been part of a fine family home. Lorimer recalled her eyes turning to his own, the face brightening as she looked at him with an expression of contentment. Even someone like that, crippled and mute, had been an integral part of a murder investigation that had given the detective plenty of sleepless nights. Nobody was better off dead, he had told his colleagues, when one of them had spoken the words aloud, daring to suggest that this particular woman had no quality of life at all. And she had proved Lorimer right, giving him a vital insight that had led to the identity of a killer. She was dead now, though, gone from this world like morning mist burning off as the sun warmed the earth, only her memory lingering on, her name a footnote in police records.

Lorimer had tried to elicit something from Kirsty about her new mentor but perhaps it was too soon for the girl to have formed any opinion. Besides, it was not his business to give away any personal details about Murdoch to his young friend. If the DS wanted to tell Kirsty about his wife, well and good. Otherwise, Lorimer would keep such things to himself. His mind wandered back to the initial interview between the scene of crime manager and three other senior officers when he had opened up about his domestic situation. There had been no plea for sympathy. On the contrary, Murdoch had been at pains to stress how his home life did not impinge on his working duties. The transfer had been simple enough and now their new scene of crime manager appeared to be hard at work, his duties including the mentoring of DC Kirsty Wilson.

*

A gentle rain was falling as Kirsty stepped out of the Honda and followed DS Murdoch up the ramp at the back of Glasgow City Mortuary. At least she didn't have to tramp the city streets as a beat cop any longer, she thought moodily, though the task ahead was not something she was particularly relishing. As the doors swung closed behind them, Kirsty looked around, wondering at the shelves of plastic containers, shuddering to imagine what they might contain. Green-clad figures flitted past, a girl with her dark hair tied back in a ponytail and a middle-aged man with grizzled locks, whistling a country and western tune.

'Aye, aye, in to see the PM?' The man grinned at them. 'Doc's just preparing for your one now.' He hesitated, glancing from Murdoch to Kirsty. 'You both new around here?' Then, not waiting for an answer he turned and motioned them to follow him. 'Viewing corridor's round this way.'

Murdoch and Kirsty followed the mortuary attendant until he stopped at a large window with a specially constructed step running along the floor.

'Intercom's switched on,' the man told Kirsty, guessing correctly that she was the rookie of the pair. 'You'll be able to hear anything she says and you can ask questions.'

'Okay.' Murdoch tilted his head. 'Who else is on with Dr Fergusson?'

'It's our favourite twosome; Doc Fergusson and Dan-the-man.' The attendant grinned.

Kirsty nodded. It had been part of their training to know just how the Department of Pathology worked; up here in Scotland the double-doctor system was mandatory to ensure corroboration. Once a post-mortem had taken place, everything that the pathologist had done and every conclusion he or she had come to might be taken apart meticulously in a court of law. She'd heard her father refer to Dr Dan, an Irish pathologist whose wicked sense of humour had been a source of anecdotes over the Wilson kitchen table.

As the body of the deceased was wheeled into the post-mortem room from its refrigerated cabinet, two figures moved quietly to take up their places next to the stainless-steel operating table. Looking at Rosie Fergusson with a green plastic apron over her scrubs and a pair of yellow rubber boots, Kirsty thought about a documentary she and James had seen on television about factory women whose days were spent gutting chickens. And wasn't it still the lot of so many women and girls up in the north-east to be fishwives, filleting their men's daily catch? Or was that just what happened in the old days? She shifted uncomfortably then Rosie's voice came over the intercom as she began to talk them through the initial stages of the post-mortem examination of one Francis Bissett. Was it such a strange sort of job for a woman, dissecting cadavers to find out what had taken place before death? Or were women actually better suited to carrying out these delicate surgical procedures?

As DC Wilson watched and listened, the whole process became an absorbing insight into the vagaries of life and death.

Later, much later it seemed to Kirsty, she and Murdoch left the mortuary with its clinical smells and artificial lighting, relieved to take a gulp of the fresh, damp air. It had been raining steadily and Kirsty had to step over a puddle that had gathered right next to the Honda.

'Where to now, sir?' she asked, glancing sideways at Murdoch's bullet-shaped head.

Just at that moment the DS's mobile rang and he left the car with a silent nod to Kirsty to stay where she was. She watched her mentor in the rear-view mirror, standing under the shelter of the mortuary doorway, his face grave he listened to whoever it was calling him. He had already taken out a cigarette and was blowing smoke over his shoulder. Not a quick call, then, Kirsty thought, curious to know if the telephone call related to any of the three cases that had commanded their attention since yesterday. Her attention was taken with the slight movement from her DS, his fingers on the mobile phone. Not just a single call waiting for him, then. The girl heaved a sigh. It was only Tuesday but it seemed as if the week ought to be over already.

At last she saw Murdoch flick away the stub of his cigarette and walk back towards the car.

'There's been a development in the robbery,' he said as he pulled the seat belt over his shoulder. 'Nottingham reckons we've got the same gang up here that did some of their shops during the summer.'

'How can they be sure?' Kirsty asked.

'CCTV image of a similar perp,' Murdoch replied. 'Digital analysis matches the footage from our cameras that they've had on file.'

Kirsty nodded. 'So what does that mean?'

Murdoch made a face. 'Means that we're going to have some English visitors crawling all over our patch,' he grumbled. 'Frankly, they're welcome to it if they can locate the buggers.'

'Do you often have a joint case with a different authority?'

'Nope,' Murdoch replied shortly. 'Our thieves tend to be a parochial shower, sticking to the terrain they know. Only once in a while do we see a gang that moves round the country like this. Ever hear of a guy called Brightman? Professor at Glasgow Uni?'

Kirsty hid a smile. 'Oh, aye,' she replied, trying to sound

cool. Not only had she heard of the celebrated professor, she considered him a friend. 'He's married to Dr Fergusson,' she told him.

'That right?' Murdoch's bushy grey eyebrows shot up in surprise. 'Well, seems he's written this book about how to map the activities of thieves and scoundrels. Rapists, murderers, even ...' He broke off to look keenly at the young woman by his side. 'He's worked a lot with Lorimer ...'

Kirsty tried not to catch the detective sergeant's eye.

'You know him too, don't you?' Murdoch said softly.

'Yeah,' Kirsty admitted. 'I've known Detective Superintendent Lorimer for ages. Through my dad. And I met Professor Brightman when I was a witness in that murder case ...' She broke off, aware of his eyes staring at her.

'Well, maybe you can persuade him that we don't need a trick cyclist to solve our cases for us,' Murdoch said, his voice laden with sarcasm. 'Back to Stewart Street, Wilson,' he added, taking out his mobile and looking thoughtfully at the screen.

Kirsty did not reply, her face reddening with an inner fury. Trick cyclist? Solomon Brightman was an eminent psychologist, not a *psychiatrist*, she told herself angrily. And she was certain that Murdoch knew the difference and was simply trying to wind her up, but why he wanted to do that was something of a mystery. Unless ...

Kirsty drove silently through the familiar city streets thinking hard. Her father was a well-liked DI and Lorimer was someone she'd known since childhood, whereas DS Len Murdoch was a newcomer on the scene. She glanced at the big man sitting in the passenger seat, texting on his mobile. Could it be that this grumpy fellow was actually intimidated by his new detective constable because of the connections she already had within Stewart Street? Kirsty blinked, wondering at the thought. Had she got this man all wrong? She had already decided that her imagination had been playing tricks on her at the scene of the robbery. After all, who would be brazen enough to nick an expensive watch like that and wear it the very same day? And was his brusque, sarcastic manner simply covering up some sort of insecurity? If so, it seemed as though she might have to reassess her first opinion of DS Len Murdoch.

The hospital room was quiet apart from the sighing sound of the mechanism beneath Irene's bed. She kept her eyes closed, not wishing to see the Perspex mask covering her nose and mouth. Everything was so difficult and she was tired, so tired ... if she could simply drift away now with no pain and no effort, then that is what she would choose.

It was the fifth time this year that she had contracted pneumonia. Would it be the last? Irene was well aware that her time was running out now. Len had held her hand in the ambulance last night, talking softly, whispering his usual nonsense about her getting better. She would never get better and they both knew it. Maybe it helped him to feel more optimistic? Irene smiled faintly. She wasn't afraid to die but she did worry about what would become of her big bear of a husband once she was gone. The boys were both overseas living lives of their own, Jack in Western Australia and Niall in Vancouver. Irene and Len had never been over to see where they lived with their wives and children, she thought sadly. Maybe once she was gone Len could make these journeys on his own?

The sigh faded as the oxygen flowed into her wasted lungs and then sleep, blessed sleep took the woman into the darkness once more.

*

It was past visiting time but nobody took any notice of the figure, stethoscope around his neck, walking along the hospital corridor in the direction of the row of single rooms reserved for terminally ill patients. The nurses at the oval shaped nurses' station barely glanced as he passed; there were so many junior doctors in the hospital, coming and going, it was hard to remember faces never mind names.

The figure stopped outside the door marked Murdoch, and paused, then slipped into the room next door. He stood for a few moments, watching the rise and fall of the sick woman's chest, the signs of life still present. His right hand shook suddenly as the mobile phone he clutched began to vibrate.

'I'm here now,' he whispered, turning away slightly as though to prevent the patient hearing his words. 'You know what to do. I'll give you twenty-four hours, that's all. Payment must be made within that time or the deal's off.'

He stood still, listening to the voice on the other end of the line, then a smile played about his mouth. 'Good. Thought you'd say that.'

The man slipped the mobile into the pocket of his trousers and nodded quietly towards the recumbent figure on the bed.

'Not long now, darling,' he crooned softly. 'Not long now.'

CHAPTER FOURTEEN

Sarah Wilding fingered the name badge pinned on to her uniform. This was what she had missed. Being part of a caring profession, having a useful job to do ... the sense of pride found in getting up in the morning and going to work had almost been euphoric this Wednesday morning. It had been easy to leave that miserable room in the bed and breakfast and head towards the train station, eager feet taking her along the city streets, umbrella held aloft to protect her new uniform. Even the long walk from Bearsden station, rain pattering down on her brolly, had failed to dampen Sarah's spirits.

She was early, far too early, really, she told herself, nervously tapping out the key code on the front door pad. Silly to get here an hour before her shift began when she might have stopped in the station for a bite to eat. But the prices at the fast-food kiosks had spoiled her appetite; every penny had to be counted carefully if she were to make it to the end of this week. The train fares, toiletries and a pack of black tights had already made a considerable hole in her budget. One of the auxiliaries gave Sarah a tentative smile as she folded her umbrella and stepped into the warmth of the building. The nurses on night shift would still be with their patients. There was plenty of time for a cup of tea and a biscuit from the caddy in the staff lounge; that would do instead of breakfast. The landlady at her digs didn't begin breakfasts till seven, far too late for Sarah when she had to be at work by eight.

The smell of bacon cooking wafted along the corridor as Sarah passed the kitchen, making her stomach rumble. Oh well, it was her own fault for coming in at such a ridiculous hour. Maybe if she could find different lodgings, somewhere with access to a kitchen, then this problem might be resolved. Was she allowed to leave the bed and breakfast, though? What would her social worker say? All these thoughts settled on her like a dark grey cloud as Sarah put her wet jacket on the back of a chair, moving it near the radiator to dry off.

'You're early!'

Sarah spun round with a gasp to see the nursing home manager standing with a tray of food in her hands.

'Sorry, didn't mean to startle you,' Nancy Livingstone laughed. 'If I'd known you were coming in at this time I'd have ...' She broke off, looking at Sarah's hungry expression as the new nurse eyed the bacon roll on Nancy's plate.

'Here,' she said, thrusting the tray on to the table. 'Eat up. Plenty more where that came from.'

Then, without another word, Nancy strode swiftly out of the staffroom, leaving Sarah with an unexpected breakfast.

She was almost finished making a pot of tea when Nancy returned, holding a plate piled high with more bacon rolls.

'The girls on night shift like to have their breakfast before they leave,' Nancy explained. 'And, since I just live up the road, it's easy enough for me to have mine here with them.'

Sarah licked her lips, tasting the salty bacon. 'Thanks,' she murmured. 'I really appreciate this.'

'You wouldn't have had time for anything to eat yet, I suppose?' Nancy asked shrewdly. 'Maybe you should just have breakfast here with us?'

Then, to Sarah's surprise, the older woman laid down the plate of food and, clasping her hands, bowed her head for a few moments.

'Thank you, Lord, for providing for all our needs,' she murmured, in a voice that seemed to speak to someone nearby, so that Sarah almost turned to see who else was in the room.

'Here, have another one.' Nancy offered the plate. 'Cook does brilliant bacon butties. Best Ayrshire bacon. None of your supermarket stuff. Just milk with my tea, my dear,' she added with a nod and a smile.

'Oh. Right,' Sarah said, rising to pour tea into two of the patterned mugs that she'd found hanging from a wooden mug tree. It was hard to know how to respond to this woman. Her kindness was palpable but the impromptu saying of Grace was unexpected to say the least.

They ate in companionable silence, Sarah relishing each bite of the food as her hunger was assuaged.

'Do the other staff know . . . ?' she blurted out suddenly.

The nursing home manager smiled sweetly and shook her head. 'It's not their business to be told about that,' she replied. 'You could be an agency nurse for all they know.'

'Oh.' Sarah gave a sigh of relief.

'Mrs Abbott was told, of course.' Nancy smiled apologetically.

She'd expected that, Sarah told herself, yet there had been no sense of having been overly scrutinised by the owner of the nursing home. On the contrary, Mrs Abbott had been quite calm, as though dealing with an ex-con like Nurse Wilding happened to her every day.

'And she didn't mind?'

Nancy Livingstone laughed. 'She knows me well enough to trust my judgement. Actually, she's my sister,'

'Your sister! Does that mean the nursing home is yours as well ...?'

'No.' Nancy shook her head with a smile. 'Bless you, no. It belongs to the Abbotts. I'm their right-hand woman, so to speak. Used to work in an accountancy firm until they asked me to help run this place.'

'You didn't mind changing careers?'

Nancy Livingstone gave her a strange smile. 'It was something I was called to do,' she said simply. 'And perhaps the Good Lord brought you here too.'

Sarah shifted uncomfortably. This sort of talk was like the stuff that pastor used to spout back in Cornton. As if being incarcerated was part of a bigger plan!

'I think I'm just lucky,' she mumbled. Then, to her dismay, she felt a tear begin to trickle down her face. 'Don't deserve ...' She began to hiccough.

'None of us deserves our good fortune,' Nancy murmured.

'But you don't understand!' Sarah protested, eyes full of guilty tears. 'If you knew what I'd done you'd never have had me here to work!'

'Oh, Sarah, don't say that,' Nancy replied. 'Catherine told me enough to know that you were not completely to blame for what happened.'

'He *died*!' Sarah gulped. 'How could I not be to blame for that?'

'Here.' Nancy handed her a box of tissues. 'The girls will be coming in for their breakfast and you don't want them to see you like this, do you?'

Sarah sniffed, taking a handful of tissues and blowing her nose. 'I'm sorry. You shouldn't be wasting your time with someone like me.'

'Listen to me, Sarah,' Nancy told her. 'There's a very important thing that the Bible says: all have sinned and come short of the glory of God. That's everyone, not just you. Think of that next time you want to beat yourself up, eh?'

Sarah nodded, struggling to contain the sudden rush of emotion that had taken her by surprise. Nancy was talking to her again, speaking in soothing tones.

'What you're doing here is very important, Sarah,' she said. 'You are well aware that each of our patients is in receipt of intensive nursing care. Many of them are stroke victims; you've seen that for yourself. One day their lives are going along a steady path then the next they're lying half paralysed in a hospital bed, some of them so helpless that they require every sort of help with their bodily functions. That's where you and all the other nursing staff come in.' She smiled gently as Sarah wiped her eyes with the edge of a tissue.

'But it's not just about making them comfortable,' Nancy continued. 'They all have need of companionship, someone to take a real interest in them as individual human beings.'

'I know,' Sarah said softly. 'Mrs Abbott said that every nurse was expected to provide a listening ear or else spend time chatting in a friendly way to the patients.'

'She'll have told you that we read to them.' Nancy nodded to Sarah. 'Newspapers or articles from journals that we know will be of interest. Things like *Farming Monthly* for Mr Imrie. He was a farmer before his stroke, you know. It's hardest of all for the ones who have led an active, physical life, don't you think?'

'Thank you,' Sarah whispered quietly.

'Oh, my dear, don't thank *me*.' Nancy beamed. 'Thank the Good Lord who sent you to us.'

Looking at this woman whose kindness had given her a second chance, Sarah made a decision. She would make something of this job, she nodded in determination. Maybe Nancy Livingstone's words were right. Perhaps she was here for a reason. And not just for herself, a whole-bodied young woman, but for these poor souls who depended on her nursing them with loving care. It was a chance to turn her life around once more.

A shadow loomed over Kirsty's desk and she looked up to see Murdoch's taciturn face staring down at her. He was dressed in his pinstriped suit again yet if anything his closely shaven face seemed even wearier than it had the day before.

'I need you to take me over to the South Glasgow University Hospital,' he said, jerking his head in the direction of the office door. 'I ...' He hesitated for a moment and Kirsty thought she saw something bleak pass over his grey eyes. Then it was gone as he snapped at her, 'Can you hurry up?'

The detective constable scurried down the stairs in Murdoch's wake, conscious of trouble ahead.

Even as she drove along the motorway there was an ominous silence between them. What was going on? He'd not spoken a word since he'd commandeered her as his driver. A swift glance saw only the man's profile, that bullet-shaped head and broken nose, a tough-looking face that seemed used to seeing the uglier side of human nature.

'Park anywhere you can,' Murdoch ordered as Kirsty slowed down to enter the parking area outside the huge new hospital that Glaswegians had nicknamed The Death Star due to its resemblance to the *Star Wars* feature. Then, to her surprise, he produced a blue disabled badge from his jacket pocket and laid it against the windscreen.

'Come with me but don't make a fuss,' he said, turning suddenly to Kirsty. 'I ... never mind, just stay quiet,' he finished with a sigh. Then he was out of the car and walking swiftly to the hospital entrance, Kirsty half running to keep up with him.

She followed her mentor through a maze of corridors, up several flights of stairs (why not take the lift? she wondered). Then at last Murdoch's steps slowed as he pushed open a set of double doors and walked towards the nurses' station.

'Mr Murdoch,' he announced quietly to a ginger-haired nurse who looked up at him enquiringly.

Kirsty saw the rush of sympathy in the woman's face as she rose from her place behind the desk. 'She's not awake, I'm afraid,' the nurse told them, including Kirsty in her glance. 'Doubt if she'll even know you are there,' she added in her soft Highland accent, leading them along a corridor and into a small room that was shaded by soft green curtains drawn against the daylight.

Kirsty wanted to gasp at the sight that awaited them; the emaciated figure of a woman, her face partly covered in a Perspex mask, several tubes snaking in and out of her body. And that sighing sound as the bed moved up and down as though it and not the patient were breathing.

Murdoch said nothing but sat down heavily on to a plastic chair next to the bed and slipped his fingers over the wasted hand lying on top of the sheet.

'Shall I leave you two with Mrs Murdoch for a while?' the nurse asked.

'Oh, I'll wait outside,' Kirsty replied hastily, the sudden realisation of what was happening making her feel a mixture of embarrassment and shyness. She had no business being here at all, she told herself, slipping out after the nurse and forcing herself not to look back at the man sitting by his wife's side.

'I . . . I'm just Detective Sergeant Murdoch's driver,' Kirsty explained once they were out of earshot. 'I didn't know . . .'

'He didn't tell you we'd called?'

Kirsty shook her head.

The nurse made a face. 'Poor soul. Some men are like that. Can't talk about it, can they?'

'What's . . . ?' Kirsty glanced behind her in the direction they had come from.

'Mrs Murdoch? Oh, we don't think she's got long to go now. On a ventilator all night.' The nurse sighed. 'She's peaceful enough. No pain. But her lungs aren't going to last much longer. We called him as soon as we were sure,' the nurse added in a tone of defensiveness.

'He knew she was . . . ?'

'Oh, sure, we've been keeping in touch ever since he came in with her the night before last,' the nurse insisted.

Kirsty nodded, remembering the dishevelled state of her mentor the previous day, the sudden change from a smart working suit to jeans and leather jacket. He must have come straight from the hospital.

'Isn't there any family?'

The nurse shook her head. 'Couple of sons. Both overseas. Probably won't come until there's a funeral.' The nurse's eyebrows rose as if commenting on the unfairness of life in general. Then she patted Kirsty's shoulder. 'Look, why don't you grab a coffee from the machine along in the day room? I'll come and collect you when it's time for him to leave. If you need me before that, just ask for Nurse Milligan, okay?'

Kirsty nodded and walked slowly along the corridor, blinking in the artificial light. How strange to be busy at work with Murdoch for two whole days and not to know what was going on in his personal life. Did that account for the grumpiness? The sarcastic manner? Suddenly she was willing to ignore the several instances of DS Murdoch's overbearing manner in the face of his dying wife. And yet, try as she might, Kirsty still could not rid her mind of the image of the scene of crime manager stooping over that tray of watches.

It was barely twenty minutes later that the ginger-haired nurse came and sat beside Kirsty, a mug of coffee clutched in both hands as though to warm her fingers.

'I've got a wee break,' Nurse Milligan explained. 'Thought you might like a bit of company.' She shot Kirsty a sympathetic smile. 'She's still here. But, like I said, she won't regain consciousness.'

'This ward, is it for terminally ill patients like Mrs Murdoch?'

'Aye.' The woman made a face. 'We're not MacMillan nurses but we all have specialist training in palliative care. There's a higher ratio of nurses to patients up here than anywhere else in the hospital. It's sad, really. We don't get to know our patients for very long. Most of them are transfers from other wards. Like the one who passed away during the night, God rest her soul. Next room to Irene Murdoch,' she said with a frown. 'It was funny. One minute she was okay then the next ...' The nurse shrugged and shook her head.

'Must be a hard job. I couldn't do it,' Kirsty told her.

'And I couldn't be a polis, that's for sure. You must see the dregs of society all the time,' she said shrewdly.

Kirsty laughed. 'Well, I attended my first post-mortem yesterday.'

'With him?' Nurse Milligan jerked her head in the direction of the ward.

'Yes, he's my boss,' Kirsty explained.

'Did it bother you? Seeing a dead body, I mean?'

Kirsty shook her head. 'Not really. The pathologist is so interesting and we need to find out ...' She broke off and laughed. 'Actually, I can't say anything about this as it's part of an ongoing investigation.'

The nurse looked thoughtful. 'Can I tell you something?' she began. 'It's about the patients here.' The woman looked around suddenly as if to check that nobody could overhear her. 'It's as if ...' She shook her head, the bright curls bouncing under the overhead light. 'It's silly. I just ... och, I don't know. I keep thinking that too many of our patients are all going off ... well, too quickly. Like that one last night. And now, poor Mrs Murdoch.' She looked at Kirsty and then moved closer, whispering behind her hand. 'It's as if there's some ... angel of mercy putting them all to sleep.'

'Really?'

The woman rose and grinned ruefully. 'No. Not really. It's just a notion I've had. Don't listen to me. It'll be the superstitious streak in me. Or else I've been on too many shifts back to back this week, I suppose. It tells eventually.' She smiled and shook her head in a self-deprecating manner. 'Better see how Mrs Murdoch is faring. I really don't think it will be very long. Will you be okay here?'

Kirsty nodded, glad to be left alone with her thoughts. What a strange nurse! Imagining that there was some sort of spirit creeping away with her patients. Kirsty gave a shudder. Was Nurse Milligan trying to hint that there were unlawful activities going on in her part of the hospital? Would she have called in her suspicions to their local police station? Probably not, Kirsty decided. Yet, having the opportunity to speak to a police officer here in the ward must have been too good a chance to pass up.

She stood up and strolled across the room then looked out of the window at the city streets far below. The people were like tiny creatures from this perspective. Were we just like colonies of little ants, coming and going, our destinies a matter of chance? she wondered. No, that wasn't right, was it? Human beings were more in control of their own fate, surely? But not always, Kirsty Wilson thought. She was becoming used to seeing some lives being ended before their natural time. Like that young drug dealer, Frankie Bissett.

She glanced back at the corridor where an orderly was wheeling a trolley along, the patient completely covered with a white sheet. Was this the patient who had died the previous night? Or a different one? There were always rumours about what doctors did at the end of a patient's life. Mercy killings, some folk reasoned. Some things were perfectly legal, like the instructions not to resuscitate. But there was a borderline between what was permitted and what was considered an act of taking away a person's life. An act that was simply called murder.

He didn't make a fuss, simply nodded at her from the doorway and said, 'She's gone.' And, as Kirsty moved towards him, ready with a sincere word of comfort on her lips, he held up his hand as though to ward off any unwelcome platitudes. 'Just take me out of here, will you, Wilson?'

It was more than three hours after they had first arrived that Kirsty found herself driving DS Murdoch back from the hospital, a light rain swishing under the windscreen wipers despite sun shining through gaps in the clouds.

'Do you want to go home, sir?' she asked gently.

'No, Wilson. Not yet,' he murmured throatily. 'I'll have things to do later.' He coughed then turned to look out of the car window as they passed the science centre near the River Clyde, the trees on either side golden in the afternoon light. 'Let's get back to Stewart Street. Need to sort out this Nottingham business and see if there's been any development with Bissett's PM. Besides, my own car is there.' He looked back for a moment and gave her a rare look of gratitude. 'Don't think I could've driven over here myself,' he admitted huskily. Then, pulling out a crumpled pocket handkerchief, Murdoch blew his nose and stared out of the window once more as though embarrassed to be seen displaying his emotions.

Kirsty was glad of the noise of traffic and the need to concentrate as they approached every junction. This was real life, something she could feel and breathe, not that overheated waiting room where she had lingered, waiting for this man's wife to take her last breath. Yet even as she drove further into the city and tried to blot out the starkness of Irene Murdoch's death, she felt a strong need to grasp Murdoch's arm, give him some sort of comfort. It was a female thing, she told herself, this urge to console. But it was an urge she had to resist. Len Murdoch had put up an invisible barrier the moment he had come out of that hospital ward and his young detective constable had the sense to respect that.

It seemed too good to be true, Sarah thought, later, tucking a stray strand of blonde hair into the clip at the nape of her neck.

The day's shift had ended sooner than she realised, the sound of female laughter coming from the staff lounge increasing in volume as the nurses on back shift arrived. Just two more days then she would have the weekend off before returning to work again on Monday for four o'clock, her late shift ending at midnight.

'The night shifts always seem the longest,' Grainne, a short, dark-haired Irish nurse, had admitted. 'Midnight till eight in the morning is everyone's least favourite shift. But, sure, we each have to take our turn.'

Sarah had nodded, understanding the need for round-the-clock nursing. And there would be a taxi provided for any of the nurses that didn't have their own transport, the manager had told her.

As she donned her raincoat, Sarah felt a sudden qualm at leaving the nursing home after her day's work. Ever since that encounter with Nancy Livingstone in the staffroom this morning, she had felt happier than she'd been for a very long time, as though the tears had somehow been cathartic, washing away her misgivings. Already it felt to Sarah Wilding that she belonged here. She'd begun to warm to the patients under her care, especially Mr Imrie, the man who had been a farmer. His eyes had followed her as she'd sat down beside him to read from his newspaper. The twisted mouth had moved but no discernible words had emerged, just a weak sort of groan. Then he had let his head fall back into the bank of snowy pillows as though the effort of trying to speak had exhausted him. What was he thinking? Sarah wondered as she left the nursing home and unfurled her umbrella. There was still intelligence behind these eyes, words and thoughts forever trapped in his damaged brain.

When the big dark car stopped by the kerb, Sarah slowed down, thinking that perhaps one of the nurses might have spotted her and was offering a lift back to the station. But it was a stranger, a man she'd never seen before, she thought, moving her umbrella and bending down to see the driver's window being lowered. He must be lost, wants to ask me for directions: the thought rushed through her head.

'Sarah Wilding?'

'Yes, who . . . ?'

Before she had time to take a step back, two burly-looking men burst out of the back of the vehicle.

Then Sarah felt her arms being pulled roughly as she was bundled off the pavement, the scream on her lips muffled by a pair of gloved hands, the umbrella tossed aside, somersaulting sideways across the deserted street.

Something sharp was digging into her side. A knife. It must be a knife.

She gulped, trying to move away from the pain but she was held fast in the grip of the two men on either side.

'Who are you?' Sarah cried. 'What do you want?'

'All in good time.' The man in the driver's seat turned to her with a grin. He had a strong face, a long jaw with a square, determined chin, dark hair that crept over his coat collar and a scar running down his right cheek. A scar that might have been made by a knife or a broken bottle, Sarah decided, her professional eye glancing as he turned back to watch the road ahead. His was a face she would remember if she were ever asked to describe it.

'Where are you taking me?' she protested, fear making her voice thin and tremulous.

'Somewhere nobody can hear you scream.' The man on Sarah's right laughed, pulling her arms so tightly behind her back that she cried out in pain.

The one on her left nudged her deeper into the middle of the back seat, his elbow pushed against Sarah's stomach.

Glancing at them in turn, Sarah saw one of them grinning through a set of broken, blackened teeth.

She shivered. Several of the inmates at Cornton had suffered from bad teeth; it was a sign of a deprived background, anybody knew that. But somehow Sarah sensed that this man had also done time, the violence emanating from him was almost palpable.

The one on her left was tall and skinny, his head covered in a black beanie hat, old acne scarring his angular face.

'What you lookin' at?' he hissed, a flick of spittle landing on Sarah's face making her turn away in a mixture of disgust and terror.

They were going to kill her.

She was certain of that.

Otherwise, why would they let her see their faces?

Sarah closed her eyes and trembled, panic rising through her body.

Oh God, oh God, help me, she implored silently.

You deserve it, a little voice insisted. *For what happened to Pete.*

I don't want to die, Sarah told herself. I've done my time. I've paid the price for my mistakes.

'Right, here we are.' The voice from the front of the car and a sudden jolt as they stopped made Sarah's eyes fly open.

They were parked off a country road somewhere, pulled into a grassy strip beneath a stand of chestnut trees whose shadows screened them from any passing traffic.

To the left was a dark pine wood and Sarah's eyes widened in terror.

Were they going to take her in there? Use that knife …?

'Ready, boys?' The man turned and nodded to the men who were holding Sarah by her arms.

'No! Please! Don't hurt me!' she whimpered.

'Well, maybe if you're nice to us we'll be nice to you, eh, Sarah Wilding?' The driver with the scar had twisted round now and was looking her up and down, making her feel naked and exposed to his roving eyes.

That was what it was about. They meant to rape her, Sarah thought.

And yet, this was no random abduction. They knew her name.

A glimmer of hope entered her heart: so far there had been no move to pull her out of the car, drag her into these shadowy woods.

'Something you need to do for us, Sarah Wilding,' Scarface told her. 'A little bit of help to show how sorry you are about brother Pete.'

The man on her right sniggered as Sarah's mouth opened in shock.

'See, we need someone like you to help us with our business,' Scarface went on. 'Nothing too hard for a clever girl like you.' He put out his hand and began stroking her cheek.

Sarah flinched at his touch, making all three of them laugh.

'You wouldn't want that pretty face all messed up now, would you?' he sneered, grabbing a handful of her hair and drawing her towards him.

Sarah shook her head, trying to utter *no* but the word was locked in her mouth, that menacing face leering into hers, his breath smelling of curry and garlic.

'All we want is for you to do us a little favour from time to time, that's all,' he said, his mouth close to her own. 'That too hard for you?'

'N-no,' Sarah gasped. At this moment she would promise these men anything, anything at all if they just let her go.

There was that sharp pain again, in her lower back, near her kidneys. A knife?

'What do you want me to do?' she whimpered.

Scarface nodded to the men beside her and Sarah felt their bodies slide a little bit away from hers.

'Good girl. Right, here's the deal.' He glanced from one of Sarah's captors to the other, a crooked smile on his face. 'And remember, go anywhere near the cops and they'll chase you. Nobody's going to take the word of an ex-con, now, are they?' he chuckled. 'And we know where to find you if you do anything silly.'

CHAPTER FIFTEEN

'That's not what I expected,' Rosie Fergusson gave a low whistle as she read the toxicology report. 'Need to let Murdoch know.'

She dialled the number in Stewart Street then listened as the call was transferred by the switchboard.

'Hello, Detective Constable Wilson speaking.'

'Kirsty? Is that you? Where's Murdoch?'

'Oh, Dr Fergusson. He's not in.'

There was a pause and Rosie could hear a sigh.

'It's really sad news. His wife passed away yesterday. He's off on compassionate leave for the next few days.'

'Oh, no. What happened?'

'She was very ill,' Kirsty explained. 'It was expected. I hadn't a clue about it but Detective Superintendent Lorimer knew.'

'Hm, listen, Kirsty, who's dealing with the Jane Maitland case? That elderly lady who died in her bed? I've got the tox report back and I need to speak to someone about it.'

'Well, I was on that case with DS Murdoch, but maybe you'd want to talk to Lorimer himself.'

'Aye, maybe that would be best under the circumstances. I'll
see that he finds you and tells you what he wants done.'

'Lorimer.'

'It's Rosie. Listen, terrible news about DS Murdoch's wife.
But that's not why I'm calling. He and Kirsty had a case the other
day, an elderly lady who had died under what may have been
suspicious circumstances.'

Rosie went on to explain about the unknown caller in the early
hours of Monday morning, someone not scheduled to visit the
woman in her own home.

'There's a high level of morphine in the bloods, enough to
have killed her.'

'Jane Maitland was receiving regular morphine injections?'

'Yes, but not dosages like this.' Rosie's tone was grim. 'I think
we have something fishy going on here. Either she had a private
arrangement with one of these end-of-life groups or else there's
something far more sinister going on.'

'Right, leave this with me. I'll have a word with DC Wilson
and make sure that someone else can take over this case while
Murdoch is away.'

'Right, I'm emailing you the tox report as an attachment now.
Let me know the outcome, won't you?'

Lorimer put down the phone with a frown, turning his attention to the computer screen and the incoming email. Murdoch
had called in to say he'd be taking just a few days off. So perhaps in the interim Kirsty would appreciate the presence of a
far more senior officer. He smiled as he glanced at the calendar
on his wall. There were several things he might need to re-
arrange, but the thought of handling a live case with his young

friend was a temptation that the detective superintendent found irresistible.

There was a murmur as the tall man swung open the door of the large CID room where several detectives were seated at their desks. And not a few eyebrows were raised when Lorimer stopped beside their newest detective constable.

'DC Wilson.' Lorimer smiled down at her. 'Just had this from Dr Fergusson. Think we need to take a closer look.'

Kirsty took the paper from his hands and read the lines of the toxicology report detailing the levels of substances found in the late Jane Maitland's bloods.

'Crikey!' She turned her face up to Lorimer's. 'That wasn't an accident, was it?'

'Could be one of two things, I reckon,' Lorimer said, sitting down in the vacant seat next to Kirsty's. 'Either Miss Maitland had made some sort of arrangement with a private organisation, and we're talking voluntary euthanasia here, or someone masquerading as a health professional gave her a lethal dose without her knowledge.'

'Murder,' Kirsty said quietly.

'That's what we need to find out. Though at the moment I'd favour the former line of thought. There were no signs of a forced entry, correct?'

Kirsty nodded as Lorimer continued.

'And as the woman was bedridden that suggests whoever came in had a key. I've applied for a search warrant for the woman's home. Could be we find paperwork that gives us an immediate answer to this question.' Lorimer shrugged. 'Should be able to access the house later today. Think you could do with me for company?' He grinned.

Kirsty's wide smile was answer enough.

*

So it was that DC Kirsty Wilson found herself in the passenger seat of Lorimer's silver Lexus, the leather upholstery sheer bliss, especially when the detective superintendent flicked on the heating on both front seats.

'How have you been finding CID so far, Kirsty. Does it live up to your expectations?'

Kirsty gave a short laugh. 'Well, I didn't expect it to be so busy,' she admitted. 'A jewellery heist and two deaths all on my first day. Back in my uniform days it was more routine than that.'

'Always expect the unexpected,' Lorimer rejoined. 'Bet your dad told you that often enough.'

'Aye, and "crime doesn't take a holiday", "round every corner of the road there's a motorist not looking where he's going". Heard them all at one time or another.' Kirsty grinned. 'Still, it didn't prepare me for such a heavy workload.'

'That's what can happen in CID,' Lorimer said. 'We try to concentrate on one case at a time but crime has a habit of throwing stuff at us in a way that makes our life pretty difficult. And our manpower is always under a strain.'

'Did you know the victim in the Byres Road flat, Frankie Bissett?' Kirsty asked. 'DI Grant said he was a well-known dealer.'

Lorimer nodded. 'Aye, but he was small-time. Used to hang out with Billy Brogan and his crowd before Billy went off with other people's money. Frankie was never big time but he would have been on the fringes of organised crime all right. Someone knows what happened in that flat. And why,' he said softly.

'There's more manpower going into that case than this one,' Kirsty remarked.

'Has to be,' Lorimer replied. 'Frankie's death looks like an execution pure and simple and we need to find out everything we can about the circumstances behind it. Sooner we know all about the people who lived there with him and all of his known associates, the nearer we'll be to finding answers to who and why. Now, this lady, Miss Jane Maitland, what have you learned about her so far?'

'Well, she lived on her own. Had been in that lower cottage flat for years, according to the woman upstairs. She'd suffered cancer for quite a long time. Spread all through her lower abdomen. She'd had surgery but preferred to stay at home in the end. Had a care package in place.' Kirsty shrugged. 'It's all in the report. The district nurse who called it in was really helpful.'

'And she said nothing that made you suspicious?'

'The nurse?' Kirsty exclaimed. 'Goodness, no. I never thought that she might have been the one to have administered that dose of morphine. After all, why would she draw attention to the patient's death like that if it had been her . . . ?'

'Why indeed. Maybe she would have left things as they were if the nosy neighbour – Mrs Doyle – upstairs hadn't made a fuss?'

'Well, she might have assumed it was a natural death. The poor lady was very ill.'

'And how long had she been in that state, lingering on?'

'Oh, I see what you mean,' Kirsty said slowly. 'If someone wanted to hurry up the process they might have taken steps to give her that lethal dose.'

'And it might have been Jane Maitland herself,' Lorimer countered, as the big car slowed down and rounded the corner of the house where Kirsty had arrived only a few days before.

'I think we will pay a quick visit to Mrs Doyle first. Let her know that we have a search warrant and a key.' Lorimer smiled. 'Plus I'm curious to meet the woman whose suspicions started this all off.'

*

'Aw, it's you again. And this is . . . ?' Ailsa Doyle looked up at the tall man at Kirsty's side, her heavily kohled eyes flashing with interest.

'Detective Superintendent Lorimer,' he told her.

'Ooh, *detective superintendent*? So there *was* something bad about the auld yin's death?' Ailsa said, raising her eyebrows in a knowing look. 'Come on in, eh? Ah've jist put the kettle oan. Tea do youse?'

And, without waiting for a reply, she walked back through the hallway, Lorimer and Kirsty in her wake.

'Wean's sound asleep,' Ailsa whispered. 'That's how I wis gonnae take myself a wee break. Jist come on through tae the kitchen, will ye?'

The kitchen was a surprise to Kirsty after the disarray of the front room on her previous visit: rows of neat white cupboards and tidy work surfaces with a bowl of fresh fruit in one corner beside a sterilisation unit.

Ailsa flicked the switch of a stainless-steel kettle and drew out a large brown earthenware teapot that, by contrast, looked as if it might have been handed down through the family.

Lorimer watched as the young woman measured three spoonfuls of loose tea from a silver caddy into the warmed teapot, an old-fashioned way of making tea that seemed at odds with this modern-looking young mother with the pink hair and row of ear studs.

'First oot the pot or builder's tea? Whit's yer preference, officers?' Ailsa turned to them with a faint smile as though she had read Lorimer's mind.

'As it comes,' he replied. 'Milk, no sugar, please.'

'Same here,' Kirsty agreed, seating herself at the small table that jutted out from the wall.

'Have you lived here long, Mrs Doyle?' Lorimer asked, sipping the tea from a mug that had a picture of a sailing ship on one side and an anchor on the other.

'Couple o' years. Since we got married. He's away at sea.' She nodded over her shoulder at the photo of a young man grinning from a pinboard that was fixed to the side of a cupboard. 'Merchant Navy.'

'So you would know Miss Maitland quite well?'

Ailsa Doyle looked shrewdly at Lorimer and put down her mug carefully. 'Aye. Fact is ma mammy lives ower the street so we've kent auld Miss Maitland downstairs fur ages. She's no' been over the door fur years, except when she wis in the hospital,' she said, turning to Kirsty. 'Did ah tell ye that last time ye came?'

Kirsty nodded, though in truth that was a detail in her notebook that she would need to check.

'We have a search warrant for Miss Maitland's home,' Lorimer told her. 'There are several things we need to ascertain.'

'Something dodgy going on?' Ailsa smirked as though the event of two police officers investigating the death of her elderly neighbour was a bit of excitement in an otherwise tedious existence.

Lorimer shot her a stern look and she had the grace to lower her eyes and blush. 'Did Miss Maitland ever talk to you about her condition?' he asked.

'Och, I'd sometimes pop in with the wean whenever wan o' the nurses or the home help wis there. She couldnae come to the door so we didnae see her ither times.'

'None of the neighbours had a spare key?'

'Naw, jist the district nurses, the home help and her parish priest. Ah did have their phone number though and I wis wan o' they – what' d'you call thems – that emergency company, the one

110

with the necklace thingmy ... they had ma number in case she needed me to call the doctor or that.'

'And had that ever happened? Did she ever alert the company in an emergency situation?'

'No' as far as I know,' Ailsa replied.

'And what about family? Did any family member have a key for the flat?'

'Whit family!' Ailsa Doyle sniffed, searching in her trouser pocket then bringing out a packet of cigarettes. 'She had nae-body. Never married, nae brothers or sisters that I know of.' She shrugged. 'Kept herself tae herself maist o' the time. Private sort of wumman. Hardly ever any visitors, usually jist the nurses or the lassie that came on a Monday tae dae her washing. She took in the Tesco delivery an' all,' Ailsa Doyle remarked. 'An' sometimes Faither Fitzsimmons wid go in tae see her.'

'Mrs Doyle, I'm going to ask you something and I want you to think hard before you answer me,' Lorimer said slowly, fixing the young woman with his blue gaze. 'Did Miss Maitland ever talk about wishing to undergo voluntary euthanasia?'

Ailsa Doyle's mouth fell open and she shook her head. 'God, no! She wis a good Catholic woman. She'd never have done something like that.' She pulled out a cigarette from the packet, fingers shaking. 'You think she'd had enough?' she asked, her glance flitting between Lorimer and the female detective.

'That is one line of inquiry,' Lorimer said smoothly. 'If you hadn't been so vigilant, the district nurse would never have called us in.'

Ailsa had lit her cigarette and was exhaling a line of smoke to one side. 'See the man that came ... thon fella I seen early on ...? Ah've been thinkin' aboot him.'

'Yes?' Lorimer asked, his tone quite neutral.

'Well.' Ailsa frowned. 'I wis lookin down at him, right? An' it wis dark. But I 'member something about him. Like a wee baldy spot aroon his hair.' She glanced up at Kirsty. 'See that's ma trade. Ah'm a hair stylist. Jist do homers the noo, right enough since the wean's came. But it's the sort o' thing I notice aboot folk. Thurr hair. An' this bloke wis dark haired wi' a baldy bit aroon the crown. Happens tae some fellas. Maist o' them'll gel thurr hair intae spikes, disguise it, eh?' She took another drag on her cigarette. 'But ah think this fella wis maybe a bit older. Forties, maybe? An' he walked *out* – know whit ah mean? Like my Gary. See, Gary's tall an' he walks out, big strider, know whit ah mean?'

'He wasn't walking away quickly?' Kirsty asked.

'Naw, jist whit ah says. A lang stride, kinda loping. No' in a hurry tae get away, like. Naethin suspicious,' she said with a tinge of regret in her voice.

'Mrs Doyle, you've been a wonderful help,' Lorimer said warmly, putting down his mug. 'I'm sure there will be a simple explanation for Miss Maitland's demise but many thanks for being such an observant neighbour. And thanks for the tea,' he added, standing up and nodding towards Kirsty.

As they made their way down the single flight of stairs, Lorimer was aware of a keen pair of eyes following their every move. Ailsa Doyle might not be the most educated of young women but she certainly didn't lack a natural intelligence. And, right at this minute, Lorimer was sure that the young mother was working out just what might have happened to her elderly neighbour.

The smell of wet wool had disappeared to be replaced by a faint musty smell as Lorimer opened the door to Jane Maitland's cottage flat and switched on the hall light.

'We need to see her priest, Father Fitzsimmons. And the home help. Maybe they'll be able to throw some light on Miss Maitland's state of mind prior to her death,' Lorimer told Kirsty. 'And tell us who else might have had a key. We'll get on to that as soon as we're finished in here.'

'It's still warm,' Kirsty remarked. 'Nobody's turned off the heating.'

A small pile of mail lay on the entrance, including a note marked TESCO.

'Wonder what they did with her groceries?' Kirsty murmured to herself. 'Don't suppose the driver was expecting the police to be here when he arrived.'

'Right, DC Wilson.' Lorimer stopped and looked down at the young woman, his blue eyes glittering in the artificial light. 'What are we looking for?'

'Evidence?' she asked. 'Something to tell us what happened early Monday morning?'

'That, certainly. But more than that.' Lorimer nodded, walking along the hall and pausing at the late Jane Maitland's bedroom door. 'We need to see if she left any sort of a note. And,' he added, 'if she didn't, then we need to look at all of the paperwork we can find. See who might have benefited from her death.'

'Oh.' Kirsty nodded thoughtfully.

'Did she have a lawyer? Had she made a will? Is there any sign of correspondence with one of these end-of-life organisations?' He gave a grim smile. 'Plenty to keep us busy here for a while,' he said. 'So, get to it, DC Wilson, see what you can find.'

'Yes, sir,' Kirsty replied, looking into the bedroom at the bedside cabinets, the telephone next to the old lady's bed and a bureau that sat opposite the bed next to an old-fashioned wooden wardrobe, its walnut burr and ornate brass doorknobs marking it as a piece of furniture that had been in vogue some time last century.

Lorimer smiled as he left the young detective constable to her search, seeing her gloved hands whip out a notebook from her handbag. She'd be systematic, he guessed, putting paperwork in order, making notes as she went along. He had seen enough of Kirsty Wilson in her young life to know that she had the makings of a good detective and he trusted her to find what they were looking for.

His own search began in the front room, a decent-sized lounge with a three-piece suite covered in matching tartan throws. A quick glance upwards showed a line of cobwebs clinging to the pleated pelmet above the bay window. Jane Maitland hadn't been able to check up on her home help, Lorimer thought. In fact, hadn't she been virtually a prisoner in her own home?

The dusty, fly-blown window told a similar tale, as did the occasional tables, a fine layer of dust clinging to the few ornaments that lay there. The home help came every Monday, her duties including light housework and taking care of the laundry, according to the notes Lorimer had read in Jane Maitland's file. Washing the bedclothes and the woman's nightwear would be a priority, he supposed, as he moved out of the empty room, noticing as he did so that the radiator in here was cold. No point in heating a room where nobody ever sat down, he realised sadly: Miss Maitland's whole existence had narrowed into that bedroom where Kirsty was looking for clues as to how the woman's life had ended.

The kitchen was a bright room facing south-west, the autumn sun glinting off the stainless-steel refrigerator and double oven. Here, at least, were signs of care and attention, the work surfaces spotless as befitted a place where food preparation must have taken place. On the windowsill outside a row of pink and white geraniums bloomed, the summer warmth lingering on. Whose hands would water them now, Lorimer wondered? Would they be left to die or was there some relative of Jane Maitland's who might come to their rescue?

The low hum of the refrigerator was the only sound, electricity being used up until someone decided to turn off and unplug the device.

Was that what had happened to the old woman? Had someone entered her home, taken the decision to terminate her life? And, most important of all, had she been a willing party to that final act?

'Found anything yet, DC Wilson?' Lorimer asked from the doorway of the bedroom. It was only right and proper to call her by this name, though 'Kirsty' sprang to the tip of Lorimer's tongue every time he began to address her.

'Nothing, sir.' She looked up from where she was on her knees examining a pile of papers. 'At least, nothing that indicates what you might call a living will. No suicide note, no correspondence between Miss Maitland and any organisation that I've found yet,' she continued. 'Still to look through that bureau, though.' She shot him a hopeful look.

'Okay, two pairs of hands will take us through it more quickly,' he agreed, moving across the room to the bureau.

It was an old piece of furniture, possibly an antique, Lorimer thought, with several different types of wood inlaid to create marquetry patterns of classical urns and garlands of flowers, its sloping top opening into a writing desk with six tiny drawers above in two rows and a spacious cabinet below, an ornate metal key in the left-hand keyhole.

Jane Maitland had been a methodical sort of person, Lorimer

decided, taking a look in each little drawer. Books of stamps, old national insurance cards, a roll of payment slips from decades before, a stapler in one drawer, a metal hole punch in another, a tin box full of paper clips, even a few Premium Bonds – small stuff packed away tidily as though their owner wanted to know exactly where to look if she needed to find anything.

The cabinet below revealed more paperwork relating to Jane Maitland's estate, however. Lorimer took out several buff-coloured files, all marked in the same neat sloping hand. *Bank Statements, Lawyer, Tax, Invoices, Investments, Charities* ... He piled them all on the bed and sat next to them, gratified to learn that the deceased had been someone with a tidy mind.

He began with the bank statements, riffling through a package of thin A4 papers detailing the woman's monthly accounts, till he came to the most recent one dated August of that year.

At first Lorimer blinked, thinking he had been mistaken, but then the figures at the foot of the page were clearly marked, statement closing balance £87,543.77

'Take a look at this,' he said, passing the entire file to Kirsty. 'And that's just her current account. Wonder what she has in investments,' he murmured, turning to that particular file.

'Who keeps that sort of money in their current account?' Kirsty said, looking up in amazement.

'Someone who hasn't been visited by a financial advisor for quite a long time,' Lorimer said quietly, examining the documents on his lap. 'The regular amounts being put into the account monthly are from pensions, as far as I can make out. She must have had all of that money lying in her bank account for long enough. And, if I'm reading these correctly then it looks as if Miss Maitland's shares are worth well over a million,' he murmured, his right hand brandishing another sheaf of papers.

116

'How on earth . . . ?'

'. . . does an old lady in a modest little cottage flat come to be so wealthy?' Lorimer finished the sentence for Kirsty. 'And what you *don't* see,' he told her, flicking once again through the more recent bank statements, 'are any large sums being withdrawn. Something just as significant for us right now.'

'You mean she'd have had to pay someone a substantial sum to supply her with morphine if she'd wanted to take her own life?'

'You'd have thought so,' Lorimer replied. 'Maybe this will give us more of a clue,' he said, brandishing the lawyer's file.

By now Kirsty was sitting beside him on the edge of the bed, head bent towards the documents.

'That's her will!' she exclaimed as Lorimer turned the pages that, like those in the other files, had been secured neatly by double plastic tags inserted through the holes in each margin.

It was certainly a photocopy of the Last Will and Testament of Jane Patricia Maitland, the original no doubt kept in a safe place at Drummond and Abernethy, the Glasgow-based lawyers whose correspondence was also in this file.

Lorimer's eyes ran down the page to where a list of bequests had been drawn up. Several charities would benefit from the old lady's passing, he saw, noting that one of the beneficiaries was the RSPB, a charity close to his own heart. So, she'd been a bird lover, he thought, his eyes drawn to the garden outside. Jane Maitland's bed was positioned opposite the window as if she had wanted to see a bit of the world. But the wire-mesh bird feeders hanging at angles from the branches of a lilac tree were empty. Nobody to feed them, he decided, sadly, nobody taking time to go outside and see to the old lady's passion.

There were small bequests to friends, a few of these crossed out over time, possibly as they had predeceased Miss Maitland, but the main beneficiary was a man by the name of Crawford Whyte to whom she had left the residue of her estate, a hefty sum, Lorimer thought, once the smaller bequests had been made.

Flicking through the correspondence, Lorimer could find no trace of a Crawford Whyte anywhere. Who was this? Some distant relative? They would need to ask the solicitors, see if there was a contact for this person who stood to inherit a vast fortune.

Or maybe someone around here might know, he thought. Hadn't Ailsa Doyle told them that her mother lived locally? Would she know any of Jane Maitland's family? Perhaps that was something he could keep up his sleeve for now.

CHAPTER SIXTEEN

She would have to wait until next week, Sarah decided, staring out at the clouds scudding across the sky as she tucked the edge of the sheet into the empty bed.

One of the patients had been transferred to a hospice only this morning, his condition deteriorating so badly. Motor neurone disease was a hellish thing to suffer, Sarah thought, remembering the man's wasted features. Here they did what they could for the patients but the hospice provided the sort of end-of-life care that was the province of very special sorts of nurses.

Sarah's thoughts drifted back to her ordeal the previous evening and the promise that she had given under duress. *But I can't do it just yet*, she'd pleaded. *Give me time.*

She would be on late shift with other nurses on her rota next Monday, at a time when the nursing home manager would have gone home and there were fewer ancillary staff around. That was the time to do it. She bit her lip. What had she been asked to do, after all? Make a list of all the next of kin of the patients who were currently at the Abbey. *Especially their email addresses*, the tallest of her captors had insisted, glaring at her intently. Not such a big deal, she tried to tell herself. *Photograph them with this*, he had told her, thrusting an iPhone into her hands. She'd taken it silently, putting it into her handbag, the tacit agreement made by that very action.

There had to be some criminal intent behind this, something that she was not going to be told. And, should anyone find out what she was doing with these people, she would be back in Cornton Vale before she knew it.

These men knew her name and they knew where she lived, the journey back from that lonely spot in the country taking her right to the door of the bed and breakfast. And they'd known she was Pete's sister. Who were they? And why did they want access to the contact details of these patients' families?

Sarah stood up, blinking back the tears that had begun to sting her eyes. She was screwed if she didn't do what that frightening man had asked, and yet she was screwed if she did.

Could she tell the police about what had happened? Sarah recalled the man's nasty grin. He was right. Who'd believe an ex-con? Nobody had believed her story when Pete had died, had they? Especially her parents.

Just get me some stuff, Sar, gonnae, please? her brother had wheedled. *They'll kill me if I cannae produce the goods.*

She could still hear his voice, that desperate fear that had driven her into a criminal act. Pete would be able to pay back his dealers, he'd assured her. It would all be okay.

And then it wasn't, of course. Pete had been found in that West End flat, dead of a lethal overdose, the drug supplied by his own sister.

Sarah shuddered. She mustn't think about it any more. Pete had lied to her but there was no way she was ever going to prove that.

'Sarah?'

She turned to see Nancy Livingstone in the doorway of the empty room.

'There's a telephone call for you. It's Catherine Reid. Can you take it in my office?'

Sarah leapt up in alarm. She'd been found out already!

'You okay, dear?' You've gone very white,' Nancy remarked, looking at Sarah's face.

'Stood up too quickly, that's all.' Sarah managed a tremulous smile. She was about to add *time of the month*, but that would be another lie and somehow she could not bring herself to deceive this woman who had shown her such kindness.

'I'll leave you to it,' Nancy whispered as they reached her office. 'I'll be in the staffroom if you need me.'

'Hello, Sarah Wilding here,' she said, lifting up the telephone on the manager's desk.

'Sarah, sorry to call when you're at work but something's come up and I wanted to ask if you could change your lodgings?'

'Yes!' Sarah gasped. 'I'd love to. It's not a great place I'm in just now. Is there any chance I could find digs nearer here? Somewhere that has a kitchen?'

There was a pause then her social worker replied, 'Leave it with me. I might be able to sort something out by the end of today.'

Sarah imagined she could hear the crackle of papers being turned, then Catherine asked, 'How's the job?'

'I love it,' Sarah said in a rush. 'Wish it was permanent,' she went on. 'But I suppose I'll need to register with an agency eventually.' She stopped, her words echoing that of the scar-faced man as he had gripped her tightly. *Once you've done what we want you register with an agency, okay? Get yourself jobs in the same sort of places.*

And he'd smiled nastily, adding, *for the benefit of us all*. A statement that had made the other man snigger.

'Well, that's good,' Catherine replied and Sarah imagined the smile of relief on the woman's face. Another client sorted out, she would think.

But, what if she were to be caught looking through files that were no business of hers? What if she were to be sent back to prison? Sarah's heart sank as she thought about the two women who were genuinely interested in her welfare; Catherine Reid and her friend Nancy, the good Christian woman who really seemed to care what happened in Sarah Wilding's life.

Drummond and Abernethy's offices were in a basement halfway up West Regent Street, the offices on the ground floor sporting window boxes that were full of late-summer annuals in scarlet, white and blue, colours that stood out against the dark red sandstone building.

The staircase to the basement was accessed by a small gate to the side of the railings that separated the offices from the street. Large windows showed activity within, men and women sitting at their desks, intent on their computer screens.

'Nice place,' Kirsty remarked, nodding at the well-polished brass plaque set into the stonework.

There was a modern keypad just inside the main doorway, its black storm doors pushed back to reveal a glass door that was etched in a familiar Art Deco design. Could it be an original Rennie Mackintosh? Lorimer wondered as he put his finger to the buzzer and waited.

The tinny sound was broken by a fuzzy voice saying, 'Hello?'

'Detective Superintendent Lorimer, DC Wilson. Police Scotland.'

There was a pause and then a different buzzing note as the front door clicked open and they stepped into a spacious foyer.

'Hello,' the voice said again and, looking up, Lorimer saw a young woman seated behind the reception desk, a pair of reading glasses perched on her nose.

'We'd like to talk to the solicitor who is in charge of the affairs of the late Miss Jane Maitland,' Lorimer explained, holding out his warrant card.

'I see,' the woman replied, shooting curious glances at the two police officers. 'Miss Maitland. Just one moment.' She turned to the laptop that was open on her desk. A few moments later she looked up at them again.

'It's Mr Brian Abernethy who's in charge of that,' she replied. 'He's with a client just now but I'll tell him you're here. Just take a seat through in the waiting room, would you?' she added, nodding towards an open doorway opposite her desk.

Lorimer ushered Kirsty through to the small lounge reserved for clients, keeping the door open so that he could hear the receptionist speaking. True to her word, Lorimer heard the names *Mr Abernethy* and *Police Scotland*, then, after a short pause, *Miss Maitland*.

'What now?' Kirsty whispered as they sat opposite one another on matching dark blue sofas.

'We wait,' Lorimer replied.

'I should imagine the solicitor will be as anxious as we are to discuss this. Can't be every day that a couple of police officers descend on him asking questions about a client,' Kirsty observed.

'Ha! You'd be surprised,' was all that Lorimer answered, his grim little smile making Kirsty's eyebrows rise thoughtfully.

'Do you know this lawyer, this Abernethy fellow?'

123

'No, but I've seen his name before,' Lorimer admitted. 'Used to be involved in criminal law before his old man died and he took over the reins here. Represented some of the less salubrious members of our society,' he added with a knowing look in Kirsty's direction.

It was less than ten minutes later that a short, portly man in a grey pinstriped suit appeared in the doorway, smoothing his thinning hair with one hand as he approached the two police officers.

'Brian Abernethy,' he said, small dark eyes searching Lorimer and Kirsty with interest. 'Please come up to my office.'

They followed him out of the waiting room, past the reception desk and along a corridor where a small flight of stairs led to the upper floor.

First impressions often counted, Lorimer thought, his eyes measuring up this little man who waddled ahead of them. There had been no handshake, no attempt to ingratiate himself with the police officers as so many strangers often did, particularly those in a professional role. Had he encountered Brian Abernethy in any past cases? Glancing at the man walking ahead of them, Lorimer decided he had been right, they had never met before. But that did not mean that one of Abernethy's clients hadn't crossed swords with him.

'We only have part of the ground floor,' Abernethy explained, leading them along a different corridor to the back of the building. 'But there are always plans to expand.' He gave a perfunctory smile, waving them into a small office that was completely panelled in dark wood, the view from the window showed the back of another building. Lorimer drew in his breath, the sense of claustrophobia making him feel uneasy. It was a weakness that had lingered from childhood, something he simply had to endure if he could not totally overcome it. Even the light from the green-shaded desk lamp and a dusty candelabra suspended from the ornately plastered ceiling failed to compensate for the lack of natural daylight.

'Please take a seat,' Abernethy said, motioning them to the two easy chairs set at an angle on the other side of his desk while he swung into the captain's chair and clasped his hands in front of him.

'Now,' he began, 'how can I help you?'

'Miss Jane Maitland,' Lorimer said. 'You will have been informed about her demise?'

'Only just now,' he said, taking up a pen from the desk and rolling it between his fingers. 'The receptionist . . . ' He shrugged.

'Miss Maitland passed away on Monday morning,' Lorimer explained. 'The Procurator Fiscal has instructed us to examine the nature of her death and we are doing just that.'

'I don't understand.' Brian Abernethy frowned. 'My client was a very sick woman. Wasn't her death . . . well . . . expected?' He looked from Lorimer to Kirsty as though either of them could answer his question.

'There are extenuating circumstances,' Lorimer continued. 'What we need to know is the whereabouts of the main benefi-ciary of her will, one Crawford Whyte.'

'Well.' Abernethy blew out his cheeks, giving him a clownish appearance. But there was no mirth in his expression as he sat back in his chair. 'That's confidential, of course. My client. . . '

'Nothing is confidential in this case, Mr Abernethy, except what Police Scotland choose to keep under wraps.' Lorimer leaned forward, his voice quiet yet authoritative. 'We need to know where we can find this Crawford Whyte and how he was related to Jane Maitland.'

'Oh, y-yes, of c-course,' the man stuttered. 'I suppose now that she's dead...?' He shrugged and gave a theatrical sort of sigh, folding his plump little hands in front of him once more, as if to restore his previous composure. 'Mr Whyte isn't aware of this,' he began, blinking at Lorimer as the detective fixed him with his blue gaze. Then, giving a tentative smile, he turned to Kirsty. 'It's quite sad, really, that he didn't know.'

'Know what?' Lorimer asked.

Abernethy gave a little smirk, pausing the way that actors do before delivering a dramatic speech and looking back at Lorimer again.

'That Miss Jane Maitland was his natural mother.'

'What do you think?' Kirsty asked eagerly as they stepped back on to the pavement on West Regent Street.

'He knew he was the beneficiary of an old lady's will but he didn't know why. Or at least he won't know why until Abernethy tells him.' Lorimer strode on down the street, his face grim. 'Wish I could be there when he does,' he muttered. 'It would be interesting to see this Crawford Whyte's reaction.'

'Well, we have his contact details, don't we?' Kirsty said brightly. 'What if...?'

'You heard what Abernethy told us. He's in London,' Lorimer said. 'Probably nobody will be with him to witness how he takes news like this.'

'Are we sure he didn't know she was his mother? I mean, if he was aware that he stood to inherit a small fortune, wouldn't he be curious about why a total stranger had left it to him?'

'Anybody would be,' Lorimer agreed. 'But Abernethy hinted that this Crawford Whyte was unaware of the extent of his inheritance.' He gave a sigh, his lips twisting for a moment. Did he believe all that the lawyer had told them? 'Let's find out just how much information this man had about Jane Maitland, eh?'

'Michael.' Brian Abernethy sat behind his desk, one hand clutching the handset, the other drumming fingers on his mouse mat. 'I've just had the police here. I need to warn you. I think they know.'

CHAPTER SEVENTEEN

'Call for you, Sarah. It's Catherine!' Nancy Livingstone's eyes twinkled as she beckoned the nurse from where she was sitting beside David Imrie.

'I'll be back as soon as I can,' Sarah apologised, patting the patient's hand as she rose from her chair.

There was something about the nursing home manager's expression as she waved Nurse Wilding into her office, something almost gleeful, Sarah thought. Could it be that Catherine Reid was passing on some good news about new digs?

'Hello, Sarah here,' she began.

'Ah, yes, well, I said I'd get back to you today if I found somewhere more suitable for you to stay. And I have.' There was a pause as Sarah breathed a sigh of relief.

These horrible men knew where she worked but perhaps she might be able to give them the slip if she changed where she lived?

'It's very local.' Catherine's voice was warm. 'In fact it couldn't be handier. But it's only with your agreement, of course.'

'Local would be great!' Sarah enthused. 'Whereabouts is it? Is it a room? Does it have access to a kitchen?'

'Yes and yes,' the social worker replied. 'But there is a catch.'

'Oh.' Sarah's face fell.

'It's at Nancy Livingstone's house. She's offered to give you a room there. Only problem is she doesn't want you to pay her any rent.'

'What? Why? I mean ...?' Sarah was at a loss to know what to say. That explained the smile on Nancy's face.

'Nancy's a widow, Sarah. She lost her husband over a year ago,' Catherine explained. 'And she rattles around in that big house all on her own. You'd be doing her a favour as much as she wants to do one for you.'

'Gosh!' Sarah exclaimed. 'I don't know what to say. I mean, it's so – so generous.'

'And so typical of Nancy,' Catherine added. 'We've been friends for a long time, Sarah, and believe me, she is one of the most giving people you'll ever meet.'

'Well, I can't say no, can I? I mean, what sort of person would pass up a kind ...' She broke off, her voice suddenly choking with emotion.

'Go and speak to her,' Catherine advised. 'I'll sort out all the paperwork here. Okay?'

Sarah nodded, too full to give any reply except for a husky *yes*.

Halfway down the corridor, she could see Nancy waiting for her, arms across her body as though hugging herself in expectation.

'You'll come?' The woman's eyes were shining and then, as Sarah grinned, she was enfolded in a hug of sheer joy.

'When's the funeral?' Kirsty asked her father.

It was Friday evening and they were sitting around the family table in West Kilbride, the topic of conversation turning to Len Murdoch and his wife's death.

'There isn't a date set yet. His boys have to come over from Australia and Canada,' Alistair Wilson replied, his fork waving in the air.

'So, not immediately?' James asked. 'Will you be expected to attend?' he asked Kirsty.

'Oh, aye, he's my official mentor, after all,' she said.

'And Bill Lorimer's your unofficial one,' Betty Wilson laughed, pushing the casserole dish towards her daughter. 'You've landed on your feet all right, my girl.'

'What's he like?' James asked. 'To work for, I mean?' He turned to his girlfriend's father.

'The best,' the DI replied simply. 'And when I think of all the people I've worked with in my career he'll be the one I'll miss most.'

It had been a hectic week, Kirsty thought, as she glanced around her mother's table, grateful for the respite of the weekend. And, although her presence was not required at Stewart Street, Kirsty's mind strayed to the cases that had commanded her attention over the past few days, particularly the one she had shared with Lorimer.

'Anyway, to change the subject,' James began, looking at Betty and Alistair. 'Any thoughts yet of where you'll be going to celebrate this man's retiral?'

'Och, somewhere nice and hot,' Betty replied, exchanging knowing glances with her husband.

'Aye, a remote island miles from anywhere. With no phone signal!' Alistair declared, making them all laugh.

'Well, wherever it is, you surely deserve the rest,' James said, raising his glass to the older couple.

Betty Wilson's face flushed with a radiant expression and Kirsty grinned at both her parents. James was right. After thirty years spent on the force, her mother having to endure his late nights and weekends away on a job, Alistair Wilson more than deserved a special holiday with his wife in some exotic location.

'Pudding?' Kirsty's mother rose from the table, smiling at her husband. The question was a rhetorical one: nobody in their right minds refused one of Betty Wilson's puddings.

Kirsty watched as her mother opened the lower door of her double oven and drew out a chocolate soufflé, its top trembling gently as she laid it down on the table. Once she had wanted to follow this path, herself: be a chef or at least work in the hospitality business. But a quirk of fate resulting in a murder inquiry had changed her destiny and now she sat here, a police officer like her father.

She smiled to herself, glancing at James as he grinned at the sight of the soufflé. Her boyfriend had also come into Kirsty's life because of that investigation. Life was strange, she decided. Was it all planned out beforehand? Or did humans shape their own particular destinies? And, the question that had nagged at her for several days: had Jane Maitland really taken her own life?

'Is that everything?' Nancy Livingstone shot Sarah an anxious look as she appeared at the door of the bed and breakfast, a haversack slung over her shoulder and a hessian carrier bag weighing down her right arm.

'Afraid so.' Sarah gave a tight little smile. 'My previous landlord disposed of all my worldly goods when I was inside.'

'He shouldn't have done that!' Nancy shook her head. 'What an awful thing to do.' She heaved Sarah's haversack into the boot of her Volkswagen Golf then added, '*Everything?*'

Sarah nodded. 'There was nothing I could do.' She sighed. 'I miss all the clothes I used to have, especially my warm winter coat.' She tried to smile as she eased herself into the passenger seat. 'It doesn't matter, really. They were only *things*.' Sarah shrugged as she drew the seat belt forward and buckled it closed.

'This is so true,' Nancy said, easing off the handbrake and glancing round before moving off into the traffic. 'Isn't life worth more than food? And isn't the body worth more than clothes?' she murmured quietly.

'Who said that?' Sarah asked. 'It sounds like you're quoting somebody.'

'Jesus,' Nancy replied simply, her eyes on the road ahead.

The journey passed in silence after that, Sarah wondering just what lay ahead. She closed her eyes as they drove through the city, sleepless nights finally catching up with her.

As the Volkswagen passed through the main thoroughfare of Bearsden, Nancy glanced at her companion. Sarah was exhausted, anyone could see that. What sort of guilt lay so heavy on this young woman's heart that she was bowed down with such weariness? *Come unto Me all ye that are weary and heavy laden*, Nancy thought to herself. Would the Lord find it in His grace to give this girl rest unto her soul? That was something that Nancy Livingstone fervently hoped as she turned the corner into a pleasant street full of large houses and then slowed down as the driveway of her own home approached.

Corrielinn was an old house that had been built at the end of the nineteenth century, a time when decorative art had been going through several changes and stained-glass artists were in demand for domestic dwellings as well as tall-spired Christian churches. It had been ridiculously expensive to buy, but Eric and Nancy had fallen in love with this house the moment they had stepped over its threshold. Perhaps it had been the long window to one side giving light on to the spacious hallway; its yellow and golden picture on the glass still drew appreciative glances from any passerby.

The soft mellow sandstone and the dark grey slate roof with its turret above the attic stairs were common enough features for Glasgow Victorian houses; it was the stained glass that set this house apart from its more conventional neighbours. It hadn't always been called Corrielinn. Once they had made it their home, Nancy and Eric Livingstone had investigated the house's past and discovered that it had been named Damascus House and had actually been owned by the stained-glass artist who was celebrated for his life-sized representation of St Paul's vision in a city centre church. However, subsequent owners had changed the name and CORRIELINN was now engraved on to the stone gatepost. A Corrie was a sheltered gully in the hills, Eric had once remarked, leaving Nancy to imagine that her dear husband was suggesting that their home was a shelter from everything outside that could encroach on their happiness. *This is where I want to grow old*, Eric had whispered all these years ago.

Nancy cut the ignition and gave a sigh. Poor man hadn't even reached sixty-five when his heart had given out after a successful career that had spanned almost four decades.

Nothing lasted for ever in this life, Nancy thought with regret. And the house would still be standing when she was gone too, its stones sheltering others from the vagaries of the outside world.

She stretched out a hand and touched her new tenant's sleeve.

'We're here, Sarah,' Nancy said quietly, watching as the younger woman awoke, blinking for a moment as though she were disorientated. 'Welcome to Corrielinn.'

*

Later, Sarah would try to describe what she had felt on entering the big house. *It shone*, she would say. *Like an inner light or a fire burning somewhere. And the peace ...* that was a word she would always use to sum up Nancy Livingstone's home. And yet, and yet ... her initial feeling was that she didn't belong here in this magnificent house (like something off the telly, a posh person's place). In fact, it had been a surprise to see a place like this owned by the nursing home manager; if anything she had expected a nice semi somewhere on the outskirts of the town, with a bit of garden to the front and back. Nancy was a good woman, her kindness glowing like these stained-glass windows. Yet Sarah felt a distance emerging between herself and the older woman as she looked around her home. What did she think she was doing, inviting someone like Sarah Wilding here to stay?

She was an ex-con, someone who had stood trial for theft and possession of drugs, charges that she had wanted to deny until persuaded by her solicitor to plead guilty. *Saves your case coming to trial*, the woman had insisted. *And you'll get a shorter sentence.*

So, how had she come to be here, in this place with its long damask curtains framing the huge windows, a bowl of amethyst and rust-coloured mop-headed chrysanthemums gracing the half-moon table in the enormous hallway?

'Do you want to see your room?'

Sarah was aware of Nancy standing to one side of the reception hall, a tentative expression on her face. She wants me to like her home, Sarah thought, looking at the older woman twisting a scarf between her fingers, a small nervous gesture that revealed her anxiety.

'I'd love to,' Sarah replied. She smiled at Nancy. 'Still can't believe I'm actually going to live here,' she murmured, turning slowly and looking at the doors leading off then the staircase that led to the upper rooms.

The half landing looked out to a well-kept garden at the side with several shrubs plus a large variegated holly tree and a vista that included distant hills. But it was the stained-glass picture that captured Sarah's attention, a vast waterfall pouring molten water into a pool below, pale skies above where a pair of swallows soared.

'That's beautiful,' she said. 'Was it made when the house was built?'

'Yes,' Nancy told her. 'It's quite old now, an antique really. Come on, your room is on the first floor, just along here.'

A quick glance showed Sarah that the staircase led even higher, up to yet another level. Maids' quarters? Or perhaps a nursery?

Her thoughts were interrupted as Nancy opened a door and stood back, letting Sarah enter first.

'Here you are, it's all yours.'

There was no comparison between this spacious room and the miserable bedsit she had left, Sarah thought as her feet sank into a thick-piled carpet. Nancy put down Sarah's haversack beside a double bed with a pretty patchwork quilt pointing towards a cream-coloured armoire and matching dressing table, decorated with rosebuds painted in pastel pink.

'Please make yourself at home,' she said, opening the wardrobe door. 'I've taken away the stuff that was in here to give you some space,' she added, indicating a row of empty coat hangers. This was Tracey's room before she got married,' Nancy explained.

'Your daughter? I didn't know you had a daughter,' Sarah said.

'No reason you should.' Nancy shrugged. 'She lives in London with her husband. Works in television.'

'An actress?'

'Bless you, no.' Nancy laughed. 'She's a production manager. Strictly behind the scenes.'

'Are you sure she won't mind me . . . ?'

'Not her decision, is it?' Nancy countered firmly. 'Corrielinn is my home, Sarah, and I can invite whoever I like to stay.'

The older woman's smile was just as friendly, but Sarah began to wonder what kind of welcome her daughter might have given to a woman so recently released from prison.

'Now, if you want to freshen up before dinner, the bathroom's just through there,' Nancy continued, pointing towards a door that Sarah had thought to be a cupboard.

Sarah pushed open the door to reveal a large carpeted bathroom complete with bath, shower cabinet and bidet in palest apricot, as well as a matching wash basin beneath the frosted glass window. There was a yellow orchid blooming on the windowsill and a pile of soft cream towels lay on the Lloyd Loom chair below. A quick glance upwards at the incomplete plaster coving showed her that another room had been sacrificed to furnish Nancy's daughter with such luxury, a luxury that she, Sarah Wilding, was suddenly determined to enjoy for as long as she possibly could.

'She's not here.' The landlady looked up at the two men, arms folded across her bosom. 'Went away with a pal, so she did, and no I haven't got a forwarding address so don't bother to ask.'

The front door slammed and Mrs Duncan flounced into the sitting room where her husband sat, eyes fixed on a football game on the television. He looked up, an expression of mild curiosity in his eyes.

'A pair of wee nyaffs!' Mrs Duncan declared. 'And not so

wee, as it happens. Bad types. You can always tell. Comes from taking in these lassies,' she grumbled, eyes darting to the front window to see that the men had indeed left. She gave a sudden shudder. 'Gives me the creeps,' she muttered, rubbing her arms.

'Well, you don't have to.' Her spouse shrugged. 'You could do the place up, get better rents.'

The harrumph from his wife effectively ended that conversation before it had really begun.

Mrs Duncan sat down heavily on the settee, fingers stretching towards the open box of Dairy Milk that Sarah Wilding had given her earlier that day. *Just to say thank you*, the girl had murmured. None of them had ever done that before, the landlady thought. But, no, thinking back to her temporary tenant's leave-taking, hadn't the gift come from that older woman who had accompanied her?

'She's done a runner,' the tall man with the scar spoke into his mobile phone. 'But she should be back at work on Monday afternoon.'

'So long as she does what she's been told,' the voice on the line replied firmly. 'Anyway, it shouldn't take you long to find out where she's gone, should it?'

'Aye, well, she's part of the scheme of things now, isn't she?'

There was a pause then a chuckle that held not a scrap of mirth. 'If she steps out of line you know what you can do, don't you?'

Scarface smiled, his hand moving down to finger the blade hidden in the lining of his jacket, the handle towards his hand. She'd been scared out of her wits, he thought, smiling as he remembered Sarah Wilding's terror-stricken face. He liked his women like that, cowed and compliant. He ran his index finger along the edge of the blade. Maybe they could have a little bit of fun once she'd dropped the list where he'd told her to leave it.

Nurse Mary Milligan sat frowning over the paperwork that lay in front of her. What would her colleagues make of this? All these patients going off so quickly? Her finger traced the line of dates on the left-hand side of the printed sheet. It was all there for them to see in black and white. The ginger-haired woman bit her lip. Statistics had been her strong point back at university, before she'd changed her course and gone in for nursing. She read the figures again. No, that didn't make sense. Statistically there should not have been nearly so many deaths all occurring on this one ward. Perhaps it might be wise to talk to someone about this, Mary told herself.

Her thoughts wandered back to that young detective constable who had come in with Irene Murdoch's husband. She'd seemed an intelligent type of lass. And she hadn't scoffed at the nurse's fanciful notions, something, Mary realised, that were not quite so far-fetched when seen on paper. Aye, she might do.

She looked up as a shadow was cast across her desk. A doctor, someone who hadn't been seen on her ward before, yet that was nothing new; there were so many medics in this place, some of them part-timers, others filling in for colleagues. This one was a bit of all right, though, a dark-haired man who stood regarding her with a laconic smile. She glanced at his left hand: no wedding band, not that it made a lot of difference these days. Perhaps he was just being clever, keeping his anonymity. Mary liked the notion of a good-looking fellow like this being careful around so many women staff.

'Can I help you, doctor?' she asked brightly, her eyes flicking towards the name badge on his lanyard. But it was turned the wrong way around and she could only see the same details that were on everyone's plastic security badge.

As if he had noticed her glance, the doctor's fingers strayed to the end of his lanyard, lingering there so that Mary couldn't see his name.

Flirting, are we? she thought and shot him a coy smile.

But his eyes were not on Mary Milligan's sweet face or pert figure, but on the paperwork on her desk.

'Ah, just what I've been asked to see,' he murmured. 'Senior consultant wants a look at these.'

He smiled at her now, his gaze disarming her for a moment so that she handed the file over without another word.

Then he was gone, the sheaf of papers in his hand, leaving Mary smiling happily after the handsome doctor as he disappeared along the hospital corridor.

The icon showed that over twenty emails were waiting in the inbox. His fingers clicked busily then a satisfied smile crossed the man's handsome face. They were beginning to see sense, all those people. Many of their sick relatives were simply draining money as well as time and energy from their nearest and dearest, something at which that second batch of emails had hinted. *Freedom*, he'd written again, and that single word had worked as though imbued with magic. And now, here they were, good, concerned folk who only wanted the best for their loved ones.

He read their pleas, cringing slightly at the well-worn clichés.

Put them out of their misery.

I wouldn't let my dog suffer what he's going through.

And, the one that always made him chuckle:

It's for the best.

And of course it was a mere coincidence, wasn't it, that each and every one of his respondents would be left a great deal better off once their darlings were gone.

CHAPTER EIGHTEEN

Rosie felt her body jerk as she awoke, conscious of the sweat clinging to her silk nightie. She gave a small moan, for a sense of dread lingered despite the dream already fading, its images blurred and indistinct.

'Hey, shh, it's all right,' a voice beside her soothed and then she was in her husband's warm embrace, his arms sheltering her from the phantoms of the night.

'Bad dream?' Solly asked, his head turning towards her so that his beard tickled Rosie's cheek.

'Mm-hm. Can't remember most of it,' she sighed. 'But I think it was triggered by one of my cases.'

'Ah, dreams,' Solly replied, one hand smoothing the curls away from his wife's forehead. 'The innermost working of the soul. Something troubling you, darling?'

'It's that elderly lady,' Rosie said suddenly, sitting up and wrapping the duvet around her chest. 'Overdose of morphine.' She turned to Solly. 'Administered by someone purporting to be a district nurse.'

'Ah.' Solly nodded. 'Great word that, *purporting.*' He slipped an arm across her waist. 'Tells me what you think.'

'*I* think we should probably enjoy our Sunday morning while Abby's still asleep,' Rosie giggled, slinking back down under the covers and nestling into her husband's warm body.

'But you also think there's been an unnecessary death,' Solly replied in a familiar tone that made Rosie sigh. That was the trouble with being married to a psychologist. Give them an idea to run with and off they went! 'You think someone gave her the drug without her permission?'

'Don't know,' Rosie grumbled. 'Up to Lorimer to find that out. Oh, and young Kirsty Wilson. Actually, it was her case first, with that DS of hers, Murdoch.'

'Why's he been replaced by Lorimer?'

'Och, it's a real shame. His wife died. She was an MS sufferer.' Rosie heaved another sigh. 'Lorimer's taken Kirsty under his wing meantime.'

'There's no way of telling what sort of intention was behind this death, then?'

'Not from any examination of her body,' Rosie agreed. 'All I can safely say is that toxicology shows a high dosage of morphine that would have rendered her immediately unconscious, death following swiftly. She was terminally ill,' she added, turning to look at her husband's thoughtful face.

'And she may simply have decided that enough was enough,' Solly murmured.

'Could be. It's not against the law to take your own life . . .'

'. . . but it is illegal for someone else to do so,' Solly finished for her. 'Unless a law is passed allowing people to have assistance.'

'Do you think there should be?' Rosie asked, running her fingers through Solly's luxuriant beard.

'Ah, big question.'

'But really? Should people be able to have help to die when they want to?'

'I'm sure it happens anyway,' Solly said slowly. 'There must be some well-intentioned GPs who give their suffering patients a helping hand. But there's also the memory of Harold Shipman, isn't there?'

Rosie curled her leg around her husband's. Who would ever forget the doctor who had killed scores of his patients, some of them for financial gain? At the end he'd taken his own life in a prison cell. 'Would you want me to help you die? I mean, if you had something awful like motor neurone disease?'

'No,' Solly said quietly. 'Life is too precious. And I mean to live it until my very last breath. Besides, isn't it up to God when we die?'

'God?' Rosie protested. 'How can you say that? You're not even a practising Jew any more!'

'Maybe not, but there are certain beliefs that appear to have lingered. And that's one of them,' he said mildly.

'Mu-um.' A voice from their bedroom doorway made them turn as one to see Abby standing there, a rainbow-coloured teddy bear trailing from one small fist.

'Come on in,' Solly said at once, turning back the duvet.

And with a bound, their little daughter leapt into the bed, clambered over her daddy and snuggled in between them both.

Rosie gave Solly a rueful look over Abby's golden head. So much for their quiet Sunday morning cuddle.

Sarah opened the bedroom curtains and stared out. Instead of bleak grey tenement buildings there was a garden, leaves on the fruit trees turning different shades of russet and red. Her eyes lifted to the hills beyond. The Campsies? She wasn't sure.

Geography had never been her strong point and even the countryside around Glasgow was a bit of a mystery to her. When she was a child they had taken the train to Wemyss Bay and the ferry to Bute, summer after summer spent in cheap digs, she and Pete guddling at the edge of the seashore. The young Sarah had collected shells in a plastic bucket while her brother dug in the sand, changing the course of the tiny rivulets by making dams. They'd been so innocent back then, she thought, tears blinding her eyes to the view of the hills.

A tap on her bedroom door made her turn.

'Morning, Sarah. Just wanted to ask you if you'd like a couple of boiled eggs for breakfast?'

Nancy hovered in the gap of the doorway, a flowered dressing gown wrapped around her body.

'Oh, that would be great, thanks. Can I help?'

Nancy shook her head. 'Not this morning, dear. Once you get to know where everything in the kitchen is, then you can make anything you want. See you in ten minutes?'

The door closed, leaving Sarah marvelling once again at her good fortune in being here in this woman's lovely home. Time for a nice hot shower, she decided, heading into the bathroom.

The kitchen smelled of warm toast as Sarah entered, her hair still damp from the shower.

The round oak table was set with two place mats, the eggs tucked under tiny knitted cosies, butter and several jars of different preserves laid out around a rack of wholemeal toast. Did she always lay the table like this? Or was it because she had a guest? Sarah wondered.

Once Nancy had murmured a grace, she smiled at Sarah and motioned for her to begin eating.

'Sleep well?'

'Like a log,' Sarah replied, buttering a piece of toast. It was not true. She had slept fitfully, troubled by thoughts of what she had to do during her next shift at work. But the little lie was kindly meant.

'Good.' Nancy grinned. 'Fancy coming to church with me this morning? Service begins at eleven.'

'Sure,' Sarah said, then immediately wondered why she had so readily agreed. Was it because she was trying to please this woman, give her something back in return for her overwhelming generosity? 'I suppose I'll need to change,' she said, looking down at her jeans.

'Nobody dresses up for church these days,' Nancy laughed. 'All the young ones come in jeans and jackets. Even the minister's wife wears jeans to morning service. Mind you, she's probably down on her hands and knees with the wee ones in Sunday school. It's just the oldies that stick with tradition and wear their good clothes.'

Sarah nodded, slicing the top off her egg, glancing at Nancy Livingstone. Did she consider herself an oldie? What age was she, anyway? Mid fifties, perhaps? Certainly not ready for retirement. She stared at the greying hair and the face devoid of make-up. At work Nancy was always smart, though not overdressed or showy in any way. She could do with some highlights, Sarah thought, scrutinising the woman opposite. And that flowery dressing gown did nothing for her. Memories of a scarlet silk kimono, a gift from her father years ago, came back. It had gone, along with so many of her other possessions, she thought, a tiny seed of bitterness creeping in to spoil her mood.

St Andrews Church was a traditional building with a lofty spire towering above its roof, no different from other Glasgow churches as far as Sarah could see. As they entered the foyer, Nancy and Sarah were greeted by a man and woman standing on either side of the door handing out leaflets. A quick glance showed that they were printed orders of that morning's service.

'Morning, Nancy,' they chorused, giving Sarah a curious though not unfriendly look as the two women passed into the church, the sound of an organ being played filling the building with music right up to its rafters.

Inside it was just the same: *Hi, Nancy* came from several people who smiled as they walked towards the front of the church.

'I like to sit in here,' Nancy said, stopping by a pew near the front of the church and motioning the girl to take her seat. Then, without another word, she bowed her head in silent prayer.

Sarah looked at her wristwatch, wondering how long she would have to sit here on this padded cushion, the smooth wooden pew hard against her back. It was ten minutes to eleven and the place was filling up. The notes from the organ became steadily slower and then died away, only to be replaced by a familiar hymn tune, one that Sarah remembered from childhood, though the actual words eluded her.

As Nancy was still apparently communing with her God, Sarah looked at the sheet she'd been handed. She read the welcome address at the start, noticed the theme for the day – 'How To Forgive' – and had just begun looking at the hymns printed inside when Nancy lifted her head and smiled at her.

'Okay?'

Sarah nodded, though in truth she was regretting her hasty decision to accompany the woman to her church. What was she doing here? An ex-con amongst all these middle-class people;

nice folk who would run a mile if they knew what sort of person was there in their midst.

Suddenly the music ceased and the whole congregation rose as one, Sarah with them, as a man walked slowly and steadily down the adjacent aisle, a huge Bible carried in his hands, the black-gowned figure of the parish minister following.

Then it was much as every church service Sarah could remember from her childhood. A friendly welcome to his flock (and any visitors – that was her, wasn't it?) followed by parish notices and then they stood once more for the first hymn.

'Praise, My Soul, the King of Heaven', rang out, the sound reverberating around her.

Sarah's mind wandered during the first prayer, eyes wide open, seeing many bowed heads all around her. What were they all thinking? Did these people really believe that someone was listening to the man up there in the pulpit, his sonorous tones invoking an Almighty Presence? The chaplain at Cornton Vale had tried to persuade the girls that God was indeed caring for them whether they could feel His presence or not. Many of the women had mocked the poor man, giving him a hard time with sexual innuendos to make him blush. *Where was God when I needed him?* they would sometimes ask, the bitterness in their tones almost palpable.

Now, familiar words were being chanted by the congregation and Sarah mumbled along, the Lord's Prayer being something that had been instilled from an early age.

'And lead us not into temptation but . . . ' she murmured along with countless other voices. Her throat dried suddenly and no further words came out.

Why could she not ask to be delivered from evil? Was she so in its thrall, ready to do the bidding of these men, that even uttering a prayer was to be denied her?

147

Sarah swallowed hard, biting her lip as sudden tears sprang to her eyes.

Then it was over, the 'Amen' like a huge collective sigh, and Sarah felt the people settle back as the minister began reading from the great book on the lectern.

It was a story about King David, the great hero who had flung a stone from his shepherd's sling to slay Goliath, the giant Philistine. But David was older now, king of his land, a powerful man who could snap his fingers and his commands would be obeyed.

'Such power,' the minister said quietly, interrupting his own reading, making Sarah pay a little more attention.

David had seen a woman, wanted her for himself and had her husband sent to the front line, quite deliberately, to be killed, the story continued. And now the minister was reading from a different passage, something about a prophet telling King David another story about a poor man robbed of his precious ewe lamb. David's indignation at the prophet's words turned to shame as he was confronted by the truth behind the story. *You are that man*, the prophet told him. Sarah's heart thumped as she realised that David had abused his power and taken a man's life out of the sheer lust of his heart.

She leaned forward a little, eyes fixed on the man in the pulpit. What happened next? Was David punished?

But the minister had laid down his book and now the choir was singing something about coming to the well.

As the last notes from the organ faded into a silence punctuated by the occasional cough, the minister began again, reading about the consequences of King David's sins.

'And this is what the Lord God of Israel says: I made you king over Israel and rescued you from Saul. I gave you his kingdom

148

and his wives; I made you king over Israel and Judah. If this had not been enough, I would have given you twice as much. Why then have you disobeyed my commands?'

Sarah listened as the minister continued reading, realising that she didn't know how this Bible story ended. Surely David would be punished? Yet she didn't remember how he had died. Execution? Wasting away in the dungeons of a prison cell? Surely that had been his fate?

'"I have sinned against the Lord," David said. Nathan replied, "the Lord forgives you; you will not die."'

Sarah sat back with a small intake of breath. Why? How could God have forgiven David such a terrible crime?

She barely looked at the words on the sheet as the congregation rose to sing the next hymn, so full were her thoughts about the Bible story. A sense of indignation filled her. Had David got off with murder just because he was a powerful king?

Then they were seated once again and a rustle of anticipation sounded through the church as the minister bowed his own head and intoned a few words.

'The Lord forgives you,' he began, his words measured and solemn, his eyes roving over each and every one of his parishioners before coming to rest on Sarah Wilding.

'Why did God forgive David?' the man continued. 'Because he loved him, just as he loves each and every one of the human beings he has created in His own image. You, me, the person sitting next to you and the folk who never come to church. Then there are all the people you find impossible to forgive. Rapists, murderers, paedophiles, terrorists ... the list goes on and on, doesn't it? Yet I tell you that God is able to forgive every single one of them.' The minister stopped for a moment, nodding as though he were agreeing with his own words.

'And how do I know this?' he asked. 'It's all in here,' he touched the open Bible on the lectern with a reverent finger.

'John, three sixteen: For God so loved the world, that he gave His only begotten Son, that whosoever believeth in Him should not perish but have everlasting life.'

There was another pause, this time for the words to sink in, Sarah thought, as she looked up at the man, his ordinary, kindly face transformed, the overhead light shining down, creating the illusion of a halo.

'God sent His Son to us, to the whole world,' the man continued, 'so that we might not die because of our sins but be forgiven instead. Jesus took all of our sins upon Him. That was why He died on the cross. These were *our* sins, *our* transgressions,' he insisted. 'And we know that our Lord conquered sin and death because he rose again!' A note of triumph entered the minister's voice.

'But did that stop sin? Did everyone suddenly become good and turn away from evil?' He shook his head. 'No. And why is that? It's because we have to make our own choice,' he went on. 'A choice to put the past behind us for ever. How do we achieve that?' He raised his hands in a questioning gesture.

Sarah held her breath. Was this man speaking to her? Surely those gentle eyes were turned directly to the place where she was sitting?

'We ask for forgiveness,' he said simply, letting his hands fall through the air as though it was a straightforward answer. 'God is always ready to forgive His children, no matter how great their sins. "Though your sins be as red as blood I will make them white as snow",' he quoted. 'And God wants to forgive us, he wants us to repent of every wrong thing we have ever done, every unkind thought we have ever had. For all have sinned and come short of the glory of God.' He smiled as though he, too, had been through this process of having to turn away from some heinous crime.

Did he know what it was really like? Sarah thought. Had he lain awake night after lonely night in a solitary bed, racked with guilt at the crimes he had committed? She very much doubted that.

'What would you have done to David?' the minister suddenly asked. 'Would you have punished him? Subjected him to the old law of an eye for an eye?'

Sarah glanced around her to see if there was any reaction to the man's words but they were all staring ahead, waiting for his next statement.

'Ah, we are merely mortals, often with revenge in our hearts and we know what it is to feel guilty about our own misdeeds. We would punish David, right? But God is greater than this. He can see into every heart and mind. He can seek out a contrite soul and take away all our sins. It is hard for us to forgive others; sometimes,' he paused and Sarah was again certain that he was looking straight at her, 'we find it hardest of all to forgive ourselves.'

Then it was over, a brief prayer giving thanks to God before the rustle amongst the congregation resumed and the uplifting of the offering was announced, marked by the organ playing a tune that Sarah recognised as 'Amazing Grace'.

'Did you tell anyone about me?' Sarah whispered, coming close to Nancy, one hand cupped across her face lest anyone overhear her.

Nancy shook her head. 'Of course not!' she whispered back, a frown of disbelief on her face. 'Why on earth would you think that?'

Then the collection bag was passed along the row, effectively stopping conversation as Sarah's thoughts whirled. That man, the minister (who was now descending from his pulpit and coming towards the communion table), he'd definitely been looking at her, hadn't he? Or had it just been her imagination? Were these words like arrows, finding their mark? For a moment there Sarah had thought they were just for her. But no, the sermon had been for everyone, not just the ex-con who sat in their midst. *He hadn't known*, she told herself, the awesome truth beginning to dawn on her. What was it the man had said before beginning his sermon? *God be in my mouth and in my speaking. God be in our hearts and in our understanding.*

CHAPTER NINETEEN

Julie was cold. The pashmina that her sister had wrapped across her shoulders hours ago was now lying on the floor to the side of the wheelchair. And nobody was there to pick it up. Julie could see it out of the corner of her eyes, the blues and greens of the paisley pattern chosen to complement her navy trousers and pale jade cardigan. Rachel was always so fussy about selecting her outfits and Julie was grateful for her younger sister's attention.

But where was she now?

A window behind her must have been left open earlier in the day for the young woman in the wheelchair could feel the draught as the breeze filtered in through the gap. Such little things were more noticeable nowadays, irritating, frustrating since her own legs would never again walk across the room, her own hands unable to perform the simple act of closing a window. With the loss of muscle control and then the inability to speak, Julie had learned to focus on things that everyone else took for granted or didn't even notice.

Her world had shrunk so swiftly since the diagnosis. Was it only last year that they had travelled to Australia? She and Rachel laughing as they had flirted with those lads they'd met on Manly Beach. How could things have changed so much?

Julie forced herself not to panic, her ventilator tube was where it should be – over her head and secured to her nasal passages – her feet were set together on the footrest, her hands protected by the sides of the chair. Best not to think too much. Best not to remember . . .

The sound of the front door opening came as a huge relief. Had she been able to make them work, Julie would have made her facial muscles turn into a smile of gratitude.

Rachel was home again. She would be safe.

The current of air became stronger as the door of her downstairs bedroom opened.

But it was not Rachel.

As the man entered the room Julie gave a grunt, all that she was able to do in lieu of speech, slivers of saliva escaping from her open lips.

'Hello, darling,' he grinned at her, making Julie wonder if she had ever seen him before, his manner was so familiar. But she could not remember that face, those dark eyes.

And how could she ever have forgotten a good-looking guy like this one, coming towards her, his medical bag in one hand?

CHAPTER TWENTY

*R*ainy days and Mondays always get me down, Karen Carpenter had sung. Her rich, low voice had not been enough to sustain the singer, Sarah thought sadly as she walked around the corner towards Abbey Nursing Home. Poor thing had died after losing her struggle with that dreadful eating disorder. The thought made her shiver, the ghostly outline of late afternoon sun sliding behind a bank of low clouds.

The day had begun well enough. Once Nancy had left for work, Sarah had wandered around the house, trying to imagine what it might have been like when Eric Livingstone had been alive, their daughter racketing about, as any teenager would do. But Nancy Livingstone seemed to have done an effective job of tidying most of their memories away. Only the photographs in the lounge (in silver frames on the polished sideboard and occasional tables) gave any hint that once the place had been home to other people.

It had, however, been a grey day from the moment Sarah had woken, a steady curtain of rain blotting out the hills. Now, shaking her umbrella as she stood on the threshold, she saw just how the weather reflected her own dismal mood.

Today was the day. She had to do what they had told her. Find the names and addresses of next of kin and photograph them on this phone. She fingered the small shape in her raincoat, making a mental note to slip it into the pocket of her uniform as soon as she could. Once it was done, she would be free of them, surely?

That scar-faced man's words came back to her, menacing, the memory of his stinking breath as he'd told her what he expected her to do.

Sarah had been too afraid to ask why, the question that reverberated in her brain at this very moment. Why was she doing this? What was the reason behind it? Was some sort of fraud involved? The people who were funding their relatives here must have money, she reasoned, the fees were an enormous burden for any family to cope with.

Yours not to reason why, yours but to do and die. The old phrase came back, making Sarah tremble as she pulled off her raincoat and shoved the wet umbrella she had borrowed from Nancy into a plastic bucket in the corner of the staffroom.

She would do it as soon as she could, Sarah decided, then looked up with a start as the door opened.

'Hi. Ready for our shift?' Grainne smiled and Sarah watched as the other nurse took off her jacket and hung it on the coat stand. 'Give you a lift home afterwards if you like?' Grainne offered, putting a bunch of keys into her handbag. 'Saves you having to wait for a taxi.'

Sarah hesitated for a moment. Did this kind offer spring from some knowledge of her circumstances? Or was the girl just being nice?

'Thanks. Midnight, eh? Seems a long way off right now,' Sarah remarked, glancing at the clock on the wall.

'Well, better make a start,' Grainne said, following Sarah's look. 'Want to take first break? Or is six-thirty too soon for you?'

'That would be great, thanks,' Sarah said quickly, her mind already moving forward to the opportunity that this might allow her. The nurses' breaks were staggered so that only one nurse was off at any one time during the evening shift. And Nancy would be away home by then, her office left open in case any of the staff needed to consult a patient's file.

The next two hours seemed interminable as Sarah saw to the needs of her patients, helping to feed them as well as undertaking the routine changing of catheters and ensuring each patient was clean and comfortable. Mrs Calder had rasped a few words in her direction as usual. *Best to put me out me out of my misery*, she'd moaned, eliciting a tut from Sarah and the extra degree of kindliness that was what they all knew this patient really yearned for. Mrs Abbott had warned her about Mona Calder. *Don't be surprised when she asks you to put a pillow over her face. Tries it on with every one of the nurses*, she'd said.

Sarah shook her head as she closed the woman's door. She had turned Mona Calder on to her side to face the television fixed to her wall, the Scottish News about to begin. The murmur of disembodied voices disappeared as she left the room, nervously biting her lip. Mrs Calder had paid not the slightest attention to the pair of medical gloves that Nurse Wilding slipped into her skirt pocket.

At last she crept quietly along the corridor, eyes glancing each way lest someone see her stepping into the nursing home manager's office instead of the staff lounge.

It was still light outside on this September evening. Light enough to take the photographs that she needed? She gnawed her lower lip as she looked around the office.

157

The filing cabinet behind Nancy's desk seemed the obvious place to begin. She pulled on the pair of disposable rubber gloves. None of the fingerprints of an ex-con would be found in here, not if she could help it.

Slowly, Sarah pulled out the drawers, the sound of the sliding files rattling like her nerves. She felt her shoulders tense, fingers shaking as they picked through the dark green folders. A sigh of relief came as she spotted the patients' names in alphabetical order.

Right first time, she thought, breathing hard. Trust Nancy to be efficient!

Yet the thought of her benefactress gave her an uneasy sensation in the pit of her stomach. Guilt had a sour taste.

Concentrate. Get it over with, Sarah scolded. How hard could this be? Twenty patients, twenty pages of names of next of kin in alphabetical order, she told herself, flicking through Jeremy Anderson's file.

Page two gave all the information she was looking for. Next of kin: name, address, telephone numbers and email, all typed neatly and easy enough to photograph.

With shaking hand, Sarah drew out the mobile phone and set it to camera mode.

One click and the photograph was taken.

Conscious of the sweat prickling beneath the arms of her uniform, Sarah shoved the file back into its place and took out the next one.

Over and over she repeated the process, pausing to listen for a footfall outside the door, terrified lest she be taken unawares.

What would they do if she were found there? What lies could she invent? Panic threatened to seize her, and for a moment Sarah wanted to thrust the folders back into their drawer and flee from the room. Only the thought of that knife against her cheek made her continue to pull each patient file out, hasty fingers turning to the necessary pages.

She had come to the eighteenth file when the sound of voices in the corridor made Sarah shrink back in terror, holding her breath. But the voices soon died away again. She looked at her watch. It was almost time for her break to end.

Hurriedly, Sarah pulled out the remaining two files and turned to the pages she needed. A couple of swift clicks, then it was done.

She closed the drawer again, hands slick with sweat beneath the gloves, a feeling of nausea overwhelming her.

Once out in the corridor, Sarah fled into the staff toilet, stomach churning.

She just made it into a cubicle on time, retching over the pan, her whole body shaking as she fell to her knees.

Wrap it in this, Scarface had ordered her, giving her a black polythene envelope. *Hide it inside the gates, got it?*

Sarah dropped the parcel into a clump of heather and looked around, fearfully, but there was nobody to be seen, no dark figure lingering around the entrance to the nursing home.

It was done. Her heart thudded as she walked swiftly back into the nursing home, skirting the edge of the building to the back door to avoid being captured on the CCTV camera that was fixed to the front.

'Two down. Bad advice from the bull. Three and five.'

'What? How should I know?' Kirsty asked peevishly. James gave a laugh and resumed his study of the newspaper crossword, his long legs slung across the arm of the chair.

It had been a long day in Stewart Street police station, mainly because the investigation demanded the sort of detail that only her computer and telephone could offer and now Kirsty's head was buzzing with a myriad of facts and figures.

'Bum steer!' James grinned at her then wrote in the answer to the clue.

Kirsty smiled back, raising her eyes to heaven. James was a whizz with puzzles whereas Kirsty simply did not have the patience for things like crosswords and anagrams. Yet she had the ability to think out of the box, hadn't Lorimer told her that one time before she'd joined the police force?

So far they had drawn a blank with the Jane Maitland case. The beneficiary was to arrive tomorrow from London and they would meet again at that lawyer's office. Wonder what he felt when he was told about his real mother, Kirsty thought to herself. There were programmes on the TV reuniting parents with their long-lost children, most of them given up for adoption by single mums coerced by their own parents. What was this fellow's story, she wondered. And how would his adoptive parents react on hearing that their son had inherited a small fortune? Well, she would know soon enough when Crawford Whyte (né Maitland) arrived in Glasgow.

'You all right? You're as white as a sheet,' Grainne remarked as she entered the staffroom just after midnight.

'I was sick earlier on,' Sarah told her truthfully. 'Something upset my stomach.' She shrugged and gave the other young woman a wan smile.

'You should've said,' Grainne protested. 'I could've given you another wee break.'

'I'm fine now,' Sarah said. 'Just need some sleep.' A simulated yawn turned into the real thing and Sarah felt her eyes stinging with fatigue.

Outside, the skies were filled with stars, shreds of clouds scudding swiftly as the autumn wind rose, scattering leaves across the forecourt of the nursing home. It would be winter soon, Sarah thought, remembering the previous winter that had been spent in Cornton Vale women's prison. She would never go back there, she thought suddenly. Let them do their worst, she had had enough, she decided, pulling the seat belt across her body and clicking it in place. The mobile phone would be picked up where she had dropped it, wrapped in its black plastic envelope.

Only the late-shift nurses were about, their car doors slamming in the quiet of the early hour as Grainne drove out of the car park and headed along the road to Bearsden and Nancy Livingstone's home. No other person was about, no late-night dog walker or any other solitary figure. Sarah breathed a sigh of relief. She'd done her part, left the parcel where she'd been told. Surely now they'd go away and leave her in peace?

Thoughts of what they were going to do with this stolen information made Sarah's head ache.

She was guilty, guilty as hell.

But, a little voice asked, *what was the nature of her crime this time?*

CHAPTER TWENTY-ONE

Margaret Fraser watched Sandy as he sniffed his way along the path that divided the row of houses from their lock-ups. The terrier stopped from time to time to cock a leg against a lamp-post, his owner alert to any possibility of the little dog crouching down, her hand searching in her anorak pocket for a plastic poop bag.

'Och, Sandy, come away from there!' Margaret called as the dog bent low, nose to the ground in front of one of the garages, its door tilted open at a slight angle.

But the dog was already wriggling his body into the dark space that had been left.

'Sandy! Bad dog!' Margaret scolded, quickening her pace as the terrier's tail disappeared beneath the metal door.

'Come here!' the woman demanded. But Sandy did not heed her command and Margaret could hear snuffling noises from within the lock-up.

Looking swiftly around to make sure that nobody was watching, Margaret stepped forward and grasped the door handle, letting its weight swing it upwards.

'Sandy . . . !'

The dog came bounding towards her, barking eagerly.

But Margaret Fraser could not move, the sight of that swinging body freezing her to the spot.

'Rachel Gardiner,' Rosie said, passing the dead woman's driving licence to Lorimer.

They were both crouching by the body that had been taken down from the overhead beams, a forensic tent masking their activity from any prying eyes.

'Suicide?' he asked.

'Probably, but there's the complication of what else we found indoors,' Rosie replied, tilting her head in the direction of the house beyond the path.

'Think she killed the woman in the wheelchair then took her own life in a fit of remorse?' a voice behind them asked.

Lorimer turned a serious glance to the young detective constable who, like them, was clad in a white forensic suit.

'That's what we need to discover. Dr Fergusson estimates Julie Gardiner's time of death to be, what? Between four and six yesterday afternoon?'

'That's right,' Rosie agreed. 'And this one died some time before midnight.'

'What was she doing all yesterday evening?' Kirsty asked thoughtfully.

Lorimer stood up and nodded. 'Go back inside and see what you can find, Kirsty. SOCOs will only let you into certain parts of the house,' he warned.

The detective constable glanced at the brass nameplate on the door jamb: RACHEL & JULIE GARDINER. At least now they knew which one was which.

The scene of crime officers were still busily gathering what evidence they could. Kirsty watched them for a moment, marvelling at the painstaking methods that could indicate so many things: footprints in the dust of a floor, the tiniest traces of fibres left on or near a body, as well as any fingerprints that might be found and matched against those kept in the Scottish database.

Her job was to find more tangible evidence, stuff that could be used to build a picture of who these people were and what had taken place the previous day.

The lounge had been transformed into a bedroom for Julie Gardiner and Kirsty went straight to a large old-fashioned dresser against the wall, her eyes measuring up the row of drawers. That was where she would keep any papers, she decided, stepping carefully past the body and pulling out the left-hand drawer by its metal ring.

'Right first time, DC Wilson,' she murmured, pulling out a sheaf of assorted papers and bulky envelopes and taking them to a corner of the room out of the way of the SOCOs.

Several of the envelopes were addressed to Miss Julie Gardiner but a quick look at the dates showed Kirsty that the more recent ones were for Rachel Gardiner, her sister, many of them bearing the letterhead of the South Glasgow University Hospital.

Kirsty skimmed through the bits of mail, noting several appointments in Rachel's name. Why Rachel? she thought with a frown. Why not the sister who was in a wheelchair?

She sat back on her heels, mouth open as the answer was revealed in one particular letter from a consultant.

... *confirming our diagnosis of motor neurone disease*, Kirsty read, scanning the letter and shaking her head as she read on. *You were aware of the familial tendencies* ... she shook her head again, eyes flicking towards the body across the room ... *do everything in our power to support you and your sister* ...

'Oh my God!' Kirsty gasped, the reality of the situation dawning on her.

Had Rachel Gardiner taken her sister's life because she wouldn't be able to cope with caring for her any more? How tragic!

She thought of her mentor, DS Murdoch, and his wife who had probably suffered for so long. Had he been a good carer, seeing to her needs whenever he was home from a job that demanded so much of his time? What must it be like to live with someone whom you know is going to die before you? And what agonies had Rachel Gardiner gone through once she had known that she, too, was going to die from this horrible disease?

'We'll know what was administered once the tox tests have been done,' Rosie said, packing her kit into the boot of the Saab.

'Well, looks as if the sister gave her something, doesn't it?' Kirsty asked.

'The scene of crime officers will be sending their report later on, too,' Lorimer reminded her. 'Evidence of other people having been in that room needs to be included if we are to form a complete picture of what really happened,' he said thoughtfully. 'There's still the problem of at least six hours between one sister's death and the other. What was Rachel Gardiner doing during that time? And why did she fail to leave any sort of note?'

'Bad day?' James looked up from where he was sitting in the armchair next to the bay window.

Kirsty nodded then yawned, tiredness suddenly sweeping over her.

'Come here, you,' James said, his lean figure loping across the room to where she stood in the doorway.

Then she was in his arms, letting her body relax as he stroked her hair.

'Not sure I like seeing so many dead bodies in one day,' she murmured, settling down beside him.

'Ach, remember what Lorimer told you,' James replied. 'It's not the dead ones that you need to worry about.'

Later, after a takeaway pizza and a shared bottle of red, Kirsty began to unfold the day's events to James.

'Seems as though the younger sister had been the other one's primary carer,' she said.

'What ages were they?'

'Julie, the one in the wheelchair, was thirty-three. Rachel two years younger.'

'And neither of them married?'

'No sign of that,' Kirsty agreed. 'We eventually looked through every bit of paperwork we could lay our hands on: birth certificates, passports, the usual, and no, there were no marriage certificates. But we did find their parents' death certificates,' she added. 'And some old press cuttings.' She shook her head. 'Wait till you hear this. They'd lost both of them on the same day. Victims of that tsunami disaster in 2004.'

'The one on Sumatra?'

Kirsty nodded. 'Their silver-wedding celebration, apparently. They were swept away. Bodies never recovered.' She gave a sigh then bit her lip anxiously.

'What must it have been like to lose both of their parents

like that?' she began. 'Imagine if something terrible happened to Mum and Dad when they go off on this holiday of a lifetime they're talking about?'

'Won't happen,' James said firmly. 'Don't let yourself think such things, Kirst. They'll have a brilliant time, just wait and see. Postcards from every corner of the globe, eh?'

Kirsty shuddered. She couldn't bear the thought of hearing such tragic news.

'How could life ever have been normal for them after such a devastating loss?' she whispered, snuggling closer to her boyfriend's side.

'Ach, must have been hellish, right enough,' he replied. 'What about the woman in the wheelchair?'

'Julie.'

'Yes. Was she already ill at that time?'

No,' Kirsty replied. 'The medical correspondence about Julie's illness only goes back to 2014.'

'Hellish disease,' James said, his arm encircling Kirsty's shoulder.

'It doesn't have to be,' she said slowly. 'Dr Fergusson told us about a friend of hers who managed to live a near normal life for more than two years before the end.'

'But don't they have breathing difficulties?'

Kirsty nodded, her mind recalling the sight of that poor woman, head forwards in the chair, the tube still attached to her nostrils and snaking over her head like some mutant life form in an episode of *Doctor Who*. It had been that, more than anything, that had made Kirsty feel a sense of horror.

'You're not going to like this,' Rosie told Lorimer.

They were seated next to one another in Rosie's office in the

Department of Forensic Medicine, an inauspicious part of the University of Glasgow that rubbed shoulders with the old Western Infirmary.

'Tox report shows a huge dosage of morphine.'

'Enough to put her to sleep?'

Rosie nodded. 'She'd feel drowsy almost immediately then her heart would stop. No pain. No struggle to breathe.' She shrugged. 'Might have been a merciful sort of end compared to what could have taken place. But,' she continued, 'morphine is never prescribed to a patient who has difficulty with breathing.' She looked meaningfully at Lorimer. 'So someone brought it into the home.'

'It wouldn't be there as part of her ordinary meds,' Lorimer said slowly.

'No chance. Either the sister obtained it or someone else administered the drug.'

'Okay,' he nodded.

'But that's not the main thing,' she went on, a grim expression on her face as she scrolled down to a different page on her computer screen. 'The forensic report shows no trace of Rachel Gardiner's prints or anything on Julie's body.'

'Washed clean?'

'No.' Rosie shook her head. 'Worse than that. Our friends at the Scottish Crime Campus obtained traces and partial fingerprints that don't fit anywhere else in that house.'

The detective superintendent raised appreciative eyebrows. The labs out at Gartcosh, said to be the finest facility of its kind in Europe, delivered results in record time nowadays. 'A stranger, then?' Lorimer asked thoughtfully, sitting back and staring at the screen.

Rosie shot him a look, her lips twisted in a crooked smile. 'Not such a stranger to the forensic lab,' she began. 'They found fibres that match ones taken from Jane Maitland's body.'

Kirsty stood near the back of the room, looking towards the tall man at the front. Things had changed now, she thought. And, despite the grim findings from the two deaths, she was experiencing a surge of excitement.

This was a big case, a real challenge. And she was going to be on the team led by Detective Superintendent Lorimer.

All around her, men and women were concentrating on the senior officer's words.

'There is an assumption we could make,' Lorimer began, 'that these people had arranged for their own deaths to take place.'

A small murmur went up as the men and women took in this statement.

Lorimer stared out at them all, his blue eyes catching each and every one of the officers.

'We don't make assumptions in this job, however,' he went on. 'We deal in the currency of facts.'

Kirsty nodded to herself. It was a phrase she had heard her own father use time and time again. Now she knew where Alistair Wilson had picked that up.

'Fact one,' Lorimer began, turning to the wall behind him where several pictures had been secured. 'Jane Maitland was given a lethal dose of morphine by some person unknown to the health authorities.'

'But was he known to her?' one of the male officers called out.

'That's something we still need to establish,' Lorimer agreed. 'And so it comes under the heading of assumptions yet again. Did the old lady arrange for her own demise?'

'Or didn't she?' Kirsty whispered, quietly so that nobody could hear her remark.

'Fact two.' Lorimer turned to the wall again, pointing at the photographs of the two sisters, one slumped over in her wheelchair, the other dangling from the beams of the lock-up. 'We know that someone administered a large quantity of morphine to Julie Gardiner. And, given the trace fibres found on her body, we can correctly assume that the same person was responsible for giving that lethal injection to Jane Maitland.'

'Are we looking for some sort of end-of-life organisation, then?' a female officer asked.

'That is one of the lines of inquiry that we have to follow,' Lorimer agreed. 'It is a huge coincidence that each of these terminally ill women were given dosages that would kill them by the same hand. *If* we can show it was by the same hand,' he reminded them.

'And if it wasn't a voluntary sort of euthanasia?' the woman persisted.

'Then,' Lorimer said, his rugged features set in a serious expression. 'We're looking for a murderer.'

CHAPTER TWENTY-TWO

The room was silent apart from the gentle breathing of the man in his bed. A single light shining down from the lamp angled above so that the figure nearby could see clearly enough to carry out this deed. The late shift had gone home now and the figure hovering over this patient smiled as he watched him sleep.

One little injection into his arm and he would stay asleep for ever. No more frustration, no more battling to speak, no struggle to swallow his food as it was spooned into his slack mouth. It was a mercy to put him out of his suffering.

David Imrie turned once in his sleep then groaned as the needle was inserted into his arm.

Then, without warning, the patient's eyes opened and an expression of alarm filled them as he saw the man bending over him.

An incoherent cry gurgled in David's throat, his hands trying desperately to rise, to fend off the stranger. But the sick man was no match for the poison spreading through his veins. The hands fell back, the eyes closing as the drug took effect.

A sigh, then a silence reaching into eternity.

'Goodnight, then, darling,' the man crooned, taking the needle and wrapping it carefully in its original paper container, hands double-gloved just in case anyone should try to find out the identity of the person who had given David Imrie this medication.

The glass doors opened silently then he slipped out into the darkness, leaving only shadows behind him.

'I'm sorry to tell you, but one of your patients passed away during the night.' Nancy Livingstone drew Sarah aside as she stepped into the nursing home.

'Oh? Who was it?'

'Mr Imrie,' Nancy replied. 'Such a nice man.' She shook her head then frowned. 'No sign of a stroke, though. Seems he simply slipped away in his sleep.'

'Isn't that strange?'

Nancy shrugged. 'Well, I don't know if you'd call it strange,' she began. 'But my sister doesn't think a post-mortem will be justified.'

'I am sorry,' Sarah said, as they walked side by side along the corridor. 'I liked him. He was a nice man. Always trying to smile.'

'And he appreciated you reading all these farming articles to him, my dear,' Nancy went on, touching Sarah's hand. 'I'm afraid this is the downside of working here. Having to say so many goodbyes.

'Anyway, I must love you and leave you. Have to see to all his paperwork before I go home today.' She gave Sarah a tired smile as the nurse entered the staff lounge and took off her jacket.

Sarah sat down heavily on one of the chairs, a sudden trembling making her legs weak.

David Imrie was dead! Could it possibly have anything to do with that list she'd taken from the office several nights ago?

Grainne breezed into the room and stopped dead.

'Hey! What's up with you? Not feeling sick again, are you?'

'Mr Imrie died in the night,' Sarah told her.

'Och, Sarah, you have to toughen up a bit if you're going to continue working here. Most of them are on borrowed time as it is, lassie,' she said briskly.

'Suppose so,' Sarah agreed, rising to her feet and straightening her uniform.

Yet as she began the preparations for her shift, Sarah Wilding's every action was laboured. There was no reason for it, she told herself. But try as she might, she could not help being overwhelmed by a deep sense of guilt.

'Hello?'

'Is that Maggie Lorimer? Annette Imrie here. I'm afraid I have some sad news.' As Maggie listened to the woman's voice she put out a hand to steady herself.

'David?'

'He passed away during the night, seemingly,' Annette Imrie told her. 'A blessing really.'

'I suppose so,' Maggie replied slowly. Annette didn't sound sorry at all. In fact, she sounded as though she was almost glad to tell Maggie about her cousin's passing. 'Though he wasn't in any pain, was he?' Maggie asked doubtfully. 'Patrick must be relieved about that at least.'

'Ha!' The woman gave a short mirthless laugh. 'He's relieved about a lot more than that, I can tell you.'

'Oh, of course ...' Maggie sighed, understanding the note of triumph that had so jarred with the breaking of this news. 'The farm!'

'Indeed. We don't have to sell up and move into some grotty little council estate.'

'Well.' Maggie paused, not quite knowing how to respond.

'You'll let me know when ... the arrangements are made for a funeral? Sad coming so soon after Uncle Robert's death.'

'We'll let you know, of course,' Annette said crisply. 'Must go. Other calls to make.'

Maggie put down the phone and sank into her favourite arm-chair. If only they had known about David's stroke sooner, she and Bill might have visited her cousin more often. She shuddered, remembering the man's wasted face, his once ruddy cheeks pale and wan, that muscular body so much smaller beneath the white sheets. Her mum had suffered a stroke and ever since then the idea of being even the slightest bit paralysed had filled Maggie with horror.

And yet it was a different unease she felt at that moment. Not because of the news of her cousin's death but rather the manner in which it had been related.

When the telephone rang again she gave a jump.

'Patrick? Oh, Annette just called to tell me ... I'm so sorry ...'

'Maggie, listen to me,' Patrick began, his voice low and serious. 'There's something I want you to do for me.'

'It's me.'

Lorimer heard the voice of his wife on the other end of the line, her breathy tone alerting him immediately that something was wrong.

'David's dead,' she told him. 'Died in his sleep, apparently,' she added.

'Oh, I am sorry,' Lorimer began. 'Poor man. But he'd suffered so much, hadn't he?'

'David?' Maggie sounded distracted. 'Oh, yes, yes of course. But so had Patrick. I mean, losing your father and your brother in such a short space of time ...'

'Aye, that's true.'

'Darling, Patrick wants you to call in at the nursing home,' Maggie told him.

'Me? Why?'

'Well,' Maggie replied slowly. 'He says he'd like a post-mortem to be carried out. Sudden death, you know.'

'*Was* it sudden?'

'Patrick seems to think so.'

'What about the Abbot woman? What does she say?'

'They weren't going to involve the police,' Maggie replied. 'Patrick wants you to talk to her. Can you do that, darling?'

The light was fading from the sky as Lorimer drew into the driveway of Abbey Nursing Home, his mind still on the case of the women who had died in their own homes. By choice? That was the question that had to be answered, he thought, stepping out of the Lexus and heading towards the front door.

Pots of late annuals graced each side of the entrance, striped petunias and masses of trailing lobelia as blue as the twilight that was fast descending. A garden bench sat by the edge of a grassy lawn, facing west. Had Maggie's cousin ever sat there, thinking about the green fields beyond? It was a nice enough place to be, he thought. If you had to be kept somewhere that was not your own home: next best thing to a hospice, more than likely. Poor David.

The door opened and Mrs Abbot waved him inside. 'Detective Superintendent,' she began. Her expression was one that he recognised; the solemn, professional look of sympathy for the bereaved, something he'd had to wear on his own face far too often.

'So sorry for your loss,' she murmured, her words echoing

those he had spoken to relatives of murder victims in so many past cases.

'He seems to have slipped away very peacefully, however,' she continued as they made their way along the same corridor that he and Maggie had taken on the day of her uncle's funeral.

'Mr Patrick Imrie called me,' Mrs Abbott said, stopping outside the patient's room. 'I understand that he would like his brother's body to undergo a post-mortem examination.' She wrinkled her nose in distaste.

'I believe that's right, Mrs Abbott. In a case of sudden death, however, it is up to the Crown Office to make that sort of decision.'

'Oh, well, that's all right, then, isn't it? I mean, one could hardly call David Imrie's death sudden.'

'He was expected to pass away?'

Mrs Abbott made a face. 'They're all expected to pass away sooner or later,' she told him with a frown. 'It's our business to make their last weeks or months as pleasant and comfortable as possible.'

'Rather like a hospice?'

The woman nodded. 'Our patients all receive palliative care but here,' she waved a hand around at the corridor with its double line of doors, 'we are a bit more specialised than a hospice. Most of our patients come to this nursing home as the result of severe strokes and they can be here for quite a long spell, really. A hospice, on the other hand, might house patients with a bigger variety of illnesses.'

'Like cancer?'

'Indeed.'

She opened the door to reveal an empty bed. The curtains on either side of the French windows were drawn back, but not secured in their tie-backs, Lorimer noticed.

One stride took him to the doors and he gave the handle a twist. 'Were these doors opened after David died?'

Mrs Abbott came forward to join him, her hand touching the drapes. 'I'm not sure,' she admitted. 'Some of the nursing staff have this notion about letting a soul escape,' she confided in a low voice. 'A bit of superstition, I know. But they will open a window to let it out.'

Lorimer nodded, looking closely at the lawn outside and the border of earth that was empty of flowers.

'Have you a gardener working here?'

Mrs Abbott laughed. 'Not really. My husband does the heavy stuff and I deal with the plants. Why do you ask?'

But Lorimer was already outside the room, his eyes fixed on the dark soil.

'Did you take out the old summer plants recently?'

'Well, yes, as a matter of fact, I took some of them out over the weekend. The tubs at the front will probably last a while yet, though.' She folded her arms and looked at him, obviously puzzled by these questions.

'Rake the borders, did you? Ready to plant some bulbs later on?'

'How did you know?' Mrs Abbott laughed. 'Goodness! It's like being talked to by Sherlock Holmes,' she added. 'But of course, you are a detective . . . ' She tailed off as Lorimer turned to her.

'I'd like to speak to the nurse who was on duty last night, if that's possible. The one who discovered that David had died.'

'That was Hilary Connell. She'll not be in until midnight,' Mrs Abbott said slowly. 'The late shift's on just now. I'll see if David's dedicated nurse can help you. Shall I? She'll have been on till midnight last night.'

Lorimer nodded as she turned to leave the entrance to the gardens and go back inside. But his eyes were fixed on something that the woman evidently had failed to see: several large footprints embedded in the loose soil, inches from the glass doors that gave on to David Imrie's room.

'This is Detective Superintendent Lorimer,' Mrs Abbott said. 'And this is Nurse Wilding. Sarah, the detective superintendent wants to ask you about Mr Imrie.'

Lorimer saw the colour fade from the young woman's face and the stricken expression as she shrank against the wall of the corridor.

Something was wrong here. Something was very wrong.

'Sarah? Are you all right?' Mrs Abbott asked, shaking the girl's arm.

'Just upset,' the nurse answered. 'He was such a nice man. Bit of a shock . . . '

'You didn't expect him to die, then?' Lorimer asked.

'Oh, no! He was fine when I left. Sound asleep, breathing quite normally.'

'You'd spent time with him yesterday evening?' Lorimer wanted to know.

'Of course. And there was nothing to suggest that anything was wrong.' She turned to Mrs Abbott. 'He'd had his dinner and supper. Really enjoyed them too,' she insisted.

'The food in here is of the highest quality,' Mrs Abbott told Lorimer smoothly. 'Our cook is also a qualified dietician.'

'And you're certain that he'd had a good evening?' Lorimer continued. 'Nothing to cause you any concern?'

'No, nothing at all.'

The girl looked bewildered, frightened even, her large eyes wide, flicking from her employer and back to his face before dropping her gaze.

'Did he sleep with the curtains open?' Lorimer asked.

'Well, yes, he did,' Nurse Wilding replied. 'He didn't like to be shut in.' She turned to Lorimer, her pale face suddenly defiant. 'He'd been a farmer, you see. He loved the feeling of being part of the fields and the trees outside.'

'He told you this?'

A brief smile lit up her features. 'I guessed some of it,' she said. 'Asked him about things like that, talked about nature and stuff . . . mostly wee nods and shakes of his head. But we communicated,' she insisted. 'Just because he'd had a stroke didn't mean he'd lost his senses.'

'Detective Superintendent Lorimer's wife is Mr Imrie's cousin,' Mrs Abbott explained. 'And the family have requested a post-mortem.'

'Oh, that's why you're here!'

Lorimer watched the nurse as she gave a sigh, her whole body visibly relaxing.

Then she opened her mouth as though to speak but closed it again suddenly, eyes cast down once more.

What had she been on the point of saying?

And what had Nurse Sarah Wilding assumed about the arrival of a senior policeman at the nursing home? Lorimer watched as the young woman walked swiftly back along the corridor then disappeared into an adjacent room.

'Thank you, nurse,' Mrs Abbott called after her then led Lorimer away towards her office. 'Do come in, Detective Superintendent. And let's see if we can chase up Hilary Connell.'

The night-shift nurse confirmed what Sarah Wilding had told them: David Imrie had been fine all during the night. But when Hilary Connell had returned from a break to look in on her patients, she had found Maggie's cousin lying on his back, his skin already cool to the touch. The local GP had been called out early next morning and he had signed a death certificate, citing sudden heart failure as cause of death.

'And where is David now?' Lorimer asked Mrs Abbott once he had finished speaking to the nurse.

'At the undertaker's,' she told him. 'Normal procedure. If the family want to see their loved one here then we keep them in their rooms.' She gave a shrug.

'Patrick didn't want to come by here today?' Lorimer guessed.

'Farmers are busy people. Isn't it hard for them to get away at all?'

Lorimer nodded, wondering. Had Patrick felt a sense of guilt at not coming to see his brother's body? Was that why he had requested a post-mortem? Or was it the suddenness of it all? From what he had heard at their father's funeral, Patrick was contemplating selling up to pay for David's care, showing that the family had anticipated David continuing to live at this nursing home for years to come.

'I think you should know that I will be making a report to the Crown Office, Mrs Abbott,' Lorimer said slowly. 'Post-mortem examinations usually establish the cause of death given by the medical practitioner, so I don't think you have any cause to worry.'

Sarah watched as the big car slunk quietly along the drive and out of the main gates. His wife's cousin! She breathed out a grateful sigh. Just a quirk of fate then that the tall man was a policeman. Pleasant manner, right enough, not the bullying type she'd encountered once before. And these blue eyes, intense, as if he could look straight into her soul.

Sarah shivered. It was just a coincidence that all of this had happened, wasn't it? Things would go back to normal, surely? Another patient was already scheduled to arrive in a couple of days' time; the waiting list for this place was huge, she knew, remembering so many other names on that list.

'That was Maggie on the phone. Wants to know if she can do anything to help,' Patrick Imrie told his wife.

'Hm.' Annette Imrie gave a small sigh. 'Can't think why. Suppose we'll see them all at the funeral again.'

'Well,' Patrick began. 'That's not going to happen any time soon, love.'

'Why not?' his wife replied sharply.

'Bill Lorimer's confirmed that David is to have a post-mortem.'

'But that's horrible.' Annette rounded on him, her eyes snapping in sudden fury. 'To do that to your own brother! Oh, Patrick, don't let them do it!' she pleaded.

'Hey, calm down, love. It's a routine sort of thing that's done after a sudden death,' Patrick explained. He stretched out to take her arm but she shook him off.

'It just prolongs everything,' she said crossly, tossing her head. 'Better to have a quick funeral and try to get everything back to normal.'

'Och, don't be like that. Anyway,' he gave a weak grin. 'Just remember what this means. We don't have to sell up now. We can stay here, keep running the farm properly.'

'Yes,' she agreed, 'I suppose you're right.' Annette gave him a crooked smile. 'And isn't that what your dad would have wanted?'

CHAPTER TWENTY-THREE

Len Murdoch slumped into the chair, dropping the address book on to the floor. Surely that was the last of Irene's friends that he would have to call? He was already sick of the steady stream of platitudes, spoken in similar hushed tones as though to raise their voices would somehow break his spirit.

He picked up the remote control and flicked on the television, his eyes wandering over the Sky menu until he came to a news bulletin.

Maybe it was time to be back at work, he told himself, listening to the latest reports from the Middle East, the rape case in London involving a minor celebrity that had dragged on for months. Then the picture changed and he saw the familiar face of a Scottish presenter, her professional tones bidding him good evening.

He was already out of the loop, Len realised, watching the different news items as they appeared, crimes amongst them. Even in the short time he had been on leave, things had moved on.

His fingers flicked back to the menu and he scrolled along until he came to the sports channels. This was more like it, something to take his mind off the present anguish. It had always worked before, watching horses as they galloped along the track, his eyes fastened on the one he'd put his money on. Irene had laughed when he'd placed that first bet, all those years ago. Bonny Irene, the racehorse was called. He'd put a tenner on it and won a couple of hundred back. And it could have stopped there, beginner's luck, something to boast about in the pub with the lads. But of course it hadn't.

He switched off the television and closed his eyes.

Now Irene was gone. And the taste for the horses had turned sour in the detective sergeant's mouth.

'We're seeing Crawford Whyte today,' Lorimer told Kirsty, bending over her desk.

He raised a shirt cuff and looked at his watch.

It was a nice watch, Kirsty thought; a plain round face with Roman numerals. An Edox, whatever that was, not one she knew. Looked good, though. Had watches like that been on the Patons' list of expensive stolen items? She didn't think so. And besides, Lorimer wasn't the sort to wear a flashy watch.

'Be ready to come to the lawyer's office in fifteen minutes, okay?'

She nodded and smiled as he walked out of the room. They were dealing with this case together, the raid on the jeweller's shop having become a joint cross-border operation.

And yet, and yet … the feeling of her very first call-out as a detective constable rankled with Kirsty Wilson. It was, she told herself, unfinished business. But was that because nobody had been arrested? Or because she still held a suspicion that Murdoch had been guilty of lifting an item from the scene of crime?

*

183

It had been a long time since he had arrived in this city, memories of a bleak, grey place where the rain was constantly falling. So it came as a surprise to the man looking out of the window when the train slowed down and stopped on the railway bridge above the river.

It was a bright day, the sun at its highest point, only faint wisps of white clouds stroking the blue skies above Glasgow. The city skyline had changed beyond recall. To the west there were new bridges spanning the river with modern flats along its banks. One low-lying building closer to the train reminded him of the long row of barges he often saw on the canal as he travelled on the Stansted Express. A circular building high up caught his eyes, its sparkling windows facing in every direction over the city. What a view the office workers must have from that place! His eyes roved further along the horizon spotting the curved shapes he vaguely recognised (hadn't he seen them on television?) until they rested upon more familiar landmarks like the towering shape of the University of Glasgow, unmistakable with its spiked spire soaring into the clouds.

He'd underestimated this city, forgetting that its fall into the doldrums of post-industrialism was long past. This was a regenerated place now, he saw, sweeping his glance across the view from his window, a place where big deals were done and big ideas were fulfilled, not least those of his own.

Somewhere in this city he was going to find Brian Abernethy's office and do what he had to do. He wouldn't hang about, the man thought. This was no hick town, after all. Abernethy had warned him about the police officers already snooping around. He'd give them the benefit of his charms then hightail it south again as fast as he could.

The traveller sat back in the first-class carriage as the train began to move again, taking him into the heart of Glasgow Central station, catching his reflection in the window. What did he see? A man past middle age, still good-looking, though his once blond hair was turning grey. Heaving a sigh, that was partly satisfaction at having completed this part of the journey, he tried to smile at the prospect of returning home later that night. He would be a rich man at last, he thought, fingering the velvet collar of the Crombie coat he'd bought on an impulse. His credit card would be able to stand that expense, he'd persuaded himself. Once he'd come into the money left to him by the late Jane Maitland. But the smile never reached his pale blue eyes, a frown of anxiety appearing between his eyebrows.

'Detective Superintendent, how nice to see you again,' Brian Abernethy gushed as Lorimer and Kirsty entered the lawyer's office.

A fair-haired man in his early fifties stood up and turned to the new arrivals, a pleasant smile fixed to his face.

'Crawford Whyte,' he said, coming forward to shake hands with both Lorimer and Kirsty.

'Detective Superintendent Lorimer and this is Detective Constable Wilson,' Lorimer told him as Whyte approached his young officer.

'How do you do,' Whyte said, giving the slightest nod to Kirsty, his smile increasing as he looked her full in the face, making the girl blush.

He was a practised charmer, Lorimer decided, watching the man as he offered a seat to Kirsty. The hand that smoothed his hair as Whyte took his place to one side of the desk was devoid of rings. There had been no mention of whether or not the man was married but the lack of a wedding ring was of no significance

185

whatsoever. Lorimer himself did not wear a ring on his wedding finger, long-ago memories of his dad having caught his own ring in a car door once, resulting in surgery to his finger, had put the policeman off.

Abernethy had begun to read from Jane Maitland's will, the papers in front of him, giving Lorimer the opportunity to have a good look at Crawford Whyte. It was amazing what a trained officer could find out just by observation, he'd reminded Kirsty on the way through the city. A person's body language might give so many more answers than spoken questions, if you knew what to look for. And Lorimer did.

There was an eagerness in Whyte's manner, that slight bend in his back as he leaned forward as though to be sure of capturing every last syllable that came from the lawyer's mouth. And, whenever the name of the deceased was mentioned (which was often, of course, in this legal document), Lorimer looked to see Whyte's response. Grief? Regret? A modicum of interest even? But there was nothing at all.

Had he known about Jane Maitland being his mother long ago? Or had the shock and surprise of being heir to a small fortune gobbled up any residue of filial feelings?

The man's demeanour was pretty easy to read whenever money was mentioned. He seemed very keen to drink in all of these words, something that showed as he uncrossed his legs, bringing his seat a little closer to Abernethy's desk, one hand absently patting his trouser pocket. It was an unconscious gesture, the unspoken desire to possess this inheritance for himself.

But if Whyte's body language told one story, his words tried to tell another.

'Such a sad end,' he murmured at a point when Abernethy read out the date of Jane Maitland's death, the insincerity of his declaration making Lorimer glance across to Kirsty to see if she had noticed. The girl raised her eyebrows a fraction, the tiniest sign that yes, she had seen just what was happening here.

'But perhaps even sadder than you might think,' Lorimer said, breaking into Abernethy's monotone as the lawyer resumed his reading.

'Oh?' Abernethy looked up from the documents on his desk as Whyte turned with a frown.

'What on earth do you mean?' the Englishman demanded, a querulous note to his voice, as though the senior officer had no right to interrupt.

'Your late mother's post-mortem gives us reason to think that her death was not as first believed.'

'Yes?' Brian Abernethy folded his small hands on top of the papers, a look of irritation crossing his podgy features.

'Toxicology tests show that the late Miss Maitland had been given a very high dose of morphine,' Lorimer told them, staring at Whyte. 'That was what killed her.'

'Good Lord!' Whyte sat back, one hand on his chest, cheeks suddenly turning pale. 'You don't mean . . . ?'

'Your late mother was in a lot of pain, Mr Whyte,' Lorimer said evenly. 'She may have decided that enough was enough.'

'Are you implying that my client arranged for her own death? Are we talking assisted suicide here?' Abernethy blustered.

Lorimer shook his head, his eyes still fixed on Crawford Whyte. 'We haven't come to that conclusion yet,' he replied. 'And until we can, there is also the possibility that your late mother was murdered.'

The man's mouth gaped open but he seemed to have problems uttering a single word.

'What evidence have you got for that, Detective Superintendent?' Abernethy bristled indignantly.

'I'm not at liberty to disclose this at present,' Lorimer replied smoothly. 'However, we would welcome a little chat with you, Mr Whyte,' he said, nodding at the Englishman beside him. 'Just to clarify certain things.'

It was a silent trio that walked back through the brightness of the city streets, past lunchtime office workers chattering as they emerged from their morning's toil. On the way out of the office building, Crawford Whyte had protested about having to catch the evening train, a note of desperation in his voice that made Lorimer curious. Now he was quiet as they walked along, Kirsty leading the way, the two men walking side by side.

Let him sweat, Lorimer thought, seeing the blond man take out a handkerchief and wipe his brow. His well-cut suit and smart coat were too much for a fine autumn day like this, the detective superintendent thought with a smile. So many of the folk from south of the Border expected it to be freezing cold all year round and were often surprised when they found that the west coast could be mild and warm. There was something about the man that reminded him of a fellow he'd put away some years back, Charlie Dawson. The Englishman had that same initial swagger, same surface charm, but no backbone, no ability to keep up the façade once he'd been rumbled.

Would Whyte have anything to reveal about the mystery surrounding Jane Maitland's death?

Or was he simply unhappy that he was not leaving Brian Abernethy's office with the assurance that a seven-figure sum was being transferred to his personal account back in London?

The ring at the front door made Sarah jump. Then, not bothering to slip on her shoes, she hastened downstairs, remembering that the postman came to deliver letters for Nancy at this time in the day. A parcel, perhaps? Something that needed a signature?

The figures outside the frosted glass door made the young woman pause for a moment as she reached the foot of the stair. Two men stood there, dark shapes that made her freeze. She shrank back against the wall as one of them raised a fist and began banging on the glass.

How had they found her?

Had someone tailed Grainne's car after she had given her a lift back to Corrielinn?

Sarah's heart thumped painfully against her ribs, terrified to make the slightest movement.

Then the banging started again.

'We know you're in there, Sarah!' one of them called out.

Her eyes flicked to the telephone table in the hall. It was too close to the door; they would see her approach, think she was going to open the door then ... what would happen?

She needed to think fast, do something that would make them go away.

'Sa-rah!' The unmistakable sound of her tormentor's voice came through the glass door as he stood there, one hand up as though to shade his eyes, to see more clearly past the large reception hall into the dimness of the interior.

She sat still. Had they noticed her descent? Were they waiting for her to make the first move?

'She's no' therr,' a different voice grumbled and the two men stepped back from the door talking in such low voices that Sarah could not make out their conversation.

The flap and bang of the letterbox made her jump. Something had landed with a soft thud on the floor but she kept herself hidden, curiosity to see what it was overcome by her fear.

Then, to Sarah's relief, they were gone.

Slipping quietly back up the way she had come, Sarah knelt down as she reached the half landing, afraid that her shadow might be seen beyond the stained-glass window.

She held her breath as she slid down flat, crawling along on hands and knees until she came to the next set of carpeted stairs.

There was another window by this staircase, its heavy drapes held back by thick tasselled cords.

Sarah stood up slowly, hidden by the swath of curtains.

Did she dare risk a quick peek?

From this vantage point she would be able to see part of the driveway then the road beyond the garden gate.

Where had they gone?

Were they down below, waiting for her, watching this very window?

She moved to the side, terrified that even the slightest movement might alert them.

Then she saw it. That car that she'd been bundled into.

But, thank God! It was being driven away.

As Sarah watched it disappear from sight she exhaled an enormous sigh. They hadn't seen her!

Swift feet took her back down the stairs to the object lying on the carpet. Scrawled on the buff jiffy bag was her name printed in black lettering, SARAH WILDING. With trembling hands she opened it, letting the familiar mobile phone slip from her fingers. Why had they brought it back? What more did they need from her? At least she hadn't opened the door to them, she thought, sweat breaking out across her body.

Yet the initial relief was tempered by the knowledge that they now knew her whereabouts and the fear that they would certainly come back already gnawing at her.

CHAPTER TWENTY-FOUR

Nancy Livingstone watched as the police car drove away, her usually calm face troubled. They had brought a forensic officer with them, a lovely young woman who had slipped into white coveralls before shutting herself in David Imrie's room and doing whatever it was she had to do. Although Nancy wasn't one for these TV crime programmes, and her knowledge of crime scene investigation was definitely second-hand, she knew all about post-mortem examinations and the requirements of the Procurator Fiscal's office. Having been married to a QC, Nancy had insight into many things. Conversations across the dinner table had been full of stories about those who had fallen into bad ways. And yet, like Nancy herself, Eric Livingstone had rarely made judgements about these people outside the courtroom.

Keep busy, Nancy told herself, going to the big filing cabinet and drawing out the paperwork that she would need to photocopy for the police. She sat down behind her desk with a heavy heart. Poor David Imrie! People outside had no conception that patients who had suffered major traumas like he had could still enjoy what remnants of life a stroke had left them. He'd seemed happier these past few days, Sarah Wilding's attention something that had made a difference.

She was a good nurse, there was no doubting that, and Nancy knew that she would be glad to write a glowing reference if the time came when the young woman decided to move on. Meantime … she paused, staring out of the window at the gardens and a stand of silver birches, their tiny leaves flittering down like yellow confetti. There was something calming in the sight, something that set her world back upon its axis. The changing seasons would come and go, leaving humankind still aching to understand their place in all of this.

Would Sarah find the peace that she undoubtedly craved? Would she be able to put the past behind her? The criminal record would always be there, of course, a blot on her character for society to see. And yet there was something fine about that young lady, something that Sarah herself could not see, hampered by her guilt. Nancy had seen how she no longer dwelt on her time in prison and the events that had led her there, at least during her working hours.

It was a treat to see Sarah talking to the patients, giving them her undivided attention, that sweet smile that lit up her pretty face. And of course, she'd been stricken by the farmer's death, Nancy thought, drawing out the pages of David Imrie's case notes that were required by the police.

If Crawford Whyte was intimidated by being inside a police interview room then he certainly wasn't showing it, Kirsty realised. A real cool customer, this one, with his cobalt-blue suit, its knife-edge creases suggesting that it was perhaps a recent purchase, and that swanky Crombie coat slung around his shoulders. A real city gent, she thought. Or at least that was the impression he wanted to give.

The interview room was a dismal place compared to Abernethy's office. Small, functional, its walls a sickly yellow with the windows obscured by an external air conditioning unit that rarely worked, it had been the scene of many stand-offs between the police and hardened criminals. Glancing at Whyte who was sitting back on the metal chair, she began to wonder about the man. In a different sort of situation would he be a 'no comment' kind of guy? Remembering the deference that he had shown Brian Abernethy, Kirsty guessed that if Whyte were to be accused of anything criminal he would be the type to demand to see his lawyer and sit fuming silently until he arrived.

But here, with Lorimer sitting opposite the man and her own seat at an angle so she could observe them both, Kirsty saw Crawford Whyte cross his ankles and fold his arms, completely at his ease. With the detective superintendent smiling in a genial manner at him, Whyte evidently felt no threat whatsoever. But then, Jane Maitland's son knew nothing of Lorimer's reputation when it came to questioning people, did he? *Watch and learn, Kirsty*, she told herself, *watch and learn*.

'Mr Whyte, thank you for being so helpful in spending a little of your day here,' Lorimer began in a tone that was possibly deferential but really came across as smooth and bland.

He shuffled some papers from a buff-coloured file on his side of the chipped wooden table. 'Your late mother,' he said, examining the paperwork as though he had to refresh his memory. 'When was it that you learned of her identity?' That frown, the flick through the paperwork as though the answer was in fact hidden there if only he could find it. Kirsty hid a smile as Whyte unfolded his arms and sat forward.

'Oh, I never knew anything about my natural mother until she died,' Whyte assured him hastily. '*She* knew about me, however.' He smiled as though the thought gave him some satisfaction. 'Through the Salvation Army apparently. Didn't want me to be contacted, just wanted to know where I lived and ... things ...' He shrugged, finishing lamely.

Aye, Kirsty thought to herself. The old lady was well respected up here, had lived a decent life. She would want to know that she wasn't leaving her fortune to some toe-rag.

'Yes,' Lorimer replied, still searching through his notes, giving the impression that he was just a bumbling Glasgow copper. 'Yes,' he repeated. 'Her will was made out in the spring of last year.' Lorimer raised his eyes and looked at Whyte for the first time since they had entered the room. 'When she was diagnosed with terminal cancer.'

'Really?' Whyte's voice rose and he cleared his throat to cover up the sign of sudden nervousness.

It wasn't a voice that she could warm to, not like James's Geordie accent, Kirsty decided. No, Crawford Whyte sounded too aloof for her liking, his clipped tones making her wonder if he was capable of any strong emotion at all. *Funny how much you can tell from a voice*, her dad had always claimed.

'Well,' Lorimer drawled, sitting back and stretching his long legs under the table. 'If you had a lot of money to leave, wouldn't you want your nearest blood relatives to have it? I would.'

'Of course,' Whyte replied, one hand rubbing the space at the back of his shirt collar as though he was feeling a little uncomfortable.

'Do you have a family yourself, Mr Whyte?'

'No,' the man replied. 'An ex-wife who's remarried.' He shrugged. 'No kids.'

'And your mother would have known this.'

'Would she?' Whyte looked surprised.

'Oh, I think so, sir,' Lorimer said, eyes once again drawn to his paperwork as though he was reading that very thing. He picked up a page and nodded. 'She wanted to know that her money would be in safe hands,' he murmured.

Whyte gave a weak grin and shuffled his chair forwards a little. 'And what safer hands than these,' he said, holding out his arms, the shirt cuffs glinting with square golden cufflinks. 'After all, being in the banking business, you know, it's always been a pretty well-regarded profession.'

'Yes?' The single word and the blue gaze fastened on the man held more than a modicum of doubt; it held all the weight of banking failures so publicly displayed over these past few years, something that nobody was going to forget in a hurry.

'I earn an honest living,' Whyte insisted.

'If you had known of your mother's existence prior to her death, what would you have done?' Lorimer asked, the question catching Whyte unawares.

'I. . . ' He looked sideways at Kirsty who managed to keep her face completely serious, giving away nothing of the glee that she felt at the sudden change of tack on the detective superintendent's part.

'I'm not sure,' he said at last. 'Look here, what has all of this got to do with my inheritance?' he asked, curling his right fist into a ball. 'I simply came up here today to see my lawyer, sort out the things that required signing and then go back home again.' His voice had taken on a querulous note now but he dropped his gaze as Lorimer stared back at him silently.

'We think your late mother was murdered, Mr Whyte,' Lorimer replied quietly. 'And until such times as we know exactly who committed that act, there is no chance whatsoever that you will be permitted to have access to a single penny of her estate.'

Took the wind right out of his sails, Kirsty would tell James later, watching Crawford Whyte visibly crumple beneath the detective superintendent's scrutiny. He's only after her money, she had already decided. He didn't care about having a mother somewhere up in Glasgow. Didn't want anything to do with her. And was it true, she suddenly thought, that Jane Maitland's son had only discovered her identity after she had died?

As she stepped out of the police station, Kirsty rummaged in her pocket as soon as she heard the ring tone of her mobile.

'Hello?'

'Is that Detective Constable Wilson?' a lilting voice began.

'Who's calling?'

'It's Mary Milligan.' There was slight pause. 'You do remember me? Mrs Murdoch's nurse from the Western?'

'Of course,' Kirsty replied, a memory of the ginger-haired woman flashing into her mind.

'It's just . . .' The woman hesitated then lowered her voice as though afraid to be overheard.

'Look, can we arrange to meet somewhere. Soon? There's something I need to tell you.'

CHAPTER TWENTY-FIVE

She spotted the man through the plate-glass window as he walked through Royal Exchange Square. It was DS Murdoch, slouching along the pavement, head bowed as if struggling against a westerly wind, hands thrust deep into his raincoat pockets. Glasgow was a village, Kirsty thought to herself as she sat inside the coffee bar to wait for Mary Milligan, elbows on the Formica-topped table, hands folded thoughtfully under her chin. It was a place where you might run into folk that you knew any time at all. She had been about to wave, but the moment had passed too quickly and her natural hesitation made her glad. She really didn't want to speak to him. Besides, what would she say? *When's the funeral? How are you coping?* Neither of these things were any of her business and Murdoch would be the first to tell her so.

Fifteen minutes, Mary Milligan had promised, and so Kirsty had arrived a little early, taking this corner table that would give them some privacy to talk whilst still allowing Kirsty to look out and see what was happening in the street. From where she sat, Kirsty had a good view of the door and her eyes kept straying towards it, searching for the ginger-haired woman.

There had been something in her voice that had pricked

Kirsty's curiosity. That breathless rush, as if she had been in a hurry or else had wanted to make that telephone call before her courage failed. Was that it? Had Kirsty detected fear in her tone? Maybe.

She looked up again. This time she was rewarded by the sight of the woman in the doorway looking distractedly around the coffee bar. Mary's face lit up with a smile when she spotted Kirsty.

'You came!' she said as she chose the seat opposite the policewoman, setting down a large tote bag and peeling off her coat.

'Of course,' Kirsty replied. 'I said I would and here I am.'

Mary turned to look around the coffee bar, her teeth gnawing on her lower lip. Then, as if satisfied that all was well, she drew in her chair and leaned forward.

'Better get our coffees first, eh?' She looked back into the coffee bar just as a young man approached to take their order.

'Skinny latte for me,' Mary said. 'Same for you . . . ?' She hesitated.

'Aye, that's fine, thanks,' Kirsty said, realising that the nurse only knew her as Detective Constable Wilson.

'Anything to eat?' The young man smiled encouragingly but both women shook their heads, smiling suddenly at one another as though acknowledging the same desire to stay off unnecessary carbohydrates.

'It's Kirsty,' she told the other woman once the waiter had left them alone again. 'Kirsty Wilson.'

'Well, pleased to meet you.' Mary gave a tremulous smile.

Kirsty looked at her watch then back at Mary Milligan, a tiny signal that was meant to suggest she soon had to be somewhere else.

'Well,' Kirsty said, 'what was it you wanted to tell me, Mary?'

The woman opposite took a deep breath then exhaled slowly.

'Something's going on, Kirsty,' she began, leaning closer across the table. 'And I swear to God it isn't my imagination.'

'Uh-huh?' Kirsty nodded encouragingly.

'See, there's been a few funny things happening and I've only just had time to do a wee bit of detective work of my own.' She smiled shyly. 'It all began before Mrs Murdoch died, your boss's wife,' she added unnecessarily. 'D'you remember I told you that so many of our patients were going off? Well it was odd, I mean, statistically speaking, you know. It's not normal to get a cluster picture like that unless there's some sort of epidemic,' she insisted.

'You sounds as if you've studied that sort of thing,' Kirsty observed.

'Aye.' Mary shot her a rueful grin. 'Dropped out of my economics degree. Decided the human race needed my tender lovin' care not my mathematical brain.'

'Snap!' Kirsty grinned. 'Same here. I joined the police after quitting my course at Cally,' she admitted.

'Caledonian University? That's where I studied nursing,' Mary remarked. 'What made you do that?'

Kirsty's grin faded. 'Something happened.' She shook her head. 'Friend of mine was murdered,' she went on, her voice dropping to a whisper.

'So you'll know all about murder, then?' Mary began to look across the table and nod but her eyes slid away under Kirsty's gaze, a sign of shyness at discussing such a subject? Or something else?

'See, Kirsty, I think that's what's going on in the hospital. I think some of our patients are being ... helped on their way, if you like ... but, yes, *murdered*.'

199

Kirsty's eyes widened and she wanted to protest that such an idea was ridiculous but the other woman's expression was deadly serious.

'Och, I know this sounds mad. But I think I've got proof,' Mary hissed.

The two women drew back into their chairs as the waiter brought their coffees to the table and set them down.

'Go on,' Kirsty said quietly.

'Well.' Mary picked up her mug of coffee, nursing it in her hands as though to warm them, tilting her head to one side, considering how to begin. 'There was this doctor. Real dishy, he was, I'm telling you! Hadn't ever set my eyes on him before but that can happen. We have so many young doctors in that place and they change all the time, honestly it's hard to keep track of who's who sometimes.'

Kirsty sipped her coffee, never taking her eyes off the woman opposite.

'Well, he comes to me the other day as I was looking at the stats, you know, the list of patients and my own notes about how I think there's something fishy about so many deaths, right? Swans off with it in his hand, tells me he's been asked for it by our consultant.' Mary moved closer to the policewoman. 'Only the consultant's not been given it at all! See, I checked and our man never requested that document, never sent anyone to me that day.'

'So who was he?' Kirsty asked.

'God knows.' Mary shrugged. 'A doctor?' She pulled a face. 'Good-lookin' fella in a short-sleeved shirt, identity badge round his neck. Only it was turned t'other way so I didn't see his name,' she admitted.

'Could that have been deliberate?'

'I've thought about that over and over,' Mary sighed. 'And I've asked around to see if anyone knows the man I saw.'

'And?'

Mary gave a half laugh. 'As far as I know he doesn't even exist,' she said. 'But, Kirsty, tell me this. How did he know I was making out that report? And what else do you think he knows about me?'

The woman's eyes had widened as if in real fear now, her thoughts taking shape as words.

'Have you got a copy of that report anywhere?'

'Yes,' Mary replied. 'It's on the hospital computer. Most of our department can access it any time.'

'So other people could have made a copy?'

'Not without our log-in password.'

'But someone must have known you were anxious about this,' Kirsty insisted. 'And if it was someone inside the department they would only have to have printed out their own copy.'

'I know,' Mary said, her eyes dropping to the table.

There was something she wasn't saying, Kirsty suddenly realised, something that Mary Milligan was holding back. Kirsty shifted in her seat, feeling a little less comfortable in this woman's presence though she would have been at a loss to explain why.

'And your consultant? Have you spoken to him about your fears for the safety of your patients?'

Mary shook her head. 'He didn't have time to listen to me,' she said sadly. 'They're very busy people you know,' she added defensively.

'So, what is it you want me to do, Mary?' Kirsty asked slowly.

Mary Milligan reached across to the chair and picked up her bag. Setting it on her knee she drew out a folded sheet of paper.

'Here,' she said, offering it to Kirsty. 'That's a copy of my report. I'd like you to take a look at it and tell me if I'm barmy.' She grinned sheepishly.

'And if I think there's something worth investigating?'

Mary drew a deep breath before replying. 'Then I'd want to make an official approach to the police about certain deaths that have occurred in my ward,' she replied. 'Including Irene Murdoch's.'

'What?' Kirsty sat up suddenly, astonishment on her face.

'Aye, I knew you'd react like that,' Mary said, a tinge of anger in her voice. 'But see, why d'you think I asked you to come here and not your boss?'

Kirsty shook her head.

The ginger-haired woman set down her coffee mug with a bang, spilling some of its milky contents across the Formica. Then she leaned closer, fists clenched upon the table as she lowered her voice.

'That's because Irene Murdoch's husband is the only other living soul I told about this.'

Maggie Lorimer had thought long and hard about the poem. Was she simply being self-indulgent in the wake of her cousin's death? Or was it that the conversation over the dinner table these past few nights had centred on the subject of assisted suicide?

Edwin Morgan, the poet, had lived a long time, hadn't he? Ninety years old at the last and still so mentally alert that he had even published a book of poetry just before the end. Their very own Glasgow laureate, their Scots Makar, she would tell the pupils. They'd wrinkle their noses and frown, Makar? Whit's that, Missus Lorimer? And she'd tell them about the ancient makars like Dunbar and Henryson, maybe even try them out with some poetry from these so-called Scottish Chaucerians. And of course she'd encourage them to find out about the 'Big Seven', poets whom she had studied at university. Out of them all she'd only ever heard Norman MacCaig and Edwin Morgan reading their poems. Maggie's mind drifted back to her student days. Oh to be so young and carefree again! She smiled at her whimsy, shaking her dark curls.

Right, 'In the Snack-bar', it would be, Maggie decided, picking up her copy of Morgan's work. The poem had been studied by countless school kids over the years but like Owen's 'Dulce Et Decorum Est', that didn't diminish its powerful message.

She began to read the familiar words, her mind forming pictures of the old blind man in the snack bar. She'd highlight some of the images, ready to make them think about what they portrayed.

> *He stands in his stained heltless gabardine*
> *like a monstrous animal caught in a tent*
> *in some story.*

Then, of course, the way that the poet becomes involved with the man, asking for help to go to the toilet. The words made Maggie focus harder.

> *. . . I concentrate*
> *my life to his: crunch of spilt sugar,*
> *slidy puddle from the night's umbrellas,*
> *table edges, people's feet,*
> *hiss of coffee machine, voices and laughter,*
> *smell of a cigar, hamburgers, wet coats steaming,*
> *and the slow dangerous inches to the stairs.*

She sat up suddenly, eyes moist with tears. Of course she would point out the figurative language. Of course she would show how Morgan evoked the senses, empathising with the old blind man.

But, as Maggie Lorimer wiped away the tear that trickled down her cheek, she could not help wondering what life had been like these last two years for her cousin, David, the man she remembered as ruddy cheeked and full of stories about the animals on his farm.

'Tomorrow, first thing if you can be there,' Rosie said.

'Okay, I'll be there. Kirsty too.'

'By the way, how d'you think she's coping with the post-mortems?' Rosie asked.

'She seems fine. Not squeamish. Quite interested, I would think. She's made of sterner stuff than you'd think to look at her.' Lorimer laughed. 'Not just a wee lassie any more, is she?'

'No,' agreed Rosie. 'Okay, see you at the City Mortuary. Bye.'

Lorimer put down the telephone and thought about the young DC. Aye, Kirsty was shaping up nicely. She'd be a credit to her dad one of these days, follow in his footsteps all right. Might even see the day when other officers would be calling her ma'am. He smiled at the notion. It wouldn't be long till Alistair Wilson's retirement do, a party in the Arthouse, a hotel in Bath Street that had undergone several incarnations in its history and was now one of Police Scotland's favoured watering holes for such events.

Thoughts of parties faded as the image of David Imrie came to the detective's mind. His wasted face, the poor body wrecked by that massive stroke . . . what sort of life had he endured at the end? He bit his lip guiltily. Was that the way to think of him? As having *endured* his existence? The nursing home appeared such a pleasant place and that young woman, Sarah Wilding, had seemed genuinely sorry to see her patient pass away. It was as if she were mourning the end of a friendship. So who was he to judge whether David Imrie was better off dead than alive, even though his life had changed irreparably?

. . . And your loved ones will be at peace.

He stopped typing and sat back to read the words of consolation.

'Hits the right spot,' he murmured to himself. 'Makes them glad to have spent some money on the dear departed.'

The man's eyes wandered to the bulging briefcase by his side. So many well-intentioned people in this world were conspiring to make him very wealthy indeed. The medical bag with its phials and syringes was shut tight, its contents ready and waiting for his next visit. A thrill ran through his body as he imagined the scene. It was not just the money that gave him this sense of pleasure, oh no. He wrinkled his nose as though he could already smell the stuffy bedroom and the decaying body of his next victim. His heart raced faster at the thought of their last few moments, when he had the power of life and death in his hands.

And there was nobody going to stand in his way, least of all Pete Wilding's doe-eyed sister.

CHAPTER TWENTY-SIX

Corrielinn was in darkness, the house shut up for the night, curtains closed against the rising wind that threatened to rip the leaves from the trees in this first autumn storm. Inside, the two women slumbered, Nancy tucked under her duvet, hands folded beneath one cheek, Sarah curled foetus-like in her own bed, her long fair hair flowing over the pillows.

A rattle sounded at the landing window, the wind shaking the old frame. A whine as the wind gathered strength, filtering through spaces under doors, down the ancient chimney pots. And still the women slept on, both weary after their day's work, deep, deep down in some unconscious realm where even dreams could not touch them.

The crash and thump made Sarah sit up with a start.

What the hell . . . ?

Then the sound of tinkling glass had her running barefoot from the room out to the corridor.

A jagged dark space was all that remained of the waterfall, fragments of stained-glass tumbled on to the carpet below. Sarah stood, mouth open in shock as she saw the huge stone lying there, paper tied around with some sort of twine.

Quickly, she darted to the adjacent window and pulled back the curtains.

But there was nobody to be seen. No figure hurrying away. No sound of a car's engine departing on the road outside. Just the wind howling like a banshee, the leaves blown up high against the yellow lamplight.

Sarah knelt beside the rock that had been thrown through the stained-glass panel. Hands shaking, she slipped off the string from the missile and pulled the paper away.

We know where you are

She let the message fall, blood draining from her face. They'd come back, that fearful scar-faced man with his crony. And now they meant to do her real harm.

'Sarah? What ...? Oh no, oh no, what's happened? Was it the wind ...? Oh ...!'

Nancy Livingstone stood, hands on her cheeks at the sight of the damaged window. 'Who would do such a thing?' she gasped, kneeling down, pushing at the fragments of splintered glass on the floor then turning to gape at the jagged hole in the window. 'My beautiful window! Oh, Eric ...!'

Tears spilled down Sarah's cheeks as she saw the distraught look on Nancy Livingstone's face.

'I'm sorry, I'm so sorry,' she whimpered.

'It's not your fault, dear,' Nancy soothed, taking the younger woman's cold hands in her own.

Sarah pulled away from her grasp. 'Oh, but it is,' she cried. 'It's all my fault, Nancy!'

'*You* didn't ...?' She looked from Sarah to the mess on the floor, a puzzled frown on her face.

Sarah shook her head. 'Of course not.' She bit her lip then whispered, 'But I think I know who did.'

If she had been impressed by the woman's kindness, Sarah Wilding was now somewhat in awe of the way she dealt with this crisis. Dressing hurriedly, Nancy went out to the garden shed to find tools and pieces of old hardboard, offcuts from a job that her late husband had carried out years before, she claimed. Instructing Sarah to find a dustpan and brush, Nancy busied herself in making a temporary covering across the window, the wood concealing not just the hole where the stone had broken the stained glass but the entire picture.

'Can it be fixed?' Sarah enquired hesitantly, but Nancy had shaken her head, not looking at the girl sweeping up the broken glass.

'Doubt it. Need to see what the insurance company thinks. Now,' she declared briskly, once Sarah had filled an empty cardboard box with the glass. 'I think we both need a cup of tea.' She shot Sarah a quizzical look, head to one side. 'And you can begin to explain who you think did this horrible thing.'

For once Sarah would have been happier back in her silent cell at Cornton Vale and not sitting opposite this woman in her bright kitchen, the Portmeirion teapot sitting between them on the table. Yet, when she dared look up at Nancy it wasn't to see a pair of accusing eyes staring at her but rather a tired-looking woman regarding her with sympathy.

'What's it all about, Sarah? Are you in some kind of trouble?' she asked gently.

That quiet voice full of concern was too much.

Sarah covered her face and broke down in sobs, the sense of

grief and loss overwhelming her so that she simply could not speak.

Then she was in Nancy's arms, the woman patting her back as if she were a child, hushing her, telling her that everything would be fine, everything *was* fine ...

Somehow they ended up side by side on the old two-seater settee, Nancy pulling a fleece rug over them both, the older woman cuddling the distraught girl as she howled in despair.

'I killed my brother,' Sarah gasped as the sobs subsided. 'They knew that. They knew what I'd done ... '

'Sarah, listen to me,' Nancy said firmly. 'You are guilty of nobody's death. Pete took an overdose. You know that. The courts know that. Goodness, Catherine Reid knows that! So why do you feel guilty about his death?'

'It was me who got the drugs for him,' Sarah mumbled into the edge of the blanket. 'He told me they'd kill him if I didn't.'

'Who? Who told him that?'

Sarah shrugged then began shivering. 'I don't know. Maybe there *were* no drug dealers threatening Pete. Maybe he made that up to get me to steal the morphine from the hospital.'

She uttered a huge sigh then Nancy felt her trembling beneath the fleecy blanket.

'I don't know now.'

'But you blame yourself.'

She nodded.

'Listen to me, Sarah. I've read the court transcript of your trial. Your brother was a serious addict. Your defence lawyer said at the time that if it hadn't been you who got him the drugs then it would have been someone else. Pete *wanted* that stuff. Wanted it badly and he didn't care if it put his sister into any danger. Did he?'

Sarah shook her head, eyes cast down.

'You were sentenced for theft, not for the death of your brother,' Nancy continued.

'*They* blame me,' Sarah whispered. 'Mum and Dad ...'

'... And you blame yourself,' Nancy finished.

Sarah nodded silently.

'Everyone is guilty of something,' Nancy whispered. 'And you've paid for making a wrong choice, haven't you?'

There was no reply.

'Well, haven't you?' Nancy insisted. 'In the eyes of society you have served your sentence. It's over. Now you have to come back to show that same society that you can live a good and fulfilling life, just as you have been doing since you started at Abbey. Hm?'

Sarah sat up and turned her tear-filled eyes to the woman who was looking at her with such loving kindness.

'But that's not all I've done, Nancy,' she whispered. 'And I still need to explain who threw that rock and broke your beautiful window.'

It was later, much later, after a second pot of tea and some buttered toast, that Nancy Livingstone stood on the landing, looking with sadness at the hardboard obscuring the damaged window. Sarah was asleep at last, the girl's soft breathing letting Nancy leave her bedside and slip into the hallway. She moved towards the other window and peeped out, hands clasped together.

Dawn was showing, a pale bright light above a sooty horizon. The night would soon be over. And, whatever fears these men had instilled into that young woman's heart, she wanted to assure her that sharp-edged knives and threats of violence were no match for the powers that held Nancy Livingstone's world together.

CHAPTER TWENTY-SEVEN

Detective Superintendent Lorimer parked his car in front of the double garage and looked up. It was a fine, stone house and, as his eyes carried on taking in details like the crow-stepped gabling, Lorimer was curious about its provenance. Old habits die hard, he chuckled to himself as he swung his long legs out of the car. His art history training had never really left him.

Mrs Livingstone had called him on his direct number, asking that he come to her house. An attempted break-in, was that what she had said? At any rate there had been something about a smashed window during the night. And, no, she hadn't called the local police station.

Looking up, Lorimer could see pale hardboard covering a long space where the window had been. Narrowing his eyes and shading them against the rays of the sun, he noticed bright bits of colour reflected within the window frame. Not an ordinary window, then, but something much more precious, he thought, striding to the door and ringing the bell.

To the detective's surprise it was not Nancy Livingstone who answered the door but Sarah Wilding, the nurse who had been so upset at David Imrie's death.

'Hello. Didn't expect to see you here,' Lorimer said, stepping forward as the nurse ushered him inside.

'I'm staying here at the moment,' Sarah explained. 'My last digs weren't up to much and Nancy wanted a lodger.'

She avoided eye contact with him, Lorimer noticed, as the blonde girl scampered off upstairs, calling on the lady of the house and leaving him standing alone in the hallway.

A quick look around him sufficed to let the detective see he was in a well cared for home. The polished side table with its huge bouquet of chrysanthemums, the richly patterned carpet (a tree of life design, he thought) and a glimpse of an original oil painting along the nearest corridor all spoke of a comfortable lifestyle. He took a couple of steps closer to the painting, its style tugging at his curiosity. Yes, unmistakable once you saw it; the turquoise waters and flying clouds above a dark brooding land mass. A Tom Shanks, unless he was very much mistaken.

'Detective Superintendent.'

Lorimer whirled round as Nancy Livingstone came up to him, her footfall so silent that he had not heard her arrival.

'Mrs Livingstone!'

'Can we go into the lounge, perhaps?' she began. 'Or would you like to see the damage upstairs first?'

Lorimer followed her glance. 'Upstairs, I think,' he agreed and waved her to proceed before him. 'You said it happened about four o' clock this morning?'

'That's right,' Nancy agreed. 'Sarah sleeps over there.' She motioned to the nearest door along the corridor. 'She heard it first.'

'Have you any idea who would do something like this?' he asked, as they stood together on the landing, looking at the damaged window. 'Have there been any other instances of vandalism in the neighbourhood? Friday nights can be notorious for things like that.'

'No.' Nancy shook her head. 'I think this is an isolated incident.' She looked at the detective superintendent and nodded towards the stairs. 'Shall we go down now? There are things I would like to discuss with you.'

Lorimer frowned as he followed her back downstairs. She was being very calm about this. No hysterics, no wringing of hands or voicing any recriminations about the perpetrators of this act of vandalism. And all his senses were on alert to find out why.

'You met Sarah at the door,' Nancy said, waving a hand towards one of the pale cream settees that sat at an angle to one another in the spacious lounge. Lorimer resisted the temptation to stare at the walls, where several decent-sized paintings were on display.

'Yes, she said she was staying here. You take in lodgers?'

Nancy managed a thin smile. 'No, not really. But Sarah needed a better place to stay and . . . ' She shrugged. 'It's a big house for one person to live in, I suppose. Detective Superintendent, can I come straight to the point?' She sat forward a little, making sure that he was paying close attention. 'I think Sarah Wilding is in danger,' she said quietly. 'But I need to have an assurance from you that what I am about to tell you will not have her put back in prison. She's had enough sorrow in her young life and I think she is on the path to a better way now.'

Back in prison? What on earth was going on here? Lorimer shifted uncomfortably. He was unused to being stared at so directly and yet there was no malice in the woman's look, more a determination to make him see things her way.

'If this is a police matter—' he began.

'It's also a personal matter,' Nancy broke in. 'I called you because I wanted your help, not to make an official report. Sarah was released just a few weeks ago and she has been doing really well.'

'I see.' Lorimer leaned back and crossed his legs, waiting for her to continue.

'Sarah Wilding was imprisoned for stealing drugs from the hospital where she used to work,' Nancy told him. 'She did it to help her brother. An addict.' She shook her head and pursed her lips in a gesture that was more despairing than condemning of human frailty and the tall policeman found himself liking her for it.

'Well, he died of an overdose.' Nancy sighed. 'Waste of a young life.'

'It's a common story these days, I'm afraid,' Lorimer agreed.

'He told his sister that he needed the drugs to give to some dealers. Told her they would kill him if he didn't.'

'And she believed him?'

Nancy nodded. 'I'm afraid so. And now she blames herself for his death.'

Lorimer thought back to the emotion that the blonde nurse had displayed at the nursing home. She was a bit fragile, wasn't she? And maybe now he was finding out why.

'What has this got to do with the damage upstairs?' Lorimer asked, although his mind was already turning to possible scenarios of his own.

'Sarah has been threatened by some men who claim to have known her brother,' Nancy said carefully, dropping her gaze for a moment, something that Lorimer picked up on immediately. Was he being given an edited version of what had happened?

'Go on.'

'They visited this house only yesterday, shouting through the front door. But Sarah pretended not to hear them.'

'And how did they know she lives here? Has she been in contact with them?'

Nancy sighed and shook her head. 'This is the hard bit, Detective Superintendent. I'm afraid that these men have been coercing Sarah Wilding into something she didn't want to do.'

There was silence between them, the ticking of the clock on the mantelpiece sounding loud to Lorimer's ears. He was a patient man but there was something going on that needed to be said and he wasn't going to shift from this chair until that happened.

'I think,' he said at last, 'I'd better talk to Sarah herself.'

Nancy stiffened where she sat and he could see from the way her eyes flitted to the door and back that the nursing home manager was anxious. Why? What was it about this young woman that had elicited such a measure of concern?

'I don't want to make any formal complaint against Sarah,' Nancy said at last. 'She may have made an error of judgement but I understand why she did.'

'If your lodger is found to have committed a crime—'

'She did something without permission,' Nancy broke in. 'Any part she may have played in a crime would have been quite unwitting,' she insisted, her voice clear and calm, a smile even hovering upon her lips.

'And if I decided that she had committed a crime . . . ?'

'I think there is a greater judge over us all, Superintendent, don't you?' Nancy said quietly. 'One who will eventually decide who is the sinner and who has been sinned against.'

Lorimer stifled a sigh. She was one of those Holy Willies, then. And she'd taken an ex-con into her home to try to show her the way to salvation. Yet sitting opposite and regarding him gravely, Nancy Livingstone did not give Lorimer the impression that she was soft in the head, no matter how kind her heart might be. Rather, there was a no-nonsense air about her that he was inclined to respect.

'It is possible that Sarah may have been involved in the death of David Imrie,' Nancy began, then held up her hand as Lorimer was about to reply. 'Hear me out, please.'

Lorimer took a deep breath and waited.

'Sarah was abducted by some men who held her at knifepoint and forced her to promise that she would copy the names and details of our patients' next of kin,' Nancy explained. 'I told you that she was in fear of her life and I meant it. These are very dangerous people, Superintendent. And I imagine that you would like to apprehend *them* rather than a frightened young woman,' she added drily.

'I still need to speak to Sarah. Hear the story from her,' Lorimer sighed.

Nancy Livingstone stared at him then dropped her gaze and nodded. 'I'll go and fetch her,' she agreed. 'And then I think I'd better put the kettle on. Would you care for some tea or coffee?'

He was standing by the window when he heard the light footstep behind him. Turning, he saw the girl standing in the middle of the room, twisting her hands nervously together. Her eyes were red rimmed. Tears of contrition? Or had she been sobbing in fear of being returned to Cornton Vale again so soon after her release?

'Sarah, come and sit down,' he said gently, waving a hand at the long settee that faced the fireplace.

For a moment he thought that the girl might turn and flee from the room. She looked so young standing there in her stocking soles, no make-up on her pale face and hair tied back in a ponytail. He'd seen plenty of ex-cons in his time, tough women who would narrow their eyes when he looked at them, mendacious creatures, some of those whose lives were punctuated by spells inside HM prisons. But this girl looked different, almost as though her experience inside had left her untouched and still vulnerable. He could see why Nancy Livingstone had taken such a shine to her. Wasn't she the perfect material for a religious type to get their claws into?

As soon as the thought came to him, Lorimer felt ashamed. That was not worthy of him. Everyone deserved a second chance, didn't they? And he was all in favour of organisations like SHINE and SACRO that helped prisoners fit into the outside world.

'What did Nancy tell you?' Sarah whispered, sitting in the farthest corner of the settee from the tall detective.

'I know a bit about your recent history,' Lorimer admitted. 'But I need to know more about what has been happening to you since you left Cornton Vale.'

The girl looked at him with wide, frightened eyes.

'I want to help you if I can, Sarah,' he continued gently. 'But I can't do that unless you are prepared to trust me.'

He smiled at her, softening the blue gaze that had crushed many hardened criminals.

'I wouldn't have hurt Mr Imrie,' she whispered at last. 'That's the last thing I would've wanted. I didn't know ...'

'It's all right, Sarah. Just start from the beginning and tell me everything.'

Lorimer drove back into the city, his head full of tumbling thoughts. He had instructed the girl to hold on to the mobile in case they made contact with her again. There would be time to have it examined by their own technical people, see if they could trace any of the calls, but he reckoned that it was better kept in Sarah Wilding's possession for the time being. By rights he should arrest the girl, but there had been no official complaint about her copying these patient files. Only Nancy Livingstone knew, the girl having broken down in tears, confessing her guilt. And the nursing home manager was not about to reveal this to her sister. Perhaps, he thought cynically, because Mrs Abbott would be less lenient with the former inmate.

Why had anyone wanted these patient files? And had this anything to do with Maggie's cousin's death? Was Sarah Wilding playing a dangerous game here? Okay, she'd been held at knife-point (something that could not be proved in a court of law) and was in fear for her life. But she'd trusted Nancy Livingstone. And, though he was reluctant to admit it to himself, there was something about that woman that William Lorimer grudgingly admired. Not only did he feel she was telling him the truth, but he was certain that she only wanted the best for the girl. And, if he were to make this a part of his official inquiry, then Sarah Wilding might well find herself back in Cornton Vale.

'Why?' Sarah stood in the doorway of the kitchen, looking in.

Nancy turned from the sink where she had been cleaning veg-etables to make some soup, a weekend task that, she told Sarah, gave her a lot of satisfaction.

'Why what?'

'Why do you want to protect me?' Sarah came into the kitchen and sat down at the wooden table. 'What do I mean to you? I mean, you hardly know me and yet . . . ?'

'Oh, Sarah.' Nancy wiped her hands on a dishcloth and came to sit next to her. 'I want you to have that second chance. Don't you see? You're so full of remorse for what happened with your brother. And if you don't try to put all of that behind you, then you may be sucked right back into whatever it was Pete was involved in.'

'Did that policeman say what he was going to do?' the girl asked dully.

'No. But if he *had* been going to make something of it, wouldn't he have taken you down to the police station? Besides, nobody has made an official complaint against you.'

'That's because you haven't told Mrs Abbott,' Sarah said.

'And until I need to do that, my sister will remain none the wiser about how these files got into the hands of those men!'

'But why would you bother with someone like me?' Sarah murmured, looking down at her hands.

'Because you're worth it?' Nancy asked with a smile. 'Can I tell you a story?'

Sarah tried to return the smile, lips trembling. 'A once upon a time?'

'If you like.' She settled herself at the table and looked into Sarah's eyes. 'Once upon a time there was a shepherd who had a flock of sheep. A hundred of them, all ages and sizes, lambs as well as ewes and rams. Well, one day he saw that one of them was missing. A wee lamb.'

'Someone had stolen it?' Sarah suggested.

'He didn't know,' Nancy replied. 'But he left the flock and set off over the rough hill country and called out all the time to see if he could find it. Eventually he heard a weak little cry.'

'His wee lamb?'

'Right. And it was stuck under a tree root in a place that was difficult and dangerous to access. He would be putting his own life in danger just to rescue that little creature.'

'And did he? Or did he do the sensible thing and leave it where it was?' Sarah replied, her eyes giving Nancy a knowing look as if she could tell which way the tale was proceeding.

'I think you know what choice he made, don't you, Sarah?'

'So he found the lamb, carried it back and they all lived happily ever after.' The girl's voice held a note of cynicism.

'Don't you want a happy ending, Sarah?' Nancy asked, her expression quite serious.

The girl shrugged and looked away.

'Or do you still feel that you don't deserve to have another chance at life?'

Nancy rose from the table and resumed her chore by the sink, now taking the leek and carrots and beginning to slice them into little pieces.

Sarah sat still, gazing at the woman's back. Nobody had ever given her future a second thought. Well, maybe Catherine Reid ... and of course she was Nancy's friend, wasn't she? She looked at the woman busily peeling a carrot, its skin one long orange strip curling on to the chopping board. They were different from the people she had known, even the nurses whose profession was to care for others. But this was personal.

This woman cared enough to make the young woman consider her question carefully. Was she a little lamb worth saving? Sarah had dim memories of the Bible story and its underlying meaning.

And how she responded to this old, old tale was going to determine just what steps she took next.

CHAPTER TWENTY-EIGHT

When she awoke it was to a sense of bewilderment; the *where am I* feeling that comes from the day after a holiday when home appears strange for those initial seconds.

She was in her own bed ... well, that was a moot point, wasn't it. Sarah sighed. It was the bed that had belonged to another woman, Tracey Livingstone. It was only hers for the duration. Another sigh. How long could she remain here? The incident of the night-time rock crashing through that lovely window had made Sarah think hard about her future.

Not for the first time did she regret her rejection of SHINE, the organisation that existed to help female offenders get back on their feet. *I'm not like them*, Sarah had told herself. *My life isn't in chaos like theirs*. She had compared herself with the junkie women who had mental-health issues, kids at home running mad ... she didn't have such problems in her life. If only she had known then how things would turn out!

And yet, Sarah mused, she did have a mentor, didn't she? Catherine Reid, her social worker, had put her in touch with Nancy and the woman who slept along the corridor was better than anyone SHINE could have provided.

God is good, Nancy had said last night, a simple phrase as she'd kissed Sarah's cheek and said goodnight. But she meant it, Sarah thought, turning in the bed and coorying more deeply under the duvet. Today was Sunday. Would she go to church with Nancy again? The thought depressed her a little. To be sitting there with all those worthy folk seemed like a cheek. Sarah Wilding, ex-con, in amongst the good, respectable people of Bearsden!

Yet the notion of spending Sunday alone in the house made her shiver. What if they came back and found her here? No, going to church and feeling like an outsider was a penance worth enduring.

'Here.' Nancy thrust an armful of clothes on to Sarah's neatly made bed. 'Tracey told me ages ago to give them to Marks and Sparks. They pass them on to Oxfam, you know.' She smiled and shrugged. 'Must be some reason I kept putting that off,' she laughed. 'Perhaps they were meant to come to you, Sarah!'

Then she was gone, sweeping out of Sarah's room.

She had knocked the door first, Sarah thought. Even although the entire house belonged to Nancy Livingstone, the woman had given Sarah the dignity of her own privacy.

She lifted the pile of clothes and began to look at them one by one.

That skirt! Sarah's eyes widened as she ran her fingers over the navy blue mock-suede. It was exactly the same as one she had left behind at the flat. She checked the label. A ten! It was even the same size. A shiver ran through her as she recalled Nancy's words. Had she been meant to have these clothes? Her face brightened as she turned them over; skirts and tops, a fitted boiled-wool jacket in cherry red, three pairs of trousers (she laid them against her leg, nodding happily at their correct length) and what looked like a brand-new raincoat. All M&S labels, all stuff that she would have wanted to buy for herself. *Had* bought, she giggled, picking up the suede skirt. She would wear this to church. With that pale blue blouse and her own V-necked jumper. A quick glance at the window showed a clear September sky with no trace of cloud. Would it turn to rain later? She put on the red jacket over her pyjamas and fastened it up with a sigh of pure pleasure. Sod the weather! She would look nice in church today!

Then, her smile fading a little, the thought came to Sarah that perhaps this was why Nancy had given her these things. Did she want her house-guest to look presentable in front of all her friends? She bit her lip. There had been no doubtful glance cast her way last week, had there?

No, Nancy just wasn't like that. Sarah nodded decisively. Not a bad bone in that woman's body, she told herself. Unlike the young woman she had befriended.

CHAPTER TWENTY-NINE

Most police work was pretty boring, Kirsty decided, rubbing her eyes.

She'd been handed the action of going through Rachel Gardiner's laptop and reading every single email message from before the night she had hanged herself.

'What am I supposed to be looking for?' she had asked Lorimer, and he'd given her a grin and replied,

'You'll know when you find it.' A remark so enigmatic that she'd wanted to groan.

Well, she had gone back several days now and had seen messages written to Rachel from all the usual places; high-street stores, holiday companies, medical suppliers ... and, of course, emails to and from men and women who sounded like friends or even colleagues.

It was odd, Kirsty thought, to be working in a job that gave her access into someone's life like this. Some emails showed a certain stream where friends had been included in a group email. One in particular made her pause.

Please don't give up, Rachel. Maybe something can be worked out to

help you. Worth a try? We miss you. And the sender, someone named Moira, had signed off with a smiley emoticon.

They knew then, Rachel Gardiner's workmates. They'd been aware of her diagnosis. How must it have felt to break that sort of news to your friends? And how would friends like this Moira person feel once they knew that Rachel had taken her own life rather than face the end of such a debilitating disease?

Another email of compassion, Kirsty thought, yawning as she prepared to flick it away.

But something stopped her. She blinked and read it again.

Be happy that the worst you can imagine will soon be over. Be grateful that the choice you decided to make was the right one. Working together with you let me see what a compassionate person you are. Now you must face the future with no regrets. And your loved one will be at peace.

There was no signature. No silly face. Just this email sent from someone, no, some organisation, calling itself quietrelease.com.

Could this be what Lorimer had wanted her to find? A frisson of excitement ran through Kirsty to be replaced with a moan as she typed the address into the search bar to no avail. The search engine yielded pages of things headed *Quiet Release*, mostly for spa breaks and osteopaths, but the website didn't seem to exist. With a sigh, Kirsty focused on the screen.

There was nothing. Not a sausage, she sighed again as she reached the last search result. No company offering to release a loved one from their pain (was that what she had been expecting?) And yet ... the very fact of there being nothing on the internet surely pointed to it being some clandestine organisation? Something set up out of compassion for patients who were suffering? Or, Kirsty wondered cynically, run for profit by someone?

Now that she had something to go on, Kirsty scrolled down, looking back at more emails, her eyes focusing hard to find something similar in Rachel Gardiner's inbox.

It was more than an hour later, trawling through the trashed messages, that she found it.

'Yes!' Kirsty said aloud, making a couple of heads turn her way though she was too intent on the screen to notice.

This was what she was looking for!

'You want tae see Lorimer?' A woman with tightly permed grey hair under a frilly cap and wearing a pale green overall stopped in the corridor, hands on her trolley full of cakes and snacks.

'Yes, I ...' Kirsty took a step forward. Who was this wee woman staring at her so intently with tiny eyes that reminded Kirsty of a curious robin?

'Well, you'll no' see him the now, hen. He's busy with the chief constable. Better come back later on.'

The woman with the trolley screwed up her eyes and stared at the detective constable. 'Hey, are you no' Alistair Wilson's girl? Wee Kirsty?'

'Yes ...'

'Och, I ken noo. My, but you're fair grown up, lass. And ah see ye've lost a' that puppy fat,' she nodded approvingly.

There was something about the woman, some memory that the detective constable was dredging up from her mind.

'Are you Sadie?' Kirsty managed to get a word in at last. 'Sadie Dunlop?'

'An' who else would I be? Lady Gaga?' The woman snorted and made a face.

'I thought you'd retired,' Kirsty said.

'Aye, well, I tried that fur a wee while but it wis boring,' Sadie admitted. 'It's ma first day back. The canteen's all changed, so it has, so ah decided tae start a trolley service. Jist Mondays tae Fridays.' She folded her arms and looked at Kirsty with her bright bird's eyes. 'See all of these polis depended on me and my cakes, know whit I mean? Course you do.' She wagged a finger at Kirsty. 'You're Betty Wilson's lassie. Best baker of a' the wives. Here,' she nudged Kirsty again, her sharp elbow digging into Kirsty's arm, 'did you no' go to Cally Uni tae study hospitality?'

'I did.' Kirsty grinned. 'But I saw the light and came here instead.'

'Och, away wi' ye!' Sadie laughed. 'Here. Gie's a haun wi' this damn trolley. Ah'm settin aff tae your bit now. CID.' She smiled and Kirsty dodged as the woman aimed her elbow at her again.

'Will he be long, do you think?' Kirsty asked as they made their way down in the lift.

'Is the Pope a Catholic?' Sadie chuckled. 'Never knew a Big Chief to come and see his nibs unless it was important. So, aye, they'll likely be a while in there.' She raised her eyes to the roof as though she could see into Lorimer's office.

'Here.' Sadie lifted a chocolate éclair and handed it to Kirsty. 'See if that's no' better than the ones yer ma makes.'

Kirsty wiped the last of the chocolate from her lips and threw the paper wrapper into the bin by her desk. Aye, she'd tell Sadie next time she saw her that her chocolate éclairs were every bit as good as her mum's.

The girl looked at the printouts on her desk with a sigh. It wasn't proof exactly, but it was a start. That was one of the things about all the actions handed out at each stage of a case; the plodding stuff was like gold mining. Loads of mud and dross then that wee shining nugget. Was that what she had found?

Free yourself from pain. Free your loved ones from all their
unnecessary suffering. If you can spare them this then your
life may be worth living once again.
Contact Quiet Release at the following number.

Kirsty paused. She had been going to wait until Lorimer read
this before she took any further action but now ... like Sadie
Dunlop Kirsty's eyes searched the ceiling. He was up there with
the chief constable. If she were to try for herself ... ?

Fingers shaking with excitement, Kirsty dialled the number
that she had found on Rachel Gardiner's laptop screen.

'The number you dialled has not been recognised,' a haughty
woman's voice told the detective constable. 'Please check and
try again.'

And, numbed with disappointment, Kirsty did as instructed
only to be told the very same thing.

It was too easy, of course it was. What had she expected?
That this organisation, this lot who were possibly involved
in assisted suicide outside the legal channels, would gaily
give out their telephone number? Once Rachel Gardiner had
responded (and it looked as though she had) they'd have found
a new number. Probably worked with a whole pile of disposable mobile phones, Kirsty decided gloomily. So, the question
was now, how were they ever to find this group? And what sort
of people were they?

Father Joseph Fitzimmons put down the telephone with a
sigh. Everyone believed that being at the top of a ladder gave
them power, didn't they? It was part of human nature, he
supposed, and human nature was a great deal of what his job
was about. He was an experienced priest with more than forty

228

years' service behind him but that did not mean that he was immune to the sudden shocks that people could still present him with. Sometimes, especially after a busy spell in the confessional, Joseph Fitzimmons thought that he had heard it all. Take Miss Maitland, for example. He had not expressed any astonishment at hearing her confession – that she was a single mother (or had been at a time when such things were still frowned upon) – had washed over him.

He clasped his hands and stared into space, twirling his thumbs thoughtfully.

That Detective Superintendent Lorimer was a decent fellow. Not all of the policemen he had encountered had spoken to him in such respectful tones. Some of them had looked bitter whenever Fr Fitzimmons refused to reveal what had taken place between himself and a known criminal during confession. Cursed him under their breath, even. But this policeman was different.

Poor Jane Maitland, Joseph sighed. They had discussed many things on his visits to see his parishioner. And that one of their topics for discussion had been assisted suicide. She would never have sanctioned that. Never. She had been adamant that she wanted to live out her life on her own terms, pain or no pain. Only days before her death they had discussed the morality and spirituality of the subject, he'd assured the tall policeman as they sat together drinking tea in the Parish House. He had indeed been a keyholder for the old lady. Kept it hanging up on the inside of the door to his study in the Parish House. Yet, when Fr Fitzimmons had looked for it to hand to Lorimer, it simply wasn't there. *Becoming forgetful in my old age*, he'd laughed. But the loss of the key worried him considerably and he could see that the tall detective had noticed his concern.

And now this telephone call. Joseph shook his head. His old friend's son had done well for himself, climbing the career ladder to the very top. Chief constable, Joseph mused, remembering the man speaking to him from Detective Superintendent Lorimer's office. But, no matter how high a person climbed in this world, no matter what lofty rank they attained, there was a higher authority still. One that was in control of everyone's final destiny. And it was by that authority that Joseph Fitzimmons had chosen to live his life.

No, he had told the younger man. *You know that I cannot reveal anything that goes on between me and a penitent soul.*

And so, if he had secrets to keep about Jane Maitland, then they would remain just that.

'Thanks for trying.'

The man in uniform shook Lorimer's hand and gave him a rueful grin. 'Well, he's an old family friend. Thought that might swing it for you. Anyway, let me know how this progresses. Looks like you may have stumbled across something a lot bigger than you realised.'

Lorimer shut the door after his visitor and wandered across to the window. He hadn't really expected the priest to relate anything Jane Maitland had told him in the sanctity of the confessional but the chief had given it a shot nonetheless.

Looking out over the rooftops, his eyes shifting from the grey skies and the familiar outline of nearby buildings to the streets below, the detective superintendent saw just a little of the comings and goings in the city. He heard the rumble of a fire engine and its whining siren as it left the nearby station, saw people walking briskly along the road towards the city centre, watched a steady stream of vehicles heading towards the motorway. Glasgow teemed with activity at any time of the day or night, most of it for the good of its citizens, some of it most certainly to their detriment, which was why he was standing there, thinking hard.

Somewhere out there people were being killed unlawfully. How bad was it to end a life full of pain and suffering? That was a question that so many folk asked. *You wouldn't let your dog go through that kind of agony* was one well-voiced declaration. But to debate the rights and wrongs of assisted suicide was not Lorimer's business. That was up to the moralists and politicians. No, his business was to root out any criminal activity and to put a stop to that.

The telephone ring shut off his musings abruptly.

'Lorimer.'

'It's Rosie. Sorry but it's not good news.'

'Go on.'

'Maggie's cousin? Mr Imrie? We rushed through the tox results after his PM.'

There was a pause and Lorimer felt his fingers gripping the phone more tightly.

'I'm really sorry,' Rosie repeated. 'But they've discovered a high amount of morphine.'

'That's what killed him?'

'Looks like it. I'd say as much in a court of law.'

'You may have to,' Lorimer replied, looking back out of the window at the clouds darkening over the city. 'I mean to catch whoever is doing this to vulnerable folk like David.'

'Three deaths in a short space of time. Three people who may have been going to die in the fairly near future.' Lorimer looked around the room at the men and women assembled there. Every eye was upon him, every face showing signs of attention.

'Jane Maitland was a very wealthy woman,' he continued. 'We've already spoken to her beneficiary. However, I think more needs to be done on that front.

'Julie Gardiner had very little to leave in the way of assets but her sister appears to have been in contact with some organisation offering to end either her or her sister's life.'

He looked behind at the two photos of the women. Julie was sprawled in her wheelchair while the photo of Rachel hanging in the garage was a grim reminder of how the dog walker had found her body.

'We have solid forensic evidence that the deaths of Miss Maitland and Julie Gardiner are linked. The grounds around Abbey Nursing Home are still being investigated by the SOCOs but we now have the tox result from Mr Imrie's PM. If there are any prints or DNA to match what we have found on the first two victims then we know we are looking for something a lot bigger than *two* deaths.'

The silence in the room was potent, each officer no doubt thinking along the same lines to a memory of another killer, the bearded Dr Shipman, whose victims may well have numbered over two hundred. That was a fact that Lorimer didn't need to voice; a reminder of the most vulnerable members of society at the mercy of one whom they had trusted with their very lives.

Kirsty watched the man's grim expression. She was still to let him know about her meeting with Mary Milligan. Something was holding her back. And in her heart she knew that it was the thought of Murdoch being involved in his own wife's death. If she were to stir up trouble for the newly bereaved man ... She drew her lips into a thin line as though unconsciously keeping her information secret. But she had to tell Lorimer. It was just a matter of when. Certainly not now in front of all of these police officers who were Murdoch's colleagues.

'Sir,' a female DC piped up. 'We heard that Mr Imrie is a relative of yours. Is that right?'

Lorimer gave a wintry smile. 'My wife's late cousin,' he replied. 'Not a blood relative of mine so there is nothing personal going on. Hardly knew the chap. Saw him recently after his father's funeral.'

'Isn't that a conflict of interest?' Kirsty heard another officer whisper to her neighbour. But a shake of the head made her fall silent once again.

'We have intelligence that vulnerable patients are being targeted either in their own homes or, in this case, a respectable private nursing home.'

He gave a nod and swept his gaze over the team. 'One thing we cannot do is to alert every hospital or nursing home to the possibility that their patients might be being bumped off,' he told them grimly. 'That would simply cause a national panic and besides, we need much more proof about what is going on.'

He smiled over the crowd to catch Kirsty's eye.

'Thanks to DC Wilson we have a lead that might help us trace emails to the perpetrator.'

Kirsty felt her cheeks redden as everyone turned to stare. More than one glance looked at her in a less than charitable manner. *Nobody likes a teacher's pet*, she thought. *He shouldn't have singled me out.*

'What we must all do is to ask these places to make us aware of any emails coming from this organisation calling itself Quiet Release. And also to let us know about any unusual spikes in their death rates.'

Kirsty looked around seeing serious faces and a few nodding heads.

'Remember this is a team effort and I know that each and every one of you will put your hearts and souls into solving this case.'

The blue gaze swept the room and once more the whole place was silent.

'Before I hand out the actions, I want to say this. And I want you to know that there is no religious conviction behind my words.' He stared at them all in turn. 'Murder is the unlawful killing of a person against their will. It is a savage act whether it happens with the swing of a drunken blade or the pinprick of a needle full of morphine. Don't think that because these people were terminally ill it somehow makes ending their lives right. It doesn't. Each day they lived was perhaps a precious twenty-four hours that they enjoyed as best they could. Perhaps every day was one more day dragging on painfully until death came as a blessed release. We may never know. But what you need to remember is that from what we *do* know Jane Maitland, Julie Gardiner and David Imrie had no say whatsoever in the time and method of when and how they were to draw their very last breath.'

'I thought you were very brave,' Kirsty said, adding, 'Sir,' as Lorimer shot her a look.

'Ach, it had to be said,' Lorimer told her, motioning Kirsty into a seat next to his desk. 'Too many folk have divided opinions on euthanasia as it is. What everyone in Police Scotland needs to remember is that no matter what their religious persuasions or lack of them, their job is to root out criminal activity *and* protect the public from it.'

'Yes,' Kirsty nodded. 'I think we all got that, sir.'

'Right, then, your email said that there was something you needed to discuss with me in private. I'm intrigued.'

Kirsty shifted in her seat. How to begin?

'When I was at the hospital with DS Murdoch. The day his wife died. There was a nurse who wanted to tell me stuff. A Highland woman. Talked about an angel of mercy putting her patients to sleep. A superstitious type, I thought. I didn't really pay her too much heed. A bit shocked about Mrs Murdoch.'

'You didn't know she had MS?'

Kirsty shook her head. 'DS Murdoch never said.'

'Go on.'

'Well this nurse, Mary Milligan, she contacted me and asked to meet up.' Kirsty bit her lip. 'Not sure if I should have ... anyway ... turns out that she has concerns about the number of patients dying in her wards. And that's not all.'

As she related the woman's words to Lorimer, the detective superintendent steepled his fingers together against his chin and regarded her thoughtfully.

'You think there may be something in it?' he asked at last.

Kirsty thought for a moment. How much to tell him? Suspicions were just that. And how would she feel if there were no basis for the nurse's words about Murdoch? Something was stopping her from repeating them, and she guessed that it was the memory of the man's genuine grief.

She coughed to cover up her pause, hoping that Lorimer would not notice her hesitation.

'Yes, sir, I do,' Kirsty replied at last.

'We need evidence. What sort of CCTV systems are there in that ward? Find out and see if there are any images of this doctor, or whoever he is. Then we might begin to put something together.'

'Yes, sir. Is that what you would like me to do now?' Kirsty asked hopefully.

Lorimer thought for a moment. Several of the actions handed

235

out included sifting through paperwork belonging to the victims. But there was one particular thing that he needed to do himself.

'Not just yet, Kirsty. I want you to come with me on a little trip to the countryside.'

The journey was made mostly in silence and Kirsty could understand why. Who would want to tell a man that his brother had been murdered? Especially if that man was your wife's cousin.

As they'd set off, Lorimer had explained about the farm. How Patrick Imrie had been prepared to sell up to fund his brother's care at Abbey Nursing Home.

He'd had a lot to gain from David's death, Kirsty realised. And yet it had been Patrick who had requested that his brother undergo a post-mortem examination. Strange, she thought, as they passed out of the city and on to a winding road between sloping hills where the heather was fading from purple to brown.

It would be very interesting to see this man's reaction to the news. And it came to Kirsty Wilson that this was exactly why Lorimer had brought her with him.

CHAPTER THIRTY

The skies were louring over the nearby hill, a grey mass of raincloud threatening to sweep across the Carse. The wind was still high, tree branches swaying, leaves scattering as they drove past. Autumn was here now for sure, the equinox long past and October promising darker days ahead. What must it be like living out here amongst these bleak hills, surrounded by fields and fields, only the occasional cottage or dwelling house half a mile away for a neighbour? Winters would be unbearable, Kirsty thought, shivering as she imagined the distant mountains covered in snow.

Lorimer had slowed down at a bend, a tractor trundling in front of them, barring any passage on this narrow stretch as a line of vehicles approached from the other side. Then there was a gap and the big car roared past, Kirsty glancing up at the young man sitting exposed to the elements, bareheaded, his sleeves rolled up on his navy overalls. Who would be a farmer?

'They're a hardy breed,' Lorimer remarked, as though reading his companion's thoughts. 'Have to be to endure the sorts of weather we get.'

As if on cue the rain began, bouncing off the windscreen and no doubt soaking the poor lad who was now almost out of sight.

It was another fifteen minutes of watching the windscreen wipers swish back and forth before the big car slowed down and Lorimer turned into a country lane.

'Your poor car'll be in a right state after this,' Kirsty murmured as they bounced over the muddy, pitted track, its twin ruts more suited to the huge tyres on a Massey Ferguson tractor.

Lorimer did not answer, concentrating instead on the steep gradient and a blind corner ahead.

'Is this it?' she asked suddenly as a farm came into sight, its limewashed walls bordering the road. UPPER TANNOCH, a sign proclaimed.

'No. That's their nearest neighbours. Think I met them at Robert Imrie's funeral.'

Then the track descended once again to a view of flatter fields where sheep were grazing and a meandering stream that separated one flock from another.

'That's Lower Tannoch over there,' Lorimer said, pointing to a group of low-lying buildings huddled against a hillside. Kirsty peered out. It didn't look like much at first, just white walls and the side of a two-storey house, but as Lorimer drove into the cobbled yard, she saw barns and outbuildings that stretched out from the main building and beyond.

Lorimer parked next to a grey Land Rover and Kirsty breathed a sigh of relief, glad to be at this journey's end and anticipating a nice cup of tea and maybe some home baking. Weren't farmers' wives famous for their hospitality, after all?

Stepping out she shivered as gusts of wind drove the rain right into her face.

Dogs barking somewhere close made Kirsty pause as Lorimer

strode to the front door. But the pair of collies who came racing across the yard had tails wagging and tongues lolling out of their mouths. A sniff of her hand seemed to satisfy the pair and they stood quietly beside the tall policeman as he waited for the door to open.

'Bill, didn't know you were ...' The man standing in the doorway looked curiously at Kirsty.

'My colleague, DC Wilson.'

'Oh. Please come in.' Patrick Imrie stood aside and Kirsty noticed that he was wearing thick socks and no shoes. Probably keeps his wellington boots at the back door, she thought, as the farmer ushered them both inside.

'Fly! Mac! Go 'way, now!' he called to the dogs and Kirsty saw them slink back the way they'd come, no doubt to find shelter in kennels or a warm barn.

'Wild day,' Patrick said as he led them through a dark corridor and into a large kitchen with a range that gave off a welcome heat.

'Oh!' Kirsty dropped to her knees as she spotted the basket by the range, its contents several furry bodies curled up together. 'Kittens!'

'You want one?' Patrick laughed at the soppy expression on the detective constable's face.

'I'd love a kitten but we live in a flat,' she explained, getting to her feet. 'Are you looking for homes for them?'

'Only one's spoken for,' Patrick admitted, his big hands picking up a furry ginger bundle. This wee fella's going up the road to our neighbour.'

The other kittens, all mixtures of stripy greys, moved restlessly, disturbed by their brother's absence, and Kirsty grinned as she saw their blue eyes open sleepily. She'd take the whole basket, given half a chance, these wee things were so endearing.

'Cup of tea?' Patrick asked, and then she found herself sitting next to Lorimer at the huge scrubbed pine table that dominated the room. He looked a nice man, she decided, watching as he placed the ginger kitten in her lap with a wink. His dark hair had a natural wave and his eyes were crinkled at the corners as though Patrick Imrie was in the habit of smiling. The hands that had held the kitten were calloused and rough, testament to years of hard physical work.

'Annette's upstairs,' Patrick said, setting a huge kettle on the range. 'I'll just go and give her a shout. She wouldn't have heard your car coming.'

Left alone, Kirsty turned to Lorimer.

'Think he'll be like your cat Chancer when he grows up?' she asked, petting the kitten who was now settling down with a purr that reverberated through the room.

'Aye, maybe. Nice wee fellow,' Lorimer said, one hand stroking the long fur. 'Maggie used to tell me about coming here as a child. It was all the farm animals that she loved, especially the newborns.'

'I can see why they'd hate to have left this,' Kirsty whispered, her eyes roving around the kitchen. The pine dresser held a row of painted china plates on each shelf and a large jug of dried flowers; the window overlooking the yard was decorated with a string of felt hearts above a lace café curtain and a stack of magazines were piled up on an old rocking chair in the corner. It was the sort of kitchen she would have chosen for her own, Kirsty decided. Plus the kittens and the collies made it seem all the more homely.

'She's just coming,' Patrick said as he entered the room again, running a hand through his hair. Immediately Kirsty could see in the man's face that something was wrong. Twin spots of colour flushed his cheeks and the downward turn of his mouth made her wonder just what had been going on between husband and wife in the few minutes since Patrick Imrie had welcomed them into his home.

Then Lorimer was standing as Patrick's wife swept into the room.

If she had chosen an image of the farmer's wife, Kirsty would have been way off the mark, she decided as Annette Imrie was introduced to her. It was not just the well-groomed hair, the made-up face or the perfectly manicured nails. No, she simply didn't fit into this place, Kirsty thought, trying not to stare. What had she expected instead of this female with her green dress and high-heeled shoes? Someone more casually dressed, perhaps, in jeans and trainers, a flowery apron over her ample bosom? Someone, she thought suddenly, like her own mum.

'Sorry to have kept you.' Annette Imrie gave them both a brittle smile. 'I was just getting ready to go into Glasgow.' Kirsty nodded. That explained the outfit. Probably glad to be away from dungarees and wellies for a change, she decided.

'What brings you here? Were you in the area?' she asked, eyes flicking curiously between Lorimer and Kirsty.

Patrick Imrie turned away from the range where he had been pouring boiling water into a china teapot. 'Aye?' His own expression was, Kirsty thought, a tad more anxious than before.

'I think you should both sit down,' Lorimer told them quietly. 'And I think we're all going to need this tea.'

Kirsty watched as the woman sank on to a chair, fingers clasped together on the edge of the table, her husband sitting next to her.

'What's up, Bill?' he asked.

'I'm afraid it's bad news,' Lorimer began, reaching into the inside pocket of his jacket and drawing out a folded paper. 'The toxicology report from David's post-mortem shows an abnormally high amount of morphine,' he told them.

Annette Imrie's eyes never wavered, fixed on the police officers opposite and the paper in his hand, but Kirsty saw the red painted fingernails digging into the backs of her hands.

Patrick shook his head. 'Are they sure? David wasn't prescribed morphine. I mean . . . ' He turned to stare at his wife, a bewildered look on his face. 'David was never in any *pain*,' he protested. 'Are you sure they got that right? It doesn't make sense. I mean, *morphine* . . . ?'

'I'm really sorry,' Lorimer repeated. 'There's no doubting these results. And, what's more, we've got reason to believe an intruder entered your brother's room to administer that drug.'

'What?' The woman gave a cry and covered her mouth with both hands.

'Are you telling us that someone killed David?' Patrick whispered, leaning across the table, tears filling his eyes.

'That's exactly what I came to tell you both,' Lorimer said gently. 'And I'm afraid it may be quite upsetting. You see,' he broke off to gaze first at one then the other of the Imries, 'David isn't the only person whose death is being investigated. And I'm the senior investigating officer in charge of several cases.'

Kirsty slipped off her seat and walked around the kitchen, eyes on the mug tree by the sink. In minutes she had located the fridge and milk jug then she walked silently back, laying the tea on the table in front of the couple.

'Sugar?' she asked, knowing how good it was for shock, but both Patrick and Annette shook their heads, the former staring at Lorimer in disbelief.

'Who would want to kill my brother?' Patrick said at last, taking his mug of tea in both hands. 'David never hurt a soul in his life.

Who'd want to kill a defenceless man in his state . . . ' He broke off with a shuddering sob, biting his finger fiercely and shaking his head.

Annette placed one hand on top of her husband's. 'Bill will get to the bottom of this,' she said firmly. Then, turning to Lorimer. 'Won't you?'

She was dry-eyed, Kirsty saw, though if there was any emotion at all in Annette Imrie right now it was a quiet, suppressed rage, her scarlet lips narrowing in a thin, determined line.

The dogs were nowhere to be seen as they drove out of the farmyard but the two figures in the doorway stood still, watching as Lorimer and Kirsty left to journey back to the city.

'Annette?' Patrick tried to take his wife's hand but she shook him off.

'I need to get going, Pat. Late now because of them . . . ' She walked back inside, lifting her coat from the hall stand and a set of car keys from the shelf by the door.

'I thought you wouldn't want to go into town now . . . ' Patrick Imrie looked at her, his brow furrowed.

'Oh? And what difference does Bill Lorimer's visit make to that?' she snapped.

Patrick let his hands fall by his side as he watched his wife tiptoe across the puddles, open the door of the Land Rover and climb up into the driver's seat.

A roar and a plume of exhaust smoke, then she was gone, leaving the farmer standing there on his own under the weeping skies.

CHAPTER THIRTY-ONE

The man in the brown leather jacket stood smoking outside the station, sheltered from the rain that was hammering against the overhead canopy.

He glanced at his watch. The contact he'd been told to meet was late, the one who would give him that envelope full of cash. Who would it be this time? The wee rheumy-eyed down-and-out, shuffling towards him? Or the young mum striding up the sloping ramp, pushing a black buggy, a fractious toddler in tow? It was someone different every time. Had to be, Rob Dolan supposed. The main man needed to keep his identity a secret from them all. *Trust nobody*, his mate Jerry had told him when he'd been brought into the operation. *Sure as hell, nobody'll trust you!* he'd added, the scar on his face deepening in that lopsided grin.

And so now Dolan was waiting, a folded copy of the *Gazette* under his arm as arranged, hopping from one restless foot to another. Only the thought of scoring off his pal was keeping him warm. *A wee line on tick*, he'd cajoled. *Jist a wee line, eh?* But Sammy Morgan wasn't as daft as he looked. *Nae cash nae gear*, he'd been told.

Dolan looked at his watch again. Surely tae God someone

should be here by now? They'd done everything the chief had told them. Taken pains to put the frighteners on the Wilding lassie, picked up the mobile from the hospital. It was all done. And now he needed payment for taking such risks.

Pulling up his jacket collar, he flicked away the butt of his cigarette and trampled it underfoot.

'Here, that's litter!' a voice by his elbow called. 'You c'n get fined fur that, ken?'

The old woman nudged Dolan's arm, shoving a brown envelope into his folded newspaper in one quick move. Then, as swiftly as she had appeared, she was gone, walking across the road to George Square, just a shambling old woman in a thick winter coat, her shopping bag slung across her arm. Nobody would give her a second look.

As Dolan strode back into the station he slipped the envelope into his inside pocket and looked up at the board where arrivals and departures were lit up in yellow.

Jerry's train would be pulling in any time now and then he would be told the next part of their scheme. His mouth turned up in a little smile.

With a bit of luck it would involve the girl.

And this time he'd not be letting her go.

CHAPTER THIRTY-TWO

'Are you sure?' Kirsty asked the woman for a second time. 'Yes, I'm sure!'

Kirsty looked at the hospital security officer's face. Dismay was written all over it, the sort of dismay that washes colour away from the cheeks and makes eye contact all but impossible.

She was scared, the DC could see. But was it fear of the repercussions to follow the discovery that the CCTV tapes had mysteriously vanished? Or fear that the police were making inquiries about them?

'What about the ones from the other wards? And the main entrances? What about them?' Kirsty persisted.

They were sitting in a small room surrounded by monitors that showed different angles in different areas of this massive building.

'The report from last year giving details of thefts is pretty bad,' Kirsty continued. 'Is security always as rotten as this?'

The woman flashed her a look then dropped her eyes.

It's true, these drooping shoulders seemed to say.

Kirsty shook her head. Folk seemed to be able to wander into this enormous place and lift items from patients' lockers, unlocked offices, anywhere that was easy pickings. Money, of course, but clothes and even spectacles had been nicked from the wards. Thieves had no conscience, stealing from sick folk. But then there had been TVs stolen too and several vehicles that had never been found. And now this.

'I need to see all the tapes from the past month,' Kirsty told her, watching the woman's eyes widen in disbelief.

'That'll take you for ever,' she exclaimed.

'Aye, well there's a whole lot more of us back at Stewart Street just waiting to see them,' Kirsty told her gloomily.

'The CCTV cameras were all in working order,' Kirsty reported back to the rest of the team. 'But the recordings on the ones in Nurse Milligan's ward had vanished into thin air.'

'Someone knew we'd be looking out for them,' DC Jean Fairlie remarked darkly. 'They're no' stupid.'

'So, what have we got?' Lorimer asked. 'A visual description of the bogus doctor from Mary Milligan and a month's worth of tapes.'

'She'd be able to recognise him,' Kirsty piped up. 'Why don't we get her to look at the ones from the entrances? He had to go in and out one way or another.'

'Worth a try,' DC Fairlie agreed.

Kirsty shot her a smile. The older woman, twice married to police officers, and twice divorced, was an old hand when it came to sizing up a situation. She and the new DC's father had worked together on numerous occasions and Jean Fairlie had been one of the first to welcome Kirsty into Stewart Street police station.

Len Murdoch opened the wardrobe with a sigh. Black suit, black tie, well-polished shoes ... it was part of a ritual that he'd been dreading.

But the boys were here now, all the arrangements made and today he would have to keep a check on each and every one of the emotions that were churning inside. He rubbed a hand over his stubbled chin. Better not put in a new blade. Wouldn't do to arrive at the funeral with cuts all over his face.

Who would turn up? Lorimer, probably, to represent the team at Stewart Street. DI Grant was still busy with the Byres Road case and the jeweller's heist was now a joint inquiry between Police Scotland and Nottingham Constabulary.

For a moment he wondered how Wilson's wee lassie was faring. She'd been good so far, he had to admit. Kept quiet when she should, did what she was told and got on with the job. Could make a decent detective if she had a nose for it like her father. Chip off the old block? Perhaps.

Murdoch was glad that neither of his own boys had followed in his footsteps. Jack was in something related to IT, exactly what he could never quite fathom, whilst Niall was working his way up in banking. They'd be waiting for him downstairs, Len realised, pulling the tie off its rack and throwing it on to the bed. Well, let them wait. Hadn't he waited till they could get flights over here? Days and days of going over Irene's final hours. Dear God! Had either of them any notion what life had been like these past few years?

There was a cold wind blowing from the east as the funeral party emerged from the church and made its way across the rabbit-nibbled grass to the burial ground. Black-clad figures, some bowed against the weight of their years, all walked slowly behind the coffin and the men who bore it.

Lorimer kept a respectful distance behind the family members, glancing as a couple passed him by, their gloved hands linked together, the woman's hair covered in a black scarf, the man's coat collar turned up against the freshening breeze. There were a few other officers he recognised from Murdoch's previous postings, a retired DCI from Kilmarnock and a couple of younger officers from Cumbernauld. Earlier they had given Lorimer a nod in passing and now each man gravitated towards the other until all four were in a small group of their own.

'Sad business,' Arnold Coates remarked as they stopped to watch Irene Murdoch's interment. 'He never let it interfere with his work, though. Have to give him that much credit.'

Lorimer threw him an enquiring look but it was DS Alan Littlejohn who answered his unspoken question.

'Och, you can't help but feel sorry for him, but still ... poor light-fingered Lennie,' Littlejohn whispered in a soft tone, but still loud enough for Lorimer to hear him. Had that been intended? Or had Littlejohn's words simply drifted across on that gust of autumn wind?

'Shh!' Donald Rutherford frowned at his colleague.

Lorimer glanced at them but neither man returned his stare. Why had Donald Rutherford shushed his friend? Was it to shut him up because he was saying too much? Or because the priest had now stepped forward closer to the open grave? All four men fell silent as the coffin bearers stopped, ready to receive the undertaker's commands.

Once all the cords were taken and the coffin lowered into the ground, there was a moment of prayer from the priest then the solemn invocation as he threw a handful of soil, the sound of it hitting the solid-oak casket like a scatter of hail.

What were they, after all? Dust? Lorimer looked up at the clouds moving swiftly across the grey rain-laden skies. Just a little while here, fighting against the forces of evil, then that long sleep.

249

What was the mystery of death? Where would all his energy go once that final breath had been taken? This white-haired priest seemed so certain that there was something after this life, didn't he? And yet, it was only at times like this that Lorimer wondered if that were possible.

It was to show his respect. To offer his condolences, Lorimer argued with himself as he parked the Lexus at the back of the pub where the purvey was to be held. Besides, it had been simply a matter of courtesy to offer a lift to Arnold Coates. *Came by taxi*, the older man had told him with a grin and Lorimer had taken the hint. He'd noticed Littlejohn and Rutherford getting into the same car and suspected that they too were heading this way.

'Ah, old bones getting stiff these days,' Coates grumbled as he stepped out. 'Nice model,' he remarked, eyeing the big silver car. 'Especially these heated seats.' He chuckled. 'You've done well, Lorimer.'

Lorimer smiled thinly but did not reply. Sometimes suspicious looks were thrown at his luxury car, comments made about how much it cost and how nice it must be to have that sort of money; jealous barbs that held unspoken questions about how a mere policeman could afford a Lexus 450. *No kids*, was his stock answer to any ingenuous enough to ask. Plus he always bought a second-hand model.

But Arnold Coates seemed to have read his mind as he continued. 'Some folk must wonder how you do it,' he said. 'No substitute for a family, though, is it?'

Lorimer simply nodded as they entered the pub and headed for the function suite where a couple of waiters stood with trays of drinks.

'Need to find a table. Can't stand for too long these days,' Coates grumbled, leading Lorimer to the back of the room.

'Here, let me take your coat,' Lorimer offered and then watched as the older man slowly fumbled with the buttons, his arthritic joints making every movement painful.

He folded their coats and pushed them on to a shelf behind the corner table then sat beside the former DCI.

'Shouldn't speak ill of the man on a day like this,' Coats began, leaning towards Lorimer. 'But there are certain things that you ought to know about Lennie Murdoch.'

Lorimer's brow furrowed. 'What did Littlejohn mean? About light-fingered Lennie?'

'Aye.' Coates picked up his whisky glass, took a mouthful then set the drink down again thoughtfully. 'Not good to spread rumours. *Unfounded* rumours, mind.' He gave Lorimer a sharp look. 'See,' he leaned closer and Lorimer could smell the whisky off the old man's breath, 'Lennie always seemed to be around whenever there was something missing.'

'You mean a piece of evidence?'

'God, no! That would have been instant dismissal. No, Len Murdoch was cleverer than that. Chose his moments well, I reckon. Helped when he became a scene of crime manager, of course.'

'Go on.'

'Well, rumour had it that there were money problems at home.' Coates shrugged. 'Nobody quite knew why but some said it was because of the wife's condition. Maybe she needed expensive care? Who knows. Anyway, most of us turned a blind eye.' He chuckled. 'No, that's not strictly true. Some of us had our suspicions. But there was never any way we could have proved what he was up to.'

'And what was that?'

Coates raised his bushy eyebrows in surprise. 'You mean you've never heard . . . ?'

A shake of the head was Lorimer's only reply. He could see that the ex-cop was enjoying spinning out this tale, letting the detective super wait until he came to the nub of it all.

The two men sat back for a moment as a stout young waitress laid plates of sandwiches and cakes on their table.

'It was thought, only *thought*, mind you,' Coates wagged a finger at him when the girl was out of earshot, 'that our Lennie lifted the odd item from scenes of crime.'

'How did anybody think that?'

Coates raised the whisky again and sipped it, his eyes on the glass, avoiding his companion's gaze.

'He'd suddenly be flush,' the old man said at last. 'Make it his round down the pub. Claimed to have got lucky with the gee-gees.' Coates gave a snort. 'No one gets *that* lucky! Besides,' he held up a hand and whispered behind it, 'always happened a week or so after some expensive item couldn't be accounted for. Mostly in a jewellery raid, you know?'

Lorimer blinked suddenly as though he had been struck. Murdoch had recently been at a scene of crime where a raid had taken place. And his neighbour on that occasion had been none other than Detective Constable Kirsty Wilson.

'Here, better go and say our piece,' Coates said, rising to his feet. Lorimer followed his glance as the bullet-headed detective sergeant came across the room towards them both. Words would have to be spoken; trite phrases of condolence that Murdoch must be hearing over and over. For a moment Lorimer truly wished that he had gone back to Stewart Street instead of coming here.

He shook Murdoch's hand and stepped back as other men in

black coats slipped to the detective sergeant's side, murmuring their condolences. More stock phrases, Lorimer thought as the men moved away and another stranger came towards Murdoch, his coat collar up around his ears.

'So sorry for your loss,' he heard the man say. 'But you must be glad that she had a quiet release.'

Lorimer gave a start. *Quiet release.* Wasn't that the name of this illegal organisation? He'd been about to sit back down with the old DCI but now he quickened his step, struggling to move through the crowd, apologising as he knocked into some of the mourners, desperate to catch a glimpse of the dark coat and dark hair above that turned-up collar. Was that the man he had seen earlier at the cemetery, holding hands with his wife, or whoever his female companion had been?

Where was he? The door from the room was closed. Had the stranger disappeared back into the throng?

He looked over the crowded room but the man was gone.

Lorimer shoved at the door and sped along the corridor, his policeman's sixth sense urging him on.

Out in the car park several people were leaving yet, although his eyes searched all around, there was no trace of the man who had uttered those words to the bereaved detective sergeant. Heart thumping, Lorimer clenched his fists, as he watched the cars leaving, no sign of the stranger in any of them.

If only he had been quicker! He cursed softly under his breath, some inner voice telling him that he had been close to seeing the man behind these murders.

Quietly, the tall detective retraced his steps. Courtesy dictated that he should make a proper leave-taking of his detective sergeant and besides, he wanted to ask if anybody knew the couple who had attended the burial.

He picked up his coat, glad to note that Littlejohn and Ruther-ford had joined the older man at his table.

'Saw a couple at the cemetery. Woman and a man with a dark coat, collar turned up. Any relation to Murdoch?' Lorimer asked diffidently, bending down to direct his question at Coates.

The older man shook his head. 'Nobody I know,' he shrugged. 'And I think I know most of the folk in this room.'

'Well, must be off, take care.' Lorimer nodded, eager now to make his escape. Perhaps he'd been wrong about the man offer-ing Murdoch his condolences. Maybe it had been a neighbour, someone that the police fraternity wouldn't recognise. Maybe these words spoken to Murdoch had been sheer coincidence? And yet, at the back of his mind, there lay the knowledge that some-times a killer took the risk of appearing at his victim's funeral. And the disquiet he felt made him look up at the car park, eyes searching for any CCTV cameras, something that might have captured that man and his wife leaving the pub. But to his dismay, there were none.

Soon the detective superintendent was driving back to work. There was a pile of paperwork on his desk waiting for his atten-tion and a meeting with the head of Professional Standards. One of their rookie cops had taken it into his head to try to restrain a prisoner in the cells with the consequences that the bloke had cried assault and now the young man's superiors were having to deal with the question of whether PC Jackie Cunningham had taken his boot to the man's ribs.

Lorimer's opinion was that the police constable had done just that in a moment of hot-headed zeal, a moment he now bitterly regretted as he awaited his fate. Lorimer sighed heavily. One stupid mistake and a young man's future as a police officer might be cancelled out. But, if Cunningham were to be let off lightly, would that give out the message that kicking the shit out of prisoners was somehow acceptable? Probably, which was why the guy's suspension would no doubt lead to dismissal after his tribunal.

Lorimer bit his lip. What was he going to do about Kirsty? If the girl had any clue at all about Len Murdoch's habit of filching stuff from a scene of crime then it was her bounden duty to report him. And, if she failed to do that, *she* was the one who would find herself in real trouble. There was only one way to find out, he thought grimly, and that was to ask her.

He must always be seen as impartial no matter how kindly he felt towards his detective inspector's daughter. Kirsty was going to be a good cop. He could sense that. She had already shown how adept she was at picking up on people's emotions. That was always going to stand her in good stead; sensing when a person was telling the truth was something that came with experience though. And he wondered what she would say if he confronted her with the rumours he had heard after Irene Murdoch's funeral.

Kirsty read the email again.

Need to ask you some sensitive questions regarding Paton's jewellery raid.

He knew. Somehow the man she respected almost more than anyone else in her life had found out the secret that had been tormenting her for weeks now.

Lorimer had been to the funeral. That was fact number one, Kirsty thought frantically. Had he spoken to Murdoch? Of course he had. But surely they would not be talking shop? No way, not on the day of a funeral. So what had happened to give rise to this email that chilled her blood?

She glanced upwards at the ceiling. Professional Standards were in today to see Lorimer about that incident in the cells. It had taken place before her arrival at Stewart Street and so it was only through the rumour mill that Kirsty had heard what had happened. Was it something to do with Chief Superintendent Miller coming to speak to Lorimer?

What about the fact that the jewellery case was now in other hands? Kirsty had no idea how it was progressing now that the Nottingham Police were involved. Did they somehow suspect that something was wrong with the inventory of stolen items?

And, if she were honest, could she be sure that she had seen the man who had buried his wife today taking a hugely expensive watch and putting it into his scene of crime bag?

The day dragged on into dusk and still he had not called her.

Kirsty stood up and yawned, stretching as she felt the strain across her shoulders from sitting too long over her laptop. The CCTV images had been copied and sent to several of the officers and so far they had not identified the mysterious doctor who had left Mary Milligan's ward. She'd need to bring in the ginger-haired nurse, Kirsty decided. But not tonight. She rubbed her eyes. Enough was enough. It was time to pack it in for today and go home where James would be waiting for her.

The thought of her boyfriend made her smile brightly.

And then the telephone rang.

'Can you come up for a few minutes, DC Wilson?'

'Yes, sir,' she replied. 'On my way now.'

Kirsty's throat was tight with nerves as she climbed the stairs to Lorimer's office. Would she open the door to be confronted by Chief Superintendent Miller, a woman whose reputation as a no-nonsense type made the young DC tremble? Valerie Miller was in line for one of the top jobs, she had heard. And she wasn't one to suffer fools gladly, least of all a wet-behind-the ears detective constable.

But, when she knocked on his door and heard him call *come in*, Kirsty was relieved to find Lorimer on his own, standing looking out of the window.

'Sir, you wanted to see me?' She moved forward but Lorimer continued to look out of the window as if he was studying something interesting down in the streets below.

'Went to Irene Murdoch's funeral,' he said, still not turning to look at her. 'Heard some rather unpleasant things about DS Murdoch.'

There was a silence then Kirsty saw the tall man draw a hand across his brow.

'You wouldn't know anything about that, would you, DC Wilson?'

Lorimer's voice was quiet, the tone neutral.

She'd heard that voice before. The matter-of-fact way he spoke when the subject was actually of grave importance. Like now.

Kirsty knew what he was asking. *Did you have any reason to suspect that DS Murdoch was a thief?* Except these words were never spoken.

Kirsty's heart thumped.

He was giving her a chance. Looking out of the window, refusing to meet her eyes, not wishing to read the expression on her face lest she gave herself away.

'No, sir,' she lied, hating herself for her deceit but suddenly knowing that this was the answer that Lorimer wanted from her.

'Good.'

There was another silence then she saw him clasp his hands behind his head as though considering something. Was he going to turn around? Confront her? See the guilt shining in her eyes? But then he spoke once more.

'That's all. Goodnight, DC Wilson.'

'Goodnight, sir,' she replied, choking back the desire to utter *thank you*, realising as she fled the room that not one question had been asked about the jewellery heist.

Lorimer blew out his breath as he turned away from the window to see the door closing. Did he believe her? Probably not. What decent human being would put a fellow officer in the mire on the very day of his wife's funeral? Certainly not a kind-hearted girl like Kirsty. But the meeting had been a small warning to her, he thought. And maybe one day he would be able to speak to her about the suspicions that were already in his mind.

CHAPTER THIRTY-THREE

Professor Solomon Brightman was accustomed to being called to assist in cases where there might be patterns to follow, cases of multiple murder. He had read everything about the notorious Dr Harold Shipman, had even lectured upon the subject and made references to the man in his own writings, but until now Solly had never expected to be professionally involved in a case like that.

Rosie had told him about the old lady and Maggie Lorimer's late cousin, of course, plus the tragic deaths of the two sisters. It was a puzzle and Solomon Brightman enjoyed the challenge of solving such things. *The who and the why*, he often told his students, adding that the *how* was usually fairly obvious. *Motive, means and opportunity* was the police mantra and that was something that exercised the psychologist's mind at this very moment as he travelled from the University of Glasgow to meet his old friend Lorimer.

Never having had the desire to drive was an advantage, Solly often mused as he looked out of the taxi window. There was the KRK store by the roundabout, not far from where Kirsty lived with her Geordie boyfriend, James. The pair had often come to

259

babysit for Rosie and Solly, the young couple taking the short walk across Kelvingrove Park to the Brightmans' terraced home with its splendid view to the west. Now he smiled at the sight of Lobey Dosser, the cartoon character astride his two-legged steed, El Fidelo, immortalised in bronze. The cartoonist had enjoyed a cult following with his cartoon strips of Glasgow cowboys. And Glaswegians held the memory of those with a special fondness. What had Lobey Dosser's opponent been called? Solly tried to think as they passed the shops and pubs in Woodlands Road. Rank Bajin! That was it! The play on a Glasgow worthy's comment: *he's a rank bad yin!*

Solly's grin faded as they travelled through St George's Cross and headed further into the city. Somewhere some rank bad person was taking the lives of vulnerable, innocent men and women and he wanted to know why.

'It has to be about money,' Solly said, spreading his hands in an expressive gesture.

'How do you work that out?' Lorimer asked.

They were sitting on easy chairs by the window in the detective superintendent's office, a couple of cups and saucers lying on the side table between them.

Before he could answer, there was a knock on the door that made each man look out and a rattle as Sadie Dunlop pushed her trolley into the room.

'Here, look who it is!' she exclaimed, leaving the trolley and coming across to give the bearded psychologist a peck on the cheek.

'He got you in tae solve a mystery, eh?' Sadie nudged the man and grinned across at the detective superintendent who merely smiled and shook his head. Sadie was incorrigible, a wee Glasgow wifey who stood on no ceremony, treating every person in the division exactly the same. Only the current chief constable had ever made Sadie speak to him with the deference due to the man's position, it was rumoured.

'See whit ah've goat the morn,' she told them, one hand waving over the baked goods that adorned the two tiers of her trolley. 'Fresh scones an' pancakes, lemon drizzle cake, fruit gingerbread an' a selection of cream buns. All the éclairs are finished,' she added with a triumphant toss of her grey curls.

'Oh, a couple of scones, please.' Solly beamed at the little woman.

'Any Danish pastries?' Lorimer murmured, getting to his feet and peering at the trolley.

'Ha! Think Sadie's forgot your pastries?' She laughed, bending down and lifting a greaseproof paper from the lower tier to reveal a paper plate with one large pastry on it. 'Saved it jist fur you,' she added, handing it to Lorimer with a smile.

'Spoil him, so ah do,' she told Solly. 'Anywise, better be getting on. See an' help our man here get tae the bottom of whatever it is, eh?' she added shrewdly, giving both men a cheery wave as she rattled out of the room.

'So Sadie's back?' Solly remarked as he picked up his buttered scone.

'Aye. Don't seem to be able to pension her off at all,' Lorimer replied with a mock sigh.

'Hard to think of her not being around, though,' Solly remarked. 'Must be a good age now?'

'In her seventies, I'd guess,' Lorimer replied. 'Could tell you if I looked up her file.'

'No need. I was just wondering ...' Solly broke off as he chewed the scone thoughtfully.

Lorimer watched his dark eyes behind their horn-rimmed spectacles. There would be a lengthy pause as the psychologist considered his next statement.

'Old people. What they do with their lives, how they cope with retirement . . . ' He shrugged. 'Tell me something about Miss Jane Maitland.'

'Well,' Lorimer began, lifting up the Danish pastry and eyeing it with relish. 'You know she was worth a small fortune?'

'I told you it would be about money,' Solly murmured. 'Go on.'

'She was a single lady who seemed to have lived a quiet, blameless life. However,' he paused to take a sip of coffee, 'not everything was exactly as it seemed to be in Jane Maitland's past.'

'Is it ever?' Solly gave a rueful smile.

'Hm. She had accumulated a great deal of money. Mostly from stocks and bonds. Must have had a good head on her shoulders as she didn't have any financial adviser to guide her. Did it all herself.'

'Some people love playing the stock market.'

'Indeed. Though I doubt that many make such vast sums as this lady appears to have done. She was worth over a million.'

'Gracious!' The psychologist's bushy eyebrows shot up. 'And she lived in a humble little cottage flat.'

'With no pretensions or little luxury that was evident from what we could see.' Lorimer shrugged. 'Anyway, it turns out she has a son. Born on the wrong side of the blanket, so to speak. Not a soul up here knew her secret apart from her lawyer and the parish priest.'

'You've met him? The son, I mean.'

Lorimer nodded. 'Name's Crawford Whyte. Was adopted as an

infant and claims that he only found out about his birth mother after her death.'

Solly smiled at his friend. 'But you don't believe him, do you?'

Lorimer gave a short laugh. 'No. I don't. There's more to Mr Whyte than meets the eye. And I'll tell you something else.' He leaned forward, pointing his index finger. 'I have the feeling that the lawyer had dealings with Whyte before that visit to Glasgow when we met him.'

'Oh?'

'Och, there's nothing concrete, nothing to go on, just a feeling . . .' Lorimer sighed.

Solomon Brightman smiled silently to himself. If Detective Superintendent Lorimer had a strong feeling about a particular person then it was odds on that he was going to be under his scrutiny until something positive emerged.

'Right,' Solly said at last. 'Let's see what I can do to help.'

It all made for interesting reading, the psychologist thought some hours later as he sat in his spacious office back at the University of Glasgow. The afternoon light shone through the bay window, coloured patterns from the stained glass shining upon the tall bank of books that surrounded the professor.

There had to be more deaths. Nobody was going to go to the trouble of setting up a campaign to assist the dying and simply select a few willing persons. Money. That was what would be at the root of it, Solly had already decided. There were several motives that made a person take the life of his fellow man; jealousy, desire for power, revenge or the lust for money. And it had to be a motive that had been well thought out, well planned in advance, ergo an act that carried *intention*.

263

'Let's see how you would begin,' he murmured aloud, as though addressing the perpetrator.

Anybody watching the bearded man sitting in his comfortable chair by the window might be forgiven for assuming that he was simply daydreaming, one hand stroking his chin, a faraway look in those dark eyes. Yet they would have been quite wrong, for the train of thought in the professor's mind was absolutely logical as he sought an answer to his preliminary question.

Mary arrived at the door and hesitated. On the glass were engraved words of welcome in several different languages, reflecting the diversity that belonged to Glasgow these days. It was the same in the hospital, she thought, pushing the heavy doors open and entering Stewart Street police station. So many different people from so many different places; it was hard to keep track of all these ethnic groups at times. But she had nodded at reading *failte*, a Gaelic word that she did recognise.

'Hello?' Mary leaned against the glass partition at reception and smiled tentatively at the uniformed officer who turned to see who had arrived.

'Afternoon, miss,' the man said. 'What can we do for you?'

'Oh, I'm Mary Milligan and I'm here to see Detective Constable Wilson?' Mary's voice rose in a moment of pride.

But the man seemed not to care in the slightest who she was as he shuffled some papers on a side counter then came back to her.

'If you would let me see some identity, Miss Milligan, then we'll fix you up with a badge.'

Mary rummaged in her handbag and produced her passport as DC Wilson had advised. It was the matter of moments to sign in a large register and take the proffered ID badge. Then she was being ushered through another door, the big policeman chatting idly about the weather as they walked along a corridor and up a flight of stairs.

'I'm here to try to identify somebody,' she confided breathlessly as they reached the end of yet another corridor.

'Oh, aye?' The policeman did not seem to be in the least interested and simply pushed open a door and signalled that she should enter before him. Mary frowned, annoyed at his apparent indifference.

'A Miss Milligan to see DC Wilson,' he announced.

Then Kirsty was there, walking towards her and leading Mary through this large room to one end where several people were seated over computer screens.

'Thanks so much for coming in. We've been going through all of the hospital CCTV tapes that we could,' Kirsty explained. 'Now it's your turn.'

'Oh.' Mary looked up at the detective, grateful that at last she was being treated as a special visitor, someone of importance 'Where shall I sit?'

'Just here. That's my desk at the moment,' Kirsty replied with a tired smile. 'D'you fancy a cup of something? I saved a couple of cakes from the wee lady who comes round every day with her trolley.'

'Aye, go on, then,' Mary answered. 'Sounds just like the hospital. We have porters who come around with stuff all the time. A coffee would be grand. Milk and two sugars, please.'

No wonder the young detective had looked tired, Mary thought some time later, rubbing her eyes. It was hard work peering at that screen, trying to make out each figure as it left the main door of her building. The place was a rabbit warren, she'd always told folk that when they'd fetched up lost in her department. You could come in one way and wander the corridors for hours before leaving from a completely different exit. She'd told the detective girl as much, receiving a worried look for her pains. And now she was staring at this damned screen, aware that they were all hoping she'd recognise the good-looking man who had beguiled her that day.

He probably won't just be wearing a short-sleeved shirt if he's leaving the main entrance, Kirsty had told her. And so they would guess that it was doubly hard to see if the man was *her* man, her mystery doctor.

In the end it was a moment of common courtesy that ended her search. The figure in the tweed coat hesitated at the top step and lifted a hand to allow an elderly lady to pass down the steps before him, turning slightly to one side so that Mary saw his handsome profile. She liked the look of this one all right.

'That's him!'

In a trice Kirsty was beside her. 'Let's see again,' the detective said, the excitement in her voice making Mary feel a sense of triumph.

Over and over the detective replayed the same part of the tape, freezing the screen to show the man in profile.

Mary and Kirsty grinned at one another. 'Ya wee dancer!' the detective exclaimed, punching the air with her fist. 'Thanks, Mary. Thanks ever so much.'

'Will he be someone your lot know about already?' Mary asked.

Kirsty leaned down until her face was closer to the ginger-haired nurse's. 'Can't say anything about an operation while it's ongoing, I'm afraid. But I will tell you this much. If we find this man and he's charged with an offence then you'll maybe be asked to give evidence in court.'

'Really?' Mary perked up. 'Like on one of these TV dramas?'

she asked breathlessly.

Kirsty gave a wry grin. 'Depends on which ones you watch,' she replied.

'He's not on any police database,' Jean Fairlie sighed, glancing across at Kirsty. 'Either it's his first time or he's a clever bugger.'

'Oh, well, at least we've got an ID to show the other members of the hospital staff.' Kirsty made a face. 'That's got to be a help.'

'Aye and bloody time consuming an' all,' Jean complained.

'But if this fellow's going around putting sick people to sleep . . . ' Kirsty protested.

'Och, maybe he'd doing them a favour,' Jean grumbled. 'I mean to say, you wouldn't hesitate to take your dog to the vet when it's in pain, would you?'

'Don't have a dog,' Kirsty mumbled crossly.

'You know what I mean,' Jean persisted.

'But you heard what Lorimer told us,' Kirsty went on. 'These people are being targeted by a killer. It's not something they've asked for.'

'How do you know?' Jean said, folding her arms across her chest. 'Maybe they'd asked their loved ones to find a way to end it all. I know *I* would if it came to the bit.'

'But what if they're simply being bumped off for the convenience of a relative. Like with these poor sisters. It wasn't Rachel who killed Julie. It was someone else. The DNA proves that.'

'Well, maybe she could only afford to pay for her sister to be humanely put to sleep,' Jean argued.

'And topped herself with remorse?' Kirsty looked askance.

'No.' Jean narrowed her eyes. 'Topped herself because she knew she was going to end up the same way and there was nobody to help *her* when the time came.'

'Either way we're looking for someone who's running an illegal organisation,' Kirsty fumed. 'It might be a moral choice to end your own life but it's something completely different if someone makes that choice for you. And against your will!'

The two women looked at one another for a long moment then Jean Fairlie gave a shrug and turned back to her computer.

'Okay, wee yin, you win,' she said at last. 'Better get ready for his nibs handing out the next actions. And I can guarantee that mine will be trailing around that bloody great hospital with a photo in my hand.'

CHAPTER THIRTY-FOUR

'She's on night shift,' the man said, huddling against the hedge outside Abbey Nursing Home, phone pressed to his cheek. He peered at his watch. It was half past midnight and the moon was showing a ghostly face behind shreds of racing clouds. 'Left the big house an hour ago and arrived here just before twelve.'

'Call her on the mobile,' came the reply. 'Tell her that she needs to come out and talk to you. Or you'll be speaking to that boss of hers, the Abbott woman.'

'Sure.' The man grinned as he looked towards the building, its porch light bright against the darkness all around. Somewhere in there Sarah Wilding was attending to her patients. 'And then?'

There was a pause.

'Then she'll find out just how serious we are, won't she?'

When she felt the vibration of the mobile, Sarah gave a little jump of surprise. She had already checked on all of her charges, who were sleeping soundly, and was in the process of preparing a list of things that the nurses on day shift would need to do; the fact that the mobile phone was in her uniform pocket was something she'd entirely forgotten.

269

'Hello.' Her voice wavered.

'You know who this is,' a man's voice snarled in her ear. 'I'm right outside this place, just along from the gates, got it? Be there in five.'

'No,' Sarah whispered. 'I don't want anything more to do with you people.'

A soft laugh sounded as she prepared to hang up and switch off the mobile. 'No? Oh, Sarah, you're going to do exactly what we tell you, doll. Or do you want that nice Mrs Abbott to know what you've been up to recently? Fancy going back inside, is that what you want? Be here in five minutes, got it?'

There was a lengthy silence as Sarah's thoughts whirled. She needed time to think, needed to let someone know what was happening.

'That's impossible,' she replied hoarsely. 'I'm in the middle of something right now.'

She cut off the voice of her tormentor. She needed to let Nancy know what was happening, she'd promised … but not on this phone, just in case …? Panic made her head pound as she looked at the phone in her hand. Could they trace her calls? It wasn't a chance that she was prepared to take but she had to make this phone call.

Heart beating fast, she sped along the corridor towards Nancy's office. She could use the landline there, couldn't she?

But when she tried the door it was locked.

Damn! Of course, since the break-in none of the staff was taking any chances. She stood for a moment, thinking hard then crept quietly along to the staffroom.

Several coats were hanging on the coat stand behind the door, Grainne's hooded mackintosh to the front. Didn't she keep her mobile in that outside pocket?

With trembling hands, Sarah unzipped the pocket and felt inside. Yes! She breathed out. Thank goodness it wasn't one of these smart phones but an ancient thing that the nurse kept just for making calls.

Sarah dialled the number and waited. Nancy would be in bed at this hour and although she hated herself for disturbing the good woman, she prayed that she would get up and answer the landline at Corrielinn.

'Hello?' a sleepy voice asked.

'Nancy. It's me. Sarah. They're back and I have to go outside to see them.' Sarah shivered as she spoke, her eyes on the window of the room. Was anybody out there, watching her through those thin curtains?

'Sarah! You mustn't! Don't go near these people. I mean it!' Nancy's tone was adamant.

'I have to,' Sarah cried. 'Or they'll tell your sister what I've done and I'll be sent back to Cornton Vale.'

'No!' Nancy almost shouted. 'Don't go out. Listen. Detective Superintendent Lorimer wouldn't want you to put yourself in any danger. Now here's what we're going to do.'

'Didn't show.' The man slouched downhill towards the main road where the car was waiting. 'What now?'

'Call her again. Be there when she does come out,' an authoritative voice replied. 'And then you take her for another little drive.'

Lorimer groaned as he sat up, hand already outstretched to pick up his phone.

The digital clock by his bedside read five minutes to one.

'Lorimer.'

'Detective Superintendent, it's Nancy Livingstone here. We need your help.'

The dawn was still some hours away as Lorimer drove across the city, its lights twinkling against a black velvet sky tinged with that familiar sodium glow. Night in the city. Time when the bad folk came out to wreak havoc on innocent citizens, time when he and his own kind had to be vigilant in tackling the different sorts of crime that tainted his beloved Glasgow. Blue and purple arcs of light shimmered on the waters as he crossed the Clyde and headed towards Stewart Street. A call was not enough. He had to see some of the night shift face to face, explain a little of the situation. Hopefully it was a quiet night for the officers there and he would have the necessary back-up when the time came.

Lorimer sped across the bridge, wondering whether Sarah Wilding had the guts to carry out their plan.

When the mobile vibrated once again Sarah let it ring a few times before picking up.

'We've got an emergency here,' she said, trying to inject as much strength into her voice as she could. 'You'll have to wait until the doctor's been. I can't come out till then.' Her hands shook as she waited for a reply. Had she sounded scared? Probably. Her knees were beginning to tremble and she wanted to sit down and weep.

'When will that be?' The response was gruff and curt.

'I don't know,' Sarah replied. 'We've been told he's on his way. That's all I know. Look, I must go.' Then she pressed the off button and sank into a chair by the radiator, pressing her hands on to its surface to ease the sudden chill to her blood.

The tall policeman would come straight into the car park and she would be waiting to let him in. What would the other nurses say? How would she explain the presence of a senior police officer in the middle of the night?

'Sarah? Are you okay?' Grainne stood in the doorway of the staffroom, a quizzical look on her face.

Sarah shook her head. 'There's a problem, Grainne,' she began. 'Mr Imrie's death is being investigated by the police. They think he's been murdered,' she began slowly, watching the other nurse's eyes widen.

'So that's why all these forensic folk were here. We wondered. Are you telling me that you know something about this?'

'It's a long story,' Sarah continued. 'But the nursing home has been a target of some sort and there's a policeman coming here right now.'

'I don't understand.' Grainne came to sit beside her colleague, one hand resting on the back of Sarah's chair. 'Why has that made you look as if you've seen a ghost?'

Sarah looked down at her hands and shook her head. 'I can't say,' she murmured. 'I've just been told to follow instructions,' she added, knowing that what she was telling Grainne was true though so much was being left unsaid.

The two men sat in the front of the black BMW, its engine running to keep them warm. From the open driver's window came a thin line of smoke, the hand holding the cigarette resting on the glass. It had been more than an hour since Jerry had first called the nurse but their instructions were clear. Stay put and pick her up.

He exhaled the last of the smoke and flicked the butt away, watching its molten tip describe an arc in the darkness until it hit the ground to join several others lying on the grassy verge.

'Car comin',' his companion said suddenly and both men stared into the dark road as twin headlights appeared, cresting the hill and revealing a large silver car.

'Must be that doctor,' Dolan hissed, turning the knife in his hands, making its silver blade catch the moonlight.

'Shut it,' Jerry replied, pressing the button to close his window. Dolan had been annoying him all night, his constant foot-tapping and humming under his breath, signs that the man was wired to the bloody full moon. Maybe what they said was true. The man by his side was behaving more erratically than usual.

Jerry Cunningham gripped the steering wheel, his bare knuckles whitening. If Dolan screwed up he'd be the first to give him a proper doing. But Dolan would scare the shit out of the Wilding lassie even more when she saw him in a state like this, Jerry thought with a sudden grin. And the blade that Rob Dolan carried would be sufficient to persuade the girl to do exactly as they told her.

Sarah shivered as she pulled on her coat. Grainne had asked questions of the tall police officer who had given the impression that Sarah was somehow helping the police. Grainne hadn't asked in so many words but she could see the other nurse wondering if Nurse Wilding was in fact an undercover police officer. Fat chance, Sarah thought. How did they do it? she asked herself as she slipped out of the staffroom. Impersonating criminal types, infiltrating dangerous groups of people? It was something she could never imagine herself doing and yet here she was, putting herself in a situation that required as much courage as she had ever mustered in her young life.

Sarah wrapped her fingers around the object in her raincoat

274

pocket that Lorimer had given her. *Use it if you need to*, he'd told her, and she'd nodded, glad to have something tangible to hold on to.

She watched as the detective left the main door and closed it behind him. Now she really was on her own, Sarah thought. And taking a deep breath, she followed him out into the night.

The Lexus was already driving away when Sarah stepped into the road that led down to where the men were waiting and she felt a spasm of fear course throughout her body.

She was quite alone now.

Glancing up, she saw the full moon, its unblinking face beaming out of the darkness. Step by step she walked along the path until she came to the corner and caught sight of the car tucked at an angle beside the hedge.

Wait until they come to you, Lorimer had instructed her. *Don't get into their car, whatever you do.*

'Took you long enough.' A familiar voice spoke out of the dark followed by the sound of a car door closing.

'We had an emergency,' Sarah said, shielding her eyes from the sudden glare of the car's full beam.

'Get in the car,' Cunningham ordered.

But Sarah stood motionless, fear and Lorimer's strict words pinning her to the spot.

'D'ye hear the man, hen?' The figure of a smaller man loomed out of the darkness and lunged at her, the blade of the knife bright in his raised fist.

Sarah plunged her hand into her pocket and took out the pepper spray. Then, as Dolan made to grab her she aimed it straight into his face.

'Arghhh!' His scream resounded through the night as Dolan dropped the blade and put both hands to his streaming eyes.

'Ya bitch, ya wee bitch!' he yelled, bending over in pain, his cries mingling with the unmistakable sound of police sirens.

Immediately the car's engine growled and the BMW took off into the night, leaving Dolan moaning on his knees, scrabbling for the knife.

Then, as she heard the sound of the siren growing louder, Sarah began to run.

Lorimer let the other car pass him on the back road. The driver of the BMW would assume that he was just the doctor, a ploy he had thought up to allow his car access to the nursing home and back out again without raising any suspicion.

Now he was following the other car and peering through the gloom to get a closer look at its registration plate.

'Sierra bravo ten. Mike, yankee, delta,' he announced clearly, letting the other car slip a little further away.

The officer back at base acknowledged his call and Lorimer cleared the line. They'd put a trace on the BMW now and, should the driver become suspicious of the silver Lexus in his wake, he'd turn off and let the patrol boys do their bit.

The car looked to be heading back into the city, but as they reached the crossroads it took a right. Was he going to turn left again? Make for the Erskine Bridge?

There was a roar as the car in front took off along a straight stretch of road then Lorimer could hear its tyres squeal as it took the first of several bends on the road towards Mugdock and into the countryside.

Lorimer followed, keeping his lights low, just a country doctor going back home to Killearn or Strathblane, perhaps, if the driver of the BMW thought about it at all.

The road narrowed and plunged between trees on either side,

the big car taking the corners too fast, the driver having to correct the BMW as it went into a slight skid.

Lorimer let it go, keeping his eyes on the red tail lights ahead, not wanting to be spotted as the trees fell behind, the countryside opening up ahead. But the Lexus sped on smoothly, the road slipping under it like a ribbon of grey silk in the moonlight. His eyes peered through the darkness, watching the red lights appearing and disappearing with each hidden dip in the road, the twin points of colour like tiny demonic creatures leading him to some terrible doom.

It was tempting to gun his big car, to creep up right behind this character who had been involved in the death of David Imrie (and God knew who else). For a mad moment Lorimer wanted to tailgate the other car, drive it into a ditch, see the fear in the man's face as he pulled him out of the car.

A sudden rage possessed him, making his foot press down harder on the accelerator. He would do it.

Then, high on a hill, waiting for them both, he saw the twinkling blue lights of the waiting patrol car, making Lorimer slow down once again, his anger cooling as he focused on his next move.

The driver in front had spotted it too, for he slowed down and drew into the side. Would he try to turn on this narrow road?

He had to stop him before the man could begin any manoeuvre. There was only one thing for it, Lorimer decided, leaning forward and peering at the hedgerows on either side.

Yes! There was a gate about twenty yards between the BMW and his own car.

He braked hard and pulled the wheel around then reversed a foot or two, placing the Lexus right across the path of any oncoming vehicle before switching the lights to full beam and activating his hazard warning lights.

277

The figure emerging from the BMW looked across at him and Lorimer was sure his lips moved in an oath. He hesitated for a moment, then, taking a step backwards, ran full tilt and vaulted the hedge.

Lorimer grabbed the wooden post and swung his long legs across the top of the five-barred gate. Then he began to step across the patch of glaur, feeling his thick-soled shoes sinking in the mud where many cattle had stood waiting for the farmer to bring their hay. By the time his feet had found dry ground, the driver of the abandoned car was halfway across the field and heading towards a gloomy patch of woodland higher up.

Lorimer broke into a run, recalling the days of his youth when he had belted up the rugby field, ball in hand, in an effort to score a try. His feet pounded across the grass, leaping over tussocks, his longer legs giving him the advantage as he closed in on his quarry.

Above them a full moon emerged from the clouds, its light enabling the tall policeman to see the running figure that began to slow down as the field sloped upwards.

He could hear the other man gasping for breath as he approached. He wasn't fit, Lorimer thought. Only fear and a rush of adrenalin had given him the necessary impetus to flee.

It was then that the man he pursued made the mistake of turning to look over one shoulder, the motion throwing him off balance for a vital moment.

Lorimer threw himself forward, the rugby tackle bringing the other man crashing down with a hollow thud as the breath was knocked out of his body.

Then the sound of other feet stamping across the ground came closer and the detective breathed a sigh of relief as he pulled the man to his feet, grateful to see several uniformed officers approaching.

'You're no doctor!' the man gasped as Lorimer pulled back his arms and clipped the handcuffs around his wrists.

The man glowered at the detective, his scar livid in the moonlight.

'Quite correct,' Lorimer agreed, pushing him towards the nearest uniformed officer. 'Take him away,' he commanded. 'I'll see him once he's had time to cool off in the cells.'

CHAPTER THIRTY-FIVE

Rob Dolan sat snivelling into a soggy paper tissue. The memory of the previous night stung as much as his sore eyes. Damn that bitch to hell! His fist scrunched the tissue into a vicious ball. He would make sure that she suffered if it was the last thing he did. There were ways and means; women inside that he could contact who would do his bidding, the promise of some gear when they came out dangling like bait.

Dolan shut his eyes, the ache lessening now. One of the uniforms had given him a couple of paracetamol and watched him as he swallowed the pills with a plastic cup of water. He'd been left for what remained of the night in the cells here in Stewart Street police station, lying awake on the mattress, his mind seething with thoughts of revenge.

Now he was in one of the interview rooms, a different uniformed officer standing guard at the door, legs apart like a soldier on duty. Dolan had tried to catch his eye but the polis wasn't having any of it, staring straight ahead as if a guy like Dolan wasn't worth the bother.

Who would he see? Last time he'd been bust it had been that big guy Murdoch who'd collared him. Dolan shivered. He'd heard that Murdoch had relocated to Stewart Street. He sniffled again, hoping that it wouldn't be the tough-looking detective that walked through the door.

'Aw, Jesus, whit the ... ?' Dolan's oath died on his lips, one hard stare from the tall figure entering the room silencing the prisoner.

'Well, well, if it isn't Robert Dolan,' Lorimer said, taking off his jacket and slinging it on the back of the chair opposite.

Dolan began jigging his leg up and down, the need for drugs to calm his nerves growing steadily.

'Aw, Mr Lorimer, c'n ye no' see whit a state ah'm in? That lassie had no right daein' whit she did,' Dolan girned.

'And what lassie would that be?' Lorimer asked quietly.

'Och, Pete's big sister.'

'Pete?'

'Pete Wilding. He's deid. OD'd, didn't he?'

'What were you doing outside Abbey Nursing Home last night, Mr Dolan?'

The man began shaking his other leg up and down, up and down, faster and faster. 'Ah want ma brief, so ah do,' he declared, his eyes flicking from Lorimer to the silent policeman by the door. 'Ye's cannae haud me here against ma will.'

To Dolan's chagrin, the detective superintendent laid his hands upon the table and burst out laughing.

'Whit's the joke? Eh? Eh?' Dolan scowled and folded his arms across his chest.

'Oh dear. If there were two of you, Rob, you'd make a grand comedy act,' Lorimer declared, pretending to wipe tears from his eyes. For a moment he shook his head as though expressing disbelief at the follies of the criminal fraternity.

Then he leaned forward, the expression on his face altered completely.

'Would you like me to charge you, Rob? Abduction, coercion, accessory to murder . . . which one shall we begin with?'

The blue stare fixed Dolan to his seat then the prisoner looked away. 'Ah want ma brief,' he muttered again, but this time there was no trace of bravado in his voice.

The lawyer who had been summoned to Stewart Street at Jerry Cunningham's request was well known to Lorimer.

'Pauline.' He smiled and put out his hand. A wintry smile and a cursory handshake were his only reward. 'Nice to see you again. How are things?'

Pauline Dick sighed and shook her head. 'They'd be a damned sight better if I didn't keep getting folk like Jerry Cunningham calling me up,' she growled, a fifty-a-day habit making the woman's voice low and gruff. 'Finishing a case on at the High Court this afternoon so I could do without this.'

'Well that's where he'll be heading eventually, I reckon,' Lorimer replied. 'Meantime he's all yours this fine morning.'

When he opened the door and stood back to allow Pauline Dick to enter the room, Lorimer could see Jerry Cunningham sitting in the chair, back ramrod straight, arms folded in a gesture of defiance. What would it take, Lorimer wondered, to see those arms fall by the scar-faced man's side?

'Good morning, Mr Cunningham,' he began. 'You know Mrs Dick, of course?'

'*Ms* Dick,' Pauline butted in, drawing off her leather gloves and stuffing them in her briefcase.

Lorimer glanced at the lawyer's left hand, now bare of any wedding rings. Ah, well, he thought. She'll be in no mood for any nonsense after her acrimonious divorce.

He switched on the tape and sat back. 'Detective Superintendent William Lorimer,' he began, then gave the time and date.

'Jerome Thomas Cunningham, you have been charged with the following. Abduction of a female person, holding said female at knifepoint, breaking property and being an accessory to the murder of David Imrie.' Lorimer intoned the words as though he were a bookie reading out a list of runners for the three-forty at Cheltenham.

'No comment,' Cunningham replied, staring defiantly at Lorimer and completely ignoring the woman who sat at his side.

'You were outside Abbey Nursing Home last night,' Lorimer continued. 'Like to tell me why?'

'No comment,' Cunningham said again, a trace of a sneer in his voice.

So, it was going to be like that, was it? The smarmy bastard wanted to play this old game, did he? Lorimer thought.

'We'll be taking a DNA sample from you shortly, Mr Cunningham,' he announced. 'I'm sure it will match the traces on the little pile of cigarette butts we retrieved from where your car was parked.'

There was a slight tremor down one side of the man's face, the livid scar tightening. He'd hit home. Or had he?

Cunningham glanced at Pauline Dick then shrugged in a parody of nonchalance.

'We also have a mobile telephone in our possession,' Lorimer said slowly. 'Records from which will match the conversations you had with the same female whom you threatened on three separate occasions.'

Cunningham's shoulders lifted a little, a sure sign of tension. But that chin still jutted upwards and those dark eyes looked at the tall detective then away.

'What have you got to say about that?' Lorimer asked.

'No comment,' Cunningham repeated then gave an exaggerated yawn and began to examine his fingernails as though they were of greater interest than the man sitting opposite or the words being recorded on to tape.

But the gesture was not lost on Lorimer. The arms were no longer tightly folded and the signs of uncertainty were there for anyone who cared to read them.

'We've taken on Professor Brightman to help us in our investigation,' Lorimer said. 'You know him, don't you, Jerry?'

Cunningham stopped picking at his fingernails and stared at the detective, lips parted slightly.

'What's that got to do with me?' he asked truculently.

'We normally don't invite the estimable professor to help us unless it is in cases of multiple murder. Cases which he is really rather good at helping to conclude.' He smiled, catching Pauline Dick's eye. The woman sighed deeply and looked at her watch. He could see that Cunningham's refusal to cooperate was beginning to annoy her.

'*Multiple* murder?' Pauline Dick asked suddenly, her dark eyebrows shooting up in surprise.

'Oh, yes,' Lorimer continued, his tone laconic, sitting back with hands behind his head as though he were enjoying the performance. 'We have reason to believe that Mr Cunningham here has been an accessory to several murders in the city. And,' he unclasped his hands and leaned forward suddenly, making Jerry Cunningham flinch. 'We have forensic evidence to back this up.'

'I didn't do anything to anyone,' Cunningham bleated, turning to Pauline Dick, his hands now falling by his side. 'It wasn't me!'

'If I could have a few minutes alone with my client?' Pauline Dick sighed.

'Interview being paused at nine fifty-three,' Lorimer said, flicking the switch, an expression of calm satisfaction creasing his face.

*

It had been a long night. After the arrest out in the Stirlingshire countryside, Lorimer had returned to the nursing home to check that Sarah Wilding was safe.

The main door had been opened by a pleasant-faced nurse who ushered him into Nancy Livingstone's office where the nursing home manager was waiting for him.

'I sent her home,' Nancy explained. 'We covered the rest of her shift between us.' Then, looking at Lorimer, she clasped her hands and brought them to touch her lips. 'What will happen to her?' she had asked quietly.

'I don't know,' Lorimer admitted. 'That's for the Fiscal to decide. But I will be stressing how Sarah Wilding was forced into an action against her will, and against her better judgement. We can only hope that there will be no charge brought.'

'If she hadn't copied those details your relative would still be alive,' Nancy Livingstone said quietly.

'Aye, there is that. But I think they'd still have found a way to access the records. We've got a team trawling every nursing home in Glasgow that deals with patients like yours. Some hospital wards too. We think that there's a whole outfit targeting vulnerable patients and their relatives. And there may be more nurses like Sarah who have been unwitting pawns in their sordid game.'

'I see.' Nancy Livingstone had shivered as though the idea disgusted her sensibilities. 'Who could do such things . . . ?'

'Have you ever heard of an organisation calling itself Quiet Release?' he'd asked. 'Any of your patients' relatives mention it to you?'

But the woman had shaken her head, her unblinking response showing that not only had she never heard of them but that she could not conceive of such wickedness impinging on her world.

He had driven back to the city through the dawn light, the

pale yellow sunrise a bright contrast to the charcoal outline of Glasgow's familiar skyline.

Lorimer rubbed his eyes, thinking of Rob Dolan and the doctor who had smeared some ointment on the drug addict's eyelids before taking a mouth swab. What he would give for the chance to go home and lay his head on the pillow of his own bed! Preferably with Maggie by his side. He gave a sigh. Cases like this took him away from his wife for long spells. But she was used to it, he hoped, gnawing at his fingernail as he remembered Pauline Dick's bare left hand.

Dolan had spilled the beans at any rate, put Jerry Cunningham right into it. They'd communicated by phone, Dolan had said at last, wee cheap mobiles that they'd been instructed to discard from time to time. But Dolan had taken it on himself to keep them, he'd admitted, taking them to his dealer in exchange for a fix.

Now it remained to be seen whether Cunningham would persist with his 'no comment' routine or try to dig himself out of a hole that looked deeper and deeper with every bit of his partner's confession.

'Interview resumed at ten twenty-eight,' he intoned, not even bothering to catch Cunningham's eye as the man sat down beside his lawyer.

'Mr Cunningham wishes to make a statement,' Pauline Dick declared, nudging the man by her side. 'Tell Detective Superintendent Lorimer what you told me, Jerry,' she sighed.

The scar-faced man scowled, first at the woman then at Lorimer.

'I can't tell you what I don't know,' he began. 'It was all done by telephone.'

'What was all done by telephone, Mr Cunningham? Please explain for the tape,' Lorimer said.

'Well, folk don't want to see their relatives suffer a lingering, painful death,' Cunningham continued, sounding as though he had memorised a familiar script. 'So this guy starts up his business to help them. Right?' Quiet Release, Lorimer thought. But would Cunningham name it and the people behind it?

'I have no idea who he is, honest,' he gulped, looking swiftly from Pauline Dick to the tall detective. 'But I can tell you who gave us our instructions.'

Lorimer tried to keep his face poker straight as the prisoner continued.

'I know this guy,' Cunningham said. 'From way back. Brogan his name is. Done time with him in the Bar-L.'

'Billy Brogan?'

'Same fella,' Cunningham agreed. 'He contacts me and asks if I want to make a bit of dough. Course I agreed. Who doesn't need to make a living?' he asked, shifting his chair forwards as his apparent confidence grew.

'Go on,' Lorimer murmured.

'We were told where to go and find these poor souls,' Cunningham said, looking up at Pauline Dick as though to check that the version of his tale was what they had agreed. 'Report back to Brogan and then move on to another place.'

'And how did Sarah Wilding fit into this?'

Cunningham shifted uncomfortably. 'I knew Pete back before he took that overdose,' he admitted. 'Knew his sister had been done for theft and supplying.' He bit his lip and looked at Pauline Dick again but she refused to meet his eyes.

'I told Brogan about her and he got back to me with all the information about her, release date and everything. Don't know how he got that.' He shrugged.

Lorimer did not respond. Some woman in Cornton Vale had no

doubt supplied that information, not something he might ever be able to prove, however.

'I was to follow her and find out where she was staying. Brogan says that the boss wanted to see if she'd be talked into helping us. Doing the needle bit. For money, of course.' Cunningham shrugged again, as if that sort of transaction was normal in his world, which of course it was. 'But then I discovered she had a job in that nursing home and it seemed that the boss had a change of plan.'

Who is he? Lorimer wanted to seize Jerry Cunningham by the throat and shake the answer out of him but the detective superintendent remained as impassive as before, knowing that such an action would be counterproductive.

'Tell me what you were instructed to do,' he said instead.

'Aw, we just sort of . . . ' Cunningham visibly squirmed in his chair then, at a nudge from Pauline Dick's elbow, he continued. 'Well, all right, we lifted her after her shift. Gave her a wee frightener. Told her to copy the patient records on to a phone.'

'This phone?' Lorimer held up a clear plastic production bag, the mobile phone that Sarah Wilding had been given inside.

Cunningham frowned and narrowed his eyes. 'Think so,' he replied.

'And you also smashed a window in the house where Sarah Wilding was lodging,' Lorimer stated.

Cunningham nodded.

'Please speak for the tape.'

'Aye, Dolan and me. We just wanted to give her a scare. Remind her that we had something on her. I suppose that wee nyaff's told you already?' he grumbled but Lorimer did not respond to his question.

'You came to Abbey Nursing Home a second time with the intention of harming Sarah Wilding,' Lorimer said flatly.

'It was just a bit of fun,' Cunningham protested.

'Explain why you called her last night during her working shift and demanded that she come out, threatening her into the bargain,' Lorimer said coldly, holding up the phone once more to show that they had all the evidence they needed to prove the man's guilt.

'All right,' Cunningham snapped. 'The boss thought that Sarah might still come in handy. Wanted to see if she'd raid the drug cupboard in the place where she worked.'

'What sorts of drugs?'

'The usual. Morphine.' Cunningham shrugged as though the answer was obvious.

'But he didn't know that none of the patients at Abbey Nursing Home require such a drug,' Lorimer told him, watching as Cunningham's eyes widened. 'So, tell me, Jerry. Who is this *boss* you seem to think so highly of?'

'Do you believe him?' Solly asked as they sat in the professor's spacious office off University Avenue.

'Aye,' Lorimer sighed volubly. 'More's the pity. Cunningham and Dolan were lured into this. They don't know the identity of the person or persons behind Quiet Release and, to be honest, I don't think they even wanted to know.'

'Safer for them not to,' Solly agreed. 'What about your old friend Billy Brogan?'

'Billy doesn't have the brains to dream up something like this but I bet he could supply the muscle power that it required.'

'Where is he now?'

Lorimer shrugged. 'Not in Barlinnie any more. Served his time for that case we were both involved in. Last known address was with Frankie Bissett in Byres Road. We've been looking for Billy ever since they found Frankie's body in that bathroom. Now we have to wonder if poor wee Frankie was somehow involved in all of this.'

'Do you think he's still in Glasgow?'

'Who knows?' Lorimer gave a yawn and stretched his arms above his head. 'Don't think he's done a bunk to Mallorca like he did last time.' He gave a rueful grin, the memory of Brogan's escapade making him chuckle. 'Intelligence suggests he's gone to ground somewhere in the city.'

'Do you think he'll have any notion who is behind Quiet Release?'

Lorimer shook his head. 'No, Brogan wouldn't be given that sort of information. Our best bet is working with the phones and the laptops to see if anything can be traced. Our technical boys and girls are probably the ones who'll solve this one, Solly.'

The professor walked towards the large bay window, his hands clasped behind his back, a thoughtful expression in his dark eyes.

'And meantime, innocent people are still being put to death,' he murmured, gazing down at the street at the gathering dusk where leaves were blowing in the chill October wind.

CHAPTER THIRTY-SIX

M urdoch was back.

The first Kirsty saw of the detective sergeant was the leather jacket slung on the back of a chair, his grey head bent over a pile of folders.

She approached him cautiously, uncertain now of the relationship between them. Was he to continue being her mentor? Or would she still be under the guidance of the man who had inspired her to join up in the first place?

He didn't see her right away, so Kirsty had a few moments to look at the detective sergeant's face as he pored over some documents. His cheeks were pale, as though he had spent too much time indoors, and there were tiny nicks along the jawline where he had cut himself shaving. Murdoch's tie was already loosened and she could see the line of grease along the edge of his shirt collar. When had he last had help at home? She was just imagining the man's domestic situation when he looked up at her.

'Wilson.'

'You're back, sir,' Kirsty said, realising as she spoke how hollow her words were. But Murdoch's demeanour was a barrier to any form of sympathy.

'Aye. And see they've given over our case to Nottingham,' he replied with disgust. 'You've been busy, though,' he added with a curl of his lip. '*And* keeping company with upstairs.'

'Yes, sir.' Kirsty bit back any further explanation. Was that a trace of jealousy in Murdoch's voice?

'Better having him as a mentor, d'you think?' Murdoch growled, confirming her suspicions.

'Don't really know, sir. But the current case is pretty complicated. It's been keeping us all busy at any rate,' she replied.

'Aye, so I see.' Murdoch swung his laptop around so that Kirsty could look at what he had been doing. Rows and rows of nursing homes and their addresses had been printed out and she assumed that the DS had been given authority to investigate them all.

Are you sure you want to do this? she almost cried out. What must it be like investigating these sorts of nursing homes? And how many of the patients would be MS sufferers like his late wife?

'Nearly put Irene in one of them,' he said, glancing at Kirsty as though he could read her mind. 'But we decided to keep her at home for as long as we could.' He shrugged. 'Same difference in the end, though. Pneumonia usually gets them.'

Was that right? Had poor Mrs Murdoch died of pneumonia after all? And had Mary Milligan been wrong about Murdoch's involvement? Kirsty frowned for a moment, glancing at the thin line of Murdoch's mouth as he undoubtedly struggled to keep his emotions in check.

'Better get on, sir. So much paperwork,' she ventured.

'Aye, you'll be chained to that desk for a while, I reckon,' he replied. 'No point in taking you to any more scenes of crime while this one lasts.'

Kirsty hesitated. There was no sign of regret in the man's

voice and he had already turned away, one hand on the computer mouse.

It took a matter of minutes to find what she was looking for.

Multiple sclerosis was so different for its victims but many of them did indeed end their lives due to pneumonia. She read on, not fully understanding every technical term that described the disease. Did pneumonia set in as a result of those wasting muscles? Kirsty just wasn't sure. She glanced across at the detective sergeant who was engrossed in something on his computer screen. He'd looked grief-stricken that day at the hospital. But after the long years of Irene Murdoch's horrible illness, wouldn't there have been a modicum of relief as well?

Kirsty gave herself a mental shake. It was stupid to think that Irene Murdoch had been one of the patients targeted by that end-of-life group. The patients in her ward were dreadfully ill people, almost expected to pass away, like that lady next door to Murdoch's wife who had died in the night. And surely the woman's nurse was simply being fanciful about her patient's demise? *It gets to you*, she remembered her father saying one night at the dinner table. *Sometimes it seems like the whole world is full of criminal intent.* Was that what was happening to her? Was her world now being coloured by every case she dealt with? She thought of Jean Fairlie for a moment. Was she destined to become like the hard-bitten older woman? Seeing life as a trek through crime and grime?

It was none of her business, Kirsty told herself. Len Murdoch's wife had been dying for a long time. Surely it was better to let her suspicions go and give the poor man a modicum of peace?

Murdoch's phone rang just then and Kirsty glanced across at his profile, the solid jawline and jutting brow. He would be a formidable opponent, she suddenly realised, glad that she was on his side and not facing him across the table in an interview room.

'Right, Wilson.' He spun in his chair and looked across at Kirsty. 'A wee development.' He grinned. 'Looks like we'll have you at a scene of crime after all.'

The Honda was parked where it usually sat, face out for a quick exit from the police car park. Kirsty caught one-handed the keys that Murdoch tossed, her reward a nod of approval from the detective sergeant.

'Off we jolly well go, Wilson,' he said, strapping on his seat belt. 'Sudden death over in the West End. Just off Great Western Road.'

'Oh?' Kirsty could not help wanting to know more.

'Fellow in a nursing home,' Murdoch replied. 'One of the ones that have been targeted,' he added, tapping an index finger against his nose.

Kirsty drove out of the conglomeration of buildings and headed west, the road curving this way and that until she came to the boulevard that led all the way down towards Loch Lomond.

'Take a left here,' Murdoch suddenly commanded, and Kirsty did as she was bid, puzzled at the diversion.

'Stop in there,' he said, sliding out of his seat belt as a row of shops appeared just ahead.

Cigarettes, Kirsty guessed, spotting a newsagent's shop. But she was wrong. Murdoch slammed out of the car and walked a few paces past the shop and entered a Ladbroke's betting shop instead. Kirsty blinked to make sure her eyes were not deceiving her. Perhaps there was a professional reason for this visit. Did Murdoch need to visit an informant in there? Or was he simply putting on a bet?

He was out of the premises a few minutes later, stuffing something into the inside pocket of his leather jacket.

'Drive,' he commanded curtly. 'First right and right again.'

Yours not to reason why, Kirsty told herself, her inner voice tinged with cynicism.

'In here,' Murdoch told her minutes later, but his command wasn't needed, the large sign by the stone pillars proclaiming ROSE PARK NURSING HOME.

Murdoch was out of the car in seconds, hauling his scene of crime bag from the back seat.

'Your Quiet Release people have tripped up this time.' He grinned as Kirsty came to his side.

'We've had officers warning loads of nursing homes about that,' Kirsty replied.

'Aye, and it looks like we hit pay dirt.' Murdoch nodded, striding towards the main entrance. 'One of the patients had his own laptop. You'll find out when we're in,' he added with another nod as he pressed the bell and waited.

'Detective Sergeant Murdoch, Detective Constable Wilson,' Murdoch told the military-looking gentleman standing at the opened door.

'John Dunwoodie,' the man said, glancing at the warrant card that Murdoch held out. 'Terrible business,' he added.

'Is there somewhere we can change?' Murdoch asked, looking around the wood-panelled entrance foyer. 'We need to put on our forensic gear,' he explained.

'Good gracious,' Dunwoodie murmured, stroking his moustache with a thoughtful finger. 'Just like that TV programme ... what d'you call it?'

'Somewhere to change, sir?' Kirsty spoke up at the man with a hopeful smile.

'Of course.' Dunwoodie straightened his back and pointed to

a door in the corner. 'Toilets over there. Ladies and gents,' he added with a cough.

'Your staff have been told to leave the patient's room?'

'Yes, sir,' Dunwoodie agreed. 'As soon as we suspected that something was ... not quite kosher ...' He broke off as the two detectives headed for the bathrooms, Murdoch pulling a set of whites from the scene of crime bag for Kirsty.

From the door to his room Kirsty could see Edward Clark's body lying on the bed, the duvet pulled back to show his upper body and the syringe that was still embedded in his arm.

'Must have been disturbed and scarpered before he could take that out,' Murdoch said grimly. 'We don't touch a thing,' he warned Kirsty with a glare. 'Not even to close the poor bugger's eyes.'

Kirsty nodded, staring at the dead man whose mouth was partly open as though in protest, his eyes still wide with fright.

'They did the right thing,' Murdoch muttered as he began laying treads from the doorway right up to the side of the victim's bed. 'Called us right away,' he added. 'Wish more people were as accommodating. Right, Wilson. Doc will be here any minute but before that, tell me exactly what you see. Think of me as a judge asking you questions,' he added sternly.

'There's an open window,' Kirsty replied right away. 'It's a ground-floor room and so if an intruder gained entry that way he could also have left the same way.' She stepped across the metal treads and looked out of the window. 'Room faces to the side. Gardens all along this part of the building and a hedge with a wire mesh that would prevent anyone from gaining access,' she continued. 'But I can see where he left.' She turned with a glint of triumph in her eyes. 'Right there.'

Murdoch was at her shoulder in a moment, following her pointing finger.

There was a deep bend in the wire fence and several branches from the thick privet hedging were scattered upon the ground.

'Looks like someone made a hasty exit,' she said, meeting Murdoch's eyes.

'Wish we knew which way he went after that,' Murdoch replied, his eyes gazing along the road that led to the well-heeled district of Hyndland on one side and Great Western Road on the other. 'Could be anywhere,' he muttered.

'DS Murdoch. We meet again.' A voice behind made the detectives turn as one to see a diminutive white-suited figure carrying her medical bag.

'Dr Fergusson.' Kirsty's face broke into a smile.

'If you could let me in to see the victim, please,' Rosie asked. And both detectives retreated from the room, letting in the pathologist who had come to examine Edward Clark's mortal remains.

John Dunwoodie came towards them as Kirsty and Murdoch crossed the vast hallway.

'What's happening?' he asked.

'We'll know more once Mr Clark's post-mortem examination has been done,' Murdoch replied stiffly. 'But for now DC Wilson here will be taking some details from you, sir.' Murdoch nodded to Kirsty as he left the hall and made his way outside.

Needs a smoke, Kirsty told herself. *Or else he's giving me the authority to ask some questions. But he should be here. He should be with me to witness anything Dunwoodie tells me.* It was odd, she thought. Just as he had left her with Ailsa Doyle; a carelessness that she couldn't fully comprehend in someone who was supposed to be mentoring her closely.

John Dunwoodie led her into a small office that was dominated by a large old-fashioned leather-topped desk and captain's chair. Floor-to-ceiling wood panelling made the room appear even more cramped, a feeling not helped by the matching wooden filing cabinet by the desk or the stack of grey moulded chairs heaped on one side. A modern white Apple Mac sat on the middle of the desk, a huge printer on top of the filing cabinet. It was, Kirsty mused, as if a bygone age was being gradually infiltrated by technology from the twenty-first century. And John Dunwoodie himself looked as if he'd have been more suited to a different era, his tweed jacket, grey waistcoat and military moustache reminding the detective constable of films set in the post-war years.

'You run the nursing home?' Kirsty began, sitting on one of the grey chairs that Dunwoodie had pulled out for her.

'My sister and I,' Dunwoodie agreed. 'I'm what you might call the administrator. She deals with the medical side of things. Dr Christine Dunwoodie,' he added, as though the name might mean something to Kirsty.

'And you've run Rose Park for how long . . . ?'

'Eighteen years,' Dunwoodie replied. 'It used to be our family home. Inherited it from the parents, don't you know.' He absently scratched at his moustache. 'Christine had been overseas. *Médecin Sans Frontiéres*. Needed a complete change. So we had the old place adapted for use as a nursing home. Worked well,' he added. 'Lots of good reviews on the internet.'

Kirsty smiled courteously. It wasn't the sort of place she'd have liked her own mum or dad to come to. Okay, the room where she'd seen Edward Clark's body had the look of any modern hospital room – plain, functional and rather clinical compared to the dreary dark-stained wood everywhere else. But, if this had been a family home, she could understand the desire to keep it the way they remembered from childhood. And John Dunwoodie with his old-fashioned clothes looked the type who disliked change of any sort.

'When did Mr Clark become one of your residents?'

'Oh, let me see now. Must have been last month.' He rose from his place behind the desk and pulled out a drawer from the filing cabinet.

Kirsty waited patiently as he riffled through the metal folders.

'Yes, here we are. Fifth of September. Relatives wanted him to have more care. Kept falling. One of the side effects of his condition, I'm afraid,' he added.

'And what exactly was Mr Clark's medical condition?'

'Oh, he'd suffered a series of minor strokes.' Dunwoodie nodded. 'Lived on his own so they thought it best to have him cared for where he would come to no harm.'

Kirsty stared at the man who apparently had no conception of what he had just said.

'But he did come to serious harm, sir,' she murmured. 'In fact, from what we can see it looks as if Mr Clark may have been murdered.'

Dunwoodie shifted uncomfortably in his chair. 'This doesn't have to get out, Detective Constable? The newspapers, I mean . . . ?'

'We wouldn't give any information to the press unless it was to further our investigation, sir,' Kirsty answered truthfully. Though what decision Lorimer came to about letting the press office run with this story was anyone's guess.

'You called us as soon as Mr Clark was found,' Kirsty continued. 'Who was it who was first on the scene?'

'Our only male nurse, chap called Joshua Ngebe. Lovely man. Qualified as a psychiatric nurse before specialising in palliative care,' Dunwoodie murmured. 'Do you want to see him?'

'We will want to speak to him, yes,' Kirsty agreed. 'But perhaps you could tell me a little more about the emails on Mr Clark's laptop.'

'Ah, it was Nurse Ngebe who found them,' Dunwoodie declared. 'He and Clark used to play chess on that laptop of his. The email just popped up, seemingly. Don't know how that works,' he mused, glaring at the computer on his own desk as though it were some sort of alien device. 'Prefer to stick to paper and pens myself,' he added with a nod.

Joshua Ngebe was one of the handsomest men Kirsty had ever seen. He stood tall and straight, a grace about his carriage that was in keeping with the large gentle eyes and warm handshake.

'Detective Constable Wilson, I hope I can be of help,' he began, his accent revealing an educated man from somewhere that Kirsty guessed as Oxford or Cambridge.

'I hope so too,' she told him. 'Tell me, what brought you to Rose Park? I'm guessing you're much too highly qualified for this sort of work.'

'Ah, the discerning detective.' Ngebe laughed. 'Yes, you are quite correct. I was to have completed my medical degree when I was unfortunately stricken with multiple sclerosis. It can be a progressive disease,' he explained. 'But I've been one of the lucky ones.' He shrugged. 'There are times when my legs give way,' he tapped his trouser leg. 'And then I need crutches for a while and time off to rest.'

'So you gave up on medicine?'

'Not exactly.' Ngebe's dark eyes looked into Kirsty's. 'I did go back. Took a sideways path into psychiatry then trained as a nurse. This sort of work suits me.' He shrugged again.

'Because you can empathise with the patients.'

Ngebe grinned, showing perfect white teeth. 'Something like that. My wife is a GP,' he said. 'So we have a nice lifestyle and she makes sure I don't overdo things.' He chuckled.

'Now, getting back to Mr Clark,' Kirsty continued. 'Mr Dunwoodie tells me that it was you who found these emails about Quiet Release.'

Ngebe's face became suddenly serious. 'The police notified us about this organisation only recently,' he said. 'We were to be vigilant and let them know if anything came to our nursing home from these people.'

'And when did you see the first email?'

Ngebe frowned. 'Must have been two days ago,' he admitted. 'It wasn't sent to him directly, you see. Somehow he'd been copied in to it. I asked him about it and he just laughed. Said it was some crank organisation trying to target poor souls who wanted to end it all.' The nurse sighed. '"Not for me just yet." These were his exact words,' Ngebe said softly, his mouth closing in a grim line. 'He made a joke of it. Said his nearest and dearest would trash anything like that.'

'But there was another one,' Kirsty insisted.

Ngebe nodded. 'Last night, just after we'd completed a game of chess,' he said. 'Popped up on the screen. Message asking about "freedom from pain", of all things. Edward was never in any pain,' he told Kirsty. 'Unless you could count the number of times I'd beaten him at chess,' he added with a sad smile.

'So you ignored the messages?'

'On the contrary. I logged them for Mr Dunwoodie. I assumed he would notify the authorities.'

Kirsty tried to keep her expression as neutral as possible but the dark-skinned psychiatric nurse gave her a knowing smile.

'He didn't, did he?'

She bit back a reply, knowing that to discuss any point of the case was out of order.

'Thank you, Mr Ngebe,' she said, holding out her hand and receiving the man's warm grasp. 'I think Mr Clark must have enjoyed having you as his nurse.'

'Well, he certainly did last night,' Ngebe replied softly.

'Oh?'

Ngebe's smile widened a little as he let go of Kirsty's hand. 'He was delighted to beat me at chess for once.'

That explained Dunwoodie's manner, Kirsty thought, heading out of the main door in time to see Murdoch flick a cigarette across the flowerbeds. The man should have alerted the police as soon as Clark's nurse had logged that email. Probably thought it was the work of a crank or a time waster. Or maybe he wasn't as au fait with sending emails as that smart new laptop on his desk suggested.

'Sir.'

Murdoch turned around at the sound of Kirsty's voice.

'Pathologist finished yet?'

'No, sir. But I think there's something you ought to know,' she said.

Murdoch listened as Kirsty related the two separate conversations.

'Good work, Wilson. Stupid idiot, though.' He jerked his head back towards the nursing home. 'He'll have that man's death on his conscience for a good time to come, I reckon.' He raised his head at the sound of a vehicle pulling up outside. 'Oh, looks like

302

we've got company,' he stated as they caught sight of the van bringing the scene of crime officers. 'Hope they tape right across this entrance,' he added as an elderly woman paused to let her small dog urinate against the stone gatepost. 'Need to keep out all the nosy parkers,' he added loudly, making the woman sniff indignantly and haul the dog away on its lead.

CHAPTER THIRTY-SEVEN

The door opening at the back of the room made several people turn to look. A young man stood there, his hands full of newspapers.

'Jimmy.' Lorimer paused to address the press officer. 'Thanks for bringing these down.'

From the worried expression on Jimmy Nichol's face, each of the officers staring at the young press officer walking towards the detective superintendent could see that the man did not relish sharing the latest news with the assembled officers. Most of his colleagues had already seen the main papers online but there were still a few curious glances directed Jimmy Nichol's way. And Lorimer was examining each and every face in turn, hoping for answers to the question he hated to ask.

'Sir,' Jimmy said, handing the rolled-up papers to Lorimer.

Without exception the case had made front-page news.

POLICE PROBE INTO PATIENT DEATHS was the *Gazette*'s take on the lead article, while others proclaimed WHO IS DOCTOR DEATH? and POLICE SEARCH FOR DEATH SQUAD.

Lorimer's face grew darker with each headline.

Then, looking once more at the officers standing before him, he lifted up the newspapers in both hands so that they could be seen.

The whole room fell silent.

'Who was responsible for this?' Lorimer asked in a voice brimming with anger.

Kirsty looked around her as if to read some guilt on one of their faces but saw that all of her fellow officers were doing exactly the same.

'Someone in this team was responsible for leaking information to the national press,' Lorimer continued, his voice low but full of menace.

There was an unnatural hush in the room then Jimmy Nichol cleared his throat and nodded to Lorimer.

'I've already been on to all their news desks, sir. The call they got was anonymous.' He shrugged as if to say *nobody's done it for the money*. 'Could it have been someone connected to the men you've arrested?' he asked doubtfully, obviously keen to find an explanation other than an internal leak.

'What do you think, Jimmy? I take it you've read the entire pieces with your usual care?'

Jimmy Nichol flushed. 'Yes, sir. They all came in after midnight.' He paused then turned to the men and women opposite, some standing, others lounging against the wall or a nearby desk. 'It's detailed information that these press boys have been given.' He looked back at Lorimer with an expression of apology. 'I suppose it can only have come from inside, sir. References to the victims could have come from outsiders but there is just too much in the way of procedural detail for it to have come from anywhere else.'

Lorimer felt his heart pounding as he clenched then

unclenched his fists. Making a scene would do nobody any good, perhaps alienating more of his team. But at that moment he wished he had the person who had leaked this news right in front of him.

A swift glance showed only troubled faces, their collective dismay tuning with his own. Yet one dissembler amongst them was clever enough to hide their true feelings.

'You know who you are and why you have done this thing.' Lorimer spoke quietly. 'And when I find out who it was then I assure you that there will be no place for you in Police Scotland.'

With a nod to the press officer, Lorimer turned and walked away, the young man scuttling in his wake.

'Why?' Lorimer slammed his fist on to his desk, making the young man jump. He had read each of the front pages and the inside columns too, several of the papers having editorial comments about end-of-life legislation.

'Who would do something like this?' he asked Jimmy, shaking his head as if bewildered by the bombshell that had struck his investigation.

Jimmy shrugged his shoulders. 'Well, no money changed hands. As far as we know,' he added, his tone laden with cynicism.

'You think there's been a fat brown envelope passed to one of my officers?'

Jimmy began to shrug again but the gesture became more of a squirm under the detective superintendent's steely blue gaze.

'I really couldn't say, sir. But we both know it happens,' Jimmy replied. 'It could be something else, though.'

'Yes?'

'Some disaffected person who doesn't want the investigation to come to a satisfactory conclusion.'

'What are you getting at, Jimmy?'

The young man leaned forwards, his clasped hands moving up and down as though to make a point. 'It's my job to know what the papers say, sir, and there's been a plethora of articles about euthanasia over the past months. Bound to be, given the proposed legislation here in Scotland,' he continued. 'What if...' he cocked his head to one side thoughtfully, '... someone on the team is all for it. Euthanasia, I mean. What if they've seen a loved one suffer and think that this Quiet Release lot are actually doing society a favour?'

Lorimer sat very still, gazing at the young man's earnest expression. It was an idea too awful to contemplate that one of his officers had deliberately wrecked the process of a major investigation like this. And yet there was something in Jimmy Nichol's words that made sense. He tried to conceal his thoughts from the young man staring at him intently. For there was one officer whose name immediately sprang to mind.

When Kirsty Wilson entered the room, Lorimer was standing once again with his face to the window but this time he turned and motioned her into a chair opposite his own, the desk between them signalling the formality of the occasion.

'I need to know about Len Murdoch,' Lorimer began with a sigh. 'Anything you have picked up from being with him, anything that might indicate whether he had money worries?' he enquired, then frowned to himself as Kirsty pursed her lips. This was hardly fair, bringing the girl in to grill her about the man who had been her mentor. But then whoever had leaked the information to the press had behaved in a despicable, underhand way and he had to be sure that Kirsty was not hiding anything from him.

'He's known to like a flutter on the horses,' Kirsty began. 'In

307

fact he seemed to be picking up his winnings when we were en route to the Rose Park Nursing Home.'

'Did he do that often? Make a detour to the bookies?'

'No, sir. Just the once as far as I know. But he did make quite a lot of calls on his mobile out of earshot. But then . . . ' Kirsty tailed off. 'I think he was in contact with the hospital a good bit before Mrs Murdoch died. You'd need to see his phone to check,' she continued, then put a hand over her mouth.

'It's all right, DC Wilson,' Lorimer said tiredly. 'That is not out of order to suggest something like that. Hopefully we won't have to go that far. If DS Murdoch *has* given information to the newspapers perhaps he might feel aggrieved enough to pack in his career anyway.'

'He doesn't have that long to go till retirement?'

Lorimer shook his head. 'Started not long after your dad,' he told her. 'He only has a few more months of service remaining. But he'll forfeit an awful lot if he is dismissed from the police at this stage of his career.'

'Do you think it was him?' Kirsty asked in hushed tones.

'I have absolutely no evidence to suggest that,' Lorimer told her. 'It could be anyone who feels strongly about this whole debate,' he sighed. 'Doesn't have to be someone with a relative who has gone through a bad time. Could simply be someone with a deeply held conviction.'

'But that's awful!' Kirsty exclaimed. 'How can anyone condone what these people are doing to innocent victims?'

'Easy to ask when you're young and healthy like you,' Lorimer smiled faintly. 'But older officers who've seen the worst that humans can do to each other might well have a different take on how to end a person's life.'

*

Kirsty had passed the canteen lady before she realised.

'Hey, wee yin, no stopping tae get a cake from auld Sadie?'

'Sorry, I was miles away,' Kirsty apologised, rattling her jacket pocket for the change she had left there just for this very occasion.

'What'll it be today, hen? Something to sweeten you up? Looks like someone's stole yer scone.' Sadie chuckled, but her eyes were full of concern despite the joke as it was obvious that something was troubling the young woman.

'Yes, please. A scone,' Kirsty replied vaguely, not picking up on the Glasgow expression for looking down in the dumps.

'His nibs been giving you a hard time, that what it is?' Sadie asked shrewdly, cocking her permed head towards Lorimer's office door.

'No, no, just very busy,' Kirsty replied with a forced smile. It would not do to gossip with wee Sadie Dunlop, she thought. Surely Sadie wouldn't have ... no, Kirsty dismissed the idea as soon as it had drifted into her mind. Sadie knew better than that. She was well used to the ways of the police and everybody knew what respect she had for Lorimer.

As Kirsty descended the stairs to her own department she knew that Lorimer had also asked her to see him for a different reason, one that had not been voiced. She would have to keep a close watch on DS Len Murdoch, see if anything untoward happened that might give a clue as to whether the detective sergeant had indeed been the one responsible for today's newspaper headlines.

CHAPTER THIRTY-EIGHT

The telephones never stopped ringing.

All over the city, hospital wards and nursing homes were checking their patient records (especially those recently deceased) to see if there had been anything extraordinary to show to the police. And the gentlemen and ladies of the press were having a field day, reporters sent to South Glasgow University Hospital as well as Abbey Nursing Home and Rose Park, the staff in each trying to fend off these unexpected visitors to their doors. It was hopeless, of course, like trying to stem the tide, since relatives of existing patients as well as those recently bereaved were being doorstepped.

By the end of the day Detective Superintendent Lorimer was heartily sick of the constant voices on the end of his office phone, the continual complaints giving him a genuine headache. Jimmy Nichol had been instructed to send out a press notice that attempted to repair as much of the peripheral damage as possible but in truth it was too late. That the 'police were continuing with their inquiries whilst holding two men on suspicion of being involved in unlawful killings' was no longer newsworthy, but it was all he had to go on right now.

With a sigh that became a groan as his chair scraped under him, Lorimer reached for his jacket and coat. It was time to head for home where Maggie and Chancer would be waiting, his ex-directory number ensuring that he would at least have a bit of peace from the calls. Slipping his mobile into one pocket, Lorimer was tempted to switch the blessed thing off but his sense of duty was stronger than the desire for some peace and quiet. He closed his eyes, hoping for some relief from the worsening headache. *I've got the best job in the world*, he'd often told people and yet right now the detective superintendent would have gladly walked out of this building and never come back.

'Hi, you.' Maggie came towards him, arms outstretched. As he held his wife, feeling her beating heart and the warmth from her body, Lorimer felt a sudden sweep of emotion. How grateful he was for this lovely woman!

'Saw the papers,' Maggie said shortly, looking up at her husband's face intently. 'Everyone in the staffroom was talking about it.'

Lorimer exhaled a sigh. 'It's been a hell of a day,' he murmured. 'Whoever did this . . .' A shake of his weary head was all he could muster.

'Well, I think a large whisky before dinner is called for, don't you?' Maggie said, turning to the sideboard and opening the door where several bottles of fine malt were stored. 'And there's chicken broth. With fresh parsley.' She smiled, picking up a bottle of Bunnahabhain, one of her husband's favourite Islay single malts, and reaching for a crystal whisky glass. 'And the remains of a lasagne if you're hungry enough . . . ?'

*

Later, replete with the food and whisky, Lorimer sat sprawled on the settee, his long legs stretched out in front of him. They had watched the evening news on television, neither of them uttering a word as the pictures of Abbey Nursing Home flicked across their screen. All over Scotland people would be seeing this debacle, he thought, and making pointed comments about the ineptitude of their police force.

Ach.' He made a face as though there was a bad taste in his mouth. 'I can't conceive of anyone stooping so low as that.'

Maggie leaned forward from her place beside him and took his hand in hers.

'For a man who's seen the worst of human nature that's a strange thing to say,' she told him. 'Think of the conmen who've doorstepped old ladies, drug dealers who have no conscience about their customers overdosing, killers who've taken the lives of innocent people . . . '

'Aye, but this is different,' Lorimer said slowly, sitting up and putting his arm around Maggie's shoulders. 'These folk had so little time left to them. Their last precious days were robbed. And what for? So some greedy bastard could pile up wealth for himself? It makes me sick!' he said, a sudden anger creeping into his tone.

'Or *her*self,' Maggie murmured. 'What has Solly said about it?'

'Oh, the usual,' Lorimer sighed. 'Don't get me wrong, the man's a genius. He does think that a man is behind this and yes, he is certain that the motivation is money. Think about it, Mags,' he said, stroking her hair gently. 'He sets up this organisation online, uses some shady characters to grub around and find out where to obtain drugs and do dirty work.'

'Did either of the men you arrested actually administer the morphine, though?'

312

'No. That's somebody else we need to find. The so-called doctor that Mary Milligan identified. But I bet you anything you like that he isn't the person behind it all.'

'Why?' Maggie turned her head and looked at him.

'Too risky. There may be hundreds of folk all over this city, all over the country, who have been targeted. Our tech people are still trying to find a lead from the Gardiner girls' computer.' He sighed. 'I think this is bigger than we realise, Maggie. And the few people who have been identified as being unlawfully killed are just the tip of a very large iceberg.'

Across the city, Solly sat watching as the latest news unfolded. Money, he had declared to Lorimer. That was behind all of this. And yet something lately had been troubling the psychologist. What if the primary motivation had changed into something far more dangerous? What if the person administering these lethal injections had developed a different sort of appetite? Not just for the acquisition of lots of money but simply because he enjoyed the act of killing? Such a person would be very dangerous indeed, someone who would relish being a risk taker, someone who would believe themselves to be invincible.

The television screen was now showing a map of the British Isles and the gales sweeping in from the Atlantic, but Solomon Brightman was oblivious to the weatherman's warnings, his thoughts focusing on the profile of the killer they sought.

Annette Imrie sat in the semi-darkness of her husband's study. The hand holding the grey plastic mouse trembled as she scrolled down the pages of emails on the new account that had been set up. One by one she deleted the messages then sat back, relieved to see a blank screen once more.

313

A noise at her back made the woman jump.

'Patrick! I thought you were asleep!'

'What are you doing?' Her husband's voice was tinged with suspicion.

'Nothing, darling. Just surfing the net to see if I can find a decent outfit for poor David's funeral. Surely it won't be long now?' she asked, rising from the chair and coming to stand beside him, pressing her sinuous body against his own.

'Come back to bed, darling,' she crooned softly. 'So much to do tomorrow. You need your sleep.'

Patrick nodded wearily, but, as they left the room, his eyes fell on the bright, blank screen. And he felt a heavy weight like a stone in his heart.

Lorimer pressed the button on his steering wheel as the mobile began to ring. It was still dark outside, the dawn light only beginning to show on the eastern horizon as he drove into the city.

'Bill?'

Lorimer frowned. Whose voice was this? And who was calling him by name?

'It's me, Patrick,' the man's voice continued.

'Patrick.' Lorimer tried not to sigh. 'I suppose you've seen the news?'

'Oh, yes, of course we did. But that's not why I'm calling you.'

'Oh?' Lorimer knew that he was hearing something grave in the man's voice. Something like defeat.

'I need to drop something off to you. Where are you right now?'

The morning light was a flush of lemon across the city skyline as Lorimer drove across the hilly country road. Patrick had mentioned a place between the farm and Lorimer's office where they should meet, a village not far from a lonely stretch of ground where the detective had once found a burned-out ambulance, the body inside a clue to solving a series of murders. He slowed down at a corner and took another winding road, glancing to his right as if he would still see that scene. But all he saw was a glimpse of white rumps as a pair of hinds grazed peacefully amidst the long autumn grasses.

The road wound down and around to the village below, then he stopped at the main road, looking carefully for any passing traffic. A minute along this road he saw the grey Land Rover sitting in the lay-by and slowed down, parking the Lexus behind it.

Patrick Imrie got out and opened the back door.

'I think you should have a look at this,' he said dully, handing Lorimer a heavy bundle wrapped in a layer of blanket.

'What ... ?'

'It's our laptop computer. Annette ... ' Patrick broke off, turning away so that Lorimer could not see his face. 'She ... ' The farmer's head was bowed now, the tweed cap shading his eyes. 'I think she was in touch with that organisation,' he mumbled. 'Quiet Release.'

'Don't say anything more,' Lorimer told him, touching his arm lightly. 'We'll speak to you and Annette later if there is anything compromising here.'

'She only wanted things to stay the way they were, I'm sure of that,' Patrick said slowly, glancing once at Lorimer then looking away again.

'Don't let her know about this,' the detective told him. 'And make sure she doesn't go on any little excursions too far from home.'

'What will happen?' The farmer looked directly at Lorimer now, his brow furrowed, the bushy eyebrows drawn down.

'Not for me to decide,' he replied. 'And these things take time,' he said gently. 'Go home and get on with whatever you need to do on the farm. And try not to dwell on this.' He tapped the computer under his arm. 'It's my responsibility now.'

The journey back to Glasgow was slower, commuter traffic building up as Lorimer neared the outskirts of the city. Fat drops of rain splashed against the windscreen like unshed tears then, as he slowed down behind a line of vehicles, the heavens opened and the car was dashed with sweeping torrents as the promised storms began.

CHAPTER THIRTY-NINE

'We're going out.' Murdoch stood beside Kirsty's desk staring down at her. It was a command, terse and brief, and the detective constable rose immediately from where she had been poring over her laptop to follow the man out of the room.

'Where...?'

'Pub,' he answered shortly, giving her a sudden grin that made his harsh features a little more likeable. Then he tapped her shoulder. 'Don't look so bemused, Wilson. It's all part of your training.'

Most after-hours socialising was done in the same city-centre bar when officers would meet to discuss the day's work over a pint or two before heading home, at least those who, like Kirsty, took public transport. She'd been out on the town several times before, mostly with her father, as different officers sought out Alistair Wilson before the detective inspector retired for good. But Murdoch had never been amongst the crowd and certainly not at this hour of the day.

Instructed to drive east, Kirsty found herself in a part of Glasgow that she remembered well from her stint in uniform. The old tenement buildings were just the same, beyond the swishing windscreen wipers, many windows boarded up as the developers sought to tear down and renew this area. Regeneration had taken place because of the Commonwealth Games, Glasgow's proud moment on the world stage, the Athletes' Village now home to many families. But it was not to any fancy new pub by the riverside that DC Wilson was directed but an old place on the corner of a street much further along London Road.

'Park round the corner,' Murdoch told her, as she glanced at the double yellow lines beneath the streaming gutters. 'We won't be that long, but why take the chance, eh?' He grinned again and Kirsty began to wonder just what awaited them here at this public house, its ancient metal sign proclaiming THE BIG YIN, a faint picture of a bearded man below just discernible in the teeming rain.

'Don't ask questions, Wilson,' Murdoch said suddenly as he unclipped his seat belt. 'Just watch and listen. Okay?' He tapped the side of his nose and slid out of the Honda as Kirsty resisted the urge to raise her eyebrows to heaven. What on earth were they doing here at this time in the morning? Okay, she glanced at her watch as she closed the door and pulled her raincoat hood over her head, it was officially legal to sell alcohol . . . but why had Murdoch brought her here?

The interior of the pub was dark but warm and dry, a welcome refuge from the torrent beating against the windows. An older man was standing behind the bar flicking through a sheaf of papers, his bare arms sporting a myriad of blue tattoos. He looked up when Murdoch strode inside.

'All right, Jock?' Murdoch nodded to the barman.

'Aye, yourself?' The man nodded back but clearly did not expect a reply, his eyes immediately returned to the documents in his hands.

Murdoch walked across the empty room to a corner table where an old man was sitting nursing a half pint of beer, the empty whisky glass beside him testament to a desperate need to fortify himself. Against the weather? Kirsty wondered. Or because DS Murdoch was now drawing up a stool and sitting opposite?

'Whisky and water for Tam and me,' Murdoch announced. 'And an orange juice for the young lady.'

Kirsty turned to see the barman, who had crept up silently behind them. She tried to make eye contact but the man called Jock had already gone back across the room to fetch their order.

'This is Miss Wilson,' Murdoch said, making the old man look up at Kirsty with his rheumy eyes. 'Tam McLachlan,' Murdoch said shortly by way of introduction.

'How do you do?' Kirsty said, stretching out her hand, but to her annoyance Murdoch slapped it away.

'Don't touch this auld beggar. Never know where he's been,' he said sharply. But the grin belied his action and the old man began to titter as he lifted up the glass to his lips.

Certainly Tam McLachlan was no oil painting, that was for sure, Kirsty thought, looking at him with renewed interest. Several days' growth sprouted from his chin and broken red veins made a pattern across his nose and cheeks, the telltale sign of a heavy drinker. Now Kirsty guessed exactly why she had been brought here. Tam McLachlan was not just any old codger. He was evidently one of Murdoch's snouts from the past.

'My round, I think.' Murdoch pulled some notes from his rain-coat pocket and handed them to Jock the barman as he arrived with a tray, flipping beermats on to the old wooden table before placing down their drinks. It was hardly worth the bother, Kirsty thought, looking at the scarred tabletop, its varnish worn away by years of neglect.

Murdoch waited until Jock had gone away again then he held out his glass and clinked it against the old man's.

'Here's to you, Tam,' he said.

Kirsty sipped her orange juice, noting the other man's gap-toothed grin, the decay in his mouth a sign of poor nutrition or simply neglect. Or, she thought suddenly, had Tam McLachlan lost some of these teeth in other ways? Brawls in the street? Fights amongst gangs? He looked too old and spent now to do much harm, the wrists skinny as he held his whisky glass, but perhaps in his youth he had been a different person.

Murdoch fumbled in his pocket and brought out a roll of twenty-pound notes that he placed on the centre of the table. The old man's eyes gleamed with sudden greed and he put out one claw-like hand.

'Not so fast, Tam.' Murdoch's great fist covered the old man's fingers tightly. 'You know the rules. Have to earn it first.' He took away his hand and Kirsty saw him replace the money in his pocket, Tam's eyes following the gesture.

'Right. Billy Brogan,' Murdoch began.

'Aw, Mr Murdoch, I dinna ken where Billy is,' Tam moaned, his eyes sliding sideways in the way of every liar Kirsty had ever seen.

'Do we believe him, Miss Wilson?' Murdoch turned to Kirsty, a mock innocence in his expression.

'No,' she said, shaking her head as she lifted the glass of juice. She didn't add *sir*. This wasn't an official scene and besides, Murdoch had introduced her as Miss Wilson, not DC.

'See, Tam, the young lady thinks you're telling porkies. Now, you don't want to be impolite, do you? So,' Murdoch leaned across the small round table and took the old man's jacket between two meaty fists, 'tell us what we want to know. Where's Brogan?'

I didn't see that, Kirsty told herself, notching up one more tick against Murdoch. The man had his ways, old-fashioned and unprincipled they might be, but it was nevertheless breathtaking to see what would emerge from this confrontation.

'Agh, Mr Murdoch, you're choking me!' Tam pleaded then gave a cough, sitting back heavily as Murdoch shook him free.

'Brogan,' Murdoch said. 'And I won't ask you again, Tam.'

'More than my life's worth, Mr Murdoch,' Tam McLachlan whined, his eyes lighting on the detective sergeant's raincoat pocket.

There was silence for a few moments then the old man slumped in his seat, an air of defeat resting on his shoulders.

'He wis in the Byres Road flat with Franny Bissett,' Tam whispered at last.

Kirsty froze, the memory of that stinking cadaver coming back with a jolt.

'They had some sort o' a deal goin' on,' he continued, taking a gulp of the whisky and eyeing his now empty glass meaningfully.

Murdoch ignored the unspoken entreaty. 'What kind of deal?'

'Something to do with a big import,' Tam said quietly. 'Brogan was into it big time. Wee Franny was jist his runner.'

'What happened in that flat?'

'How the hell dae ah know, Mr Murdoch?' Tam protested. 'Brogan wis jist staying there wi' Franny when he cam oot the Bar-L back in July. But ah do ken this.' The old man moved closer to the two detectives so that Kirsty caught a whiff of his sour breath. 'Brogan wis dealing before he left the jail. It wis some job that started when he wis inside. Naebody kens jist whit is wis. But if I had to guess I'd say that our Billy-boy was holed up with that cellmate o' his.' Tam nodded, a glint in his eye. 'Guy done for armed robbery.'

Murdoch stared at the old man for a moment then snapped his fingers in the air.

'Two more halfs, Jock. Big ones this time,' he called.

'How long have you known him, sir?' Kirsty asked as they drove back into the city.

'Too bloody long!' Murdoch exclaimed. 'Was a time when Tam McLachlan gave decent information about the goings-on in that part of town. Had a nose for trouble, that one, but the drink got to him, as you can see. Muddles things up a bit nowadays. But I'm willing to bet that this wee nugget is pure gold, even from Tam's wasted brain.'

'Billy Brogan seems to have cropped up before,' Kirsty mused aloud.

'One of your pal's old cases.' Murdoch snorted. 'Lorimer and your dad were both working on that one, as I recall. Bloody shambles, if you ask me,' he humphed. 'But they got Brogan all right. Put him away for a few years anyway.'

Kirsty remained silent after that, following Murdoch's directions as they navigated through the streets, turning south towards the address that Murdoch had eventually prised from the old snout.

The road wound around the curve of a park then Kirsty found herself driving in and out of a series of old streets, their run-down tenements a far cry from the East End's regeneration.

'Loads of foreigners,' Murdoch remarked as they passed a gypsy-looking man and woman outside the mouth of a close, a baby swaddled in a blanket across its mother's chest. 'Place is hoaching with druggies and whores,' he added with disgust.

'This was your old patch, sir?'

'Aye,' Murdoch replied but said nothing more, his eyes

intent on reading each house number as they crawled along the street.

'Round the corner,' he said at last, after leaning forward and giving a quick glance at the upper windows. 'And just sit where you are. These men might have guns. We'll need back-up for this one.' He looked across at Kirsty and gave her a grim smile.

It was less than half an hour later that the cars arrived, armed officers heading round to the back of the tenement and others swarming through the front close.

'Stay put,' Murdoch ordered, strapping the bulletproof vest to his chest.

Kirsty opened her mouth to protest but Murdoch silenced her with a scowl.

'Your dad would have my guts for garters if anything happened to his wee lassie,' he grunted. Then he was gone, running in the wake of the armed officers, leaving Kirsty wondering just what would happen if Billy Brogan had a weapon.

The man wasn't doing anything other than his job, Kirsty told herself as the uniformed officers led Brogan and another swarthy-looking man away to the waiting police van. But she still owed it to Lorimer to see what she could learn.

'Good to know we'll be a bit further along the road in finding out what's behind this Quiet Release thing, sir,' she began.

'Aye,' Murdoch agreed, sitting back and fumbling in his pocket for his packet of cigarettes.

Kirsty rolled down the passenger window without being asked and glanced across as Murdoch lit up.

'Must have been hard for you, personally, I mean, sir,' she continued bravely.

323

'How d'you mean, Wilson?' The DS turned away to blow smoke out of the window.

'Seeing your wife so ill and knowing later that someone was close by, taking other patients' lives,' she ventured.

There was silence between them for a few moments and Kirsty wondered if she had gone a step too far but then a faint smile played about the man's mouth.

'Irene loved life,' Murdoch said at last. 'She'd never have condoned assisted suicide. Even to the very end she wanted to be here.' He turned and stared at the girl by his side. 'See, when they say they want an end to it all, most of them mean an end to the pains and discomfort, not an end to their existence. It's not the same thing at all,' he muttered. 'And if we could have found a cure or even a way of prolonging her life, we would have done anything . . . ' He broke off, staring over the river as they crossed the Kingston Bridge away from the place where his wife had taken her final breath.

'Do you think I should have helped her to end her life, Wilson?' he asked softly, turning to stare into Kirsty's eyes.

'No, sir,' she answered.

'Good,' he said shortly, taking another drag on his cigarette. 'Not everyone thinks that way. See, I was one of the lucky ones. I got a chance to say goodbye to my loved one.'

Murdoch's brow furrowed as he tossed the butt of his cigarette out of the window. 'I can tell you, Wilson, I'm one hundred per cent behind Lorimer on this case. I want to catch the bastard that's doing this to sick people. Taking the choice of life or death out of their hands. Stopping them from being able to say their last goodbyes.'

CHAPTER FORTY

Detective Superintendent Lorimer looked around the inter-view room. It should have been Murdoch here instead of himself but the detective sergeant and his young colleague were seated on the other side of the glass wall that separated this room from where they sat waiting for the interview to begin, able to hear and see all that was going on but invisible to the occupants of the room. A little apart from the table and empty chairs sat the bearded psychologist, his presence a little unusual perhaps, but Lorimer wanted the man to witness all that was going to happen in the next hour or so.

Both men looked up as a uniformed officer led Billy Brogan into the room, followed by a tired-looking Pauline Dick, whose services Brogan had requested.

There was a swagger to the man's gait as he came into the room and sat down, scraping the chair under him as if eager to begin.

A spell in prison had not done anything to improve the drug dealer, Lorimer thought, looking at Brogan. The man's once sandy hair was turning grey, cropped close to his skull to mask the diminishing hairline. His arms were folded defiantly as he stared across the table at Lorimer. Once upon a time Billy Brogan had been a small-time dealer until his thieving ways had landed him in a lot of trouble. Something had changed while he'd been inside, Lorimer thought, regarding the man silently. There was a hardness around that thin-lipped mouth, a knowing look from those pale blue eyes so similar to the ones that the detective had read over the years. *I'm a hard man*, his expression seemed to be saying. *Crack me if you can.*

Too right, pal, Lorimer told himself grimly.

'Interview beginning on Wednesday the twelfth of October,' he began.

A sudden thought of the following week flashed into his mind; they had pencilled in for a break while Maggie was off school for the half-term holiday. If they could wrap this up in the next few days ...

Kirsty watched the scene before her, conscious of the man by her side who was munching his way through the second of a plate of scones and jam that he'd lifted from Sadie's trolley. Comfort food, she told herself. Or maybe he'd not eaten breakfast. How did you cope in the aftermath of a loss like Murdoch's? The thought was pushed aside as they saw the detective superintendent move some papers around on the table, a look of affected boredom on his handsome features.

'How does he *do* that?' Kirsty whispered.

'Years of practice, Wilson,' Murdoch grunted. 'Watch and learn, eh?' he added with a chuckle.

Either Brogan had forgotten the tall detective's methods or he was too cocksure about his own ability to dissemble, for the man leaned back in his chair, drumming the heels of his trainers against the linoleum as though he were home and dry already.

'Francis Bissett,' Lorimer began, not looking at Brogan but at the notes in front of him. 'Slashes to the throat, fatal injury being the severing of his windpipe. Left to die in the bathroom of his rented flat in Byres Road.' He looked up suddenly as though he had just remembered the presence of the prisoner.

'Your flat too, Billy.'

'Aye, jist for a wee while,' Brogan replied, his jaws moving up and down as he masticated a piece of chewing gum.

'After your release from Barlinnie on July the twenty-sixth,' Lorimer agreed, his bank manager's voice dry as dust.

Brogan sighed and nodded, clearly bored already by the conversation.

'Please speak for the tape,' Lorimer instructed, not deigning to look at Brogan.

'Yes, I stayed with Franny Bissett for a couple of days,' he agreed. 'So what?'

The impertinent addition made Kirsty draw in her breath. Surely Lorimer would pounce on that piece of cheek? But no, he seemed not to have noticed.

'And what date did you leave Byres Road?'

Brogan shrugged and shot a look at Pauline Dick who nodded to him to answer the question.

'End of the month,' he said, glancing sideways and licking his lips.

'Effing liar!' Murdoch growled by Kirsty's side. 'Bet you were there when poor wee Frankie copped it, you nasty piece of shit.'

Kirsty raised her eyebrows. Tam McLachlan had referred to the dead man as Franny, like Brogan, but the cops had known him as Frankie, as if there had been another side to him. *A better side?* Kirsty wondered. Nobody she'd met in the course of her work had been totally evil, had they? Wasn't there always a redeeming feature in even the worst criminals?

'We have reason to believe that you stayed a lot longer than that, Billy,' Lorimer said mildly, stopping at a particular piece of paper and staring at it intently as if the evidence to support his statement was right there in front of him.

'Who says?' The words came out as Brogan raised his chin defiantly.

Lorimer smiled at him. 'Oh, you know we cannot divulge our sources, Mr Brogan,' he said. 'Let's just say we have been reliably informed that you left the Byres Road flat and took up residence in Cartside Street in mid August, around the time of Frankie's death.'

He flicked through the papers again and, as if reading from the one he held up towards him, intoned, 'August the nineteenth, to be exact. Just before all the students came back to look for flats in the area. Good time to move, I suppose.'

Brogan shuffled his feet, clearly rattled by this piece of news. 'So what? Never been very good at dates and that,' he blustered.

'So you agree that your residence at Cartside Street did in fact commence on August nineteenth?'

'Whit?' Brogan frowned at the formality of the detective super-intendent's words, echoing as they did the sort of parlance that Brogan might come across in a court of law.

Clever, Kirsty told herself. *Make him feel he's in the dock already.*

'Aye, well, that's right but ah wis staying with a burd before that,' he said, one leg bouncing up and down, a sure sign of the man's growing anxiety.

'Name and address?' Lorimer asked, his pencil poised above a clean page of the notebook in front of him.

'Eh, um . . . Marianne,' Brogan said, a note of desperation in his voice. Then, sitting back he looked down at his lap, clearly cross with himself.

'Tut, tut, Billy,' Lorimer said with the ghost of a smile playing about his mouth. 'You can do better than that. Your sister, Marianne? That the first name that springs to mind? Oh dear, Billy, could it be that you have a guilty conscience about your poor sister?' Lorimer's tone was mocking now and Kirsty realised why. Brogan's sister had been transferred from prison to a secure mental unit following the murder case that had involved the brother and sister. Had he ever visited her? Kirsty mused. But her thoughts were interrupted as the detective continued his questions.

'Rob Dolan told us that you had recruited him for a job,' Lorimer said suddenly, laying down the notebook and folding his hands upon the table.

Brogan glanced nervously at Pauline Dick whose face had taken on a familiar stony expression. Kirsty felt sorry for the lawyer. What must it be like to constantly be at the beck and call of types like Brogan, Cunningham and Dolan?

'No comment,' Brogan said, the line of his jaw tightening.

'Mr Dolan also said that you were aware of the identity of the person whose idea this was. The person behind Quiet Release.'

Brogan dropped his gaze and leaned towards Pauline Dick, whispering in her ear.

'You must speak for the tape, Mr Brogan,' Lorimer insisted. 'Mr Brogan has just spoken inaudibly to his lawyer, Ms Dick,' he added lugubriously.

'If I tell youse . . .' Brogan looked up nervously. 'Do I get witness protection?'

How the detective superintendent managed to keep a straight face when Murdoch burst out laughing at her side was anyone's guess, Kirsty thought, marvelling yet again at the detective superintendent's sangfroid.

'Any information you provide us with today will be taken into consideration by the Crown Office,' Lorimer assured him, the tones he now used more like those of a kindly head teacher to a wayward pupil.

'I jist know who paid us,' Brogan said, his eyes flicking from Pauline Dick to Lorimer then across to the bearded man in the corner as though he had just clocked him at that particular moment.

There was a silence in the two rooms then, Kirsty and Murdoch leaning forward intently as they waited to hear, Lorimer sitting patiently, a small smile of satisfaction on his face as though ready to reward the man opposite.

'Wee fat man,' Brogan told them. 'Lawyer up in West Regent Street. Said his name was Barry.'

'And how often did you meet this gentleman?'

'No' very often,' Brogan admitted. 'He'd see us in the Amber Regent for a Chinese meal and hand over the cash. Followed him one time, though. That's how I knew where he worked.'

'Us?'

'Aye. Naw, jist me and him.' Brogan looked at Pauline Dick. 'Will I get time off for telling all this?' he asked hopefully.

'Brian Abernethy,' Kirsty whispered gleefully from the next room. '*Has* to be him!'

West Regent Street was crowded with office staff spilling out into the street when Lorimer and Kirsty walked briskly up the hill. Len Murdoch had been given the task of questioning Brogan further, this time about the death of Francis Bissett. Would he still be tempted to cry no comment about that? Kirsty wondered as she walked as fast as she could to keep up with Lorimer.

The doors were still open when they arrived, the same receptionist sitting behind her desk

'Mr Abernethy?' Lorimer told the woman. 'May we see him, please? He isn't expecting us,' he continued, holding out his warrant card to remind her of their official presence.

'He's not here,' she told them with an air of surprise. 'Didn't you know? Mr Abernethy has sold the practice and gone overseas.'

'A forwarding address perhaps?' Lorimer asked, but his face did not express any hope of being given this and he was right.

'It all happened so quickly,' the receptionist told them. 'One day he was here, the next he was gone, just an email to let the rest of the staff know what was happening. I've been kept on till the new owners move in.' She looked from the tall man to the young woman. 'Why? He isn't in any trouble, surely?'

'Can we see his room? There may be papers that we need to take away,' Lorimer explained.

The woman put her hand to her mouth in a gesture of dismay.

'Oh dear,' she said, biting her lip. 'I thought it was strange, doing that, I mean ... there aren't any papers left ...'

'What do you mean?' Lorimer asked.

'He left it in such a mess,' the woman whimpered. 'All the drawers pulled out, everything empty.' She looked at them both as though she might begin to cry. 'And bags and bags of everything by his desk.' She shook her head miserably. 'You see, when we eventually unlocked Mr Abernethy's office we found that everything had been shredded.'

'A dead end?' Kirsty asked as they retraced their steps down to the city centre.

'Not necessarily,' Lorimer told her, then fell silent. The technical staff were working hard on the Imries' laptop computer. What they might find there could easily push the investigation forwards. But for once Lorimer was loath to share this information with his younger colleague. Maggie first, he told himself. Especially if it was news of the worst sort.

The late news programme was just finishing on BBC Scotland when his mobile vibrated in his trouser pocket.

'Lorimer.' He spoke into the phone as he rose from the settee, ignoring Maggie's questioning glance. She'd know soon enough if this was what he was expecting to hear.

'Go ahead,' he said, walking out of the sitting room and into the hallway. 'I'm listening.'

The detective's face was impassive as he heard the woman's voice reading from the report. As he had anticipated, the laptop had been pretty easy to search, the messages from Quiet Release simple to retrieve. He closed his eyes as the replies from Annette Imrie were read out to him then heaved a quick sigh.

'Thanks,' was all he said. 'Excellent job. Thanks for getting back to me so quickly. Appreciate it.'

He closed the phone and slipped it back into his pocket then stood at the window, looking out into the darkness. The rain that had fallen steadily all day had abated, leaving skies that were clear, stars sparkling in the heavens. When all was said and done they were all just creatures with an allotted span. Some would slip away in their latter years, frail and tired, others were gone far too quickly, like the baby boy who'd been born to them all those years ago. There was nothing fair about life or death, Lorimer told himself. It was a matter of luck where you were born and what sort of life you made for yourself, wasn't it? The Imries had been men of the soil, he had chosen a different path, but they had all had the good fortune to live in a country at peace with the rest of mankind. Why then were there folk who persisted in destroying that peace? People like Annette Imrie, whose misdeeds were about to be unfolded to the woman waiting patiently for him?

Maggie sat in the toilet weeping. The death of her cousin was bad enough, she'd told him. But to think that his own sister-in-law had been instrumental in having David murdered! Bill was downstairs now, the promise of a cup of tea a weak apology for the disastrous news he had given her.

'Why?' She whispered the word aloud. 'What harm had the poor soul ever done to you?' She thought about the red-haired woman at the funeral, her anger against the sick man palpable. It hadn't taken too much guesswork to see what Patrick's wife had achieved. And he'd taken steps to ensure that she would be caught. Maggie stopped crying and blew her nose. What sort of relationship did that pair have? The hard-working farmer and the younger woman who would not have looked out of place in a fashion shoot. *His second wife*, Maggie reminded herself. Some men were poor choosers, weren't they? Stephanie Imrie, the first wife who she remembered from the lavish wedding in Stirling, hadn't lasted the pace. She had never been cut out for the role of a farmer's wife. At least the woman had had the sense to see that early on, unlike Patrick.

Maggie wiped her face with a damp facecloth and dried it hastily, smears of mascara darkening the pink towel. Sod it! Well, it would go into the wash.

She unlocked the door and walked across their bedroom. Bill had lit the bedside lamps, leaving a small tray with a mug of tea and a biscuit by Maggie's side of the bed. The duvet was turned back too, an invitation to crawl under the covers if that was what she wished.

It wasn't Bill's fault, Maggie reminded herself, sitting on the edge of the bed. It was just part of the job. And hadn't it been Patrick who had called? Asking to speak to Bill, pleading with him to take a look at the circumstances of David's death, wanting there to be a post-mortem. Had the ruddy-cheeked farmer known even then? Had Annette given herself away at any point? How he must have despised his wife! Or had Patrick been party to a scheme to take his own brother's life?

Maggie sat very still. She didn't believe it. Didn't *want* to believe it. But somehow the truth behind her cousin's death had to be discovered.

And, as she warmed her hands around the mug of tea, Maggie Lorimer knew that her husband would do just that.

CHAPTER FORTY-ONE

Once again it was Detective Constable Wilson that accompanied Lorimer to the farm amongst the Stirlingshire hills. He did not anticipate any problems but the local constabulary had been made aware that an arrest was about to be made on their patch.

The rain from the previous day had left huge puddles and the big car slewed through them, causing sheets of spray to arc high into the air. Kirsty shivered then put out a finger and turned the heated seat up to its maximum level. Lorimer glanced at the small action. It was not just the colder days that made her feel like this, he guessed. It was the thought of what lay ahead, the arrest of a woman she'd once met in her own home.

The same two collies ran to meet them as Lorimer and Kirsty left the car and headed to the farmhouse door. But this time there was no shout from the building and he let the dogs sniff around his legs as he and Kirsty stood waiting for an answer to his knock.

'D'you think they're in?' Kirsty asked at last, looking up at him.

'Land Rover's there,' he said, a tilt of his head indicating the vehicle parked in the yard.

At last he tried the door handle. It turned easily and the door swung open, the pair of collies bounding through as if to show them the way.

'Hello?' Lorimer called into the darkened hallway.

There was no answer.

'Go through to the kitchen,' Lorimer told Kirsty. 'See if there's any sign of them.'

The farmhouse kitchen was as warm as before, the big range heating the entire room, the basket of squirming kittens wakening as the dogs bent down to sniff them before loping out of the room again.

Lorimer followed the collies out and along a corridor where they came to a halt outside a closed door.

For a moment his eyes met the young detective constable's.

'Something's wrong,' Kirsty ventured, picking up on the expression on his face.

Lorimer hesitated for a moment then one of the dogs began to whine and scratch at the bottom of the door.

He turned the handle but nothing budged.

'Patrick? Are you in there? It's me. Lorimer.'

For a long moment nothing happened but the persistent scratching of the dog, then the door opened and they saw the farmer standing there, the hands hanging by his side covered in blood.

As Lorimer stepped into the room, Patrick stood aside, a pair of heavy wire cutters grasped in his right hand. His face was drawn and pale, as he looked from them to the figure sprawled on the sofa.

Annette Imrie was hardly recognisable, the blood from a wound on her head streaking rivulets down her face and soaking into the neck of her white jumper.

'Is she dead?' Kirsty whispered, looking up at the farmer who was slumped against the wall as if his legs would hardly support him.

'I don't know.' His voice cracked

Lorimer was bent over the woman now, one hand feeling her wrist.

'She's still with us,' he said, glancing at Kirsty. 'Get an ambulance here. Now.'

He stood up and grasped Patrick's arm, taking the tool out of his hand, then led him away from the room

'Why ...?' Lorimer shook his head in despair as Patrick bent to push the dogs away.

'I tried to stop her leaving,' Patrick Imrie gulped. Drawing a hand across his eyes. 'I didn't mean to ...' He broke off as Lorimer took him into the kitchen.

'Sit down, Patrick,' the detective told him gently, seeing the man trembling all over. Shock was beginning to set in and he wanted to hear what this man had to say before he became too upset to talk.

'Kirsty,' he asked, as the DC appeared at the door, 'can you put the kettle on?'

He turned back to Patrick and spoke quietly to the distraught farmer. 'Tell me what happened, Patrick.'

'I told her that you were coming to speak to her.' He heaved a weary sigh that seemed to reverberate throughout his whole body.

Lorimer waited for him to continue, aware that Patrick Imrie was now reliving the horror of what he had done.

'She just went berserk,' he whispered. 'Screaming and yelling that it was better for David to be dead and us to have a decent lifestyle ...' He broke off, the words choking in his throat.

Lorimer studied the man's face as Patrick swallowed hard.

A tough man of the outdoors he might be but the death of his brother and the knowledge that it had been effected by his own wife had broken his spirit.

The farmer gave a long sigh and sat up a little straighter, his face still white, but he glanced at Lorimer and nodded.

'Hard to explain what happened,' he told the detective superintendent. 'Something in me just snapped. I'd been outside mending a section of fence. These were in my hand ...' He pointed to the heavy metal wire cutters that Lorimer had laid down on the floor.

'If she hadn't said these things about Davie ...' The farmer put his head in his hands, covering his face with bloody fingers, and began to sob.

Beyond the sound of his cries the faint but unmistakable rise of a siren could be heard.

'Police or ambulance,' Lorimer said quietly. 'Kirsty, go and tell them where to find Mrs Imrie.'

Left alone with the farmer and the blood-soaked woman lying unconscious on the sofa in the other room, Lorimer put out a tentative hand to the man's arm. His stomach churned and the dull ache of a returning headache made him pause for a moment. *It was his job*, he told himself, *just his job* ...

'I'll have to arrest you, Patrick. You know that, don't you?'

Patrick Imrie nodded, his eyes downcast. 'What about the farm?' he asked suddenly. 'Who'll look after the beasts? The dogs?' He spread his arms around, a look of confusion in his face. 'There's so much to do ...'

Should have thought about that before you lashed out, Lorimer thought to himself, but there was no way he could utter such harsh words as he watched the disbelief on the man's face. He had seen it all before: the hasty blow delivered in fury then the look of horror as reality sank in. *I didn't mean to do it . . .* the phrase that often followed such acts of passion. He wanted to tell him that everything would be okay, but that was never going to happen. Annette Imrie might die and everything this man had worked for would be taken away from him.

'I'll see your neighbours in Upper Tannoch,' Lorimer promised. 'And perhaps you'll receive bail . . . '

The look that Patrick Imrie shot at him filled Lorimer with dismay. He might be part of this man's family, albeit by marriage, yet at this moment as he prepared to read him his rights Detective Superintendent William Lorimer was a threatening figure of authority to the farmer, nothing more.

After the police car and ambulance had removed both husband and wife from the premises, Lorimer motioned Kirsty into the farm kitchen once more. The kittens were staggering about on shaky paws, their tiny tails upright as they crawled over one another to find their way back to the warmth. Lorimer watched as Kirsty picked them up one by one and replaced them in the basket. A movement by the window alerted him to a tortoiseshell cat that had jumped up at the sill and was rubbing itself against the glass.

'In you come,' he said, opening the window and letting the mother cat jump noiselessly down. Soon she was lying on her side, the purrs of contentment emanating from the kittens as they nursed.

'Better let the neighbours know about this lot, too,' Lorimer sighed. 'Don't know if Patrick Imrie will be back any time soon to look after these creatures.'

'What'll happen to him, sir?' Kirsty asked as they walked out of the farmhouse.

'Well, you were present when I read him his rights, DC Wilson,' Lorimer said, his mouth closing in a tight line. 'Depends on how bad Annette is,' he went on quietly. 'He'll likely be looking at a charge of assault to severe injury. Then there is the matter of whether or not he knew what his wife had done.'

'What do you think, sir?'

Lorimer shook his head. 'To my mind Patrick knew nothing about this end-of-life organisation. It seems to have been his wife who had taken the initiative when they emailed the farm. But she may tell a different tale. *If* she recovers,' he added darkly. 'I just hope that my wife's cousin gets himself a decent lawyer.' He opened the car door, ushering Kirsty inside.

He looked over the expanse of fields, the cattle over on a far park, sheep mere dots against the green hillside. 'It's a hard life at the best of times.' He swung himself into the driver's seat. 'Farming's a lot more than just baskets of kittens,' he said, his eyes full of something sad as he looked across at Kirsty. 'Come on, we've got a visit to make to the Imries' neighbours. Then we need to get back to Glasgow to see where we go next.'

It was dark by the time Lorimer reached home again. He sat in the big car with its engine turned off, staring into space. He'd left a message on Maggie's phone giving her only the barest details. How was he going to tell her about Patrick and Annette? The woman had regained consciousness and was sedated, a police guard outside her room until such times as Lorimer could return to question her. *And charge her with conspiracy to murder*, a small voice reminded him. And Patrick? How could he tell Maggie that her cousin had attacked his wife and was now languishing in a cell subject to being taken before a judge the following morning?

She was standing at the cooker stirring something in a large pot when he entered the long open-plan room that was divided into a study-cum-living room and kitchen, divided by a long breakfast bar. The overhead light shone down on her head, making a halo of brightness above her long dark curls.

'Hey, gorgeous.' In a few strides Lorimer was at Maggie's side, his arms encircling her waist.

'What happened?' Maggie did not turn around but kept stirring the pot of broth, her eyes fixed on the wooden spoon as though she were afraid to meet his eyes.

Lorimer let go of her with a sigh. 'Not good news, I'm afraid. I'll have to see Annette in the morning. If she survives,' he added bleakly. 'Then I expect to have to charge her.'

'What about Patrick?' Maggie stopped stirring for a moment, lifting the spoon and letting the soup drip from its rounded edge. 'You said something about him attacking her? That can't be right, surely?'

He said nothing as she looked at him through weary eyes.

'It's true, then,' Maggie said dully. 'Patrick found out that Annette had colluded in David's death.'

'If only he'd waited for us to arrive,' Lorimer said, a note of regret creeping into his voice. 'We'd have taken her away, questioned her and then none of this other stuff would have happened.'

'But why? Why did he attack her today and not when he found out what she'd done?'

'Oh . . .' Lorimer let out a huge sigh. 'He was keeping such a control of himself, I imagine. Then she let fly at him. Verbally, I mean,' he added as Maggie raised astonished eyebrows. 'Usual story, I'm afraid. Just snapped and lashed out at her.'

'Dear God.' Maggie let the spoon fall into the pot then came and placed her head on her husband's chest. 'What a mess,' she whispered. 'What a hellish, hellish mess!'

341

CHAPTER FORTY-TWO

Ailsa Doyle pushed the pram along the street, the sound of her child's cries lessened by the music playing in her ears. Her mother would kill her if she knew but Ailsa didn't care. She'd hide the headphones in her pocket before she reached her mother's door, let the wean scream at the top of his voice so all the neighbours knew what a great pair of lungs he had.

But when the young mother reached her mother's house she was surprised to see a police car parked outside. Pushing the pram up the garden path, Ailsa looked at the front of the house to see if there was any movement from inside. Aye, she thought. Polis are in there cadging a cuppa from the auld yin. She placed a foot on the brake and bent down to cradle the baby in her arms, taking his blanket and wrapping him up against the chill October wind.

'You in here?' Ailsa said loudly as she barged into the front room where three pairs of eyes looked up at her.

'I've goat company,' Ailsa's mother sniffed in obvious disapproval. 'I'm assisting these two officers with their in-qui-erries,' she drawled, trying to sound posher than she was.

'Oh, aye?' Ailsa grinned. 'Here, haud the wean a mo, will ye?' She handed the baby to her mother who took him but looked back at Ailsa with an expression of annoyance on her face.

'Huve youse heard ony mair frae ma maw than whit ah telt that detective lassie and thon big guy, Lorimer? Eh?' Ailsa demanded, plonking herself down on a vacant easy chair and lifting a packet of cigarettes from her pocket.

'No' in here, hen,' her mother admonished her. 'Mind the wean.'

'Mrs Doyle?' one of the officers, an older hard-faced woman, asked. 'Ailsa Doyle?'

'That's me,' Ailsa agreed. 'Ah'm the one who saw that man leaving Miss Maitland's house. Okay?'

'I'm Detective Constable Fairlie and this is DC Munro,' the woman told her. 'We wanted to ask your mum about Miss Maitland's past.'

'Oh.' The wind seemed to be taken out of the girl's sails momentarily. 'Mind if I stay and hear about it?'

The two detectives looked at one another, then Jean Fairlie shrugged. 'Don't see why not. You'll just tell her anyway, isn't that right, Mrs MacSherry?'

'Ah never knew about her early life,' the older woman began. 'Jist since she came to stay here. She'd be about thirty, thirty-five then, maybe. No fella, jist herself.'

'And when would this be?'

'Oh, now ...' Ailsa's mother pondered the question, counting on her fingers. 'Oor Ailsa's twenty-three this year, Tam's four years older, Charlotte's thirtieth comes just before Christmas and Eddie's forty next August.' She nodded in satisfaction. 'And ma Ricky's forty-four on my birthday. I'll be sixty-five,' she said proudly. 'Naebody could believe it when that yin came alang,' she added grinning at her daughter. 'Anither wean at that age.' She hooted with laughter.

Then her face fell for a moment. 'She must've moved here about 1972. Forty-five years we lived across the street from her, wid ye credit that. There ah wis, happy with ma bairns and pair Jane Maitland all alone in the world. She used tae love comin' in tae see them, you know.' Mrs MacSherry looked down at the grandson in her arms with apparent contentment. 'Loved bairns, so she did. Pity she never had any of her own, I used to tell her.'

'What did she say whenever you made that comment?' DC Fairlie asked sharply.

'Nothin'.' Mrs MacSherry shrugged. 'She jist went a' quiet like and sad. Mibbe she'd had an unhappy romance?' She began to rock the baby in her arms. 'Anyway, that was then. We saw mair of her at weekends when she wasn't working, o' course. But even after she retired there was always a wee gift brought over for any o' the grandweans. She wis nice like that, very thoughtful.'

'She never mentioned any of her own family by any chance?'

'Naw, pair sowel had naebody,' Mrs MacSherry shook her head.

'Aye she did,' Ailsa interjected. 'She telt me wance she had a nephew. Big shot down in London she said.'

'When was that?' DC Fairlie asked.

'Oh, now . . .' Ailsa chewed her lip thoughtfully for a moment. 'Must've been after she was ill. Cos I remember I was in her bedroom giving her a cup of tea . . . aye, about this time last year, jist efter Halloween. I'd asked her about the fella, whether he had kids an' that, but she didn't seem to know very much.'

Ailsa walked back slowly to her own home. They'd speered plenty after that, wanted to know things that her mother simply could not remember. But why, Ailsa Doyle wanted to know, were they asking all these questions about children? Was it something to do with the old lady's will? And had she left her wee house downstairs to this nephew from London? Ailsa frowned. She had been asked to put her signature to a document that day when the wee fat lawyer had called in. It had been the poor wee soul's Last Will and Testament. Was that why the polis had come back? Or was there something else in the old lady's past that had brought them here? Something that Jane Maitland had kept hidden even from Ailsa's own mother?

Father Fitzsimmons frowned as he unfolded his hands from his prayers. The missing key had completely slipped his mind but now he had remembered the empty hook behind the door and the fact that nobody had returned it to its place. His housekeeper did those sorts of things, leaving Father to the spiritual side of his ministry. Except that she hadn't. Mrs Brown, a widow of many years and a stickler for order, had not come across the large brass key, she had told him firmly. And now the priest sat pondering its whereabouts. Jane Maitland had entrusted it to him, welcoming the priest's visits, especially towards the end.

With a sigh, Father Fitzsimmons lifted the telephone and dialled the number on the small rectangle of cardboard that the police officer had given him.

A few minutes later he replaced the phone on its cradle and put his fingers to his lips. If Detective Superintendent Lorimer was right, then there had been a thief inside the Parish House, possibly a person known to either Mrs Brown or himself. The thought made him close his eyes with a sigh and he folded his fingers together once more.

'It all began with her,' Solly said. 'Jane Maitland had a great deal of money to leave to her illegitimate son.'

'And now Brian Abernethy's done a runner,' Lorimer said gloomily.

'What about the son? Mr Whyte? Has he been able to help you at all?'

Lorimer shook his head. 'Spoke to him as soon as we knew Abernethy had scarpered. He sounded astonished when we told him.' His face twisted in a sardonic grin. 'Wanted to know if his inheritance was safe and went very quiet when I told him that all the documents had been shredded.'

'Will he get his money?'

'Oh, I think so. It may have to go to probate if there is no other copy of Jane Maitland's will, however. Her money is tied up in stocks and bonds plus that hefty amount gaining tiny interest payments in the current account.'

'Isn't that strange?' Solly asked, stroking his beard thoughtfully.

'What?'

'That she kept such a vast amount in her account. And no large sums withdrawn?'

Lorimer sighed volubly. 'We'll never know why she did that,' he said. 'Perhaps she intended making payments to different people before her death? A lump sum for the church or to friends and neighbours who'd been kind?'

'Sums that couldn't be taxed?'

'Maybe.' Lorimer shrugged. 'It was Abernethy senior who had been her solicitor until he died last year. Then his son, Brian, took over.'

'And found he had a terminally ill client with a great deal of money that she wanted to leave to the man she thought was her long-lost son,' Solly mused. 'Even though he was a complete stranger.'

'Father Fitzsimmons called me this morning,' Lorimer told him. 'The spare key to Jane Maitland's house is still missing.'

'Hm.' Solly tapped his finger against his cheek. 'Now who would have had easy access to that particular key?'

Once again Lorimer found himself face to face with Rob Dolan. The room in Barlinnie Prison was bright after the darkened walls outside and the prisoner sat opposite blinking hard.

'How are you, Rob?' Lorimer began.

'You're no' here tae ask after ma health, are ye, Mr Lorimer?' Dolan screwed up his eyes and glowered at the detective.

'Right first time, son,' Lorimer agreed. 'Need some more information from you, though.'

'Will it count when ah come tae court?' Dolan shot back.

'I'll include it in my report to the Fiscal, certainly.' Lorimer smiled.

Dolan looked doubtful for a moment then gave a sigh. 'Whit d'ye want?'

Lorimer leaned forward and spoke quietly. 'I would like to know if any of you were in the Parish House at St Martin's.'

'Oh ...' The word was drawn out as Dolan stared back at the detective. Then he grinned. 'Took youse long enough tae figure that wan out, eh?'

Lorimer sat silently, his raised eyebrows the only gesture necessary for the prisoner to continue.

'Aye, well.' Dolan ducked his head, avoiding the detective superintendent's cold blue stare. 'Me an' a couple of pals, we asked the Father if he needed his grass cut. Brogan's idea, see. He knew frae this wee lassie at the church that Father Fitz used tae visit the auld wumman. Had her key, see?'

'And it was an easy enough matter to lift the key and pass it to Brogan,' Lorimer said.

'Aye. But we were supposed tae be given it back again. An'

347

we never,' Dolan complained. 'Orders were tae pit it back where we'd found it.' He shrugged and licked his lips. 'You havenae goat any sweeties on ye, eh?' Dolan's eyes fell upon the brown paper bag lying near Lorimer's hand.

'Oh, that?' Lorimer glanced at the packet. 'Mars bars.' He lifted the parcel into the air. 'But you don't like them, do you, Rob?' he teased.

'Whit more c'n ah tell ye?' Dolan said, his eyes following the brown paper bag as Lorimer laid it down again.

'You can tell me who was given that key, Rob,' Lorimer said softly, a tone of menace in his voice.

'Sure as God's ma witness, I passed it on tae Brogan. That wis aye the way of it,' he protested. 'Me an' Jerry were jist the go-betweens, the fixers, know whit ah mean? An' Brogan never gied us that key back like he wis meant tae.'

'Yes, Rob, I know exactly what you mean. Here.' Lorimer tossed the sweets across the table. 'And if there is anything else you've forgotten to tell me I'll find out from your pal across the way.' He cocked his head towards the wall that separated this block from the one where Billy Brogan was housed.

'Eh ...' Dolan clasped the paper bag to his chest as if it contained a month's worth of cocaine. 'That lassie ...'

'Sarah Wilding?'

'Aye, her. Supposed tae be asked tae do some of the needle jobs. But Brogan said there'd been a change of plan.' It was Dolan's turn to lean across the table. 'See what I think.' He tapped his forehead solemnly. 'There's a fella out there who's a doctor or a nurse. Knows how tae dae all that stuff. And I bet Brogan knows who he is.'

Sarah Wilding was supposed to do *some of the needle jobs.* The phrase resonated around the detective's brain.

There could be more than one doctor or nurse employed by this organisation, he suddenly thought. The handsome man described by Mary Milligan might have been a completely different person from the man seen leaving Jane Maitland's home that September morning. And had it been someone else in the two nursing homes that had wielded these needles?

For a moment Lorimer stopped to imagine the extent of this organisation. Solly had hinted that its tentacles had had a much greater reach than any of them yet knew. And, if that was so, were they looking for a team of medics who had taken money in exchange for putting people to sleep? How many folk had suffered this fate already? And would it be possible to find the mastermind behind Quiet Release, to put a stop to this business once and for all?

'Brogan's been utterly useless,' Lorimer told the man sitting opposite. 'I'm sorry, sir, but I think you are right. We need to throw the net a lot wider to find Brian Abernethy.'

The chief constable took a sip of his tea from the white porcelain cup and then set it down on the table. 'The chain of command appears to have been well thought out,' the man in uniform said at last. 'Abernethy may be the man behind the whole scheme. Or there might be someone even higher up pulling his strings. What's your thoughts on this, Lorimer?'

Lorimer stifled the desire to sigh. Sir Robert Caldwell had every right to question the way this case had proceeded and yet it had not been easy at first to tie some of the deaths together. 'I'd like to talk to Crawford Whyte again, sir. Might do no harm to obtain a search warrant for his home and office. See what we can find on his computers.'

'Hm.' The chief constable pursed his lips as though considering

349

this. 'And what about the technical staff? Haven't they come up with anything at all yet?'

'No, sir, not so far. What we do know is that every email address for Quiet Release was abandoned after each death. They knew what they were doing,' he said sourly. 'IP addresses kept being changed so the main user couldn't be tracked. And they were meant to use different mobile phones for each new job.'

'Very well, get on to the Fiscal for a search warrant. A trip to London and back . . . ' Caldwell shook his head. 'Better get some results, Lorimer. The budget's stretched tight enough as it is.'

There was so much that had to be verified. Crawford Whyte's statements had been backed up by Abernethy and by the local Salvation Army officers who had traced the Maitland family on the dead woman's behalf. So why did he have this nagging feeling that the man from London had been telling them less than the whole truth?

Maggie was poring over a pile of jotters when he pushed open the door to the living room. She looked up with a tired smile then waved a pen in the air.

'Just got three more to finish then I'm done for the night,' she told him. 'Soup's in the fridge.'

Lorimer bent down to give her a peck on the cheek then slung his coat over the back of a chair and headed through to the kitchen area. A plate of soup and a whisky, he decided. Then pack a few things before heading off to bed.

He was asleep by the time Maggie entered their bedroom, tip-toeing across the carpet to her side of the bed. Her husband's dark hair flopped across his forehead, the dark circles under his eyes testament to so many long days and restless nights. Tomorrow she would be stopping work for the half-term break but he would still be driving himself onwards, desperate to see the conclusion of this case. Lately she had begun to worry about the man who lay slumbering on their bed. His sort of work was always hard but there was a strain in his face that did not seem to go away nowadays, as though he was fighting some inner pain. Was it just because the case had come so close to home? Or were there other demons inside her husband's head, ones that he kept from the woman he loved?

CHAPTER FORTY-THREE

Sarah was glad to be back on day shift, being taken from Corrie-linn and back by Nancy who was a soothing presence at Abbey Nursing Home. She still had terrified dreams about that night, Scarface lunging at her, a knife being drawn down her cheek, the blood hot and sticky. Nancy had given her something to help her sleep but Sarah still awoke at around four in the morning, heart thumping from the nightmare images, a sense of darkness swirling around her.

I prayed for you, Nancy had told her afterwards. *I knew the Lord would protect you.* Sarah had nodded dumbly, grateful for this woman's simple faith but wondering if it had not in fact been the tall policeman to whom she owed her life.

Mrs Abbott had been kind too, but in a brisk no-nonsense fashion, letting Sarah know that hard work was the best way to forget the horrors of her past. Just how much Nancy's sister knew, Sarah wasn't sure. But she was glad of the job and had thrown herself back into caring for these patients whose lives were being shortened by their illnesses.

Today the glazing company would be fitting a new pane to

replace the beautiful stained-glass window. *Just a temporary measure,* Nancy had said. *I may find something else to put there in time.* And Sarah had burned inside, guilt gnawing at her.

She looked at her watch with a sigh of relief. Just enough time to give them all their medication then the next shift would arrive and she and Nancy could return home.

However, when Sarah entered the staffroom she was surprised to see Catherine Reid sitting there, a magazine in her hands.

'Hello.' Catherine looked up with a smile. 'How are you?'

Sarah gave a little shrug. 'All right,' she said. 'Fine,' she added.

'Really?' Catherine Reid had raised her eyebrows and was regarding Sarah closely.

'Well . . . you know . . . ' Sarah broke off.

'Yes, I do know,' Catherine replied. 'I've seen plenty of women like you who've been forced into making bad choices. You need to try to forgive yourself, Sarah. Really you do,' she said firmly. Then, as though she were afraid of sounding too preachy, Catherine gave a shrug. 'Nancy and I are going out tonight. Got tickets for the RSNO. Nicola Benedetti.' She smiled. 'Been wanting to hear her play the Mendelsohn violin concerto for ages. We'll drop you off at Corrielinn first, though,' she added.

Sarah closed the front door behind her and turned the key in the lock. They were nice women, good women, but she still felt as if she didn't deserve to belong in their world. The big house seemed cold and draughty as Sarah climbed the stairs and she paused to examine the place where that stained-glass waterfall had been. That rock had been a part of her own life, thrusting its way into this house, a violent act reminding Sarah that she had no business being here in the first place. But where, she asked herself as she pushed open the bedroom door and sank gratefully on to the bed, was she supposed to go?

A wee lost lamb, Nancy had called her and right now, wrapping herself in the duvet, Sarah Wilding felt the truth of that little story. She looked around the place that had once been Tracey Livingstone's room. She did feel comfortable here, Sarah told herself, and not just because of the nice furnishings and hand-me-down clothes. It was more than that; it was the warmth of Nancy's smile, the motherly way she spoke to Sarah.

Tears crowded into the young woman's eyes as she thought about her own mother. She brushed them away, angry at her self-pity. How had Mum felt losing her only son? First to drugs, then to that overdose? How could any mother cope with that sort of tragedy? Sarah had gone over and over these questions during her time in Cornton Vale, never finding an answer. Except that she was to blame.

She sat up and pushed the pillow behind her head then leaned back and closed her eyes.

It's time to stop blaming yourself, a voice seemed to be telling her, a voice that might have been Nancy's. Might have been Catherine's.

She had done a bad thing and been punished for it, Sarah thought. But there was a way out of the darkness, a way to find forgiveness if she could only bring herself to ask ...

Sarah closed her eyes, wondering if there really was any listening ear to hear her cry.

'Dear God,' she began. 'Help me find a way back ...'

When she finally opened her eyes, Sarah blinked at the last rays of sunlight shining from the window. There had been no thundering voice replying to her prayer, only a peace filling her heart and mind.

She got up off the bed and wandered into the bathroom.

Yes, it was the same face she saw every morning, but now the lines had faded from around her eyes and the woman gazing back at her was smiling. It was a smile of hope, Sarah realised, a smile of new beginnings.

CHAPTER FORTY-FOUR

It wasn't surprising that Lorimer hadn't been the one to come to the woman's bedside, Kirsty thought as she followed Murdoch back through the hospital corridors. For all his protestations about not having a personal interest, the press would have had another field day if the detective superintendent had appeared in Annette Imrie's room to read her the charges. That was down to Murdoch. Perhaps he was the best person for this particular job, Kirsty thought, remembering the way he had tackled his snout in that East End pub.

In the end it was a pitiful sort of scene, the heavily bandaged woman peering at them from blackened eyes, her speech slow and slurred from the medication she had received. Murdoch was brief and to the point. Annette Imrie was being charged with conspiracy to murder by person or persons unknown. She had seemed hardly surprised by their visit and had said little afterwards.

'Will you be pressing charges on your husband?' Murdoch had asked and it was only then that a faint gleam had come to the woman's eyes and she nodded her head.

'Of course,' she had insisted. 'D'you think he's getting away with doing this to me?'

'Bitter woman,' Murdoch said quietly as they left the building. 'Shouldn't say it but it's the husband I feel sorry for.'

Kirsty nodded her agreement, remembering how nice Patrick Imrie had been to them at his farm, the image of the warm kitchen and those fluffy kittens coming back.

She strapped herself into the Honda and glanced across at Murdoch who was also pulling at the seat belt. For a moment Kirsty stopped and stared. Where the man's watch had been there was just bare wrist.

'What?' Murdoch ventured, catching her inquisitive look.

'You were wearing a very expensive watch just after the robbery, sir,' Kirsty said, facing him with a sudden rush of courage. 'Isn't it working any more?' she added innocently.

Murdoch stared at her, his face hard as granite, then he gave a sigh. 'Wondered if you'd seen me lift it,' he said. Then he smiled at her. 'But you didn't shop me, did you? That was nice of you, Wilson.'

'I . . . ' Kirsty's mouth fell open. 'What happened to the watch, sir?'

'Oh, I didn't keep it long, Wilson. Needed to realise some readies to pay off a few debts, didn't I?' he growled. Then, turning in his seat, he leaned across until his face was only inches from her own. 'You didn't tell Lorimer, did you? Now why was that?'

'Didn't want any trouble, sir,' Kirsty murmured. 'But can I ask you something?'

'Ask away, Wilson,' Murdoch said, sitting back against the passenger seat with a sigh of resignation.

'Mary Milligan said that she'd told you about her worries that patients were being targeted in the hospital. Yet you did nothing about it.'

There was a silence between them for a few moments then Murdoch turned and gave her a strange look.

'She said that, did she?' he said thoughtfully. 'I wonder why.' He turned to Kirsty. 'She was telling you a pack of lies, Wilson.' He frowned. 'Never said a thing to me about any suspicions. Yet she picked on you. A rookie detective. What did you think? That she was just a fanciful Highland woman with all her crazy superstitions?'

'I . . . I don't know, sir,' Kirsty stammered

'Thought she was a bit attention-seeking whenever I went up to that ward. Didn't you?' Murdoch's face had grown thoughtful as he gazed ahead.

Kirsty's head reeled with the sudden possibility that she had been played by the big, soft-spoken nurse. Who was to say that any doctor had been there at all? Only Nurse Milligan. And had Kirsty and her colleagues spent precious police time trawling through videos to find some unknown visitor to the hospital who fitted the woman's fantasies? The very thought appalled her.

'Right, Wilson. Drive. And we can forget we ever had this little conversation, okay?'

The call came as Lorimer prepared to leave the office and head out to the airport.

'Thanks,' he said after listening to the woman from the forensic laboratory. 'Much appreciated.'

He sat back down and began to type an email that would be circulated to the team, copying in Professor Solomon Brightman to the message.

DNA trace on Crawford Whyte's teacup confirms my
suspicions that he is not related to the late Jane Maitland.
Lorimer.

It would be a doubly interesting visit to London, now, the detective superintendent decided, and he was looking forward to confronting the banker about this new information. It had been a long shot to take the trace instead of asking Whyte to supply a sample, but he hadn't wanted to chase him off. His team had also uncovered some interesting facts about Crawford Whyte, one of which was that his role in the bank was that of IT specialist. Which might or might not explain why their own technical support had found it so hard to crack into the centre of Quiet Release.

CHAPTER FORTY-FIVE

He should have spent more time in the gym, Abernethy told himself as he jogged through the trees. Up ahead, the dark shape of the lodge lay screened by Scots pine and Sitka spruce. It had been a perfect place to hide out despite the internet connection being somewhat erratic up here amidst these mountains. A few more days and he would set off down south. A train from Inverness to London then the boat across to France. That was the plan. Crawford Whyte had already made the arrangements, the lawyer's reward for emptying the old woman's accounts and transferring the bulk of her money. But he had to keep out of sight, Whyte had insisted. At least until the police were certain he had fled the country. Then and only then could he begin to make his move.

Abernethy stopped and leaned down, clutching his thighs. This self-imposed regime was intended to reduce his weight, make him appear a little less like the fat man that everybody would recognise. He'd already shaved his hair off and now hated looking in the mirror at this bald man with the wobbling paunch. Once he was in France everything would change, the lawyer told himself, visions of buttered croissants and huge cups of fragrant coffee making a smile appear on his face.

With a sigh he continued to walk towards the woodland bothy where he had been staying these past few days. It was late afternoon and the sun had already slipped behind the mountains, leaving pools of darkness between the trees.

And yet there was a square of light straight ahead. Abernethy frowned. He was sure he had switched off the light before going for his run. But perhaps he'd been mistaken? These last rays of sunlight had been dazzling bright, after all. Had he not noticed the light on as he'd left?

He walked slowly and quietly up to the door and felt for the handle. Bothy doors were never locked, their presence in the wilderness safe havens for any wanderer.

As he touched it, the door swung open with a menacing creak that made him jump. Good grief! He'd even left the bloody door open! You were in too much of a hurry to get out while it was still light, he scolded himself. 'Becoming careless, old boy,' he said aloud.

Abernethy stepped into the lodge then turned as a shadow fell against the far wall.

'Oh, it's you,' he said, facing the figure standing by the open door. 'What on earth are you doing here?'

There was no answer, just a lunge towards the fat lawyer and the sound of ripping as the hunting knife tore across the man's throat.

Abernethy gave a gasp and a gurgle then his body fell heavily on to the wooden floor, blood spattering across the walls.

'Becoming careless, old boy,' the killer whispered, wiping the blade of the knife across the man's stomach before thrusting it into its leather scabbard. Then, as some midges began to circle around the room, hands were drawn to scratch an itchy head. It was a small, unthinking gesture, as careless as the way the body was left, discarded on the floor.

It might be weeks before the corpse would be found, stinking and corrupt. The killer smiled at the thought. Wouldn't that be a fitting epitaph for the lawyer?

CHAPTER FORTY-SIX

The October school holidays began early for the lads from Inverness who were tramping through the woods behind their Scout leader, whistling a tune as they went. At the very back of the line of boys, Gary Little stumbled on a tree root and fell with a shout.

'Oi, Wee Gary's copped it!' another of the lads yelled out as the boy writhed on the ground, screams of agony showing that this was no soft tumble.

The Scout leader, a worthy middle-aged man whose sons had all been through the Scouting movement, turned back and jogged towards the place where the youngest recruit was now sobbing his heart out.

'It's my leg, my leg,' he cried as the leader bent down to examine him.

'Hush now, Gary, let me take a look,' the man said, gently lifting the boy's leg.

'Arghhhh!' Gary cried out and Archie Featherstone let the leg down again. It was obvious that the wee lad had hurt himself badly, possibly broken his ankle.

'Right, boys, here's what we're going to do,' Archie said

brightly, aiming to instil confidence into them all, even the poor laddie sobbing on the ground.

The lack of mobile telephone signal was a little worrisome, however, Archie Featherstone had checked and re-checked the route map for every eventuality and knew of the bothy hidden off to the right of these trees.

'We're going to carry you, son,' the Scout leader told him. 'Boys, gather round.'

Several minutes later, the boy cradled in his arms, Archie Featherstone came to the door of the bothy.

'Open it up, lads, we'll let Gary lie on the bed. There's always a bed or two in a mountain bothy,' he added cheerfully as several boys clambered up the wooden steps in a race to see who would gain entry first.

The scream made Archie's blood freeze, then there was a scramble, boys falling over themselves to race past him, ashen-faced and open-mouthed, some of them beginning to cry.

'What is it?' The little boy in his arms squirmed, trying to see what was beyond the open doorway.

But Archie Featherstone had already turned away, hiding little Gary's eyes from the carnage that lay inside.

Rosie Fergusson watched as they brought the body into the post-mortem room. There had been no protest from her counterpart in Highland Region once the identity of the deceased had been made known. A team of officers had scoured the wooden hut, bringing back as much trace material as they could find and already it was being processed in their facility in Glasgow.

Once again it was Detective Sergeant Murdoch with Kirsty Wilson who stood on the other side of the viewing area, ready to watch the pathologist at work. The cause of death was easy enough to see at first glance, Rosie thought, looking at the open gash across Brian Abernethy's throat, but nonetheless she went through the procedure with painstaking care.

Perhaps he ought to have called first, Lorimer thought. But then he had wanted the element of surprise. And now it was the tall detective who had been given a surprise, first at the bank where Crawford Whyte no longer worked, as he'd been told by a frosty-faced gentleman in reception. Whyte had only been working there less than a year, the man had informed him. Freelance, not a bank employee. Then the second surprise here, in this flat that bore all the hallmarks of a hasty departure, as if Whyte had anticipated a visit from the police. At least he had the office computer, Lorimer told himself, setting it down on a side table of the man's bedroom. Though what would be found there was dubious. Probably wiped it clean to factory standard before he'd left the bank.

This place was deserted, that was for sure. Wardrobe doors hung open, most of the contents removed, wooden hangers suspended in the shadows. An old, worn raincoat that had seen better days and a couple of dark suits, the trousers shiny with age, had been left. The detective had a sudden vision of the smart suit and Crombie coat the man had worn on his visit to Glasgow. Of course, he had anticipated coming into money. Spent some of it before it had reached his bank account. There were no papers anywhere, nor had Whyte left a bag full of shreddings like the ones they had found in Abernethy's office.

The Met would send some of their people round to Whyte's address, Lorimer had been assured by his counter-part down here. Every cooperation that they could offer had been promised and all he had to do now was wait for their SOCOs to arrive, along with a senior officer or two. Meantime, he could have a look around the flat and see if he could gauge anything about the man who had assumed the identity of Jane Maitland's long-lost son.

Maybe it was what was *not* there that gave him most insight into this man. No pictures, no green plants, either on a window ledge or outside on the balcony. A washer dryer that smelled as if it hadn't been used any time recently. The fridge freezer practically empty apart from a half-litre carton of milk, that was past its sell-by date, and a tube of vegetarian spread that had scarcely been touched. The freezer compartment showed a thick layer of ice from its roof and a tray of ice cubes that was stuck to the base when Lorimer tried to move it.

'You've not been here for days, have you,' he murmured. 'Knew we were coming to get you, is that it?'

He sat down heavily on a kitchen chair and sighed. Was Crawford Whyte behind this entire illegal organisation? Or, like Brian Abernethy, had he been just a step higher up the chain from the three men now languishing in Barlinnie Prison? Abernethy could no longer tell them what they wanted to know and Lorimer believed that the lawyer had been deliberately eliminated to keep him quiet. What secrets had his office contained? One more avenue was open to him down here, however, and that was the Salvation Army, whose officers had diligently sought and found the man claiming to be Jane Maitland's only living heir.

The news that he had been waiting for came as Lorimer left Glasgow airport, the taxi taking him into the city once more.

Match found in hair samples at Abernethy and Bissett crime scenes, the email read.

Nothing on database to identify the perpetrator.

Lorimer's smile turned sour as he read the last line. Damn! They had so much evidence now to tie up these two murders but whoever this was who had spent time in that Byres Road flat remained a mystery. It wasn't someone on their radar, then. None of the usual hit men who had hung about with the harder criminal types in this city. Nor had HOLMES shed any light on the UK's database. Yet whoever it was seemed a practised killer, at least according to Rosie Fergusson. The wounds had been made with some sort of hunting knife and the members of Lorimer's team were already trawling through the types of possible weapon that the pathologist had suggested.

'Can you take me up to University Avenue,' Lorimer leaned forward and told the taxi driver. Suddenly he felt the need to run all of this past his old friend to see what he made of it.

'I think they'll slip up eventually,' Solly told him as he poured hot water into the little china teapot on the huge table that was often surrounded by students eager to listen to the professor's words of wisdom.

'How do you figure that out?' Lorimer asked him, gloomily.

'As I said before, it's all about money,' the psychologist replied. 'Or at least it was to most of the people involved. Now that Mr Whyte seems to have got what he was after we need to wait and see who else has to be paid.'

'What do you mean?'

Solly smiled enigmatically and began to pour the tea into two mismatched mugs. 'Your three thugs are out of the equation,' he began. 'So there will be more money in the pot for everyone else who is involved.'

'So?'

'So, my guess is that one of them will be trying to get a better share of whatever profits have been made out of the demise of these patients. Including whoever killed Frankie Bissett and Brian Abernethy.'

'But if Whyte's scarpered with all of the money . . . ?'

'Not so.' Solly wagged a finger at his friend. 'My guess is that he's taken the money that Abernethy and he were supposed to split between them.' He raised his eyebrows at Lorimer. 'You don't really suppose that there isn't an awful lot more swilling around? What did it cost Mrs Imrie? And Rachel Gardiner? Five thousand pounds apiece? Multiply that by the number of patients whose lives have been taken . . . ' Solly shrugged.

'But that's something we don't know!' Lorimer protested.

'My point exactly!' Solly beamed. 'There could be scores, no, hundreds even . . . someone has been making a small fortune out of these seriously ill people. Miss Maitland was just one example of how greedy Abernethy and his accomplice were.'

'We've found out a bit more about Whyte,' Lorimer told him. 'Real name's Michael Rogerson. Whyte *was* the name of Jane Maitland's son. The Salvation Army did a sterling job of tracing him. Their only reservation was that they thought they had reached a dead end.' Lorimer made a face. 'And I mean a *really* dead end. Crawford Whyte was stabbed to death when he intervened in a bar brawl. The Salvation Army folk reported back to the Glasgow lawyer but they said that Abernethy had told them he had heard from Miss Maitland's son. Made them think they'd made some error in their search.'

'Not like them,' Solly commented, raising his bushy eyebrows again.

'Abernethy already had a connection with Rogerson,' Lorimer

told the professor. 'Represented him in a fraud case some years back. Explains why there's no data on him. It expired years ago. They must have kept in touch. I can just imagine that conversation,' he added angrily. 'Abernethy asking Rogerson if he wanted to make some serious money. And all he had to do was impersonate an old lady's son and heir. Wouldn't even have to see her or speak to her.'

'Because by that time they knew she would be dead,' Solly added solemnly.

'But I'm willing to bet that Rogerson had more to do with this scheme than just play-acting for our benefit,' Lorimer said, grinding his teeth in a spasm of annoyance. 'He was an IT specialist. And he had some medical stuff in his flat.'

'Abernethy wasn't the brains behind this,' Solly said quietly, 'though I grant he was the one dishing out the money. No, if I were to hazard a guess, I would say that there are more people involved than this Rogerson fellow, though he was probably the one sending out the emails. There has to be someone else involved.'

'There's the man who killed Bissett and Abernethy, of course. And we can't forget that we have to find the ones with the necessary medical background,' Lorimer sighed, nodding in agreement. 'I know what you mean.' He turned his gaze over the city skyline where lights were beginning to twinkle in the gloom. 'Somewhere, Solly, some disaffected medic is still at large, possibly with a quantity of morphine at his or her disposal.'

'Yes.' The bearded psychologist nodded solemnly. 'And what concerns me is whether they have sated their desire for killing.'

CHAPTER FORTY-SEVEN

Grainne smiled at the woman as she handed her a magazine. 'What's so great about you today?' Mona Calder shivered.

But the nurse did not reply, simply gave her patient a little kiss on the cheek.

'See and keep the windows shut,' Mona ordered. 'Or someone will come in and finish me off!' she said, her eyes following Grainne around the room as the nurse went about her daily tasks.

'Now, Mona, isn't that what you've always been asking us to do, eh?' Grainne teased. '"A pillow over my head." You're a terrible woman!'

'Not the same,' Mona Calder replied, her voice shaking. 'Not the same thing at all,' she murmured, turning away but not before the nurse clearly saw the anxiety in her patient's eyes.

All over this city there were patients whose lives were constrained by their disabilities, fear sweeping over them like a tsunami. Mrs Abbot had been unable to keep the news from her patients, like so many others responsible for their care. Newspapers, television and the internet flooded these clinics and hospital wards with the suggestion that somewhere out there people were being paid to do away with the sick and the feeble.

Grainne opened the magazine and laid it on Mona's bed. 'See, there's the Royal Family. Take a look at these pictures. Aren't the wee ones growing up a treat!'

Mona Calder did as she was told, but her eyes hardly saw the smiling people in the double-page spread, her mind fixed instead on the shadow of terror that had kept her awake all night.

'Cleaned out.' Murdoch whistled as he read the report. 'See that, Wilson?'

Kirsty moved across to where Murdoch sat at his desk and looked at the latest information in the case.

'Good Lord,' she sighed. 'With that amount of money he could have gone anywhere.'

It was all there in black and white, the police IT officers having retrieved much of Rogerson's files from his office computer. He had taken the laptop back to its factory settings right enough but had been in too much of a hurry to overwrite anything afterwards. It was all there now for them to see; figures showing Abernethy's bank transfers, emails from the fund managers and, best of all, some old correspondence between Rogerson and whoever had been responsible for carrying out the actual killings.

'Likes a bit of mystery, whoever he is,' Murdoch growled, pointing the cursor at the recipient of Rogerson's correspondence. 'What the hell sort of name is that?'

Kirsty peered closer. HUSS, the name read, all in uppercase lettering.

'Could google it, sir?' she suggested, returning to her own desk.

Moments later she was back at Murdoch's side. 'Doesn't make sense,' she murmured, frowning. 'A huss is a dogfish.'

'A dogfish? Stupid sort of name to give himself,' Murdoch declared. 'Think we're dealing with a grade-A nutter, Wilson. Or else it's his little joke that something fishy's going on. Well, let's hope one of the others can come up with a better explanation, eh?'

It was the sort of day that made your eyes water from staring at the screen, Kirsty thought later, getting up and rubbing the base of her spine. It felt as if she had been sitting there for hours. More information had begun to trickle in from the forensic laboratory, some of it making the detective constable sit up a little straighter. The hair samples taken from the locus in Byres Road and the mountain bothy had been further analysed and at least one showed that whoever had left these traces used a particular type of hair gel. Kirsty's mind flew back to Ailsa Doyle's description of the man she had seen leaving Jane Maitland's cottage flat. No hair gel, she'd remarked, nothing to cover up that balding area on the crown of his head. It was something that a trained hair stylist would notice and Ailsa was as sharp as they came, Kirsty nodded to herself. Jane Maitland's killer was not the same person, then. Not the mysterious Huss who had been corresponding with Michael Rogerson, ordering emails to be sent to various hospitals and clinics in and around Glasgow, as well as to individuals in their own homes.

It was a relief when her phone rang.

'Detective Constable Wilson speaking,' she began.

'Oh, dear, is that the same lady who came with the tall gentleman?'

'Who is calling, please?' Kirsty made her voice as neutral as possible, but unthreatening lest the anxious-sounding caller put down the phone.

'It's Mrs Collins from Mr Abernethy's office. You came in to see him the other day . . . '

'Oh, yes, what can I do for you, ma'am?'

'It's awful, I'm really, really sorry,' the woman apologised, making Kirsty purse her mouth in frustration. Would she get to the point? she thought.

'You see it wasn't all shredded,' she went on breathlessly. 'I found copies in the lower basement. Things that I'd been told to get rid of quite a while ago, but I'd completely forgotten about ...' Her voice trailed off as though she were expecting a severe reprimand.

'Mrs Collins, don't worry about a thing. I'll be around in ten minutes to pick it all up. And thanks,' Kirsty added warmly. 'You did the right thing to call us.'

'Where are you off to, Wilson?' Murdoch stood up and barred her way as Kirsty made for the door.

'Abernethy's office,' she said, unable to hide the excitement in her voice. 'Something's come up. Won't be long, honest!' she exclaimed as he stood aside, a puzzled look on his face.

There were more files than the detective constable could carry by herself and so the receptionist helped her take them out to the waiting car. What might they contain? Kirsty wondered, putting the Honda into gear and driving through the city streets once more. At least she'd given Murdoch a call, let him know what to expect.

There was a small crowd waiting for her on her return, Murdoch having alerted others in the team to the find in the lawyer's basement.

If she had been wearied by the constant peering at the laptop screen, Kirsty was now energised by the chance to flick through hard copy, even though there was so much of it. Jean Fairlie had picked up her share of the files and was sitting opposite, her hands flicking over page by page as she read. And it was the older detective constable who made the discovery just half an hour later.

'Gotcha!'

Everyone stopped and turned to where DC Fairlie was sitting.

'Sir.' She was standing now with a sheet of paper in her hand, Murdoch rising from his desk. 'I think you should see this.'

Professor Brightman enjoyed puzzles. As he stared at the latest reports from Lorimer's team, his eyes fell on the obscure name that Michael Rogerson's mystery correspondent had used.

'Huss,' he murmured to himself. 'Now what is the etymology of that little word?' A dogfish was a type of shark, he knew, a strange creature with skin like sandpaper instead of scales. A predatory kind of fish, he mused. Was that the reason for this odd choice of name? It was, he thought, reading the emails closely, from a person who appeared to be educated. A doctor, perhaps? Someone who had failed his exams and been lured into this organisation with the promise of a fortune to be made? Or was Huss the brains behind the entire organisation?

This needed more careful thought and, perhaps, a different way of looking at the word.

Lorimer sank back into his chair, exhausted.

'Glass of wine?' Maggie offered, proffering the bottle of Chianti, one of his favourites.

'No, thanks.' He shook his head wearily. 'I'll just fall asleep.'

'Maybe that would do you some good,' she muttered, glancing at her husband's furrowed brow. This case was really taking its toll, she thought.

The phone ringing made Lorimer sit up but Maggie had already picked up and was saying 'Hello', her lips curving into a smile.

'It's Solly,' she said, handing him the cordless phone. 'Says he needs to tell you something.'

'Huss,' Solly began without any preamble. 'It is a dogfish but the word itself is quite an old word, really, related to the fish, of course . . .'

Lorimer listened, suddenly irritated by the psychologist's lengthy pause.

'What d'you mean?'

'It is a sort of shark, right enough,' Solly told him. 'But it is a particular type. Clever sort of word to use . . .' he mused.

'Solly,' Lorimer addressed his friend wearily. 'Can you get to the point, please? If there is one,' he added, testily.

'Oh, of course, sorry,' the psychologist replied. 'A huss is a nurse shark,' Solly told him. 'But the word on its own simply means "nurse".'

The hospital car park was full when Kirsty drew up as near the entrance as she could.

'Take a chance,' Murdoch told her, pointing to an ambulances only parking bay. 'You stay here, Wilson. Flash the badge if you need to. Now let me get inside and nab that bloody nurse!'

Mary moved towards the window at the first sound of police sirens.

Her patient was sound asleep and so she drew the curtains around the bed then pressed the red emergency button and swiftly left the room.

There was a back staircase that Mary Milligan knew well,

used mostly by porters at the end of their shifts or smokers keeping to the back of the building where they would not be caught on CCTV cameras. The woman hurtled down, taking the steps two at a time, desperate to get away. Her car was parked on the far side of the hospital grounds, a good five minutes' walk away. Would they have found it and be waiting for her there?

'Sorry, you can't park here,' the stony-faced warden declared.

'Police Scotland,' Kirsty rejoined, whipping out her warrant card and thrusting it close to the man's face.

'You still cannae park here. This is for emergencies only,' the man continued stubbornly.

'Take that up with my boss,' Kirsty hissed furiously, but the warden was not for budging.

'You need to keep this bit clear,' he said. 'Ambulances have to have access to this door.'

With a sigh Kirsty started up the car and began to weave her way through the maze of vehicles.

It was at that moment she saw the figure running in the opposite direction, arms pumping up and down, white shoes pounding the pavement.

'Mary!' Kirsty gasped. It was not a simple matter of turning the car and following the woman. Given the one-way system here it was a couple of minutes before Kirsty had managed to manoeuvre the Honda back out towards the main road.

She was just in time to see the ginger-haired nurse get into a red Mini Cooper and head along the road towards the dual carriageway.

There was a thirty mile an hour limit here with a camera to catch any speeder but neither woman paid that any attention as the Honda roared after the smaller car.

'DC Wilson,' Kirsty called out to any patrol car in the area, then gave her location and the description of the car that she was following.

She reached the first roundabout, wondering which direction the red car would take then watched as it drove in the direction of Renfrew.

Is she heading for the motorway? Kirsty wondered, ignoring the blare from an Audi's horn as she nipped in front of it and put her foot down hard.

There were still two cars between the Mini Cooper and her own. Had Mary spotted her?

She drew to a halt at the first set of traffic lights then followed the red car as it turned towards the old town centre. Not the M8, then. Kirsty alerted the traffic police at the other end of her two-way radio and moved slowly into position, still two vehicles behind her quarry.

On and on they drove, along the leafy streets, accelerating over the old swing bridge above the River Cart, the Honda creeping ever closer to Mary Milligan's car until a set of red lights forced them both to stop.

Damn! As the lights changed to green, Kirsty saw the nurse's head turn and for a split second the women's eyes met.

As the red car roared off towards the Renfrewshire country-side, Kirsty clutched the steering wheel, gritting her teeth in determination. All these months of preparation for her Advanced Driving Test were coming back now, she realised with a grin as the Honda closed in on the little red car.

Then she was side by side with the smaller car, driving as close as she dared, making the nurse glance across, a terrified look on her face.

Kirsty heard the scratch and squeal as branches of hawthorn

scraped against the nurse's car, then the thump as she forced it into the ditch.

She was out of the Honda and pulling at the driver's door in moments.

'Gerroff!' The woman staggered back then took a swing at the detective.

Kirsty ducked and then charged with all of her strength.

Her head made contact with the nurse's stomach, knocking the wind from her and then Mary Milligan was on her knees and Kirsty had her wrists secured with a pair of handcuffs.

'Mary Milligan,' Kirsty said, her breath coming in gasps, 'I'm arresting you for the murder of . . . ' Then she stopped. *How many other people had this nurse actually put to death?*

'Brian Abernethy and Francis Bissett,' Kirsty said firmly.

Then, as a familiar silver Lexus drove up followed by two patrol cars, she breathed out a huge sigh of relief.

CHAPTER FORTY-EIGHT

'This your coat, sir?' The customs officer lifted the expensive-looking garment and put it across his arm.

'Of course it is!' the passenger snapped.

'And these are your bags?' the officer continued, examining the labels attached to the Louis Vuitton cases.

'Yes. Now can you hurry up, please. I have a transfer to make,' the man said, his clipped English accent quite at odds with the Australian drawl of the customs officer.

'Sure, pal, just routine, y'know,' the officer smiled. But, unseen below his desk, the customs officer pressed a button that immediately brought several more uniformed officers to the desk where the passenger's belongings were spread out before him.

'Crawford Whyte?' A burly Aussie cop took the man's arm. 'Or should I call you Michael Rogerson? Come with me, sir.'

CHAPTER FORTY-NINE

Solomon Brightman had been looking forward to meeting the woman who was now in custody. The huss, the nurse shark who had been responsible for so many deaths. What would she be like? he wondered.

She was not the formidable person that he had expected her to be, just a tired-looking woman whose unwashed hair was drawn back from her face. It was a face that might have beguiled a lesser man than the professor of psychology. If she had smiled and turned these large eyes upon him, who knows what he might have thought? But Solly was too well trained in the art of separating appearance from reality to be charmed by a pretty face.

'Your name is Mary Milligan,' he began, sitting at the table on his own, a uniformed female officer standing, as instructed, out of Mary's line of sight.

Mary nodded, her hands folded together, the metal cuffs a necessary precaution lest she try to attack her interrogator.

'How are you feeling today, Mary?' Solly asked, his eyes reaching the woman's, noting how they slid away from his gaze, wondering what lies she was already creating in that disturbed mind.

A shrug and a twist of her mouth were all the reply she wanted to give. Fair enough. The initial questions were intended to relax her, put her at some sort of ease.

'We found Brian Abernethy's body.' Solly smiled at her. 'His windpipe was severed quite neatly, I'm told. Your work, was it?' He tried to sound as though he were giving her some sort of praise, though the images he had viewed still made him feel nauseous.

'Of course,' Mary bristled. 'Did they think I wasn't capable ... ?'

'Not in the least,' Solly assured her. 'Everyone guessed that you were quite capable of carrying that out. And Francis Bissett, too.'

Mary darted a suspicious look at the man with the dark, curled beard. 'He had to go,' she said simply.

'Did you both decide that?'

The woman frowned. 'Both?' she said, eyes sliding to one side.

'Yes, Mary,' Solly nodded. 'There is trace evidence in the flat that places you there and we also have samples that match the scene at the Gardiner sisters' home. But not yours. Someone else's.'

Mary had looked away, her face set, lips shut in a firm hard line.

Solly suppressed a sigh of disappointment. She would refuse to acknowledge that there was anyone else involved. Or would she?

'You took some big risks,' he commented, almost as if he were talking to himself. 'Must have been quite a thrill to enter a police station and help the detectives who were looking for that mystery man.' Solly's tone verged on one of admiration.

He could see Mary's mouth curving in a slight, sardonic smile. What was she thinking? That she had outwitted them?

'There was nobody else then? No handsome doctor performing

all of these acts of euthanasia? Or do you prefer to call them mercy killings, Mary?' His voice had a hard edge to it now, forcing the woman to regard him through narrowed eyes.

'Think I couldn't do it myself?' she sneered, the pretty face turning to something bitter and ugly.

Solly looked at her dispassionately. She had wanted to be the main focus of attention. Had needed to be regarded as the centre of it all, even when it meant exposing herself to danger, to being caught. It was a recognisable mental condition, one that would see the nurse admitted to a secure hospital where she would likely spend the rest of her days.

Lorimer had been right. Mary Milligan would never tell them who that shadowy figure was. The man who had slipped into Jane Maitland's home, the one who had lured innocent and vulnerable people like the Gardiner sisters to their deaths. The man who was the real brains behind Quiet Release.

'Did you love him, Mary?' Solly asked quietly.

For a brief moment the woman's eyes widened, her lips opening a fraction. Then the shutters were down once more and the psychologist nodded to the police officer who strode towards her prisoner, ready to escort her from the room.

CHAPTER FIFTY

It was the scene of celebration in more than one way, Kirsty thought happily as she and James sat side by side at the Arthouse, watching the assembled crowds enjoying her father's retirement party. Alistair and Betty Wilson were both dressed to the nines, her father in a new grey suit that Betty had insisted on purchasing from Marks and Spencer, and Kirsty's mother looking far younger than her age in a fitted lacy navy dress from Reiss. They would be off in two days' time, a long trip overland in the US to see the glories of some of the National Parks.

'Here's to them,' James whispered, raising his glass of bubbly and clinking it against her own. 'And here's to you,' he grinned. 'Detective Constable Wilson!'

Kirsty grinned back then looked around her. All her friends were there; Lorimer and Maggie, Solly and Rosie, the team from Stewart Street. Even Len Murdoch had looked in for a brief half-hour to offer his congratulations to Kirsty's father.

'My turn soon,' he'd said, winking at Kirsty and nodding at James. 'Chip off the old block, your girl,' the detective sergeant had added. 'She'll do all right.'

Kirsty had watched the big man as he left the function room, his broad shoulders and grey head bowed a little, still carrying troubles and grief. She hoped he would be okay. Would he keep away from the bookies? Realise that the weakness had almost cost him his career?

They had tied up so many loose ends now that Mary Milligan had been apprehended and confessed to her part in Quiet Release. And yet … Kirsty had listened as Lorimer had quizzed the woman for hours. Like the detective superintendent and Professor Brightman, the young DC did not believe Mary Milligan's claim that she and she alone had been responsible for all of those patients' deaths. Her claims that she had wanted to force that other nurse, Sarah Wilding, into administering these lethal injections sounded as though it was a much bigger racket than just one Highland nurse putting herself about. And besides, there was still that unidentified man to locate … and perhaps he was the same person as the handsome fellow inside the hospital, though Mary had now denied his very existence. Yet the CCTV footage they had of this man had led them nowhere. Maybe he was someone she had selected at random from the screen? Would they ever really know?

She glanced across at Lorimer who was laughing at something Professor Brightman had said. It was unfinished business, the detective superintendent had stressed to the team. Michael Rogerson, who had impersonated Miss Maitland's son, was in custody, the money he had defrauded from the old woman frozen for now. In time it would go to the widow and children of the real Crawford Whyte, the man who had been stabbed as he'd tried to stop a fight. Why Jane Maitland had kept so much money in her bank account was clearer now. According to Abernethy's records, she had wanted easy access to her money in case the son she had given up so many years ago had come back into her life. And thus

384

the seed of the lawyer's greedy plan had been planted. So many innocent people! Kirsty sighed. She looked back into the room, voices raised in laughter, the candles at each table illuminating faces smiling at one another, telling jokes and clinking glasses.

It had been a lot of hard work, she told herself, and they deserved a night out. Yet luck had played its part too: the files in Abernethy's basement had also shown the link between Mary Anne Milligan and Brian Abernethy. The lawyer had handled the case when a patient complaint had been made about the nurse, a case that had never come to court.

She glanced at Jean Fairlie, her burgundy silk dress swishing as she walked past on her way to the bar. A designer frock, Kirsty saw. Must have cost her a packet. She frowned, remembering the older woman's protests about end-of-life causes. Could she have been the one to leak that information to the press? It was a thought that she did not want to pursue, something else they might never find out. Kirsty took another sip of champagne. She was learning things about this job, she thought. Sometimes it didn't make for a quiet life to air your suspicions.

She turned to look out of the window at the streets and the twinkling lights. This was where she belonged now, this city with all the different facets to its character. There would always be chancers and rogues, mad, bad and dangerous types. But there would always be the ones on her side too, she thought, a feeling of gratitude coursing through her as Lorimer caught her eye and raised his glass with a grin.

EPILOGUE

The girl turned with a smile. 'So glad you're here already. Thought it would be Jenny, though. And she's not normally here so early.'

'All part of the service,' I smiled. 'Soon have you comfortable. Right, let's see which arm we'll have this morning.'

She looked away as I wiped the patch of skin, a twist to her thin lips anticipating the needle scratching her fine pale skin.

'Won't be long,' I said cheerfully. 'Just a little prick . . . there! That's it. Now just relax and you'll soon feel a lot, lot better,' I crooned.

I put down the needle at last and wrapped it in the paper bag, ready to dispose of it safely. My gloved hands stroked the girl's arm and I sat patiently as her eyelids grew heavy and finally closed.

All over this city there were silent, seated watchers just like me, waiting for their loved ones to die. Some would mourn, others would breathe a sigh of relief, but to me they meant nothing at all on a personal level.

I watched until the rise and fall of her breathing ceased and I was sure that she had left this world at last. Moving from my place by her bed, I put two fingers to my lips and blew her a kiss.

'Good night, darling,' I said, then made my way back out into the darkened street.

ACKNOWLEDGEMENTS

As ever, this book could not have been written without the help of many experts in their field who continue to give me information so cheerfully. Bless you all! Dr Marjorie Turner keeps me right with up-to-date things concerning pathology, and Dr Alan Bennie gave me some good suggestions about palliative care. Detective Sergeant Mairi Milne is always on hand to answer even the most obscure question about procedure. (In return for scones, but they don't count as bribes!) I owe a big debt of gratitude to Superintendent Martin Cloherty and Chief Superintendent Ellie Mitchell who gave me insight into the workings of the Professional Standards Department and facts concerning the fate of any officer who might be guilty of some misconduct. Thanks, too, Alistair Morris, whose keen memory of his life as a DS comes in very handy at all times! Sarah Wilding's story was enhanced by talking to former Head of CID and CEO of SACRO, Tom Halpin, especially about the work of SHINE. Thanks for all the insight into the mentoring work that is carried out to rehabilitate women offenders, Tom.

To Crawford Whyte, thanks for supporting the RNLI fund-raiser at which you won the right to have your name selected for a character in this book.

To Thalia, Liz and the staff at Little, Brown, huge thanks for keeping me right! Especially when the spell check gave up in despair after too many examples of Glasgow parlance.

Thanks, Moira (enjoy your retirement!) and Stephanie, Rachel, Jo and Vicky who were there to help keep my diary sorted.

Huge thanks to my editor, Jade Chandler, who seems to know how I think and always knows the right thing to say, a marvellous gift! I am doubly lucky in having not just the best editor but also the best agent in Jenny Brown. I am honoured to have you as an agent and a friend, Jenny. Long may we continue together!

Alanna, this book is dedicated to you for all the many years of encouragement and friendship. Bless you for both.

Last but never least, Donnie, for driving me wherever I needed to go, for quietly supplying all the cups of tea, for putting up with me sitting at this desk in my dressing gown at all hours of the day and night as the story took over, thank you seems a little inadequate! I am just very, very grateful that you enjoy this crazy life as much as I do!

Alex Gray, 2015